ALLEGIANCE

ALLEGIANCE

A NOVEL

WAYNE L. GREEN

CROWN PUBLISHERS, INC.

NEW YORK

G82a

Published by Crown Publishers, Inc.,
One Park Avenue, New York, New York 10016,
and simultaneously in Canada
by General Publishing Company Limited
Manufactured in the United States of America
Library of Congress Cataloging in Publication Data
Green, Wayne L.
Allegiance.
1. World War, 1939–1945—Fiction. I. Title.
PS3557.R37567A78   1983   813'.54   82-19806
ISBN: 0-517-54927-1
Book Design by Lauren Dong
10 9 8 7 6 5 4 3 2 1
First Edition

In Honor of
Congressional Medal of Honor Winner
Private JOE P. MARTINEZ
Company K, 32nd Infantry
Seventh Infantry Division
U.S. Army
Killed in Action
Fish Hook Ridge, Attu
26 May, 1943

and

First Lieutenant HITOSHI HONNA
Commanding Officer, 2nd Company
303rd Independent Infantry Battalion
Imperial Japanese Army
Killed in Action
Point Able, Attu
21 May, 1943

ACKNOWLEDGMENTS

I particularly wish to thank Pastor Lloyd K. Sewake, Dr. Crashi Mitoma and Jesse Miyao, all of Sacramento; George C. Chalou, General Archives in Washington, D.C.; Senator S. I. Hayakawa, for making possible my journey to Attu; Lieutenant (jg) Theodore Mar, Warrant Officer Ben Davis, SK3c David B. Grenot and MK3 Donald B. Lewis, all of the U.S. Coast Guard, for invaluable assistance at Holtz Bay and Chicagof Harbor on Attu; First Lieutenant Gerald W. Lyden, U.S. Army, of the Seventh Infantry Division at Fort Ord, California; my son, Gary W. Green, once a combat corpsman in Vietnam, for specific insights about medical practices under fire; Margaret Moore, R.N., of Stockton, California, for critical review of the manuscript; my wife, Elisabeth M. Green, for analysis of the manuscript, plus editing and endless hours of typing; editor Lisa Healy, of Crown Publishers, for her patience, counsel and encouragement; and most especially a certain physician's widow, for her unique kindness and generosity.

W.L.G.

PREFACE

This novel is based on fact. It was shaped by the true experiences of a certain Japanese physician who lived and loved, felt joy and pain; he served and suffered much as presented. He was a person much like you and me.

My interest in this physician was sparked a few years ago during a conversation with my family doctor, an American-born gentleman of Japanese descent. He told me of the physician who had inspired him to study medicine and of that physician's fate on the island of Attu. My family doctor, however, didn't know the whole story—the if and how and why. No one did. Someone, he said, must unravel the mystery. I became intrigued.

My research took me far afield: to the National Archives in Washington, D.C.; to the files of the Seventh Infantry Division at Fort Ord, California; to the libraries of the University of California at Davis and Berkeley; to Pacific Union College in Northern California; and to the homes of men and women who had known the physician. As a result I gathered a strong image of a devout Christian dedicated to serving his fellow man. That image clung to my mind—a composite, of course, of many impressions. It was confirmed and intensified at last by the physician's widow, a gentle, gracious and courageous lady who is now an American citizen residing in the United States. She possessed a slow sad smile as infectious as the bright twinkle in her eye, and it was she who provided me with a wealth of information about her husband, including insights into his character, personality, moods, mores and beliefs.

The physician's actual diary, quoted at the end of each chapter, speaks for itself. In addition, his experience on the last day of the battle is verified by certain eyewitness accounts in my possession.

Research finally took me to Attu itself, that bleak, windswept weather-tortured island at the western tip of the Aleutian chain. There at East Arm, at the northern end of the Japanese airstrip, I found the site of the physician's first hospital on Attu. From there I gazed at Moore Ridge, which he called Shitagata-Dai, and which divides the bay and valley in two; at the snowy slopes of Shiba-Dai, known to the Seventh Infantry as Hill X; and to the south at the high rugged crest of Hokuchin Yama, which Americans called Fish Hook Ridge. On its lower slopes, clearly marked as a gray slash amid black volcanic rock, was the zigzag path the physician used in his retreat from East Arm to Chichagof Harbor.

The long ravine at Chichagof had changed but little in thirty-five years. The deep-cut paths seemed brand new and the trench holes were still deep and square and ready for use. The site of the hospital tents upon the hill was barren of vegetation, even yet, but erosion had enlarged the holes where the tent poles had been sunk, and they now appeared as pits in the tundra two feet in diameter. Old bomb craters and shell holes surrounded the area. Growing beside the ruin of his old barracks were scores of huge green large-leafed fronds—a vision of spring amid the rain, snow, sleet, fog and never-ceasing cold winds of Attu.

There on Attu I paused to remember. In May of 1943, endless-ly circling Attu Island in a sea-battered U.S. Navy fleet oiler, I had had no idea that the battle for Attu would become·a microcosm of the Japanese experience in World War II. Not until years later, until the research on this novel was far advanced, did that concept begin to emerge.

In the body of this novel I have followed the general history of the physician and tried to capture the essence of his nature. His role on Attu, however, is played by Dr. Tomi Nakamura, a fictional character. I have given Tomi the necessary words, thoughts, deeds and motivations that lend credence to a legitimate literary purpose—to help demonstrate the broad spectrum of human experience in war.

In the final analysis, Tomi is a product of my imagination.

As it is with Tomi, so it is with all other characters presented within these pages. They are fictional and do not represent any actual persons living or dead.

November 1982

ALLEGIANCE

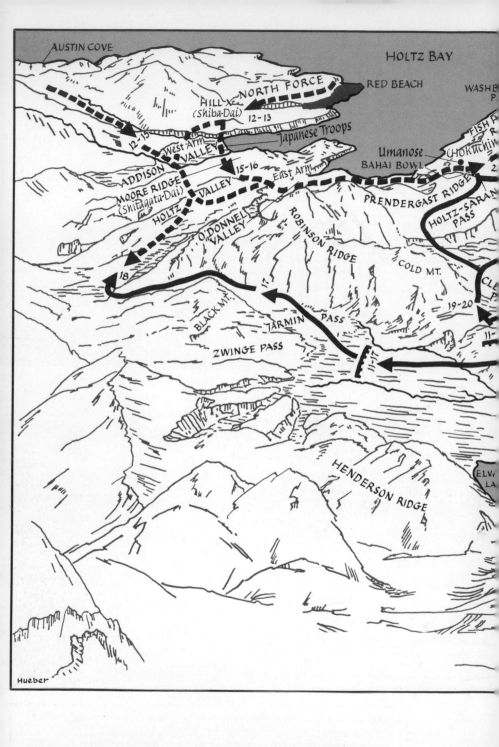

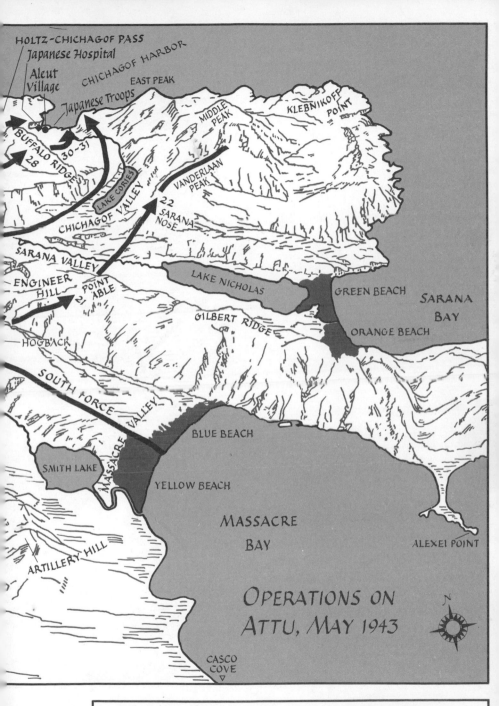

HOLTZ-CHICHAGOF PASS
Japanese Hospital
Aleut Village
CHICHAGOF HARBOR
EAST PEAK
Japanese Troops
KLEBNIKOFF POINT
MIDDLE PEAK
BUFFALO RIDGE
30-31
28
LAKE CORIES
CHICHAGOF VALLEY
VANDERLAAN PEAK
22
SARANA NOSE
SARANA VALLEY
ENGINEER HILL
POINT ABLE
21
LAKE NICHOLAS
GREEN BEACH
SARANA BAY
GILBERT RIDGE
ORANGE BEACH
HOGBACK
SOUTH FORCE
MASSACRE VALLEY
BLUE BEACH
SMITH LAKE
YELLOW BEACH
MASSACRE BAY
ALEXEI POINT
ARTILLERY HILL
OPERATIONS ON ATTU, MAY 1943
N
CASCO COVE

Solid arrows indicate the advance of the American South Force from Massacre Bay;
dotted arrows indicate the advance of the American North Force from
Austin Cove and Red Beach. Numbers on the arrows indicate the dates.

MAY 17, 1943

At 14,000 feet the twin-tailed P-38's rode the clean cold wind like majestic eagles searching for prey.

There were eight planes in all, four to a flight, with each plane and each flight in staggered formation, like stairs, echelon right. Their motors purred rather than roared, the formation cruising at easy half-throttle while constantly circling the eastern portion of the island below. Snugged taut to the belly of each plane was a bomb-shaped auxiliary fuel tank specially fitted for this mission; the tanks were not yet empty.

This was their third hour of dreary patrol, of waiting in the sky, first for the low scudding rain to sweep southward, then for a persistent ground fog to dissipate in the wind. Now, at 0600, the wide Arctic sky was bright with a new day, the high winds gusting at 60 mph and the temperature warming at minus 20 below.

Their mission: strafe. Kill Japs.

In number four position First Lieutenant Michael Andrews eased the strain on his tiring back by stretching the muscles of his lean five-foot-eight frame. Red-blond and blue-eyed, his square jaw and usual half-grin restrained by the chin strap, he peered down on the lava-black, snowcapped island. No rain, no fog. The sun's rays were now touching the highest peaks; light in the valleys would soon be adequate. So everything looked good. All that was needed was the word *Go!* from Big Boy One, one of the old battleships cruising the choppy seas below in the center of Task Force Sixteen.

Gazing down on the island, Michael thought, What a helluva place to fight a battle!

Attu was so isolated, the westernmost island of the Aleutian chain and a mere fly speck on the ocean chart. Exposed to raw weather beating southeastward from nearby Siberia, Attu suffered daily from driving rains and snows, high winds, numbing sleet and chilling fog. Michael had heard of few other places as uninviting to live upon, much less wage war. Six days ago the poor bastards of the Seventh Infantry had slogged ashore at Massacre Bay and Red Beach at Holtz Bay. Six long brutal days of cold and misery, of battle and mud and death. Now the Japs at Holtz Bay were said to be retreating. True? He shrugged. That was the latest word.

From this altitude Michael thought the island looked just like its map. Forty-six miles long and fifteen wide, most of it mountainous, icy and treacherous. No trees. Its jagged outline formed numerous reef-studded harbors, most of them exposed to wild gales and heavy seas. One major exception lay on the northern shore—Holtz Bay, deep, two miles wide and marked by a series of low hills called Moore Ridge which jutted into the bay and extended inland, thereby dividing Holtz Valley in two. The result was twin valleys, West Arm and East Arm.

East Arm—that's where the Japs were. Retreating. And that's where the P-38's were scheduled to strafe.

"Close up, close up," said Coach from the lead plane, his voice brittle with static. "Mike, you're all over the goddamn sky."

"Roger, Coach." A touch of rudder and a half-inch of aileron brought him back into position. He eyed the nearest plane—Eddie's. Michael had always thought that on the ground, wheels down, a P-38 looked like something that should pull up its pants. But here? Four hundred and ten mph at 25,000, maneuverable as an Indy racer and able to climb like a rocket. Fly it while you sleep. Though this one had the nasty gasp-producing habit of fluttering its tail in a long steep dive, and the manifold pressure of the left engine had a strange tendency to run a notch low. Synchronizing the engines was sometimes a problem. At such times the plane hobbled like a guy on a crutch. But it could be lots worse. At least the new superchargers kept ice off the carburetors.

"Room service, anyone?" asked Hank's bored voice.

"Martini for me," said Jughead quickly. "A whole pitcherful."

"Tall blonde, brunette, redhead." That bass rumble was Jake. "I'm not particular."

"*Ach, ja!*" muttered Eddie, playing his favorite role. "You kinders haff no brains. For me a glass of schnapps. *Ja! Mit zom—*"

"Keep the chatter down, fellas," said Coach. "We're being monitored by Big Boy One."

"Screw Big Boy One," said a quick falsetto.

"Screw you, too, Coach," said an unnatural bass.

"All right, you guys."

Michael's glance caught the instrument panel and a certain likeness Scotch-taped there. It showed a rakish tilt to her head, an unruly mop of natural blond hair, a little button nose, a cheerful grin and happy gray eyes. Phyllis, the light of his life. The photo, even yet, gave him the same sense of discovery and wonder that he'd felt from the very start, combined with a strange new urgency.

"Eagle One," crackled the radio. "This is Big Boy One. Do you read?"

"Roger. What's the word?"

"Your mission is go! Repeat, go! Weather is now clear over the target. At ground level, wind is gusting at thirty knots from the north. Hit 'em hard!"

"Roger. Wilco and out." Coach began a long sweeping turn to the left. "Mike, you hear that?"

"Got it, Coach," said Michael. "I'm all set."

"Take Jughead with you. The rest of us will circle west, act as bait for the AA guns. You use that long spine of Fish Hook Ridge for cover. Sweep around the headland, low and fast, and dive in from the east before the AA crews spot you. Do it right and this oughta be a snap."

"Roger." Michael took a deep breath, peering down on East Arm.

"Get those AA's and I buy the beer. Otherwise I'll have your ass."

"So what else is new?" He eased the plane down and away and began sliding left, Jughead taking position above and behind the left wing. Nose down, more throttle, the horizon cocked at an angle. Speed building—410 mph. The sea gray and huge. A dark rain cloud moving in from the north.

Down past Massacre Bay, the altimeter spinning. Eight thousand. Seven. Five. Throttle wide and the whine from the superchargers sharp in his ears. Down, down—faster, the plane bucking in the blasts of the wind. Three thousand, two, one, level now. At two hundred feet skimming the surface of the sea, it looked cold and deadly. Briefly he thought of old Gus Weiss, who a month ago disappeared in the wind on a routine mission and had never been heard from again. Gone was the die-hard Graham, who couldn't contend with the silent, clammy-gray and ever-pervading fog. Gone, too, was McGee, believe it or not a Jew, who undershot the field at Amchitka and in thirty seconds sank to his death in the bay. But nothing of the sort would ever happen to Mike Andrews, trencherman without equal and the guy responsible for the glow in Phyllis's eyes. Not he! He was too young to die. Phyllis wouldn't like it either.

The island swept past. Hard bank left, the turn-and-bank indicator registering 60 degrees, ground-speed needle pushing 540 mph. A sudden shadow speeding below. He peered ahead and down at Eagle Seven—little Jughead—cocked on his ear as Michael was and skimming the crest of the waves. Goddamn! "Jughead, those are ten-foot waves. You're too low! You need a hundred feet, minimum. Come on up!"

Silence. Goddamn kid, green and foolish, cutting a tighter

bank and sweeping low and in front to get the first crack at the Japs. Stupid, ignorant and brash. The plane below and its shadow on the waves were almost one. Couldn't he see? Didn't he know? Why wouldn't he listen? Hotshot— "Jughead, ease up! Abort! Abort!"

Even as he spoke a wave ahead reached up and flicked the Lightning's wingtip. Michael could only watch wide-eyed as the plane began cartwheeling at 500 per across the water. One bounce, two, tail-booms scooting free, one wing fluttering wide on a course of its own, the rest disappearing in a huge white final splash, seven seconds and a full mile from first contact. Two seconds more and the tower of water whipped past below and behind.

"Big Boy One, this is Eagle Four. Eagle Seven went in two miles east of East Arm. He went in hard! Repeat—"

"We got it, Eagle Four. Help is on the way." Somewhere nearby a sleek gray destroyer would already be pouring on the steam, heeling in a sharp turn with white water peeling back from the bow.

No time to think. Target three miles away. At 480 mph he had less than twenty seconds to locate the target, line up the sights and fire. In the nose were four 50-caliber MG's and one rapid-fire 20-millimeter cannon, all cocked and ready. Michael peered hard into the distance. Where are the AA's? Right? Left? In the blink of an eye the shoreline loomed and flicked behind. Slightly right—a streak of flame and spurt of smoke. There! The controls moved with his hand. A long barrel swam into the gunsights. Crosshairs just so. Fire! The plane-bucked. Tracers streamed forth, up a little, a touch right. He watched the 20's burst on target, flashing, objects blasted apart, debris in the air. A part of what might have been a man turned a lazy somersault and fell away. Back a half-inch on the stick and the plane lifted, ground speed 460. Behind him the AA gun had, he hoped, lost its gunsight. Maybe the tracking gear was smashed. Certainly the crew was dead. Score one, he thought, for Eagle Four.

He held course and speed for fifteen seconds, half the length of East Arm, then arched the plane high, a thousand, two thousand feet and over in a half-loop and let it roll upright. Nose down and gaining speed. The other AA—where? Tundra, little silver streams, muskeg grass, snowy banks—there! A barrel moving slowly in traverse, the crew frantically trying to bear on this abrupt new danger. He could see them now in the gunsight, little dark creatures who kept working while his tracers were reaching, searching, finding. Michael had time to place six 20-millimeter shells into the heart of the gun. Score two. Then quickly back on the stick, heart pumping, the plane so low that a man with a good arm could have thrown a shoe into a prop. Close. Far too close.

Zooming skyward he caught a glimpse of the next target: on a zigzag trail up the hillside to the pass leading to Chichagof Harbor—a long line of Jap troops in full retreat. Hundreds. With the AA's out of action they would now have no protection from aircraft at all.

"Eagle Four to Eagle One. You there, Coach?"

"Roger. You got the AA's?"

"Scratch both. Everything's clear. What's the scoop about Jughead?"

"Negative. No trace, no chance. Went down like a stone."

Michael gazed blankly at the sky. He felt empty and found nothing at all to say. Jughead—now a closed book. *Finis la guerre.* Happy screwing in that great whorehouse in the sky. "Coach, I tried to warn him."

"We all heard. Okay, you guys, line astern. Let's go to work."

At 4,000 feet Michael brought the plane level and found the line of planes peeling off and angling down toward the mountain trail. All had throttled back, flaps down, to give them more time to fire. He had time to circle once over West Arm before joining the line at the rear. By that time Coach and Eddie had both fired on that long serpentine line of Jap troops. Then Jake, Joe, each one in turn. On the trail snow flew like dust. Lips pressed tight, concentrating, Michael aligned his sights on that haze of stirred snow. Gently he pressed the trigger and watched the tracers reach out. More snow dust rose in his sights; he blocked from his mind all that was happening there. The mission was, as Eddie had said, "A gift to the friendly neighborhood folks who sponsored Pearl Harbor." So just lift the nose and spray the trail.

At last Michael raised his thumb from the firing button, added full throttle, and eased back on the control column. The last two of the tiny figures below had scurried into the dark of a cave but the others had caught the full force of his four 50-calibers. In close work like this it was never good to use the 50's and the 20-millimeters together. The recoil from the cannon jarred the plane, slowed it by a good 10-20 mph and tended to throw it off course. The resulting spraying effect of the 50's was often unproductive, so keeping the gunsights on target was always a first consideration.

By this time it was safe to say the raid had been a success. Everyone from general to grease-jockey should be congratulated. He could report four hundred dead Japs sprawled in the snow.

Michael felt no particular remorse or even regret. He saw no reason to. It was just too bad, that's all. Somebody always in the wrong place at the exact time. Like Jughead. That was war. They had started it. Now they were getting it back. At least the dead Japs wouldn't be killing good American GI's in the cold and mud and snow. That's all that mattered.

The plane was lifting nicely, strong and smooth, picking up speed, and would clear the summit of the pass by a good two hundred feet. Mission over. In forty minutes he'd be back at base. First he'd find the can, then a mug of hot coffee. He'd have what passed for a hot shower and force down a hot meal of whatever garbage the cooks were serving. Write to Phyllis. Sweet little wonderful Phyllis. There might even be a letter from her.

Phft! Phft! Phft! He jerked away, aware of sudden searing pain in his left arm, shoulder, ribs. He heard himself shouting, screaming. My God! Hit! He'd been shot. Blood came welling through the sleeve of his jacket. The whimper he heard was his own and he gripped the controls, amazed, confused, peering right and down, sure the sudden gunfire had come from there. On the mountain pass below a tiny solitary figure, black and vengeful against the snow, holding what might be a light machine gun. You sonuva—

Without warning the right engine lost all power, flared briefly with a long tongue of flame. Instantly the right engine housing and half the wing became a roaring red mass of flame, black ugly smoke streaming like a funeral' pyre behind.

Jesus God, there seemed a thousand things to do all at once: kill the right switch, full power left throttle—both with only his good right arm. Kick left rudder—the one remaining engine was pulling the plane about. Altitude a mere eighteen hundred feet. Mountains straight ahead. With an effort he banked the plane left and began following a long deep ravine down to the sea. Bleeding, bleeding—

"Big Boy One, this is Eagle Four. Mayday! Mayday! Fire on board! Wounded! Going down into Chichagof Harbor."

Burning—oh, God! Nothing but hard land below and freezing water dead ahead. No handy Navy destroyer to pull him out quick. Japs all around. Shit! Burning, bleeding and going down—

Almost as an afterthought he jettisoned the spare gas tank. For an instant, with less weight, the plane lifted, then lurched like a wounded deer and sagged as the remaining engine died. He stared at the dead prop, couldn't believe it. Why? He realized then he should have switched to the main tank first. Idiot! Fool! With no power the plane had the gliding angle of a falling stone.

"Eagle Four, this is Big Boy One. Say again! Say again! Over."

God, he hurt! Bleeding to death. With one hand tried to start the one engine—no go. Altitude now only a thousand, wind whistling a funeral dirge. The shore lay directly below and freezing death in the depths ahead. Angrily he swung the plane hard right along the shoreline, tried to see through smoke and flame a space flat enough and long enough in all these snowy mountains to set down. Best to keep the wheels up; maybe they wouldn't catch and the plane turn turtle.

He could feel the heat of the flames. Gas line shot through, he guessed; all that gas pouring out on a hot engine—

"Mayday! Chichagof! Chichagof, you dumb sonuvabitch! Mayday! Eagle Four burning and going down into Chichagof."

Bleeding bad. Need a tourniquet. Sonuvabitch—the only flat spot ashore was occupied by a collection of little white buildings and a large underground A-frame building similar to those in Holtz. No room there. No dice anywhere—too many Japs. They'd kill him.

"Mike, this is Coach. We're with you. Are you wounded?"

"One of the sonsabitches shot me, Coach—"

The heat was now intense, the cockpit seeping smoke. Hardly any lift at all from the right side, the flames burning the wing through. Down, down, only three hundred left. Shoulder screaming, ribs screaming. Blood all over—

Desperately he banked the plane hard right toward a shallow, too-short valley lined by snow and topped by a veneer of tundra grass. Cross controls—left aileron, right rudder, crab half-sideways and keep the flames flowing away. The plane sagging, sighing, dying in the air. Phyllis, I love you—

At the last moment he kicked left rudder and let the plane belly-flop straight on. It hit hard, held together, sliding in the grip of the mud into a bank of snow. With a lurch it stopped. Out! Out! The heat from the flames was now unbearable, smoke, fumes. Hard to breathe. God, oh, God, it's going to blow. He fumbled with the canopy, hands slippery with blood; at last it opened. Safety belt. Shoulder harness. Parachute straps—pain be damned. Up! Out! The back of his jacket burning now. Roar of flames. Smoke. Stench. Quickly!

He fell upon the wing at the left, found his feet and dove into the snow, rolling, twisting, pressing his back to the snow. The jacket hissed, its heat ceased, but there was pain all across his back. Up now. Run! Get away—

He had stumbled fifty yards away when it blew; thanks to sealed, bullet-proof tanks it took that long. No matter now. His belt served as a quick tourniquet for his left arm. Where were the Japs? Which the best way to run?

Engines. A glance upward and there they were, circling. Coach, Eddie. Jake. Joe. They couldn't possibly help him, not here, not now. . . .

Maybe they didn't even know he'd gotten out. He hugged the ground, listening for approaching Japs.

What to do? Where to go? West? Tonight, not in the full light of day. Right now he needed a place to hide, to wait. Away from the plane. Also shelter from this God-awful biting wind. Food and water before too long. Medical care—shit! Tonight he'd head toward Massacre Bay, feel his way an inch at a time through the lines. Tomorrow by this time he'd be warm and safe in American hands, somewhere in a hospital, home scot-free.

Meantime he remembered the little white houses in Aleut Village. Less than a half-mile away. Japs there? Their headquarters area? Maybe dangerous, but did he have a choice? Surely somewhere there he could find a way to get out of sight and escape this God-awful bite of the wind.

The black billowing smoke from the wrecked American aircraft had faded to a tendril of dirty brown by the time Dr. Tomi Nakamura, Acting Officer in the Japanese Imperial Army, had properly scrubbed and was ready for surgery.

Tomi knew he should not perform surgery, not right now. His left knee ached with early rheumatism, and he felt far too tired—exhausted, really—after the all-night trek from his old hospital at East Arm, up the zigzag trail and across the snowy pass called Umanose and down the long ravine to his new field hospital at Chichagof Harbor. All this with his personal effects strapped to his back and two heavy cartons of medicine on one shoulder. It was now 0630; he had not slept or eaten since arriving, but at once began to organize his workplace. He felt heavy and sluggish, his eyes dull, hands stiff. The patients, he thought, deserved more than he could give.

God is our refuge and our strength, he prayed. Therefore we will not fear.

He did not bow his head or move his lips to pray. He prayed in his mind. He was, so far as he knew, the only Japanese Christian on the island. That made matters difficult. The Buddhists, and especially the Zenists, frowningly resented any display of other religions. Except of course for Hayasaka, a young wardman, who one day had asked to borrow the New Testament.

At five-foot-five, Tomi was taller than the average Japanese. His normal weight was 135—but less than that now, due to half-rations these past two months. His hair style had changed as well, not parted on one side and combed laterally across his head but cut to the length of one-half inch, no more, conforming both to the esteemed Garrison Commander Colonel Shima's order and to the dictates of good sanitary practice. Otherwise he remained, as always, a serious man, fair in complexion, with an open face marked by a square jaw, calm eyes and a small mustache carefully trimmed. Plus wire-rimmed spectacles, the penalty of years of hard, constant study.

Weary as Tomi was, he could see that Dr. Hirose, his immediate superior, was in no better shape. In the harsh light of a gas lantern Hirose did not look like a surgeon, a promising orthopedic specialist. A short, thin man not yet forty, with crumpled hair and weary eyes, he merely looked like a father who'd been awakened one too many times by a restless child.

Hirose was grumpy. "Too little rest these days," he muttered. "The Americans lack the grace to let a man sleep."

Tomi said nothing. Hirose considered Americans a host of hard-eyed fanatic monsters bearing terrible weapons, whose only intent was to torture and kill all Japanese. But Tomi knew better. Americans were neither vicious nor truly his enemy. Imagine him, Tomi Nakamura, a devout Christian, an enemy of the land he had come to love almost as he loved Japan.

In his mind he saw a scattering of gray stately buildings on a lush hillside in Northern California, where he'd studied the life of Jesus and majored in premed. How friendly everyone had been. Bright smiles, so generous and kind. Even later, in medical school near Los Angeles—

For nine years he had lived in America, studying, watching, learning, comparing. He considered the American Constitution a magnificent Christian document. Jefferson, a giant for all time. Washington, Adams, Franklin, Paine—all had been men of religious ethics and good will. With a cadre of others of their kind they had created an atmosphere where simple folk could be their best—or worst. The truly amazing thing about America was that anyone, even the most downtrodden, had infinitely more freedom to stand up in public and curse his surroundings, circumstances, country and its political leaders than the richest and most influential Japanese gentleman.

He saw Sergeant Okasaki waiting beside the first patient. A large and bulky man in his mid-forties and a veteran of more than twenty-five years of Army experience, Sergeant Okasaki was Tomi's assistant in surgery and in the wards. He was also the unit's *Shuban Kashikan*, the NCO in charge of quarters. It was rumored throughout all Attu that Okasaki was superior to all men in strength, dedication to duty and prodigious consumption of sake.

"Is all in readiness?" He eyed the first two of the day's casualties. Both were superior privates—one with a nasty head wound that Hirose chose and the other a belly puncture that fell to him.

Behind the tables the other surgical personnel were ready and standing by, including Hayasaka, the poetry-loving scrubman who bowed his respect. A glance proved the back table had been arranged—the gloves and varieties of sponge sticks, towel clips, gowns, towels, sheets and sutures. The ring stand, too, displayed a ready assortment of needlehooks and holders, Russian dressing forceps, Michel clipholders and clips, a groove director, a probe, a ribbon retractor. Also the Mayo stand with its curved Kelly hemostats and straight Kellys, forceps, types of scissors, scalpels, ligature ties, two sizes of Babcock intestinal forceps—

Tomi leaned over the patient, a small, thin man of middle years. He was breathing in ragged gasps. Eyes dilated . . .

"Morphine?"

"Thirty milligrams, given by a field doctor six hours ago." Okasaki was reading the red "drug tag."

Six hours was too long without medical care, too long to lie hemorrhaging inside. Tomi imagined the man lying all those precious hours on some frozen slope, waiting for men to carry him away, waiting for enough light to see their way down the mountain. Waiting—then to have the fog lift and expose him and his rescuers to heavy enemy fire. Hours of waiting, lying cold, sweating, vomiting, bleeding inside, watching the thin hard light of dawn soften, grow vague and begin fading into shadows . . .

The man's skin was ashen gray and felt cool, especially the hands and feet, proving deteriorating circulation. Sweat covered the body. The skin felt clammy. The pulse seemed nonexistent. Blood pressure would be down. "What are the readings?"

"Eighty over forty and going down," Okasaki said instantly. "His pulse is one-twenty and rising."

Hypovolemic shock. "Oxygen, at once." Tomi stood erect. "Start an IV of one thousand normal saline. Use a large-bore needle, a fifteen gauge." That would hasten the flow of solution.

Sodium chloride was all right, he told himself. But Ringer's lactate was better and so was Dextron, or plasma or serum albumin. But he could use only what he had. Then hope. The thing to do was to go in there quickly, find the source of hemorrhage and close it off. Anything he did was a gamble.

The wound itself was not impressive, a small puncture lateral to the umbilicus and about the same size. A shot from a rifle or pistol had penetrated through the body, emerging superior to the entry. No external bleeding. The anterior opening had almost closed, was puckered a bit about the opening, blue-edged—

"Fifteen hundred units of tetanus," he ordered. He had no way of knowing if the patient was sensitive to tetanus. Best to err on the safe side. With no wasted motion, but carefully, he began irrigating the wound with generous quantities of warm saline solution. First, clean the wound, then let it bleed a bit and wash out all foreign substances such as loose threads from clothing, bits of dirt or grass and perhaps flecks of metal from the bullet. Any devitalized tissue would soon show itself by lack of color, lack of bleeding, lack of elasticity. So cut it away. Irrigate again, then go in and start sewing.

Perhaps the body stiffened momentarily, he wasn't sure. Perhaps a hand twitched as if to fend something off. There was no doubt, however, that the dry gasping suddenly ceased. The silence rang in Tomi's ears. "Pulse?" he asked in a calm tone.

"It rose to one-forty, a moment ago. Now—"

"*Arigato*. Thank you." For an instant he peered down on the sweaty hulk of flesh on the table. One eye had half opened and the mouth had fallen ajar. Tomi touched a damp shoulder, gazed down on a nerveless arm. If only he could have worked faster, gone in quicker, the man might . . . just might have survived. There were always a lot of ifs.

He bowed his head. The grace of our Lord Jesus Christ be with you.

Losing a patient hurt. It wasn't the first time he'd lost a patient, not even the first during surgery. Even so, it hurt, it always hurt. Each time, something went out of him; he died a little himself. Then the joy of being a physician—helping people, making them well and strong again—was gone, leaving nothing within but a huge, black lonely pit.

He glanced at Hirose, there in the yellow light easing chips of bone from a man's brain. "Do you wish help?"

"No." Hirose's quick glance, a flash of compassion in his dark eyes, showed that he, too, had known that dark pit. "This is a one-man task at the moment. Others need you more."

"Next!" In turn he treated a hip wound, shrapnel. A right arm with ulnar artery severed, nerve damage and shattered elbow; a face wound, one gaping maw of congealed blood, ripped flesh, one eye hanging loose amid flecks of bone and a driblet of bright arterial blood; a deep chest wound, the pneumothorax open, its puncture hole plugged with a soiled handkerchief; a leg blown off below the knee, the bone stained with black earth; a hand ripped and shredded, several fingers gone or hanging by slivers of flesh. Last was a dead man, a row of neat round holes stitched across his naked chest.

Later, seeking escape from the smell of blood and medicines, Tomi stood alone on the bluff enduring a strong Arctic wind whipping in from the sea, studying Chichagof Harbor. This was his first view of it. Since arriving from Holtz Bay in the dark only hours before the American planes had caught Colonel Nagumo's men climbing toward the pass called Umanose, he had slept too few hours and performed too long in surgery. Now he could see that Chichagof Harbor, like Holtz Bay, opened to the north. Its entire width was merely a mile, perhaps a bit less. Centered on a quarter-mile plain between beach and hill was Aleut Village, ten or so white wood-frame houses and a school, used now as a communications center and offices for administrative personnel. The simple once-white church was now headquarters for the esteemed Garrison Commander Colonel Shima. A large underground storage building, well roofed by a camouflage of grassy sod, lay on the western edge of the plain. Two hundred yards west, in a large flat-bottomed ravine curving up from the beach toward the mountains, were the underground hospital barracks. On the thirty-foot bluff above the ravine, the hospital tents.

It was the exposed site of the tents that annoyed Tomi. Twenty-six feet in diameter and octagonal, both the operating tent and ward tent would meet the full force of the wind, rain and the worst of weather. Also possible enemy fire.

Worse yet was the general state of the medical department on Attu. By every standard he had ever known, this hospital, if indeed it deserved the name, was poorly equipped. It lacked even the simplest of X-ray equipment and the means of typing blood—equipment they might have had, but which now lay in the hold of a ship somewhere on the floor of the northern Pacific Ocean, thanks to the diligence, accuracy and firepower of the American air arm. Neither did the hospital have serum, which had gone instead to Kiska. Kiska had the hospital; Attu could boast only of two glorified first aid stations. Poor ones at that.

He considered the operating area. Chest number one held the bandages and dressings; number two, the instruments, an inadequate twelve-cubic-inch autoclave and bottles of 95 percent medicinal alcohol; number three, the drugs and medicines. Number four, if they had one, would be the dental chest. But men who needed dental care were either ignored or sent to Kiska. Prior to the American landing, serious dental cases, involving radical surgery, were sometimes returned to Tokyo.

The greatest negligence he'd found since his arrival last March was the total lack of electricity for the hospital. Headquarters had electricity. Some of the officers' quarters had electricity. The incomplete radar station on the highest peak of Hokuchin Yama had electricity—at least until the Americans bombed the thing off its base a few weeks ago. But the hospital obviously had a low priority, if any at all. Light was provided by gasoline lanterns and candles. Water, from the stream in front of the hospital, was heated on a two-burner gasoline stove operated by air pressure; it needed pumping almost constantly. The beds were not cots but mere canvas litters supported at each end by wooden boxes. Such shortcomings would never be allowed in an American Army unit, but here . . .

He sighed his frustration. All he could do was his best.

"Honored doctor?" Tomi jumped, unaware of anyone at his side. "I do not wish to intrude upon your meditations. But I have brought you a few biscuits. I regret there is not more. And some hot tea."

It was Hayasaka, the wardman-poet, his eyes pleading, shining. Tomi had once seen a doe with such eyes in a zoo. As always, Hayasaka was quite thoughtful. Tomi thanked him and began munching the hard biscuits. Suddenly ravenous, he found them delicious.

"Honored doctor, may I speak?"

"Of course, Hayasaka. What is it?"

"Each day I read your New Testament," said Hayasaka in his gentle tone. "I become confused. How does one pray? Is it true I am a sinner? Where have I sinned? I am told one should not fear death. Yet, how can one not fear the unknown?"

Tomi gave Hayasaka all his attention. "Your sins are those of Adam and Eve. Soon I will tell you of their disobedience. Meanwhile, you are not going to die. Not yet. But even if you do, you must not be afraid. You must kneel to God. Tell him how you feel. Be humble and sincere. Ask for forgiveness of all your sins, and remember that whosoever shall call on the name of the Lord shall be saved."

"Oh! I do wish to be saved!"

"Remember, too, that all are sinners in the eyes of the Lord. But few are truly wicked."

"I shall pray. But . . . is it proper to ask for reinforcements?"

"By all means."

"Thank you! Thank you." Hayasaka beamed his pleasure. "On this occasion I am reminded of a certain haiku by Basho."

Tomi fumbled to understand. Basho—a seventeenth-century Japanese poet.

"Basho wrote: 'Gathering the rains of May, the Mogami River flows swiftly.' Is it not beautiful? So prophetic."

"Y—yes." Was this truly a prophecy? Gathering the rains of May . . . representing the forces of war? On Attu? The Mogami River—perhaps the tide running in Japan's favor?

That could not be so, as Tomi knew well. At least not here on Attu. Six days ago the American landing northeast of Holtz Bay had, in effect, outflanked the heavy fortifications at West Arm, forced a costly withdrawal, cut the surviving forces from their main supply base and confined the Japanese to the heights above Chichagof Valley. In only six days the situation had become desperate, with 11,000 big, tough, angry Americans opposing only 2,400 hungry sons of Nippon.

Reinforcements from Japan? Promised, yes. Infantry, artillery, food and ammunition already loaded aboard ships at Paramushiro in the Kurile Islands; the Fifth North Force of the Imperial Navy ready to escort the ships; the Japanese air arm standing by; submarines already in the area and stalking the enemy—so said rumor. But no deep-laden freighters rode the tides in Chichagof Harbor; no lean gray wolves of the sea challenged American battleships. As always, Americans ruled the skies. Japanese exultation of six days ago was now giving way to a morbid sense of . . . what? Had they in fact been abandoned?

At this rate, he thought, every Japanese on the island will die.

Discouraged, turning now to begin his morning rounds, Tomi noted that the smoke from the wrecked American aircraft had completely ceased. Across the valley there were many soldiers with rifles and fixed bayonets still searching for the missing pilot.

Sergeant John Murphy, in charge of the Third Squad of the Second Platoon, Dog Company, had realized at the first light of dawn that today was meant to be a good one. From West Arm he had watched that long single file of Japs high on the mountain trail crumble under the guns of the P-38's. Their bodies were still there; he could see them with the lieutenant's binoculars. Hundreds! It was encouraging to know that the ranks of the Japs were depleted by that many. During the coming advance he and all the kids had a better chance.

Two battalions strong, they were still waiting in the shell pits and bomb craters of West Arm to attack Moore Ridge. Waiting since 0600; it was now 0745. Waiting, as they had done so often these past six days for word to go ashore, to climb the bluff at Red Beach, to cross that long windswept plateau, to attack the Japs dug in on Hill X; to reconnoiter, raid and clear the whole area; to advance then without covering fire into the churned mud of West Arm and find it deserted and the Japs busily constructing rearguard emplacements on Moore Ridge. Waiting, too, for a chance to eat chow, for a stolen moment of sleep, for orders that never seemed to come.

"Just like the goddamn Army," Private Swensen growled as if reading Murphy's mind. "Reveille at some ungodly hour, stick you in a lousy hole in a fucken cold wind and nothing to eat but K-rats. F'Chrissake!"

Everybody was tired, Murphy thought. And edgy. Each man of the squad was quiet in a desperate sort of way, drawn into himself with a tight knot of fear in his gut. Everybody silent but Swensen.

"I had breakfast once," Swensen announced to no one in particular. "Year before last, it was. In August. Served in bed at ten in the morning after an all night orgy. Suzy—that was her name. One gorgeous little piece."

"Lousy damn island," growled Jeeters, peering at the distant Jap figures frantically digging on Moore Ridge. "Anyplace without sidewalks ain't worth fighting for."

Attu reminded Murphy a lot of the Nevada desert just north of Las Vegas: barren, bleak and colorless, only darker, with snow and ice in abundance and a strong icy wind that wouldn't quit. A dead land scarred by small ravines, occasional rocks and great patches of pure snow. Underfoot lay soft wet tundra and large areas of rootlike bramble that snatched at passing legs. Everything muddy. Mud on his clothes, shelter-half, sleeping bag, everything he owned.

What he really wanted was to fire up the canned heat and try to make coffee. Coffee, hot steaming coffee! He wished, too, for dry socks and a chance to wash his hands, brush his teeth. Maybe tonight, he thought. If he was lucky.

It all reminded Murphy of what he'd tried to ignore. So many things—the woolen Navy cap, so necessary, that matted his hair and eventually began to hurt his scalp; the long woolen underwear that raised little itching bumps like insect bites on every part of his anatomy; the six-day-old beard that itched like mad under his helmet strap; wet feet and stiff boots, to say nothing of dirt and mud that had crept into every crevice of clothing and scraped against tender flesh; the ever-present smell of stale sweat and the sour feel of scummy teeth. What was it the squad kept repeating? All this—and Attu.

"All this waiting really tickles my fancy," Swensen said, looking everywhere but at Moore Ridge. "I knew a dame who said that once. She told me one night, 'Honey, you really tickle my fancy.' And I says to her, 'Darling, I ain't laid a hand on you yet.'"

No one laughed. Two hours they'd waited in this cold. Within a quarter-mile Murphy could see more than a dozen captured Jap warehouses all loaded with food and supplies. Barracks, too, with stoves and coal.

Waiting was hard. For himself it didn't matter. He was thirty-four now, six-foot-one, 180 pounds, still lean and strong. He'd had the best life had to offer and lost it all. His concern now was for the squad. His kids. The only family he had left.

Five of them were new to the squad, replacements for others sent to special schools just before the division left the States. He eyed them one by one:

Corporal Baker. A college boy filled with a sense of his own importance, an attorney's son who needed to learn humility. Smart but sassy. Had lots of potential and stood up well under fire.

Hall. Sloppy and undisciplined, cheeks aflame with pimples, whose greatest need was lots of food and a good friend. His mustache was a total failure, and he smoked too much.

Jeeters, from New York. Sallow-faced and lean, who imitated Murphy's walk and speech, a kid fumbling toward manhood. A me-too kind of guy who didn't mind using people if he could.

Lewis. Who knew Lewis? Lewis was an orphan who seldom spoke and always stayed in the shadows. Obedient and overtrusting. He often displayed a blind adoration of Murphy.

Jones. A Negro sent by a typical Army fuck-up to a white unit. Jones was six-foot-five, 240 pounds and still growing. Easygoing and always grinning, he carried the Browning automatic rifle—the BAR. The other kids ignored him, most times, but nothing fazed Jones.

The remaining four in the squad had been with Murphy from the beginning, and for them he had a special affection. He had tried to guide them, be a big brother. There was Young, a Utah Mormon who detested cigarettes and alcohol in any amount. Also blasphemy. Unpopular with the new men; he preached too much about morals. He wrote home often and spoke quietly of a certain girl he hoped to marry. Brave when he had to be, and dependable.

Beside Young was Cooper, an Arizona cowboy who was always shivering and dreaming of warm desert climes. A ranch, he often said, was the greatest thing in the world. Arizona—God's country. Spoke with a soft drawl, seldom smiled, and trusted everyone with all he owned.

Next was Bennett, shy and naïve and virginal-looking, the long-suffering butt of everybody's jokes. He chewed gum constantly. Seemed to suffer from a feeling of inferiority. Bolstering the boy's ego was often time-consuming; Murphy couldn't always protect him from the squad's give-and-take, which was sometimes cruel.

Last of all—Swensen. Swensen was brash and incorrigible, hiding his real self behind outrageous boasts about women. His freckles, wild thatch of blond hair and toothy grin were very much like those of Murphy's oldest son, now dead. Which made it hard to watch Swensen . . .

A faint shout carried on the wind. Suddenly men down the line were rising, and Murphy tightened his chin strap. "Listen, you guys. Remember you can expect grazing machine-gun fire. Short sprints are best. Keep calm; take your time. Use all the cover you can find. Get down, fire a round or two, then go. Baker, remember the Japs are inclined to fire at anyone waving commands."

"We know, we know," said Jeeters with a frown, his cigarette bouncing with the motion of his lips. "How many times you gonna tell us?"

"Enough so you remember. Make sure you do. You guys all got extra socks on?" Each man now wore three pairs of fine woolen socks, found in a captured Jap warehouse. All except Jones, whose big feet and one pair of socks were all his boots could hold. "Everybody got an extra Jap blanket?"

"I-got-mine-so-I'm-jes'-fine," sang Jones with a grin.

Young kept checking his rifle sling and the straps that held his pack. Bennett furiously chewed gum and Swensen was strangely quiet.

Murphy eyed the bare smooth sand of the beach. No cover there at all. But inshore about twenty yards a five-foot-high shelf covered by rough bramble brush would be his route. Bramble brush—so damned difficult to walk through, with all of those wiry, thick, long stems that snagged a man's legs unless he lifted them high, stomping his way along. Tiring and slow. Bramble brush, however, had certain undeniable assets: it was dense, knee-deep and green-gray. Good cover.

Murphy was not a religious man. At home he had seldom gone

to church and then only because Helen had insisted—the kids and all. He considered Christianity a bald myth. Christmas to him was a time for giving gifts and eating a fine dinner, a family time. The concepts of fate and predestination were for other folk; he scoffed at such beliefs. Yet, today, gazing at the beach and the bramble brush, he thought it strange that his squad would advance on the left flank of the platoon, the platoon on the left flank of the company, the company on the left flank of battalion, and the battalion at the left of a two-battalion attack. Somehow the implications of all that was more than he cared to think about. But it would be a good day, he felt in his bones. A real good, whopping kind of day.

The weather cooperated. To the southeast a cold snow now fell on Massacre Bay, on friend and foe alike; a scant mile or so eastward sleet kept pelting Chichagof Harbor, while to the north a heavy rain was falling on ships at sea. Here at Holtz the fog was nonexistent and all was clear, though the wind came strong from the north at forty or more miles per hour. Such wind, at subfreezing temperatures, had a way of penetrating the heaviest of clothing. Already Murphy's ears ached with cold, despite the cap that covered them. A man could freeze solid, he thought, remembering the awkward poses of a few Jap bodies he'd seen, frozen hands clutching the air in agony.

The command came to move out. In the waiting, milling mass of men there was suddenly order. In an instant belts were given a final hitch, canteens adjusted to a more comfortable spot, cigarettes puffed one more time and then tossed into the tundra, rifles brought to port arms and a line emerged and moved ahead. Twenty yards, fifty yards—no Jap fire. Tromping through the bramble brush, Murphy could see a staggered line of men scuttling forward, another line forming behind and a third waiting their turn. Everyone seemed tensed for the first incoming fire. The squad was doing fine, Baker breathing heavily with the effort, Jeeters stepping right out and almost lunging through the bramble brush. Jones, the irreverent sonuvabitch, was softly singing: "Beat me, daddy, eight-to-the-bar."

On the far right the new battalion began taking light rifle and mortar fire, but nothing here on the left. A hundred-yard advance now, and no fire. Too early to start counting blessings.

Bennett suddenly fell in the bramble brush and got up cursing. Baker and Swensen had edged left and now were striding on smooth wet sand, hooting something about "suckers in the bushes." Murphy restrained himself from ordering them back. Maybe they were right. Without enemy fire, the bramble brush was too damned tiring to walk through and they had a long way to go. Cover or no cover—why do things the hard way?

Soon they were all walking on hard sand, three hundred yards from jump-off point. The Jap fire was heavier now and more widespread, mostly at the center and right. But here? Still nothing, and that began to bother Murphy. Maybe the friggen Japs were setting a trap, sucking them in. He could see no movement on the slopes of Moore Ridge. For all the world it looked like there were no Japs on this end at all.

At five hundred yards the command came to halt and dig in, for whatever reason Murphy couldn't fathom. Typical Army foul-up—waiting in this cold, balls freezing. Jesus H. Christ! Now the Japs were firing furiously on the far right. GI artillery there, and machine guns and mortars. *Pft! Pft!* Like firecrackers . . .

But here—it could have been a church picnic, except for the cold. The slopes and heights of Moore Ridge ahead seemed so innocent, a virgin waiting for the wedding night. Yet the nagging question remained: an ambush?

He eyed a certain tall peak on the east end of Moore Ridge. Any idiot with half a mind could see that a squad holding that particular peak would outflank any and all Jap positions on the ridge, in fact would command all of Holtz Valley, both sides of the ridge.

Was all this quiet a trap or an opportunity?

An old joke came to mind. Some whores forming a labor union adopted a motto—"We don't give a fuck for nothing." That's just the way he felt.

No officers in view; no one to tell him no. So why not? "Let's move out!" he yelled, grabbing his rifle and rising suddenly from his foxhole. The kids would follow, he knew. Bitch about it a bit, not too loudly, and frown, but they'd come—follow him straight to hell, really.

He began slanting down to the beach, the wind at his back. Across the tundra, through the rim of the bramble brush, into the soft sand high on the beach and at last to the hard wet surface close to shore. He kept as alert as a stalking cat, there beside the murmuring sounds of the surf and the warm smell of the sea.

A glance behind revealed the squad following in single file, rifles held at port arms, safeties off and all eyes fixed on Moore Ridge. Behind—Murphy felt surprised—straggled the rest of the platoon. For once nobody had asked questions.

What the hell? Murphy thought. The more the merrier. Let's make it a real party.

The kids were all quiet, well spread out. Along the beach he led them, past a wrecked Jap plane, a Zero float job that lay upside down on the beach. The almost sheer bluff of the ridge suddenly seemed incredibly high. The heights were green and wet, glistening in the pale sunlight, yet were ominous, deadly, waiting to gather them in.

Murphy took them through a five-foot-deep stream of icy water draining the east side of West Arm. Then the route lay hard eastward along the shoreline that jutted into the bay. Still no Japs in view. Yet they were there; his instinct swore they were.

How could the Japs not see them? Why wasn't every man in the platoon dead minutes ago? The Japs were blind, deaf, asleep—or merely waiting? Murphy didn't know and refused to worry. Worry got you nowhere. Just take what you get and ask for more.

A thousand feet eastward along the jutting shoreline he found a proper ravine. Deep, sharp-angled, narrow, slippery with dripping snow water and moss—it was nonetheless an avenue. Broadway. Main Street. Slowly they climbed, sharp eyes searching the rim above, Bennett planting his feet carefully to avoid slipping, Cooper offering a helping boost, Swensen cursing softly and grunting his way upward. Make haste slowly, Murphy thought. Don't think about a lousy court-martial.

He found himself standing on a grassy, windswept shelf about three hundred feet square. It was open and fairly level, like a mountain park, and not a Jap in sight. On its opposite side was a thirty–forty-foot knoll, the same tall knoll he'd spotted from his foxhole. So far, so good. He had this sudden urge to hurry.

His own squad and two extra men were already surrounding him, others still arriving. "Let's go." He turned and hurried toward the knoll.

Midway, a high cry rose from the far right. Spotted—dammit! Running now, desperate, scrambling up the slippery side of the knoll, he was only too aware of being too old for all this physical effort. Oh, to be young again! Sweating and breathless on the crest of the knoll, he took one quick look along the ridgeline.

"Baker, take the left flank. Jones, your BAR on the right. Open fire!"

There were forty, maybe fifty Japs a mere hundred feet down-slope and coming hard, led by a puttee-legged saber-wielding officer whose teeth gleamed white. There was no time or hardly need to aim. Murphy fired from the hip—his first target went down. Three others fell, the result of Jones's BAR. Others kept coming in short sprints, throwing hand grenades that mostly fell short, the hillside now roaring with gunfire.

"Bennett, don't shoot so fast! Aim."

GI's were joining on the left flank. More BAR's now in action and a few grenades falling among the Japs. Still the Japs came—a suicide charge?—screaming a God-awful high cry. Upslope they hurried, pressuring the left, not pausing now to fire—bayonets shining wetly. "Jones—the left flank—the BAR." Murphy detached four men to help hold the left flank. Too late! On the far left it was suddenly bayonet against bayonet, stabbing, hacking, slicing. No time to think, just jab and keep jabbing. The Jap charge seemed uncoordinated but determined. On the right and center they ran in little spurts, running and throwing themselves down, firing and running again—

Automatically Murphy fired a clip and reloaded, fired again. He saw a face dissolve, a chest blossom with red, a hand holding a grenade flying through the air. He heard little, not distinctly. A scream, perhaps a grunt. Suddenly he had no time to reload. A dark little figure had his bayonet poised almost at Murphy's gut. There was but one tiny instant of time to act without thought. A quick step, a hard lunge with all his might and the blade slid in easily from the side. A gasp, a sighing squeal, a puff of hot foul breath in his face. Murphy shoved hard with one shoulder and the Jap fell back and away.

A quick turn in the glare to parry a slashing blade. Silent, his own breath a wheeze in his throat, knee crushing crotch, rifle butt smashing jaw. The blade in and out, like slicing bread. Cutting, slashing, grunting, sweating, teeth clenched and arm wielding bayonet like a scythe. Cut the bastards down—kill! Wheel to face a new foe—feint, parry and jab. Like boxing. A thin red blade slicing the sleeve of his coat; his own steel entering a brown throat. Good job! Grunt and push him away.

His mind was aroar with shouts, cries, grunts, moans, squeals, the blast of rifles and exploding grenades. A body winced under his foot. Where were the guys, all his kids?

His hand found a clip and rammed it home. On one knee—*pow! pow! pow!* Downslope the charging little black figures fell. A grenade—pull pin and lob it. The blast threw bodies down. Another—quickly! Beside him someone fell; he had no time to look. His mind was as cold as the snow about him—a mind laughing that he had got them all this far, yet raging that the friggen Japs dared oppose him. Dammit, he was Murphy—platoon commander!

From ten feet away he snap-fired, drilled the shouting Jap commander through the chest—three hard rounds in left center. The body jerked with each round, then fell like a limb from a shattered tree. That would do it, he knew. Within seconds the surviving Japs began retreating—a rout, ignoring cover and leaving two-thirds of their original number sprawled on the slope. Yet Murphy kept sighting and firing, his mind as cool as the rifle was hot in his hands.

Then abruptly all was still, the enemy out of effective range.

The sudden silence in itself was shocking. Again he felt the wind, the cold, the damp of the air. Dull-eyed he peered at Bennett, Baker, Jones, Hall, Swensen, Jeeters, Cooper and Young. Behind dirty faces and old eyes they all seemed okay.

"Where's Lewis?" someone rasped. "Anybody see—"

They found Lewis, the orphan, the loner no one really knew, downslope amid a half-circle of four dead Japs. His head was fearfully gashed. One arm had separated at the shoulder and was lying a bloody six inches away. His eyes were open and on his thin face an expression of total incomprehension.

For a moment Murphy could only stare. Lewis! But no time for delay. He staggered erect. "Radio! Who's got the goddamn radio?" A hand rose from the right flank. "Get battalion."

In a half-minute he had the instrument in hand. "Colonel? Sergeant Murphy, Dog Company, on Moore Ridge. I'm holding this fucken hill. I got just twenty effectives. I want reinforcements." He glanced about at a score of dead and wounded GI's. "I want medics. I want ammo—"

"B Company will move out in ten minutes. What else do you need?"

"Everything—now! Tell somebody down there to get off his goddamn ass!"

Atop the peak again, rifle in hand, he gazed down on the terrain he had won. The Japs would be back, that seemed certain. But this bunch of guys would hold—that he felt was also certain. At the moment he held the key to all of Holtz Valley. Controlled it. Him, John Murphy.

You sonsabitches! he cried in silence to the fleeing Japs. I own this goddamn hill—it's mine! You want it? Come take it. Just try.

Michael didn't feel at all safe. His luck must hold until dark. Yet he was warm beneath this pile of old uniforms and as comfortable as his wounds would permit. The long underground warehouse was dim inside, silent as the proverbial tomb and completely unguarded. That's what amazed him. An American commanding officer, even the least competent, would have a half-dozen men guarding a building this size. Otherwise his own men would strip the shelves bare. Japs, Michael decided, were either honest or not very sharp.

The warehouse was a good substitute for those little white houses in Aleut Village. The church and houses were lousy with Japs. So he'd found his way here and now lay buried under old uniforms, those on the bottom clean, well repaired and neatly folded; those on top thick with mud and giving off strong odors of blood, sweat and urine. They hid him from the men who entered far too often, seized whatever boxes they needed and hurriedly left; they also kept him warm. Count your blessings, he reminded himself. No matter how few you really have.

His back, on the right side, felt like flame, especially when anything touched it. He couldn't lie on it or lean back against the wall. Lying on his stomach was complicated by the pain across his ribs—a long gash apparently caused by a passing bullet. Add the problems with his left arm. What little first aid training he remembered warned that a tourniquet must be loosened from time to time to allow blood to pass through. If not, a man could lose an arm or leg from gangrene damned quick. Every time he tried it, however, blood welled forth in alarming little spurts and he'd had to tighten it again against the flow. He had no feeling at all in his lower arm and hand, and he worried about how much blood a man could lose and still function normally.

That left him sitting up all the time. Sitting up was hard work; he was tired of it.

Outside in the tundra were a thousand little rivulets, some mere inches wide and inches deep, all filled with sparkling clear snow water. A swallow or two would help tremendously. A canteen of water, a .45 pistol, maps, compass and first aid kit had all been included in the emergency supplies for the plane, abandoned in his haste, and doubtless destroyed by fire. The K-rations—

At 3:00 A.M. he'd eaten his usual large portion of reconstituted eggs, a broad slice of fried ham, greasy potatoes with toast and jam, but only one coffee because a toilet in a P-38 at 20,000 is hard to find. Ten P.M. A long time between meals.

He couldn't help thinking of food. Juicy pork roasts. Tender beef prime rib. Turkey and gravy, a lamb stew of his mother's he'd never forget. Her overladen Thanksgiving tables. Steaks cooked to a fine turn over an open fire. Hot dogs and hamburgers and French fries. Fried chicken . . .

The thought of food brought a vision of Phyllis. Spring of '41, in the Ag Library on campus; that's where they'd met. She wore the same bobby sox, loafers, knee-length skirt, middy and open sweater as other girls, but she was somehow different. She sort of . . . bubbled, he thought. The way her face curved it was hard to know she wasn't always smiling. He knew, because he watched her from behind his books, three tables away, for three nights straight.

From her, nothing. Never a sign that she saw him, even knew he existed. Every night the same routine. She would study until eleven, fold up her books with a preoccupied air and walk out alone, skirt swinging and her round little fanny flaunting itself to the world.

Alone—that's what he couldn't understand.

Her name? No one knew. In class, at work washing dishes in the cafeteria, walking about the campus, awake or asleep, she haunted his mind. Why? He didn't know. There were lots of flirtatious girls about, but Miss Five-foot-two adorable-you wore no ring and no pin and wouldn't give him a glance.

The fourth night of sly watching became too much. Something had to give. On sheer impulse he rose from his study table, gathered his books and as nonchalantly as possible seated himself at her table, directly across from her. Close enough to brush shoes with her, if he'd tried. Even then no response, not even a frown. For half an hour he covertly studied her face, found a faint host of fine freckles on brow and cheek, truly kissable lips and a small dimple in the cleft of her chin. Her fingers were slim, the nails trimmed. No lipstick, no perfume, a totally natural girl. Her blond hair was short, cut in a casual tomboy style that left it free to swoop down over one eyebrow. Upon occasion she blasted air from one corner of her mouth, an obvious attempt, always unsuccessful, to shoo the errant lock away. She also calmly chewed pencils and frowned a bit as she read. Her eyes, he thought, were gray. Perhaps with a touch of blue. He would know if she'd only look up.

Without warning she rose, gathered her notes and books, moved to another table and immersed herself again in study. After a moment he followed, heart pounding, again sat opposite her and tried to read. The words blurred, meant nothing. Try as he would, he couldn't ignore her. Then with a start he realized she was staring at him, a level gaze that bore inward and took his measure through and through.

Beautiful warm gray eyes.

What should he say? He could think of nothing intelligent. An introduction, perhaps? He cleared his throat and without knowing what he might say heard himself whispering, "Have you seen my mind? I just lost it. One look at you and—"

Silence. From wall to wall the library roared its silence. Total rejection. He felt like a fool, found himself blushing. "I'm Michael Andrews. My friends call me Mike."

"Oh, do they?" Husky voice, contralto. One eyebrow raised as if she were looking at a bug. "I'm glad to hear you have friends."

"My mother, a dog or two and you. It's getting late. In an hour you'll have to leave."

"I'm aware of that. So?"

"So if we're going to have coffee and get acquainted, we ought to go now."

"Are we going to have coffee? I hadn't heard."

"Of course! Since I first saw you three days ago I've saved an extra nickel. So you see there's no problem."

"Naturally not. Are you all right? Normal? No fever? Tummyache? Bells in your head? Are you sure you have the right girl?"

"Absolutely! I knew instantly you were the right girl. We're going to have a long and wonderful relationship."

"Oooh! Hold it! We just started talking, like two minutes ago. You don't even know—"

"Enough. I've known you all my life. Perhaps in some previous existence as well."

"—my name. Really! And already you're getting cozy."

"You'll appreciate me better as time goes on, I'm sure. Anyway, I know everything about you I need to know."

"Such as?"

"You're the domestic type—"

"Which means I'm female. Go on."

"You're well disciplined. Organized. Brainy. An extrovert, which I like. A little bit nearsighted—you frown when you read. Very attractive."

"Were you normal, by any chance? I mean born and not hatched?"

"You're also very passionate."

"A-hah! The serpent lifts its ugly head."

"Girls with gray eyes are known to be very passionate. That's historical fact. Helen of Troy. Dido. Elaine, Ophelia and Henry the Eighth's third wife. Jack the Ripper adored gray-eyed women."

She stared. "Do you create this deathless love-prose yourself, as you go along, or does some little monkey help?"

"I'm serious. I want to know everything about you. Your favorite food. Do you snore? I sleep on my left side."

"Good for you."

"I know we're going to be good friends. At least to begin with. Then—"

"Then what? What exactly are you proposing?"

"You see? Your word, not mine. Perhaps it's destiny."

"Oh, for the love of mike—"

"Precisely! You're getting closer all the time."

She shook her head. "You know talking to you is impossible? Why don't you go away? I've got to study."

"I thought we were going to have coffee."

"I don't want any coffee."

"Y'know—" He paused to reflect. "It's historic, really. I think we're having our first argument."

"Oh, God, what have I done to be so punished?"

"You're beautiful. Now, can we start over? We should get acquainted. Be friends—just friends, okay? I'll grow on you."

"There you go again."

"Okay, okay! Truce? Friends? Please believe me."

She sighed. "Okay, I believe you. So help me God, I do! But if what you say is true, I think your mother should have kept you in the cage."

"Oh, I'm housebroken, never fear. Reliable, lovable me."

"You're so shy and unassuming."

"And a joy to behold. How about it? I still have that extra nickel."

"I don't think I should go, really I don't."

"I think you should, really I do."

"I wouldn't want to bankrupt you."

"You're not the type—too angelic and uncorrupted. Which of course I plan to correct. Besides, you wouldn't want to break up a beautiful friendship, would you? Let's get that coffee."

"Well . . . " She blew hair from her forehead and began gathering her books. "Maybe just this once . . ."

Over coffee he learned that she was just past twenty and a sophomore in chemistry. Chemistry—a girl? "Why not?" she'd said, a warning glint in her eye. "I found I'm good at chem and I like it. Why shouldn't a girl be a chemist?"

"You're right. Why not?" She was an only child, her father an assistant manager of a bank in Berkeley, her mother a high school teacher. Her goal in life: do something worthwhile—she didn't know what yet—and be happy.

"That's marvelous!" For the moment he set aside all humor, regarding her with critical eyes. This little sweetheart doll at first glance seemed created for breeding purposes only. In fact, however, she had a first-rate brain. Also an instinct for wisdom. "Y'know, as a chemist, knowing your way around a lab, you'll be a tremendous help to me."

Head cocked sideways in a most tantalizing manner, she eyed him. "Hey, don't get any wrong ideas. I intend to be very careful about whom I get mixed up with. And I don't know you."

"Yet." A dark thought then filled his mind with dread. "There's somebody else?"

"Well . . . maybe. It's a possibility. Maybe even a probability."

"Would you clean that up, please, and run it through again?"

"Stop frowning. Everything is pretty loose between Jim and me. Very uncertain. We have an understanding, yet we don't."

"That's as clear as mud. Jim, is it? You love this guy?"

She looked at him, thinking.

"Fond of him, maybe?"

"Well . . ."

He sighed his relief. "So there's no big problem. Unless you see him often."

"He's back east going to school. He's going to be a doctor, an obstetrician, and I guess he'll make all kinds of money. He's a few years older than you."

"That's important to you—money?"

"As long as there's enough."

He raised his brows.

"Not that way, not when it comes to scads of money."

"I don't expect I'll ever be rich. Plant pathologists never get rich. But there's compensations." He grinned. "I don't think Jim's much competition."

"He's an old family friend. His father is my father's boss. All my life it's sort of been expected that someday Jim and I—"

"Don't jump to any conclusions, please. As you say, you don't know me yet."

"Jim's a nice guy. He's tall. Dark hair. He has lovely eyes." She gazed at him, seemed to compare his five-foot-eight, plain features, reddish-gold hair. "A while ago you said that I, as a chemist, could help you. I'm curious—mildly, you understand. Help how?"

He nodded to himself. He'd put out the bait and she'd swallowed it. So that proved her interest in him, a little bit at least. Carefully he explained. He was now twenty-two and would graduate in June. He was a farmboy from near Fresno, two hundred miles southeast of San Francisco. His family produced their own meat, eggs, milk products, vegetables and fruit. The cash crop was grapes. When the market for fresh table grapes fell to heartbreaking levels, they made raisins or sold to wineries—

"Three different markets? Sounds like a good, rich life."

"Not that good. Some years during the Depression we made a little or broke even. Other years . . . I don't know how Dad did it."

He was the youngest of seven children, the third son. He remembered endless afternoons after school pruning and wrapping vines in the winter cold; mindless days of irrigating in one hundred plus temperatures, sometimes eating eggs morning, noon and night because they had little else to eat; years of hardship and deprivation and sacrifice. There was also laughter and love and a feeling of giving his whole strength and mind to a common cause. His early memories involved working from dawn to dark shoulder to shoulder with Dad, brothers and sisters. Except for Mom, everyone had worked in the fields.

Silently she listened, eyes aglow. "But you're here, in college, fighting your way up."

A 4-H scholarship and a few precious dollars from home had brought him here to the university's College of Agriculture. In dusty, sun-splashed classrooms and in well-thumbed texts, he found zoology, botany, the full art and science of agronomy. Reading of food problems in India, Mexico, Africa, he became possessed by a grand idea, a vision, a purpose in life so simple and utterly necessary it astonished him. He would not return to grow pretty, tasty grapes on the Andrews farm. He would specialize in plant pathology, find new ways to grow more basic food per acre, perhaps develop more prolific strains of wheat, oats, rice and barley. He had many ideas concerning commercial fertilizers, insecticides, soil conditioning, terracing, methods of irrigation, frost prevention, mechanical harvesting—

"Mike, you amaze me! Continually. You're not kidding? All this time I thought you were just another witty student with an empty mind. A guy on the prowl."

He blinked his surprise, too caught up in his own enthusiasms to know what to say. "That's what you thought—really?"

"You're a different person, Mike, when you're serious. Do you know that? I'm really surprised."

"Think nothing of it. I took lessons from Errol Flynn. I admit I'm really a superior person."

"Oh, you poor thing . . . "

Now the vision faded. In the dark of the warehouse it gradually became apparent that no one else was seeking the boxes that lined the shelves. Hadn't for a while. The Japanese were doing whatever ground troops do at night. Like snatching a bit of sleep or patrolling or maybe finding a hole somewhere out of the wind.

Slowly, painfully, he crawled from under the pile of clothing, paused to ease the tourniquet, let the arm bleed a minute, then tightened down. His flight clothing and every vestige of American uniform he shoved farther under the pile. Dressed in voluminous but too-short Japanese trousers and boots, with a thick coat over his naked, flaming back, he eased along the aisle lined by ammo boxes, administrative supplies, a half-full bin of coal, drums of oil or gasoline, a bin of broken rifles, laundry supplies and case after case of sake. No sounds, no knife in the back. At the door, open to the extremes of weather and the whims of any trespasser, he paused to study the world outside.

It was deep dusk, near midnight, almost the deepest and darkest hour of the Aleutian night. Nothing stirring; no one in sight. So far, so good.

Terrain? At Amchitka he'd often studied maps of Attu; the details now clung to mind. He should skirt the village on its west side. Then a hill—that one. Leading west from the opposite slope should be a path leading past Lake Cories into Sarana Valley. A few miles to another stubby hill. Cross it, turn south and cruise like a goddamn conquering hero all the way to Massacre Bay. Oh, for hot food, a bath, medical care . . .

Boldly he stepped into the open as if he had every right to be just where he was. Instantly he was wet, soon soaked. A fine rain driven by a 30 mph wind made the going slippery and slow. Tall wiry growths here, hip deep; he had to step high to keep from tripping. No one challenged. The wind colder than the heart of a whore. The wind howled and drowned all sound except an occasional crash of waves against the shore. A hundred yards. Two. He struggled, panting now. At the foot of the hill, having successfully bypassed the village, he began to realize how very weak he was.

No matter. He was committed now, had no choice, had to go on. Slowly up the hill, trudging, expecting a momentary shout, a challenge, even a shot. The slope not steep, not too hard, but long. At the top of the hill he paused to gaze back. Peaceful scene—church, houses, all snug and quiet, like late Sunday night almost anywhere.

Sweating now, with long strides down the long slope and narrow path. Dark low hills on the right; gleaming ebony water left. Wind. Driving rain. Back burning, oh, God! Pause to bleed his arm and Jesus Christ it's so far . . .

On the path with nothing but wind to impede him. Coach, Coach, did you see? Do you know? I'm alive, Coach! Eddie, Joe, Jake—did anyone report? Big Boy One—oh, damn you! Eleventh Air Force to Washington to Mister and Missus God-I-love-you Andrews—your son is MIA. In limbo. Please God, don't let them hurt too much.

Phyllis? When you hear, honey, have strength! Courage! Faith! Bear with me, someday I'll come back. Months, years . . . Yeah, grinning like a silly fool and hold you, never let go. Kiss, oh, yes! I'll say the damnedest thing, anything, everything, all meaning you and you alone, for better or for worse as long as we both shall live, through sickness and in health—

Oh, Phyllis . . .

Touch me. There! Again. Darling—

Oh, the sweet body of woman. Her. There. Up! Love it! Moving slow, kissing deep. Tongues. Thrust deep. Oh. You. Yes. Sweet. Deep, oh, God! Phyllis! Sudden stop. "I love you! I love you! I love you!"

But his overcoat scraped raw across his back. Burning, a sharp file rasping tender flesh. With limp fingers he let the coat fall away; the cold was less painful. How much farther? The lake still there at the left; dark hills ahead an impossible distance. All getting lighter now. Stop! Loosen the tourniquet and bleed awhile. Weak. Like a kitten. Cinch up tight. Sky growing light. Jesus, to fail so goddamn soon, too early, too easy. Jesus—

Dimly he knew he lay half-naked in the mud. Cold beyond measure. Clammy mud, slime crawling into every pore. Goddamn, to die here like this, alone. Up. Fight. Dammit, up!

He fell back sobbing to himself and gritting his teeth for another try.

From somewhere—a voice. Hard, staccato, brittle. Japs! He rolled away in the mud as best he could, hardly aware their idle banter had suddenly ceased.

Before sleeping that night Tomi struggled to write in his diary:

> May 17. At night about [0300] under cover of darkness we left the cave. The stretcher bearers went over muddy roads and steep hills of no man's land. No matter how far or how much we went, we didn't get to the pass. Was rather irritated in the fog by the thought of getting lost. Sat down every 20 or 30 steps. Would sleep, dream, and wake up again. Same thing over again. The patient on the stretcher who does not move is frostbitten. After all the effort, met sector commander, Colonel [Shima]. The pass is a straightline without width, and steep line towards Chichagof Harbor. Sitting on the butt and lifting the foot, I slid very smoothly and changed direction with the sword. Slid down in about twenty minutes. After that, arrived at Chichagof Harbor ward after straggling. The time expended was about nine hours for all this without leaving the patients. Opened a new field hospital. Walking now extremely difficult from left knee rheumatism which reoccurred on the pass. The results of our navy, the submarine and special underwater craft in the vicinity of Chichagof Harbor since the 14th: sank a battleship, 3 cruisers, 31 destroyers, transport of air-borne troops, six other transports By the favorable turn, since the battle of East Arm, reserves came back. Off shore of Shiba Dai, six American destroyers are guarding one transport.

MAY 18, 1943

It was past midnight when the last operation was finished and Hirose, together with the surgical teams, stumbled away to the barracks to sleep. Tomi delayed a moment in the ward tent, not knowing why. His left knee ached and he felt tired—more tired than he ever remembered. But not from physical strain, he knew. While operating he was always keen, alert, intent. A nerve-racking experience. Afterward it took awhile to relax.

Someone nearby suddenly moaned. One of the new amputees—dreaming no doubt of the shot, explosion, slicing shrapnel or whatever. Or perhaps even the bite of the scalpel or saw. Tomi had often wondered which imposed more pain or fear—getting wounded or being tended. From any view, one sometimes seemed as bad as the other.

He paused to adjust a saline drip, found a cold foot thrust from the blankets and tucked it under. A chart revealed a pleasing fact; the patient's hemoglobin count was maintaining itself.

A half-hour ago the corporal with the mangled face had died. The man might have lived, had he fought. But toward the last he seemed to welcome death. Perhaps somewhere in the depths of his drug-fogged, shock-blurred, fear-crazed mind he had understood, stared death in the face and opened wide his arms. Perhaps even eagerly.

To help him relax Tomi allowed himself a half-portion of cold beans and a handful of soggy rice. He remembered reading somewhere that under normal conditions five bushels of rice were required to fuel one person for one year. It was impossible to visualize. In this cold climate a ration of four hundred grams of rice per day per man was hardly enough to sustain warmth and life. Thus, if a man must work and fight, he should require much more.

Since March 30, however, long before the battle had begun, all personnel on Attu had been on half-rations. Malnutrition was one early result, especially the need for vitamin C. No supply ship could get through the American sea-air patrols, or so he'd been told.

Meanwhile he didn't want to think of all the supplies at West Arm captured by the Americans. Those tons of rice, the potatoes, the oats and barley, the canned peas, carrots, mixed vegetables and *rinkan* roots, the canned tuna and salmon and fish flakes, the brown beans and white beans and soybeans; tons and tons of strength and energy. None of it would fill Japanese bellies. So try not to think about it.

"Honored sir?" Superior Private Ouye, on night duty in the operating tent, had quietly approached and now stood at his elbow, bowing. "There are three new patients just arrived who require your assistance."

Tomi nodded and rose at once. In the operating tent he saw that two of the patients were walking wounded, one suffering from a simple fracture of the left forearm, the other a severed right ear. Both were soon treated and released again to their units. Turning to the litter case he found a man covered from head to foot with thick black mud. He appeared to be tall for a Japanese, strong and lean, and he grunted briefly as Ouye and Tomi eased him to the operating table. "Are you in great pain?" asked Tomi.

No answer. Checking the muddy torso for signs of injury, Tomi found blood clotted along a long but shallow gash across the ribs. Also, a single gunshot wound high on the left shoulder, another below a crude tourniquet above the left elbow. Along the right of the spine, from shoulder to waistline, a burn. Infection could be a problem, but the burn itself was not too bad. First degree, perhaps a portion of it second degree.

Turning to issue washing instructions to Ouye, he happened to catch the patient's stare—a stare that stopped all his movement, that caught him and held him captive. He blinked his surprise and found himself holding his breath, remembering. Was it possible?

Only once before had he seen such never-to-be-forgotten eyes, so brilliant and piercing. In Los Angeles, long ago, in a gallery, in a portrait of Jesus suffering on the cross. The eyes in that portrait had haunted him ever since—hard eyes, yet soft. Eyes that had followed him around the room. Demanding eyes, compelling eyes. Eyes that called, eyes in agony and yet filled with love.

But those eyes had been intense, liquid brown. These eyes beneath his own, the persistent eyes of his patient, were brilliant Irish blue.

Motionless, Tomi swept all sluggishness from his mind and studied the patient. The man was naked from the waist up. Beneath the mud and grime his tousled hair seemed red-gold. His brow was both high and broad. The eyes and lids, too, were European, lacking the hooded cast of an Oriental. The nose lay straight and thin, almost aquiline. And though the lips seemed firm and stubborn as any Scot's, the square blunt bones of his jaw suggested Teutonic origins. A typical product of the so-called American melting pot, Tomi thought. He knew some Japanese would say "an American mongrel."

"Don't let me die!" the man whispered suddenly in English, his voice barely audible. It seemed much like a prayer. He pointed to his injured arm and the tourniquet, his free hand brushing a glinting object askew on his chest. A silver cross nestled there, together with dull metal identification tags, amid mud and mud-matted chest hair. "For God's sake, don't let me die!"

Astonished, Tomi peered now at Private Ouye, there near the far wall. Had he heard? Ouye stood, dull and apathetic, seemingly unaware while preparing a basin of warm water.

The eyes beckoned and drew him back. Solemnly Tomi considered the problem. Duty to the Emperor demanded that he walk instantly to the radio telephone in the ward tent, summon armed soldiers from headquarters and let them deal as they would with the American. He had no doubt of the result. The Army had built no stockade on Attu for prisoners and had no excess personnel to guard captured Americans. Neither had the Japanese a plethora of food to squander on men such as this, and they owned no abundance of compassion for the enemy. Hence, the soldiers would be efficient and practical: the American would be forced erect and dragged away, his burned back soon pressed against a snowy, muddied hillside, and without ceremony his white body riddled with bullets.

Duty demanded exactly that. Yet Tomi remained in place, held by a natural reluctance to cause a man's death and also by an inner compulsion beyond his understanding. Such eyes were not to be taken lightly.

The coincidence of it—this man arriving at this particular hospital at this particular time—was close to overwhelming. Any other hospital would mean a physician in attendance who spoke no English, who would instantly call the soldiers. Any other time would mean Hirose in charge, observing, aware. Again, the soldiers. But this man had surfaced magically at this hospital and at the exact time Hirose was sleeping soundly. Everything had worked out, just so. So at first glance it would seem as if the American had traveled a long, long path, unerringly, like a brilliant shaft of sunlight, directly to the only Japanese physician on Attu who spoke English. Also the only Christian. Coincidence? The question hung in Tomi's mind.

His mind racing, hoping to gain more time to think, he turned to Private Ouye. "I shall attend to this man alone. His needs are not great. You may return to more pressing duties."

Ouye, an obedient and unassuming man, nodded and left, not

so much as glancing at the man on the table—a man whose eyes followed Tomi's every glance, every small gesture.

Tomi turned again to the patient who now was fingering the cross on his chest. Medically speaking, yes, he could save the man's life. But for how long? Surely when Dr. Hirose awoke and discovered an American present, he would at once call the soldiers. . . .

Such waste of human life! Tomi felt driven to learn more. "You are a Christian?"

The man remained quiet, his eyes—for some reason Tomi couldn't guess—growing wary.

"I will not harm you. I only wish to know if you are a Christian. That cross you wear. What is your religion? Baptist? Methodist? Mormon?"

The patient swallowed, his expression changing to a mixture of relief and perhaps hope. "When you first came in, when I saw you . . . I knew you'd understand. I just knew."

"I understand nothing yet, a defect I wish to correct. You are perhaps Catholic?"

"I'm a—my mother's Presbyterian, my father Lutheran. I guess I'm something in between."

"Aaaah! As I suspected. Then we both have faith in Jesus. Is your faith strong? Unyielding? How often do you attend church?"

"At home the whole family goes, one week to one church, next week to the other." His eyes narrowed. "Why?"

Imagine, Tomi thought while injecting a half-grain of morphine, a devout American suddenly within our midst.

"I'm not sure how much I can help you, but—"

"Don't let me die! There's a lot I have to do. There's more school and study and work. I'm not through living yet."

"Do not excite yourself. I am Dr. Nakamura, your friend. Lie still while I attend to you. First, tell me your name and rank. How did you manage to survive, to get here to me?"

The force of the eyes bored into Tomi's mind, found an echo from far away, long ago: *I am not finished. . . .*

"You'll help me, really? How badly am I—"

"Trust me! I am your friend, a fellow Christian. I will help all I can. But please answer my questions."

The man peered hard at Tomi. "Name's Andrews, Michael Andrews. First Lieutenant. I got—hit and shot down yesterday."

"A Lightning—a P-38? You were one of those strafing our troops on the mountain pass?"

Andrews nodded reluctantly, obviously expecting some dire and immediate consequence.

"But that is war, isn't it? It's what is expected. Where are you from—Los Angeles perhaps?"

"North of there. Look, you'll help me, won't you? I have work to do, important work."

Tomi paused, held by Andrews's eyes, weighing what he should do. If he were to help Andrews, save his life, it would require more than medical services. It would also mean concealing him somewhere, somehow, for as long as the battle lasted. An impossible task! Too fantastic. Yet—

He considered the consequences. By giving such aid and comfort to the enemy Tomi would become a traitor to the Emperor. An unsettling thought, for the penalty for such disloyalty was dishonor and instant death, without recourse to other authority.

No Japanese worthy of his people would consider such a course.

On the other hand—this strange compulsion he felt. The coincidence of it all. The miracle of this man's survival. Add the fact that the American had come such a vast distance, from birth to this moment, from gigantic America to tiny Attu. From the relative warmth of the southland to the cold, rain, fog, sleet and eternal winds of the north. From the high sweet air where one is free to the stench of smothering blood-soaked mud. From security among his own to great peril amid his enemies. From a burning plane, unrecognized in the dark, with his whiteness concealed beneath all that mud, then to this hospital, to this time, to Tomi himself. A survivor of all this, and more—the bullets, the flames, the crash, the cold and being brought in by Japanese troops. Truly a miracle! Somehow Andrews had lived against all odds.

Why?

Tomi sensed the answer, heard it ringing in his mind. It was fate, of course, the working hand of God. Had to be. A sign from on high—he felt this truth in his innermost being. There existed a great meaning and purpose behind Andrews. A reason. A grand plan. That plan was not yet obvious; only the future would reveal it. But given the coincidence of time, place and circumstance, add the significance of the silver cross and Andrews's invocation of God's name, and consider the promise of two Christians brought together in secret behind Japanese lines—there could be no other answer.

Michael Andrews—an agent of God.

The thought warmed him, steadied his resolve. He smiled and nodded to himself. Then he, too, was an agent of God.

He knew just what was needed, what he must do. Gladly, whatever the cost. First, the physical body. He could guess that Andrews's auxiliary artery had been slightly damaged, that six or eight stitches would do for the gash across the ribs. These first, then the burn.

Without further thought he began reaching for saline, scalpel, sulfa.

What was done was done. He'd committed himself. Only minutes ago Tomi had left Andrews well hidden. As a burn case, the American now lay shrouded from head-top to waistline in white bandages on a litter in the operating tent. He was equipped with an easily removed Texas catheter, blanketed and unconscious, to all outward appearances just another badly wounded Japanese soldier. And that was very good, for God's purpose was being satisfied.

Yet now Tomi gazed squarely at himself in a mirror. Just who—and what—had he become? Thirty-three years ago he'd been born in Hiroshima, the son of a dentist, a devout Christian who desired that Tomi study medicine in America. In Japan, a son obeys his father.

In 1929—college in Northern California. Then medical school. Yet the greatest event during those nine years in America was Sumiko, the petite daughter of an old family friend. He smiled at the memory of the special day with Sumiko in Yosemite Park, beside the falls . . . the frothing creek . . . gazing in awe at the heights of Half Dome . . . laughing in the warm summer rain. In his mind he again saw the tents and campfire, Sumiko daintily toasting her chilled feet, the minister's wife preparing her children for bed—the boys in one tent, the girls in the other. The minister bedding himself down in the car.

Suddenly they'd been alone, he and Sumiko. He kept watching the fire play teasing tricks with the twinkle in her eyes. Oh, by this time he knew—was absolutely sure—she cared! She was his for the asking. Otherwise, why was she here?

But how did a man propose marriage? In Japan these matters were properly arranged between fathers. In America all was chaotic, no system, no rules at all.

In Japan a man would never abase himself by saying, "I love you," to a mere woman. In America it was expected, demanded, seemed a national pastime. The lack of that simple phrase often caused divorces, which in Japan a man would never permit.

He might simply say, as others did, "Will you marry me?" But how humiliating to plead to a woman! She would never again respect him. Nor could he order her to marry him. . . .

Then suddenly he knew a way. Quietly he began telling her of the recent request of the church that he return to Japan . . . medical missionary . . . Tokyo, for at least six years, then back to America to make his home . . . would be leaving soon.

He became aware that the wonderful, heartwarming twinkle began fading from her eyes. They became strangely bleak, withdrawn. Soon her shoulders slumped a bit and she grew small and turned to gaze at the fire. He hadn't meant to hurt her.

"Sumiko, look at me." An order he had no right to make, not yet. Her gaze clung to his, wistfully, her eyes glistening now and she seeming to tremble.

"I think you should go to Japan with me." He'd said it! A flat statement, straight out, with no smile or pleading tone. But that was all that need be said, he knew. Later they would arrange the date of marriage.

The change in her was as sudden as it was miraculous. Without moving a muscle she became alive again—the Sumiko he knew and cherished—eyes glowing and twinkling. Her voice was soft. "Yes, I think I should go to Japan with you." And he took her hand—how velvet it was! How it clung to his! He settled himself close to her, shoulders touching. She did not rebuke him.

Then in Tokyo, January 1941, drafted into the Japanese Army. Military obligation or not, he would have preferred to remain a civilian. His main concern in life was to heal ailing bodies. Of equal importance was the need to heal errant souls and cause them to follow Jesus. The Army, however, had been unsympathetic to his arguments. "You are a Japanese citizen," he'd been told. "You will serve or face instant execution."

Then Pearl Harbor. At the news he'd been horrified, almost sick. He didn't want to fight Americans. His many friends in America—what would they think of him? Sumiko's parents in Hawaii—were they all right? He had groaned to himself, prayed. War upset, would delay indefinitely, all his carefully made plans; it changed his life. It would be years now before he could return to the United States with Sumiko and the children. He had wanted to live there, work there, become a citizen.

Sneak attack, the American radio had said. Such monstrous stupidity on Japan's part! Japan couldn't possibly win the war. Her new enemy was simply too huge, too industrial. And now motivated, fearfully so. Japan had seemed intent on committing national suicide.

Yet he'd said nothing to anyone except Sumiko, bitterly, in the privacy of the bedroom. Soldiers, especially reluctant ones, do not voice the slightest opposition to their superiors, their government, or the Emperor.

And now here—Attu. Last March meeting Captain Yamamoto, of an old Samurai family . . .

Captain Yamamoto was in command of all medical personnel on Attu and functioned in a hospital cave far up the ravine near Umanose. A tall man by Japanese standards, the captain lacked Sergeant Okasaki's *oki anaka* which, like Buddha's, was said to bring good luck when rubbed with vigor. According to common belief, stout bellies signified patience, tranquillity and contentment. Yamamoto owned neither the stomach nor the qualities. He wore Army-issue glasses, affected a Hitler-type mustache and had the irritating habit of raising his brows and pretending wisdom by staring at one coldly. All who met him learned early that he'd spent four years on the China front—a combat veteran, no less—and was by his own admission an excellent surgeon. A self-proclaimed authority on combat medicine, he had a mind closed to all new ideas. Also the man drank far too much sake, often at the wrong times. In the operating room he was what the Americans called "butcher."

The captain's frequent pronouncements to Tomi carried much weight:

● Nine years in America! Our Japanese medical academies are in many ways superior.

● Buddha is the only God, Zen the only religion. Nakamura, there is little of Japan in you.

● Civilian hospitals? There you gave aspirin to pregnant cows and candy to crying children. You specialized in enemas. You are soft, Nakamura, not at all prepared for the rigors of front-line surgery.

● Any surgeon tainted by soft American philosophies is a liability to our success in battle.

● You will regard enlisted men as little better than cattle. When wounded, the Japanese Army considers them damaged goods. Perhaps even useless. Quickly repair those who can rejoin the battle. Give them morphine and return them to the lines. As for long-term patients, do only what time allows.

Tomi's protest merely encouraged the final crushing blow: "You are medically and politically unreliable, Nakamura, not to be trusted. That is why you are merely an acting officer and not a full lieutenant, as is Hirose."

Tomi did not regard himself as soft, unworthy or unreliable in any way. Far from it! He was . . . what? He gazed at his own reflection. He saw Tomi Nakamura—an honored, cultured Nipponese gentleman, loyal to the Emperor, now guilty of harboring an enemy of Japan.

The zigzag trail up the north slope toward Fish Hook Ridge was a slippery mess and the driving rain didn't help. Between the rain and the wind, he couldn't see, and that's why Murphy had ordered the squad into the cave. Not a large cave—big enough for maybe twenty men lying flat. The floor, however, sloped at an uncomfortable angle and a six-inch-wide streamlet emerged from the depths and surged down the center. Otherwise it was dry and also warmer than he had expected. Best of all, the wind couldn't reach them. They could even make coffee.

Jones kept peering out at the rain. "Someday I'm gonna buy my daddy a tractor," he suddenly announced to everyone, for what reason no one knew. "A big red one. My mama, she gits a fancy new icebox, all shiny white, soon as we gits electricity. I got my heart set on gittin' a piece of land all our own, an' everybody a white shirt just for sittin' round on Sundays an' talkin' in." His big teeth gleamed proudly white against the dark of his face. "It-jus'-don't-seem-like-a-foolish-dream."

No one answered, all tired. Murphy's feet were growing cold. Too cold. Peering down at black leather boots designed for desert warfare, he decided that heavy moisture had seeped into his boots. Wet feet weren't good. Wet feet were the bane of an infantryman. Wet feet could incapacitate a good fighting man as well as a bullet, and almost as fast. "Everybody with wet feet change socks," he ordered.

But Murphy kept staring out at the rain, a gray glistening wall of water slanting in from the west and driven by a 40-mph wind. With a touch of Irish luck it would blow over soon. Meanwhile it hid all view of Holtz Bay.

Early this morning, finding no Japs along the length of Moore Ridge, the GI's had begun exploring East Arm and found it also abandoned; the Japs had retreated into the mountains. That's when Lieutenant Scott summoned Murphy.

Lieutenant Scott was a brand-new West Point go-by-the-book kind of officer ten years younger than Murphy, inexperienced in handling people but, by every measure, all man. It was strange to see him unshaved and with mud on his boots, his cheeks gray with fatigue and eyes red from lack of sleep.

Scott gave him a cigarette and a tin of foul coffee. "Battalion wants to maintain contact with the Japs. You'll need full packs and ammo belts. Take a radio and rations for three days. Use the trail the Japs took up that mountain and continue the advance until you make contact. Send us the coordinates for that position. Then withdraw one hundred yards and dig in; we'll support you."

So here they were, wet and cold and staring at the rain. Murphy hated the rain. Especially rain at night, rain in the cold and driven by the wind. Hard rain blurring the windshield, the wipers going *whip-whap whip-whap,* never-ceasing but ever-clearing the view ahead. He'd been driving too fast, he knew, but no longer remembered why. The three shots of whisky in his gut hadn't helped, nor had Johnny, Jimmie and little Kathleen, wrestling, giggling and teasing in the back seat. But good kids, cheerful and obedient. God, he loved them, every one. And Helen . . .

Helen hadn't been a beautiful woman by far. Not even attractive, he supposed, by other men's standards. She was short and a bit dumpy, her hips broad, breasts too prominent, nose a fraction bulbous. Her hair, a mousy brown and always combed, was nonetheless never quite neat—domestic, he had called it. Yet she was always very clean and sweet-smelling, also well organized, and she had a calm manner that took calamity in stride. Her understanding and patience had seemed immense, especially with him. Loyal to a fault, all his. A real gem all the smart-ass guys had passed up.

It was all still a blur in his mind, most of it—the sudden haze of glaring lights erupting from a blind corner. Helen had screamed, "John!" He'd cut the wheel, braked hard, felt the sickening lurch as the tires slid like ice across the wet asphalt. Then the God-awful crash, glass splintering, the car tilting. He had found himself lying on hard cement, blinking numbly toward the sky, the hard pelting rain full in his face. Dully he sensed that he lived, gradually realized that Johnny's legs had twisted grotesquely apart while his body lay pressed by the weight of the car. Jimmie? Kathleen? Oh, God! Helen was still somewhere inside. Oil in the gutter. Blood in the gutter. *Whip-whap whip-whap* went the wipers of the dead car.

Four days later, on crutches, he had buried Helen, the finest woman God ever gave to man. A closed casket ceremony. Beside her, Jimmie, complete with baseball cap and glove. That was on Monday. On Friday, little Kathleen, her red Irish hair for once well combed and her face serene. Two weeks later—Johnny, whose broken spine and punctured groin had become infected.

His whole family. And he alone was to blame.

It was weeks, months, before his bones had mended. He had lurched about in a daze most of the time, knowing the hard truth but not able to accept. Helen and the children were right there, as always—the bedroom, the kitchen, in the yard. Yet they weren't. How many times had he turned to share a sudden thought or special insight, only to find Helen's chair empty? His hand reaching for her in the dead of night. Oh, that cold, comfortless bed! The boys' room remained untouched, as disordered as ever, and the World Series that year had meant nothing, not without Johnny and Jimmie there to listen with him and cheer for the Yankees, Dodgers, whomever. Football games—why bother? Kathleen's favorite storybook had gathered dust. So, he thought, had his heart.

He had sworn then he would never drink again. Never, not even a beer. He hadn't, and he knew he never would.

By Pearl Harbor time he was again on his feet, shaky but functioning as best he could. Missing them. Lonely. Join the Army; what the hell. Nothing seemed to matter anymore. . . .

———

Like a water tap suddenly shut down, the rain finally ceased. Murphy slowly led the squad uptrail. Frozen snow crunched underfoot, sounded like someone eating celery. Black mud clung to all it touched and tripled the weight of each boot. Up higher, panting and struggling under the weight of the packs. At trailside the jagged thin ice was marked by Jap boots. Ahead, Jap bodies lay everywhere on both sides of the trail—torn, twisted in grotesque shapes, scarred by gaping wounds and blackened blood. Twenty yards into their midst, Murphy paused to stare. Shellfire and the P-38 boys had done a good job. Maybe four full companies of Japs lay just as they had fallen, most of them no older than the kids of his squad.

His breath steaming white in the air, Murphy studied the path ahead. This was the last leg of a long series of switchbacks. Fifty yards ahead the muddy trail lay between a low knoll on one side and a huge rocklike projection on the other, each the beginning of small bumps and ridges that in concert formed a considerable barrier. The opening was like a break in the fence, a natural highway and just the sort of place he himself would pick to defend.

He wished fervently that right now some squinty-eyed, buck-toothed Jap up there would open fire. A round or two, no more, just enough so he could report contact. But all was too quiet. The snow ahead glistened so hard in the sunlight it hurt his eyes and the only sound was the high roar and whine and sigh of the wind as it gusted again and again.

At intervals of ten yards behind him the kids were all watching and waiting for orders. Jeeters's eyes round and wide, Bennett's jaws moving in slow rhythm, Jones gripping the BAR, Cooper tight-lipped. Murphy took a deep breath, motioned for all to follow and began easing uptrail.

Twenty-five yards to go to the hole in the earthen fence. Without conscious thought he slipped the heavy glove from his right hand and eased the safety on the M1. An icy calm invaded his mind. He knew it was possible that this was the day he would die. Like in five minutes, or even less. Okay, so he could face that. Mere existence didn't matter anymore, not really. But if he had to die he asked only three things: that the kids in the squad all be safe; that he take lots of Japs with him; and that it wouldn't hurt. Lots of pain he could do without.

He stepped quickly through the narrow opening between knoll and rock, glimpsing a flat plateau surrounded by low mounds all forming a small crater, a bowl. To his immediate left, protected from the wind by a large niche in the rock, were three Japs squatting over a makeshift latrine.

He stared down on them, totally surprised. He'd expected at least a squad, maybe a machine gun. But this? Beady little eyes filled with wonder and brown flanks poised over a hole?

For an instant the three returned his stare, obviously as startled as he. Then the nearest lunged for a rifle nearby and Murphy fired from the hip. He had time and knew it. Both rounds caught the man full in the throat. The second man had time to half rise, taking rounds three and four through the chest; he fell back and did not move. The third man, a neat bandage circling his head, made no effort to rise or move. He merely watched and accepted death as he had life—without changing expression.

Even as the sixth round found its target, Murphy discovered he was already under fire. From several hundred yards away, across the shallow bowl, a light machine gun began chattering. Chips flew from the rock over his head. Murphy simply turned and ran, found Bennett just entering the bowl and pushed him back. "Contact!" he cried, deliriously happy; he didn't know why. "We made contact."

At his motion the squad reversed course and hurried down the trail. As they neared the site of all those Jap bodies Murphy called a halt. "Jeeters, you see that little hummock right up there? Take Hall with you, dig in and guard the path. Cooper, you and Jones go up higher, where that little shelf lies near that ravine. Two hours on and two off. HQ is in the cave."

He didn't wait to watch them dig in; they were competent and he was cold. On the lip of the cave, radio and map in hand, peering down on Holtz Valley, he called battalion: "Red Fox, this is Rover. Enemy contact at coordinates . . ."

The effects of whatever drug the little Jap doc had given him hadn't yet worn off. Michael lay in a dreamy state, angled a bit on his left side to protect his back, his left arm jutting down the length of his body. The general absence of pain was a big plus.

Maybe the little Jap doc was okay, he thought. Then maybe he wasn't. Japs were funny; a guy never knew what they were thinking. Laughing or crying, they could look you square in the eye and never change expression. Stoic. The dim light had made it even worse. No time for questions; no explanations for anything. Michael could decide nothing; he had so little evidence.

How far could he trust the little doc? How come the guy spoke English so well? Why the third degree about religion? Why would he bother to hide an enemy—aid and comfort an *enemy*, for God's sake!—and go through this elaborate charade? Risky. No American would take so big a chance. So *why?* There had to be an ulterior motive. Maybe butter him up, get him talking and try for classified information? Could be. But nothing really added up. In the States good Samaritans were a dime a dozen and each had an angle. So what did the doc stand to gain from all this?

Wait—that's all he could do. Then ask.

Meanwhile, it was bad enough not being able to see, his eyes and entire head all covered with bandages, but worse yet not to know what was going on. If he could only understand Japanese! All this bowing and scraping—weird. All around were undercurrents of thought and feeling he didn't understand. What was obvious, however, was that one little mistake, maybe a wrong gesture or lapse of some kind, and one Michael Andrews would suddenly be food for the fish. The odds on that happening seemed pretty good.

Personally he knew almost nothing of the Japanese. Only that they had bombed Pearl Harbor on a Sunday even while talking peace in Washington. Stab in the goddamn back! So, in the final analysis, suppose the chips were down, really down, and the doc had to choose between tending Michael or saving himself. Wouldn't he naturally choose . . .

So right now, what to expect? His last meal had been a full day ago. When would he eat? How—with his hands all bandaged? Where—and not be observed? What's more, nature would soon take her course. A john—he'd need a john. The catheter took care of any immediate problems but sooner or later, when his bowels again began functioning, he'd need a latrine. Where was it? When could he use it and his white flesh not be seen? So much he didn't know and couldn't ask. Mustn't speak to anyone, no matter what, and couldn't make a sound. Don't respond to anything. Be like a rock, unmoving and silent.

All about him was a strange unseen world. Glassware, tinware and metal clanging against each other. Footsteps heavy and light, pausing, moving on. Low polite voices in staccato speech, men breathing, snoring, coughing. It surprised him there were no moans, no cries of pain. Smells of medicine, rice, unwashed bodies, urine and sometimes feces. The air was heavy, not with heat but from the pressure of too many men in a too-small space. Damn, he thought; surrounded by enemies who would kill him on sight, if they knew, weak and helpless as a baby, unable to fight or run—his chances were just about nil. Scared? Yes, when he thought about it. If he could only see!

Outside the wind was blowing. He could hear its plaintive howling, often gusting like a rifle shot against the sides of the tent. It was raining, too, quite hard, if not sleeting, and that meant little if any flying today. Coach and Eddie, warm and snug in the Quonset, probably playing cribbage, drinking coffee. Same old lousy jokes. Bitch about food. Never a mention of Eagle Four. Talking about guys who didn't come back was verboten; it hurt too much. But they'd wonder: Did he get out? If so, what then?

Back home they'd wonder, too. MIA, crash-landing on some enemy-held island. Jesus . . .

Hearing the news, his father would sit with a rock-hard face and stare out on the growing vines, his hands still and the coffee cold. He would wait. Farmers do a lot of waiting. He would ask himself if the same force that made the crops grow would return his son alive. That was Dad. He would be especially nice to Mom. Never mention to her his doubts or say all that burdened his mind. On Sunday he would quietly pray in his church or hers. Dad—he'd take it hard. Then he would wait.

Ol' Mom. She'd start cooking and steam up the whole kitchen with loads of hot, spicy, wonderful food no one would ever eat. She'd clean house in a determined yet steady way, and crochet a lot for the grandkids. Busy, always busy when her heart was troubled, her jaw pinched tight against the world and a faraway look in her eye. She might, during a weak moment, retire to her sewing room, close the door, have a good cry, then return to the kitchen as if nothing of the sort had ever occurred. Michael had never seen her cry. A few times he'd suspected. Mom would never believe he was dead.

Then there was Phyllis. He knew how she'd feel—oh, yes, he knew! But how would she take it? Couldn't tell about Phyllis; very strange, marvelous, wonderful girl.

"I've been thinking of you all day," he'd begun that second night. "I've decided we're going to have three children, two boys and a girl two years apart. Mike Junior, Henry and Lorna. They'll all look like you. We'll live in a little white house and keep adding rooms as the family grows. The boys and I will do the gardening. There will be nine grandchildren, all blonds with gray eyes, and you'll be a beautiful grandmother." He smiled hopefully and sat waiting.

"Gee! All planned out. You just don't quit, do you?"

"Not where you're concerned."

"Did it ever enter your mind that I might not agree with all that?"

"You will. Just a matter of time."

"What makes you so sure? We only met yesterday."

"It's just this feeling I have. Intuition? I'm positive you're the wench for my wigwam. Agree and we'll tell this Jim-bimbo doctor-guy el finito! Or, if you like, we'll keep him for an old family friend."

"My, my, my! The oracle speaks; the world listens."

"Just you, honey. You're all the world to me."

"Look, don't call me 'honey,' okay? You haven't earned that right—"

"Yet. But I will. What's your name?"

"I thought you'd never ask. Would you believe Phyllis?"

"Hello, Phyllis." He grinned his widest. "Phyllis what?"

"I shouldn't say. Really! People just laugh."

"I promise not to laugh. Honest Injun! Phyllis what?"

"Well . . ." Her gray eyes grew smoky. "Philpot. Phyllis Philpot."

He caught himself staring. "You're kidding."

"No."

"My God, does it hurt? How did it happen?"

"Well, once upon a time there was this little girl who looked a lot like me, who met this tall, good-looking oddball who happened to be named Phillip Philpot. Why the name I don't know, never dared ask. But like stupid little girls everywhere she fell in love with the big lug, and they married. On their honeymoon— the inevitable! And here I am."

"Such alliteration—Phyllis Philpot! Your folks did it on purpose? Are they bad, frustrated poets? Or was it born of a sense of humor?"

"I don't know. But Daddy's the worst joker I've ever met."

"Worse than me?"

"Well . . ." She squirmed on the hard seat. "Let's put it this way; his mind and your mind run in the same rut—or gutter. He's a joker, but I don't know yet if you're a joker or just a joke. The main difference between you is he's taller and older. Handsomer, too." She cocked her head like a little minx, smiled, and he wanted to kiss her.

"Of course you realize there's only one thing to do," he murmured in his most serious tone. "You have to change your name. May I suggest—"

"Michael, don't—"

"Phyllis Andrews? Has a certain flair, doesn't it?"

"Michael—"

"Mike. Otherwise I won't sit up and bark."

"I've asked you not to talk that way. I'm very uncomfortable with it. It's too . . . personal. And too soon. I don't like to be rushed."

"Don't blame you a bit. But we've known each other a day now. This is our second library date. Are you my girl or not?"

Silence. She was wearing a new blue V-necked dress that revealed very well she was all woman. Thirty-four C-cup, he thought.

"I like you, Mike," she said evenly. "But I don't know you. I don't know if you're always talking nonsense—a handy line to take advantage of innocent, tender young things like me—or if you're really serious. If you're serious—"

"I am! Don't ask me how but I knew right off you're the one. I'm just being honest."

"But flippant, too. That's what confuses me."

"Being flippant is one of my better virtues. I have many others."

"There you go! I had an uncle like you once. His sense of humor got clogged one day. The bile backed up and he died from congestion of the brain. You show all the symptoms."

He groaned. "A comic yet. Where did all the straight men go?"

She had nice legs and she smelled clean. Half smiling, too. "Look, y'want the straight goods—why I think someday we'll get married?"

"Not really."

"You love me. It's that simple."

"I do? I'm so glad you told me." Idly she toyed with her pencil. "Why in the world would you possibly think that?"

"For one thing"— he pointed to the obvious—"you're here. After all the crazy, outrageous things I've said in fun—but meant; things that would make any gal in her right mind go screaming in panic for the nearest exit, you're still here."

"Intrigued, I admit. I'm really waiting to see you fall down. I just love blood and gore, splintered bones and broken finger-nails."

"And that dress is new. It's designed to attract helpless young male people like me, which it does. All this tells me that you think I'm the most wonderful guy in the world. Which of course I admit."

"You mustn't run yourself down like that."

"That's the result of my scientific mind. A fact is a fact."

"How romantic you are! Look, I'm not sure yet you're worth bothering with. How's that for honest? Good husband material, I think, is very rare. I'm particular."

"So you admit it, you're looking for a husband."

"Not so's you'd notice. Just in training, so to speak. Taking notes, comparing this one to that one, deciding what's important. And who."

"Okay, take a note. I'm important. I'm a one-woman man. I'll marry once, for a lifetime. That's it. Take it or leave it, but you're the woman."

"I'll accept that, pending confirmation. Really, the way you talk so seriously, so soon, is very unsettling."

"Admit it, Phyllis, you love me."

"Gee and gosh, dear sir, these days a poor girl doesn't have any secrets at all."

"This summer," he murmured, "I want you to meet my folks."

Her eyebrows lifted. "Down, boy! Hey, I intend to date other guys when I want. Nobody has priority. Anyway, don't make plans. Jim is coming home this summer before he starts interning. I'll have to spend some time with him."

"Jim. *Yetch!*"

"You don't have to make a face like that. He's a nice guy, kinda sweet. Doesn't push. Very sober, quiet—"

"Which I'm not, I know. But I'm loads of fun. People look at me and laugh and laugh."

His chest felt like a lump of ice. Those nice legs, that figure, her smoky eyes. He watched her every move. "Do that again."

"Do what?"

"Flip your hair that way. Know what it looks like? The color, the way it flows—like a field of ripe wheat waving in the wind."

"Mike, don't get poetic. . . ."

May 18, 1943

Now, behind his thick mask of bandages, hearing strange clinking, shuffling, bumping, grunting sounds all about, an alien tongue jabbering left and right; aware of smells he could not define and seeing only the gray shifting light that managed to penetrate the gauze, he found it comforting to think of Phyllis. His memory of her was true, honest, solid—very tangible. It was real, something to hold on to. . . .

May 18. The [Nagumo] detachment abandoned East and West Arms and withdrew to Umanose. About sixty wounded came to the field hospital. I had to care for all of them by myself all through the night. Heard that the enemy carried out a landing at Chichagof Harbor. Everybody did combat preparations and waited. 2nd Lieutenant Omura left for the front line on Hokuchin Yama. Said farewell. At night a patient came in who engaged a friendly unit by mistake and received a wound on the wrist. The countersign is Isshi Hoke.

MAY 19, 1943

Andrews, the American, kept rubbing the blond stubble of his beard. "You're late." Accusation in his tone. "I thought you weren't coming."

"I regret the delay," Tomi murmured. It was 0300 hours. The door to the tiny room Tomi shared with Hirose in the barracks was firmly shut, with Hirose on duty in the operating tent. This was the safest time—if any time could be called safe—to talk to Andrews and see to his most primitive needs. Those ridiculous bandages that made the man look like an ancient white knight were off, temporarily, to give him a chance to eat a bowl of cold rice, scratch himself and use the bedpan. In the yellow light of a single candle the gunshot wounds and stitches across the ribs appeared clean and healing nicely so far. The burn Tomi left undisturbed, fearful of possible infection.

"Listen carefully," he continued softly. "I have told everyone concerned that you are a wounded high-ranking officer, that you wish to remain anonymous. I trust that no one but myself will approach you. But if anyone should, you must not make any sound, nor signify you hear. Do you understand? I have brought some dark snow goggles, so that you may see through eye holes in your bandages, yet not be seen."

The American was quiet. Too quiet to suit Tomi. Also seemed tense. Suspicious? Perhaps uncertain, even a bit frightened. All that would be normal. There was, however, a desperate need to communicate.

"Please understand," Tomi said gently, "I am worthy of your trust. By saving your life and hiding you, have I not proved that very point?"

"How come you speak English?" blurted Andrews.

"Why, I studied in America! Nine years." There was little time for reassurance. Quickly, however, he spoke of his birth in Hiroshima, education in America and lifelong dedication to God, omitting only his concept that Andrews was an agent of God. "I am a physician," he concluded. "A healer. Also a man of principle."

"I don't know any military secrets," Andrews said coldly. "So you're wasting your time."

"Oh," gasped Tomi. Why would the American think that? "But I do not wish to know of military things. That night we first met, you spoke with intentness about your work. Important work, you said. Is it research? Medicine? Politics?"

"Why do you want to know?"

"Because we are both involved with each other. Is that not clear? We are both in great danger; your fate and mine have become one. We must cooperate! Also, I cannot work blindly. So tell me, please, what is your profession? Thirty years from now—"

The response was immediate. "Plant pathologist!"

"A—what?"

For a long moment the young American studied him, unblinking. "Do you know," he said slowly, "that half the world is starving? To me, hunger is a crime against humanity."

"Oh, I agree!" The ache in his stomach was never quite absent. Four hours remained before his next half-bowl of rice.

"And I believe that the best available weapon to combat world hunger is modern plant pathology. Shall I go on?"

Astonished, Tomi leaned forward. "I know nothing of such things. By what means— How—"

"I'm telling you. Plant pathology is a new science, and small.

But we'll grow. We want to find cures for lots of agricultural diseases. That means revitalizing various soils, crossbreeding— Hey, you know about crossbreeding?" The young voice grew stronger, face intent. "There's nothing like it! First the raw idea. Then all the debate, the planning. Engineering. The controls. You watch and measure. Then— it's a feeling I get. Sometimes I feel like God—the whole process of creating a new breed of plant. Bigger, y'know, and stronger than nature's own."

"I know. Sometimes in my own work I get such a feeling. It is very . . . compelling."

"Right! Now, I think everything we learn should be shared with the whole world. Bar none! America has the money, technology and knowledge. We're learning more and can teach others. For example, take rice. If, using present acreage, we could manage to increase the rice-growing capacity of Asia by ten percent, think of the enormous human energy released to create a higher, more productive standard of living. Okay?"

"Aaah!" whispered Tomi, now aware of the grandeur of Andrews's concept. More rice for Japan, an overpopulated country. For two decades Japan had been caught in the turmoil of rapidly changing times, its young men moving like a flood from farm to city, its agriculture therefore in decline. The nation had been in dire need of new sources of rice for its people and new markets for its growing industry. For that reason, Tomi believed, Japan had become militarily adventurous in Manchuria and China, then the Greater East Asia Co-Prosperity Sphere . . .

Tomi felt sure of it. If good food in quantity were that important to peace in the world, then it followed without question that Michael Andrews must be preserved. Andrews's quest was in fact God's purpose: to spread the wealth of full bellies and good nutrition throughout the world.

Producing food in abundance—a cause that transcended all war.

So Michael Andrews must live, no matter what problems or obstacles. No matter what cost to himself.

"Baker, Swensen, you two relieve Jeeters and Hall on guard," Murphy said. "Bennett, try to get some coffee going; those guys'll be cold. Young, you come with me."

Well wrapped against the wind and cold, rifle in hand, he moved out and found the fog thicker than he'd thought. He could see perhaps ten feet. But uptrail he found the landmark he sought, a dead Jap kid with a leg blown off and one eye lying on his cheek. From there it was straight up the mountain following the bootprints left by Cooper and Jones. About this time they'd be expecting relief.

For three minutes he climbed, then paused for breath, frowning. Maybe the fog muffled sound, he couldn't really tell. But the way he and Young were panting, plus the crunching of snow underfoot, they should have been heard. By this time they should have been challenged.

He gestured *shhh!* to Young, whose face looked gray with fatigue, and carefully eased upward. He could hear nothing strange, no clink of metal or murmuring voices. Not even a snore—though he would have raged at that. He could smell nothing odd. Yet he now stood on the shelf he'd pointed out. He felt sure of that. Cooper and Jones were mere feet away. Had to be.

He inched along the shelf until he found an empty two-man foxhole, six inches of icy water in the bottom. In the snow all around were bootmarks of a violent scuffle. Cooper, the cowboy, lay five feet down the slope, eyes wide open, his throat slashed half through and equipment gone. His pockets were inside out.

Jones? In the fog, hearts like stones, Murphy and Young searched a perimeter of fifty feet in every direction. At last they eyed each other. Jones and his easy grin was gone. They didn't dare ask where.

Lots and lots of questions, Michael thought. But no real answers. Why wouldn't the little doc level with him?

With dark glasses now covering the eye holes in his bandage, he could see quite a bit. Peripheral vision was lost but by turning his head that defect could be largely overcome. It helped that the light near the tent entrance was adequate. Even this early in the day he had already located a few basic tools he would need or could otherwise use: a small pearl-handled revolver under the pillow of the man on his right; and the radio telephone on the north side of the tent.

Any plan of escape had to take into account the personnel who could block it. The young ward attendant who seemed so devoted to the little doc—Tomi—was just a raw kid and offered no major obstacle. The other doctor, an oily, too-smooth character a bit taller than Tomi, was as yet an enigma but appeared lax in many ways and not dangerous. But the big man who wore what might be sergeant's stripes seemed the greatest possible threat so far. He was plainly curious, glancing at Michael's bandaged figure far too often, scanning the chart at the end of the litter and at one point standing quietly near Michael's feet and gazing at him a full minute. That needless scrutiny had been enough to set Michael's teeth on edge.

At least six feet tall and well over two hundred pounds, the sergeant was not completely a stranger. Michael would bet on it. His bulk, his broad impassive face—yes. Without a doubt this man had been the one standing at the crest of the pass, firing his machine gun at Michael's plane.

Even without that recognition, however, Michael would have known the man anywhere. His counterpart existed in every unit of every army, the hard-nosed sergeant who in effect made the unit function. Career sergeant, the typical professional, backbone of any army. This particular hard-nose had eyes like gimlets, ever probing. No detail seemed too small for his close attention; no small habit of the attendants escaped critical review. Even Tomi and the Oily One, perhaps without realizing, seemed to follow the sergeant's lead.

The man was perfection personified, everywhere at once. Yet no man could be perfect at any large task. Somewhere he would have a flaw, a weakness. But what? Behind his dark glasses Michael could only wonder, bide his time and study Hardnose quietly and with care.

———

She was there as soon as he closed his eyes, as always—the rebel lock of hair low on her brow and the bright eager cast of gray eyes. Over coffee she'd said, "Okay, dear Roscoe, how do you cross-breed a plant? First a formal introduction, then a hotel?"

"Okay. Each plant has a male stamen that holds the pollen. At a given time this stamen bursts and the pollen spores connect up—I simplify—with the female section, the stigma. The pollen germinates, grows a germ tube which penetrates the ovary and—"

"Hurray! And again a sweet innocent unsuspecting flower is pregnant. Great."

"That's normal reproduction. To crossbreed, however, we emasculate—"

"Oh, God, no!"

"—the stamen and introduce the pollen spore of another variety. At the proper time, of course. Very painstaking work, difficult to do. To inseminate thousands of—"

"You make it sound so sexy."

"No, you merely have a dirty mind."

She sighed, then took a deep breath and squared her gaze with his. "Mike, I think we shouldn't see each other all this next week."

It felt like a surprise blow in the gut. "You serious? Why a whole week?"

"I want to think about you. Really! I need to decide whether I should see you again or not. That means think clearly, not have you confuse me. So let's meet again one week from tonight in the library, usual time. That's a promise, okay?"

"But, Phyllis—"

"But-but-but like a motorboat. I don't want to do this but it's a must. We don't talk to each other or see each other for a week. Call it a test."

"When did you decide all this?"

"A few days ago. It was something you said. You said—oh, never mind. I need confirmation. Either way I decide, you'll thank me for it later. Good night!" And she was gone, her round little fanny that nearly drove him mad suddenly hidden by the closing door.

All week long his studies suffered. Without Phyllis, did the starving multitudes of the world really matter? He caught himself straining for a glimpse of her about the campus, the cafeteria where he worked, the movie lines on Saturday night. His appetite failed. The mere idea of her studying with another guy, maybe a football player with hulking shoulders and massive thighs, enraged him to the point of violence. Twice, responding to direct questions in class, he made fumbling, misleading recitations. Each time the professor frowned and made little marks in his book. At night her face and figure dominated his dreams and he swore he hadn't slept. He felt terrible and his friends said he looked it. Heartsick, he waited keenly for Sunday night, yet dreaded her saying good-bye.

She was there, in place and on time, the real her. Studying. He sat opposite her as usual, ignored her as best he could and kept eying words that had no order, form or meaning. His mental messages earned no response, but promptly at ten she closed her books and focused on his right eye. Objective expression. No big smile. "Hello."

"Pardon, ma'am. I'm not accustomed to speaking with strange young ladies. Not without a proper introduction. Especially very forward, unmannered strange young ladies."

"Oh." Now she cocked her head and smiled beautifully. "Miss me?"

"Well . . . so-so. Y'know."

"I see. Are you interested in what I've been thinking? My conclusion?"

"If you hurry. It's getting late."

"I missed you. Aren't you glad?"

He nodded, relief flooding through him. "All my women say that. Eventually."

"I missed you very much. That surprised me. I went out with another guy and he spent so much time being polite and gentlemanly he forgot to be interesting. Very dull compared to you.

What do you think of that?"

"I plead the Fifth Amendment."

"Mike, you're not cooperating. I came back to say I like you. A lot! But you—"

"How much is a lot?"

"You can be infuriating, did you know that? Why I bother with you I just don't—"

"How much is a lot?"

She blew hair from her brow and glared.

"A lot isn't 'love,' I know. Not yet. Maybe 'fond of '?"

"Something like that."

"Maybe even 'very fond of '?"

"Mike, do you want to listen or should I leave?"

"Tell me you're very fond of me."

"Mike, I'm very fond of you, okay? I don't know why. Yes, I do! But it's none of your business. It proves only that I'm an idiot. And that's an understatement."

"I missed you, too."

"You did? Tell me." Her eyes were suddenly smoky, her hair again on her brow. She didn't blow it away. "You really did?"

"Every once in a while. Once last Tuesday as I brushed my teeth. Again on Friday night during an attack of indigestion. It was you or gas on my stomach, I couldn't decide which."

"Nobly said, with all the intriguing romance of a diesel truck. Your mother did a bad job of raising you."

"I was reared, not raised. There's a big difference."

"Okay. Mike, you graduate this summer. On graduation day I want to meet your folks. Very casually. Just as a friend, nothing more. That's all we are anyway. Friends?"

He could argue but decided not. "Okay. But why the sudden change?"

"None of your business. Let's say it's the next test."

"Do I have to keep taking tests? I thought the blood test at the last minute took care of everything."

"Like I said, I'm particular. The way I feel about a guy doesn't count if he's the wrong kind of person. I don't know if you're

posing or if what I see and hear is the real McCoy. God, I hope
not! Or do I?"

"What's the right kind of person?"

"Like you said, a one-woman man. Because I'm a one-man
woman. That's for starters. This last week I found you're a straight
A student—"

"I got a B once in my freshman year."

"—and you're very hardworking, persistent, sober except on
extremely rare occasions, don't run around with the wrong kind of
girls—"

"Until just lately."

"You don't waste money—"

"I would if I had some."

"And your professors have approved you for graduate school.
They all think you'll succeed very well in your field. One even
said—"

"My God, woman, what did you ask them?"

"I said I was doing a psychological study—"

"That's a synonym for snooping."

"Perhaps. Meanwhile, I learned that everything about you is
solid except the crazy way you talk. Y'know what? I think your
breezy, flap-happy manner hides a first-rate mind. I think you do
it deliberately. I'm curious as to why."

The important thing, he thought, was the hours she'd spent,
her depth of thought and concern. "You forget. From the very
first I've insisted I'm a superior person. An elite—"

"Can you be serious for once?"

"Yes. Want an example? I'm very fond of you, too."

"You are? Gee! You've never really said—"

"And also very hungry. So let's go to your place and I'll let you
fix me a sandwich. Then if you're a good girl, very quiet and
unresisting, I'll kiss you good night."

"Good God," she muttered, picking up her books. "To think I
came back with both eyes wide open."

They walked out together, tightly holding hands.

———

The bell at the entrance to the operating tent suddenly rang—the call to surgery. Tomi set down his half-empty tea bowl and hurried to the operating tent. By the time he had scrubbed and was properly gowned, gloved and masked, the first patient was already on the table: compound fracture of both the right ulna and radius, also ulnar nerve contusion complicated by multiple fragment wounds.

He irrigated and began picking pieces of shrapnel from the arm. Much of the forearm muscle had been blown away, replaced mostly by dirty snow. Let it bleed freely to wash out the dirt. Help the process by irrigating. Lots of sulfa. Carefully now, align the bones, just so. Hold it, brace it. Now the splint.

Next! A smashed and bloody face marked by a score or more of broken teeth, ripped cartilage, mangled flesh and splintered bones where the nose and eyes had been. The man suddenly quit breathing. Immediately Tomi began emergency procedures, then paused and looked at the face. After a long moment he ordered the body removed.

Next! A simple femoral fracture requiring only a plaster cast, then a spinal case involving traction followed by a hopeless abdominal case with half a score of large penetrations, protruding and perforated intestines bleeding profusely. Morphine—and set him aside to die.

Next! A gunshot penetration of the liver, a serious but not necessarily fatal wound. Here, however, the peritoneum was not intact. . . .

Next! Incise, irrigate, probe, suture. Next! Quickly now, flush out the dirt, dig for shrapnel, debride, irrigate, sulfa and bandage. Next! Tourniquet to stop the bleeding, suture the artery . . . Next! Already dead from loss of blood. Next! Pus in the wound? How long since— Scalpel, tie off the veins, saw, suture, irrigate and suture the flap, and bandage. Next! Blood and bits of bone, mangled brains—hopeless. Next! The smell of blood, gasoline, alcohol, feces, sweat, antiseptic, urine, fear. The sound of heavy breathing, low groan, the saw on bone, the clink of metal on metal. A boot scraping on the floor.

Body after body, naked, cold. Contusions, lacerations, punctures. Hemorrhage, shock—oh, for serum! An old man, an officer—cardiac arrest. Next! Anaerobic infection, gangrene. This craniocerebral case, take him away. Elbow-deep in blood. Next.

Someone beside him wiping sweat from his brow. Hayasaka. Tomi glanced up in thanks.

Body on the table, an abdominal puncture. Tomi understood the dangers. Fecal fistulas. Intestinal abscesses. Sutures that wouldn't hold—and why? Limited peritonitis. The essentials were speed and thoroughness. He bent to the task, probing for the bullet. Found it. Irrigated liberally again, applied sulfa and quickly closed the wound. How many minutes? He couldn't guess. Okasaki, behind the mask opposite him, began applying a Montgomery dressing. Expertly.

Next!

A body on the table. A foot injury. Toes gone, the metatarsals all broken, twisted and mixed together. A strong working foot that should have served seventy, eighty, even ninety years—now a bloody splintered mess mixed with mud and gunpowder and Tomi couldn't guess what else. "Scalpel," he said wearily. "Clamps. Saw—"

One body replaced another, a never-ending procession. With the pressure of too much humanity, the tents grew warm and then hot and Tomi grew more tired than before. His knee ached, his mind grew numb and he fought to stay alert. His bladder felt ready to burst. Sergeant Okasaki was there across the table, an automaton, tireless, immune to all except duty. Morning became afternoon and they still came, body after mangled body. Broken bones, flesh torn. Blood flowed and tables were rinsed. Next! Fresh stocks of morphine, saline, antitetanus, iodine. Tomi shook the sweat from his eyes, the tiredness from his brain, grabbed a lungful of fetid air and steadied his hand. Clavicle, scapula, metacarpus; femur, patella, tarsus. Aorta, carotid, brachial, tibial. Tie it off, clamp it down, sew it up—he's gone, let him go. Everything numb, dull, automatic, routine. Swaying on his feet.

Against one wall a jumbled array of *sennimbari* belts—each a "belt of a thousand stitches," fashioned by tender and loving hands, worn under the uniform and around the waist, which granted to the wearer all the magical benefits of good fortune, valor and immunity from the enemy's attacks. Against the opposite wall, a growing pile of amputated limbs.

Next!

Body on the table.

A huge man, a black man, American, this one wanted for interrogation by Intelligence. Glares of outrage from Sergeant Okasaki. Imagine! A Japanese doctor aiding this creature, a contemptible, miserable American who had allowed himself to be captured. Let him die! Better yet—kill him! Tomi ignored Okasaki. The patient was unconscious. Fractured left radius and ulna. Contusion on forehead. No skull fracture but surely a brain concussion. Frostbite on both feet. But don't amputate, not yet. Try to save them; leave the feet free to the air. Just set the arm, splint it. Next!

But no other came. No new limp body emerged from the dark beyond the yellow lantern light to lie soundless and quivering upon the table. The black American had been the last.

Two Americans here, Tomi thought. One hidden, the other evident to all.

Tomi glanced at Hirose, a blood-smeared mess, gaunt and haggard, staring back with eyes glassy from fatigue. Neither spoke. As one they removed gloves, caps, masks and gowns. Together they moved from the close heat of the tent into the free cold air at the edge of the bluff. The muted roar of cannon came from the west. The Americans from Massacre Bay were said to be advancing.

Tomi breathed deep, glad that Hirose was as exhausted as himself and did not feel like talking. But then Hirose was usually silent. Sometimes, after drinking bottle after bottle of sake, he might talk in glowing terms of geisha girls and his explorations into the *yoshiwara*, the Happy Fields where one finds women for hire. At such times Tomi refused to listen, preferring to read medical reports or one of his English classics. He knew only that

Hirose was a doctor of a type he had never known before—he drank and swore and didn't always respect his patients.

Hirose's silence, however, revealed that he hadn't spoken today with Okasaki.

In the artificial light of false dawn, as Tomi had carried Michael's bedpan toward the latrine, the ever-vigilant Okasaki had seen, despite all secrecy, all precautions. Okasaki had stopped short, stepped aside at once, brows lifted in surprise at the unique sight of a physician abasing his high position by performing this lowly chore. Unheard of! the man had no doubt thought; had the honored doctor no self-respect? Tomi had merely nodded and continued on his way, tight-lipped, fleeing the puzzled, persistent gaze of Sergeant Okasaki.

Now, Tomi reminded himself, he must be more careful.

The cold wind had risen and Tomi followed Hirose into the ward tent, now jammed with fifty-three patients, all immobile. Andrews lay near the entrance, head, upper torso, arms and hands again well swathed in bandages. His dark goggles gave him a sinister appearance. The black American lay on the opposite side of the tent.

The lightly wounded and walking wounded had already been sent back to their units, there to fight as best they could until killed. This policy grated on Tomi's conscience, though he recognized the dire need of it. The esteemed Garrison Commander Colonel Shima's latest order was quite clear: "No further retreat! No soldier is to flee from his trench hole!"

Tomi understood. Every man capable of pulling a trigger was needed now, not in ten days or two weeks. The crisis was immediate and compelling, its successful resolution vital to them all. Therefore a patient whose wounds were clean and a minimum of four days old could expect early reassignment to the front. A half-man on the firing line, even temporarily, was better than no man at all.

He peered about the ward tent. The great majority of his patients were really not men at all but mere boys of twenty years or less. Children. But all seemed thoroughly imbued with the principles of *Yamato damashii,* the Japanese spirit that emphasized from earliest childhood how glorious it was to die for the Emperor. The Emperor was divine. One must give him absolute loyalty. Any precaution against death was unmanly, but one who gave his life in battle was forever honored in the memory of his descendants, or other family. His name and a miniature gravestone was added to the family shrine in the living room. Each day food would be set out for him and reverence paid to his memory. A typical Japanese soldier calmly, even cheerfully, accepted the prospect of certain death.

On the other hand, one who surrendered to the enemy was forever disgraced, his family shamed and shunned by all. The birth of this tradition Tomi had often wondered about. Did it lie in ancient, medieval times, the Samurai era, when one who surrendered was tortured to death? Or did it serve to prove that one who surrendered was weak, a coward who had no heart to continue the battle, one who was less than a man? Or perhaps it demonstrated a certain lack of loyalty to one's lord, a despicable quality in any man. Whatever, it survived in tradition: no Nipponese soldier or sailor shall ever surrender. Never! When one's gun is lost or ammunition expended, his bayonette stripped of its blade and capture imminent, then he should destroy himself, commit *seppuku—* by whatever means available.

In his nine-year visit to America, Tomi had come to view and question such attitudes in a new and different light. Now it often seemed as though Japan as a whole had obsessed herself with thoughts of death, in the Hemingway style—a national death wish.

Tomi was not afraid of death, not in itself. It was natural, like birth, to be expected in the due course of time. To Tomi, death became an eternal life with Jesus, a concept reinforced by his years in America.

He could accept the possibility of death in battle. An errant bomb or shell, a chance bullet, a white-hot metal splinter that might find him at just the wrong moment at a given place—these were the risks accepted by every man who honorably served the

Emperor. So be it, come what may. But to seek death, blindly and actively, to surrender oneself to death by committing *seppuku* in the name of the Emperor, this is where Tomi parted from traditional Japanese dogma. It separated him from those about him. Could a dead physician heal the sick and wounded? Could a dead missionary draw others into the fold? Could a dead man cherish a wife and rear his fatherless children? No, Tomi must live. The future and his work beckoned him.

He found Hirose in the operating tent impatiently instructing a young wardman in the proper manner of using a catheter. "Lubricate the tip with jelly, idiot! Then hold the opposite end between the third and fourth fingers, like this. Any fool can do it. Then insert. Use a steady, gentle pressure. Keep it going until the urine begins to flow. Now do you understand?"

The boy nodded, his face sullen. The patient made no sound or movement. He lay as if unconscious. Hirose washed his hands and wearily joined Tomi beside the stove at the center of the tent. "Morons!" he muttered. "Why can't they send us people who at least have a minimum of brains and a bit of training? And this morning, first those damned American naval guns, then the news of this cursed American aviator—"

"What American aviator?" Tomi blurted, suddenly tense and hoping blindly he was wrong.

"You haven't heard? A day or so ago, after strafing our troops, a crippled American plane was brought down within our lines. The pilot escaped, possibly injured, and is said to be lost or hiding somewhere nearby. Our troops are still searching the hills and valleys for him, without much success."

"Oh?" His thoughts whirled. He knew instinctively there was danger in asking too many questions. Jesus, do not fail me! He seized a deep breath to help still the hurried pounding of his pulse. "Then there is no danger, nothing immediate to concern us here?"

Hirose smiled in his superior way. "In a well-guarded hospital? Please, Nakamura!"

With a short, quick bow he escaped only to find Wardman

Hayasaka waiting, a bowl of hot tea in hand. Hayasaka bowed. "For you, honored doctor. In honor of your morning's labor I have also brought an illustrious poem to hearten your day. By Kenji, who wrote so beautifully before his death." Thrusting a tattered paper into Tomi's hand, Hayasaka abruptly turned and hurried away.

Slowly Tomi read:

> A man with the strength
> To resist the rain
> To resist the wind
> To resist the snow and summer heat
> He has no greed
> Never gets angry
> Always composedly smiles
> He eats four *go* of brown rice
> Some mismo and vegetables each day
> He carefully sees everything
> With an unselfish mind
> Understands and never forgets
> He lives in a small thatched cottage
> In a field in the shade of a pine grove
> When a sick child is in the east
> He goes out to care for him
> When a tired mother is in the west
> He goes out to bear her a bundle of rice
> When a dying man is in the south
> He goes out to tell him to have no fear
> When a quarrel or feud is in the north
> He goes out to tell them to stop their worthless words
> In time of drought, he sheds tears
> And walks with dismay in the summer's cool spell
> All call him a fool
> No nuisance, he never hears praise
> I wish to become such a man.

Jones. Murphy couldn't bear thinking about Jones. It was one thing to get killed like Cooper; war was like that. Or hurt, wounded, even crippled—a guy took his chances. At least there was something there, a body or part of one, either alive or dead, something to deal with. But when a man disappeared without a trace, *phffft!*, like one little fart in a windstorm . . .

He had no idea what Japs did to prisoners. He'd heard stories the like to turn his hair; he didn't want to remember them.

Today he seemed obsessed with thoughts of death.

At Fort Ord, in training, he had often wondered how it felt to kill a man. He'd felt a bit squeamish about it, the result of a lifetime of propaganda about the value of human life. Now he knew better. The truth was, human life was cheap at best, certainly expendable. Human life on Attu could be used, burned, thrown away. It was worth exactly nothing. Including his own.

Take the Japs. On Hill X he'd seen supposedly dead Japs come to sudden life, rifles roaring, shooting unsuspecting GI's in the back. Tricky bastards! So a new policy had been quickly adopted. Every "dead" Jap got a round in the head, just to make sure.

But it made a man wonder. Jeez! They coulda surrendered; they coulda lived. . . .

He'd seen red-cross-marked medics go running out to help the wounded, get deliberately machine-gunned down like ducks in a pond. Time and again. Godamighty! Murdering Jap sonsabitches! Even now his fingers twitched on an imaginary trigger.

Then in a hollow near West Arm he'd found three horribly mangled Japs who were hardly recognizable as human. On all three the legs were intact and most of the lower torsos, but the left hands and forearms were missing. The chests were hollowed out as if by a large scoop—ribs, hearts, lungs all gone, scarlet blood draining into the cavities. The heads were still attached, though without faces, and the bodies lay in a straight, precise line as if the men had composed themselves in formation before pulling the pins and thrusting grenades against their chests. Lying there amid the mud and tundra were assorted fingers and thumbs.

Suicides! It was scary—the "why" of it. What kind of people were these goddamn Japs anyway?

Last night he'd had a dream. In the dark he was running,

desperately, toward a light in the distance. The light was warm and good and filled with promise; he must reach it or die. The path was rough, lay along a steep and tiring slope and twisted from side to side. That was okay; he could handle it if the light would merely stay still. But it kept going away, far away, fading, and the harder he ran the faster the light fled from his grasp. Woke up sweating, scared out of his friggen mind . . .

Meanwhile, he couldn't help but think of tomorrow. A two-company attack. Every instinct he possessed cried that the first squad through that earth fence and into Jap fire would be his own.

For himself, it didn't matter so much. But the kids, he thought. F'Chrissake, the kids . . .

"This burn case of yours," Hirose said. "A thermal burn? Our men are so well clothed against the cold that thermal burns on one's torso are next to impossible. What were the circumstances?"

They had just finished surgery. Hayasaka's tea was hot and fresh, a delight, especially so in light of dwindling stores. Tomi had relaxed within himself, savoring the tea's heat, flavor and aroma. Now his mind suddenly raced.

"The circumstances were not explained to me. The burn case is an officer of high rank. Perhaps while bathing, a bomb or shell might have . . . But in fact I do not know. The burn area is not extensive. No excess fluids were lost and neurogenic shock was not a factor. Your concern is unfounded."

"Perhaps. Yet it's all very curious. You are using the standard closed treatment?"

Tomi nodded. First a cleansing of the burned area with hexachlorophene, rinsing then with sterile isotonic saline. Apply a sterile fine-mesh absorbent gauze, plus a pressure dressing; wait and watch and pray for no infection. "Thus far the burn has evidenced no complications."

"But I'm very much interested in the treatment of burns. In this case tannic acid is clearly unnecessary, but in North Africa the Germans report that British field hospitals are using a petroleum-based cod liver oil solution as a coagulant."

"We have nothing of that sort. The high protein diet is also impossible."

"Or a light dusting of sulfanilamide—"

"I have already applied it."

"—together with a measure of tule gras. And continuous saline baths are quite useful, according to the latest journal."

"I read the article. But the patient is progressing well." This was dangerous conversation; its result could prove disastrous. He must turn Hirose's attention away.

"I would enjoy seeing the patient with you soon," Hirose said. "I have a theory—"

"Soon?" He twisted, frowned, peering along the rows of litters. "Of course, very soon. I shall appreciate your opinion." He was aware that Hirose was staring at him as if somehow he'd become an object of great curiosity.

"Dr. Nakamura, are you well? You seem tense, quite nervous."

He could have sworn that no outer manifestation of his inner turmoil had crossed his face. Had he not maintained a usual calm? Apparently not. The result was Hirose's close inspection and a loss of status.

Frantically he searched for an explanation, an excuse. Anything! A nagging idea leaped to mind. "Dr. Hirose, may I be quite frank? To you I admit my growing concern. I feel a sense of—what is the word?—military confinement. Consider: only a short time ago we Japanese controlled this entire island. We could come and go according to whim. Then, after the landing of the Americans, our sphere of influence narrowed. The first to fall was Shiba-Dai. Then West Arm and Shitagata-Dai and East Arm. Now I understand the Americans are challenging the mountaintops above Massacre Valley, and winning. More and more of our territory on Attu is reduced. I feel at odd moments that, should I breathe too deeply, I would upset a precious balance. So! Unless reinforcements arrive soon, our defeat is certain. What is your thinking?"

"I think the Emperor has spoken," Hirose said, following Tomi's lead, his voice almost lost in the background drone of the ward. "It is certain, therefore, that we shall be reinforced when the proper moment arrives. When? The High Command shall decide. Until then our task is simple—fight, wait and endure. We must have faith." Hirose paused to eye him. "As a Christian, surely you understand faith."

There it was, the conflict that had troubled Tomi all his life. His religion versus his country. Jesus versus the Emperor. He loved both, paid homage to both, had faith in both. Must he choose between them?

The Japanese believed the Emperor divine. To Tomi, only Jesus was holy.

The Emperor, by drafting him into the Army, had enslaved his body. Conversely, by opening salvation to all men, Jesus had freed his soul. First Corinthians explained it perfectly: "For he that is called in the Lord, being a servant, is the Lord's freeman: likewise also he that is called, being free, is Christ's servant."

But Hirose would never understand. Hirose would merely snort or laugh, turn away and think him a traitor.

Of course it was good that Hirose had boundless faith in the Emperor, Tomi decided. Otherwise he would feel terribly alone.

Making his rounds, Tomi made notes on various charts. Increase the glucose IV. Measure fluid intake and output. One-quarter grain of morphine each night. Slowly he circled the interior of the tent, assessing each patient, and at last the late afternoon rounds were over. He must stand by now and monitor the patients, including Andrews, especially Andrews, as Hirose slept. He found himself adjusting a tourniquet here, an arm sling there, a bandage next, ordering saline and applying pressure, examining red tags—and there he argued against regulations. The Imperial Army Medical Code stipulated a maximum of one-quarter-grain of morphine injected at first application, an amount totally inadequate for an active, healthy male. A half-grain Tomi thought essential, especially considering the escalating traumas of shock. Often he judiciously ordered small extra injections of morphine, plus a saline drip to inhibit the effects of internal hemorrhaging.

For the most part the patients were conscious and seemed

stable and calm, accepting their lot and their pain. Except the black American. Too long for the litter by nearly a half-meter, he lay awkwardly, his bare feet propped high to catch the air. His feet were cold, he kept saying to every passing wardman; and they hurt. Tomi could imagine the pain—excruciating, without doubt. The man wanted his feet covered. No one, however, could understand him, except Tomi himself and Michael, who could only observe through dark goggles. Nor were his gestures heeded. The man was simply being ignored: let the black American continue in pain.

Name? Jones, according to the metal tags about his neck.

Tomi paused to examine Jones's chart. Blood pressure a bit high, probably caused by anger. No morphine had been administered, or tetanus, although Tomi had specifically ordered both. Eying the feet, he found the hard, white appearance gone. Now they were merely red. He avoided touching them.

"How do you do, Private Jones?" he said pleasantly in English. "How do you feel this morning?"

Suddenly Jones didn't move. He lay stiffly still, the whites of his eyes stark against the dark of his skin. He stared up at Tomi. Meanwhile Okasaki, Hayasaka and Hirose stopped all activity. The patients on both sides of Jones, in fact most of the ward, began watching in silence, curious.

"Who you?" Jones blurted, his teeth beautifully white and large.

"Dr. Nakamura, your physician." He bowed and tried to smile. "How do you feel?"

"A Jap doctor! Hey, you're weird."

"Japanese doctor, if you please. It's like the difference between Negro and nigger—you understand?"

Jones nodded once and winced, proving at once to all Japanese that Americans were indeed inferior. They did not hide their pain.

Tomi gazed down on Jones, a gigantic Negro captured unconscious in the fog near the heights of Umanose. The condition of his feet proved an incredible oversight on the part of the enemy.

Such light leather boots leaked water badly. Ice water and wet feet added to freezing nights meant chilblains, trenchfoot, frostbite—and often amputation. For example, the Americans knew—for they had taught Tomi—that a temperature of 35 degrees Fahrenheit with a wind of 20 mph produced the exact result on exposed flesh as a minus 38 degrees. Just like a deep freeze.

"About your feet, are you in pain?"

"Doc, you jus' ain't a-woofin', baby. Gimme-what-you-got, I-need-a-shot. Whisky! Jesus God!"

A gesture to Hayasaka brought the morphine. "One-half-grain," he said. "Then I'll check him later."

Jones eyed the needle. "Doc, what you doin'? You ain't gonna stick me with no junk. Nosiree! I heard about you Jap doctors. You'll stick me an' then you'll cut—"

"What do you mean, 'cut'?"

"Everybody knows. You'll-cut-me-there-an'-that-ain't-fair. You ain't foolin' me none. I got your number."

"Private Jones! I do not castrate helpless men. The amount of morphine I'm prescribing will relieve your pain. It will not render you unconscious."

"Listen to them big words. Doc, where you from?"

"Please do not interrupt. You have a case of frostbite, the destruction of healthy tissue by freezing. The problem in moderate to severe cases is thrombosis of minute blood vessels—"

"A throm-what?"

"A coagulation—"

"You mean blood clots? Why don't you say so?"

"We have thawed your feet carefully in a warm water bath. If the water's too cold, tissue damage increases with the time of thawing. If thawing is too rapid, more damage. The idea is to get your blood circulating again. The process involves considerable pain, which I'm prepared to alleviate if I can get your cooperation. And I emphasize that you will remain conscious and I won't castrate you."

"Well, y' never know." Jones shrugged apologetically. "Y'hear so much about Jap doctors."

"Japanese!"

Jones turned from the sight of the needle and winced again as Tomi thumbed the plunger down.

"You will feel better soon, Private Jones."

"Private Fust-Class, Doc! You-short-my-rank-you'll-draw-a-blank."

"I will check on your progress later. Thank you for your cooperation."

"I didn't do nothin', jus' layin' here watchin'. For-what-ah-see-there-ain't-no-fee. But I'd like to eat, Doc. I'm powerful hungry."

"Yes." Tomi sighed. "All of us are."

He turned from Jones to find the patient in the adjoining bed beckoning.

"Honored Dr. Nakamura, if you please! I am Superior Private Umeda. May I speak?"

"Of course, Private Umeda." Another amputation case, a foot. Gunpowder and black dirt ground into the wound. "You also are in pain?"

"No longer. I am concerned only about the black American. He is rude. He stares at me constantly. He laughs and points to my missing foot. Then he insults the Emperor and all Japanese. And me."

"How do you know this? Do you understand English?"

"Quite well. In school . . . it became my desire to know the enemy we were destined to fight. It shames me now to know we are fighting pigs."

"Private Umeda, how does Jones insult you?"

"He sneers. The names he calls us, they are degrading. They are unspeakable. Then he laughs."

"Americans sometimes have a strange sense of humor."

"There is nothing humorous about him. He means all he says. Why is he allowed to live?"

"The Intelligence people wish to speak to him."

"He must die!"

"Umeda, listen to me. You must take no action against this man. He is a prisoner under our protection."

"Prisoners deserve no respect. Is he not ours to do with as we wish?" He glanced at Jones and said softly in English: " 'Merican die!"

"Well, g'mornin'!" Jones grinned. "It's Mister Moto hisself. How come you decide to talk to me? I had you figgered for an uppity, high-tone, too-good-for-everybody nothin'." His eyes narrowed and he lost his grin. "Look, bandy-legs, make one move agin me an' I'll show you how we gut hogs."

Umeda merely stared back, his face a mask concealing all he thought and felt.

"Restrain yourself," Tomi said quickly to Jones. "Private Umeda has been instructed to disregard you. You must do the same to him. Above all, no violence."

He hurried from the American's derisive grin to find Hayasaka waiting, bowing. "Honored sir! A message from Sector Unit Headquarters, for you. The esteemed Garrison Commander Colonel Shima orders your presence at once at the church in the village. There is no time to waste."

"The church in the village?" All he could do was repeat, sounding stupid, he felt sure.

In the barracks he donned fresh woolen stockings, wrapped his lower legs in woolen puttees, tugged on knee-length rubber boots, added a fur-lined mackinaw, thick leather gloves and a heavy cap with earflaps. Dark glasses, a protection against possible snow blindness, completed his preparations.

Leaving the barracks, he crossed the stream and began walking through long frondlike plants. The small rills that twisted underfoot he leaped despite the pain in his knee. The distance to the church was short, perhaps a quarter-mile. To his left lay the icy calm waters of the bay. In moments of rare sunshine the bay was as happily blue as Sumiko's kimona. In the fog it looked gray and dead, a depressing sight Tomi avoided. Now in thin overcast it appeared mildly green, a fresh color of spring, of rebirth and promise.

The church stood at the eastern end of the village and the village rested on the deepest curve of the bay. The church, facing westward, was no longer attractive. First, from belfry to basement it needed a fresh coating of paint. Second, its nails had rusted, as iron and steel did quickly on wet Attu, and the horizontal pine boards had loosened in spots. The belfry sagged a bit at one corner. The steps to the entrance creaked under his boots and the main door had broken loose from its upper hinges. There were no sentries, nothing to indicate that this was, in fact, headquarters. Inside he found the air stale and smelling of decay.

The main hall was everything—a nave without sacristy or apse, without an altar or figure of Jesus on the cross, without pews or seats of any kind. In one far corner was a strewing of blankets and old civilian clothing, but in the opposite corner a number of candles illuminated three men huddled about a table. They had ceased talking and were staring in his direction. They, too, seemed uncertain in the dim light.

Was this headquarters? He saw no runners, no radio telephone, no bustling activity, no grand officer studying maps, pacing the floor and shouting orders.

Ignoring the stabs of pain in his knee, he hobbled toward the men in the corner, recognizing no one. No rank was visible on their coats, and no one spoke or moved. To whom should he bow?

A compromise—he bowed to the group. "Acting Officer Nakamura reporting. Is this Sector Unit Headquarters?"

"We have been waiting for you," said a thin man with a livid scar on his forehead. "The headquarters offices are located below in the warmth of the basement, but we shall work here. I am First Lieutenant Ujiie of the esteemed Garrison Commander Colonel Shima's staff. These are Second Lieutenants Oda and Hirano from Intelligence." He gestured toward the others, both of whom waited for his bow.

"Now, are we all ready to work?" asked Ujiie. "Nakamura, the problem is a simple matter of translation, a minor task of reading English. We wish your knowledge, skill and opinion. Here is a captured American field order and map of Attu. Read them. Study them well. Then tell us what the Americans are thinking. What do they do next, and where?"

Immediately Tomi bent to a detailed map of Attu. Squinting in the dim light, he soon saw that, to the Americans, Shiba-Dai was Hill X; Shitagata-Dai, Moore Ridge; the landing area above Holtz Bay, Red Beach; Hokuchin Yama and Umanose, Fish Hook Ridge. He found Jarmin Pass, newly captured by the enemy leading from Massacre Valley roundabout through snow and mud toward upper Holtz Valley. Buffalo Ridge, Prendergast Ridge. An arrow pointing to a key pass leading to Chichagof Harbor. Second Battalion, Seventeenth Infantry. First Battalion, Thirty seventh Infantry. First Battalion, Fourth Infantry. Gilbert Ridge and Point Able.

"This map—by itself it tells me next to nothing of American intentions. We already know they are attacking in force from Massacre Bay."

"Then compare it with this." Lieutenant Hirano, a man whose burn scar on his left cheek gave him a splotchy, sickly appearance, extended a paper. "An American field order. Tell us what they intend doing."

Tomi had no heart for this covert examination of documents. It seemed like peering into a man's wallet, or bedroom, seeking to learn secrets that at best were private. Such matters were not his concern. Medicine was more to his liking. The study of medicine, the experiments and growing knowledge, were published widely and shared by men of all nations. In medicine there existed no bloodlines, no political limitations, no false barriers. Physiology, bacteriology, anatomy—sciences involving all mankind. There should be no secrets, he thought. Not among men of good will.

He scanned the paper, fumbling to understand names, units, hours, locations, directions, the sense of this strange, coded, coldly objective military English. It seemed mystifying, a jumble of convoluted terms. Blue Bird? Witch Hunt? Main Street? Fox Trot? What did such terms represent? He began checking rhetoric against the map.

No one hurried him and no one spoke. The only sounds were the sigh of wind outside, boots shuffling occasionally against the floor and Oda's breathing near Tomi's shoulder. Someone sighed.

For a while Ujiie drummed his fingers against the tabletop. Often he glanced at his watch. Tomi was aware of the candles burning low and beginning to smell. He did not rush, preferring his own meticulous pace.

It was like working a jigsaw puzzle. First one sees only a general concept. From that emerges an outline. Then, piece by piece, a pattern. A section here, a section there. In time, color emerges and becomes relative, a part of the whole. The picture grows, comes together and loses the blur of confusion. Chaos becomes clarity. And at last, as Hirano was lighting fresh candles, Tomi stood tall and eased the ache from his shoulders.

"Respected gentlemen," he said, "this is a plan for a coordinated attack on the pass of Umanose."

"Umanose?" Ujiie said, blinking.

"The pass is the only objective?" Oda asked.

"Perhaps. This field order is limited; it concerns tactics only, not overall strategy."

"The strategy is obvious," Hirano said. "If this attack is successful, our forces will be divided. We must reinforce Umanose at once."

"We are already strongly entrenched on the peaks, ridges and crevices of Hokuchin Yama," Oda insisted. "An impregnable position. From such altitude we see everything. Our guns control all that moves below."

"This attack," Ujiie said, glaring Oda and Hirano into silence. "Give us the details."

"Two companies of infantry are required, plus artillery." Tomi glanced at each man in turn. "Before dawn the various units will move into position. The time of attack is zero-five-hundred hours tomorrow."

For a long moment no one spoke. They merely returned his gaze. Oda seemed suspicious, for what reason Tomi couldn't guess. Hirano was content to frown, study Tomi's every expression and exhale fumes of sake. Ujiie appeared poised, as if waiting for a blow.

Then Oda said, "That cannot be so. My English is not as fluent as yours, but please notice the date of attack—the twentieth of May. Today is the twentieth. No such attack took place this morning."

"Honored sir," Tomi said in his most neutral tone. "You are correct. We Japanese use the time west of the international date line. The enemy, however, uses the eastern time. To them, today is the nineteenth."

"I regard this document as suspect," Oda said. "May we depend on it? Or is it a deliberate plant, a ruse?"

"I know nothing of intrigue," said Tomi, wishing only to escape. "I also know nothing of American military methods, their code names, the units involved, nor the enemy's possible purpose in disseminating false information. I can tell you what these documents report, nothing more. Verification is up to you."

"You are very helpful," Ujiie said. "Thank you very much. You are now dismissed to return to your unit."

He bowed his respect to each officer in turn and limped rapidly from the church. Outside, the first breath of clean cold air felt wonderful.

On the front step, however, he saw the fog—a dangerous fog, penetrating, icy cold and dank, thick enough to blind a man, confuse his sense of direction and make wandering about a hazardous exercise. A man could easily lose his way and stumble about the tall fronds all night, searching vainly for shelter, getting colder and colder. . . .

If he were to preserve Michael's life, he must first preserve his own. Best to wait for dawn inside the church.

Ignoring Ujiie, Oda and Hirano, still arguing in the candlelight, he dragged a few old blankets to a neutral corner, folded them carefully into a neat bed and crawled in. His last conscious thought concerned the American, alone and hungry, waiting in vain within a prison of white sterile dressings.

Tomi was right, Michael thought. He must heal and rest. Husband his strength. Soon he would need all the strength he could gather. But sooner than Tomi thought.

Time to face it: whatever plan of escape he devised had to include the big Negro across the tent, an added complication. Okay, to include him with feet like that in an escape attempt seemed impractical. Yet the means must be found. Leaving him here among these avid, unthinking wolves would condemn him to death. The major obstacle? Coordination of effort meant communication between them.

How? Jones couldn't walk. And Jones's nosy neighbor spoke English. If Tomi would separate—

From behind him he sensed a presence. A shadow . . . Hardnose the sergeant suddenly appearing without sound, on the silent feet of a big cat. Now bending down, saying something. His big hands reached for Michael's blanket. "Aaugh!" growled Michael, hoping that might pass for language; he waved the man away, shook his head. The man stood erect, glaring down. His breathing became deep and strange. Then he strode away.

All evening and far into the night Hardnose supervised everyone, everything, kept pacing back and forth like a restless lion. With every about-face his gaze swept the length and breadth of the tent and seemed all too often to linger, however imperceptibly, on the white bandages that hid Michael's face from the world.

Damnation! Would the man never relax?

It was close to three in the morning when the decision was no longer his. The risk had to be taken; he simply couldn't wait any longer. No Tomi—the time for his appearance was long overdue. Operating? Conspiring? What was he up to? Had he been caught? Whatever, Tomi had let him down.

Dawn was not far away. He really shouldn't chance it, but overruling all other considerations was a basic fact: a latrine damned soon was an absolute necessity.

Except for the normal sounds of men in deep sleep, the tent was quiet. Even the radioman sat dozing. No Hardnose in view. Hardnose was probably in the other tent or perhaps even asleep. So now was the time.

Slowly he climbed from the litter, pausing as needed to allow recurrent dizziness to drain from his head. Erect, several deep breaths improved his confidence. He removed the Texas catheter and eased the best he could into trousers stored under his litter. Sliding his feet into boots took only a moment; no time to lace them tight. Then along the aisle, a pause at the entrance to the tent. Overcast sky, a smell of rain. Nothing stirring in the ravine below.

Water rushing down the creek, washing the blood and filth of battle from the heights; it hid all other sound. Seemed safe. No reason not to go on.

He walked deliberately down the ramp and along the hidden path he'd used with Tomi the night before, a path less than a foot wide and cut a full twelve inches deep along the hillside. A marvel, he thought, how the fronds above the path hid it from the air. No aerial photographs would show a path at all.

The boxlike camouflaged latrine loomed against the hillside. Tonight, no Tomi to stand guard. Get in, get out, that's the ticket. In the latrine he squatted over one of the four holes cut into a long plank. The nose-numbing smell of disinfectant filled the air. Clean, like a hospital. He felt sure, given enough light to see well, he would see no paper towels or toilet tissue scattered about, no cigarette butts, no urine carelessly sprayed, no crude anatomical drawings of females or graffiti on the walls.

Michael hurried. Leaving the latrine, he paused on the narrow path. In the east the sky was growing gray. Too late now to ease across this low hill, find the beach and trudge toward American lines at East Arm. Also too cold and no proper clothing. So no choice—he had to depend on Tomi, like it or not. He turned reluctantly toward the tents.

Nearing the ramp where the path broadened he saw Sergeant Hardnose striding toward him like a fullback on the prowl. Damn! What to do? How to avoid—Anything he did would be wrong, Michael knew. What if Hardnose saluted? Or did not salute? Or spoke? Where was Tomi?

Nothing to do but plunge ahead. Bluff it out, kiddo. Head

down, let it wag like a moron. Too bad you can't drool. Shamble a bit. Ignore him. Watch him suddenly step aside, his voice murmuring, then sharp and angry. Keep going; confusion is his problem.

At the top of the ramp Michael paused to catch his breath and watch Hardnose enter the latrine. He'd be there at least two minutes.

Michael stepped quickly inside the tent. All quiet except for lots of snores, which maybe would help. In the pale glow of the candle near the radio, the attendant on duty sprawled in sound sleep.

Hot-damn! This was opportunity.

As quickly as caution permitted he eased along the aisle between litters. Not much light from the candle. Slowly now. No noise, no fumbling. Reset the frequency, just so. Pick up the handset. Keep a wary eye on both the tent entrance and the sleeping attendant. Flip the switch on the right to what must be "on."

"Big Boy One," he whispered intently into the mouthpiece. "This is Eagle Four. Do you read? Over!"

May 19. At night there was a phone call from Sector Unit Headquarters. In some spots of the beach are some friendly float type planes waiting. Went into Attu village church. Felt like someone's home. Some blankets were scattered around. Was told to translate a field order presumed to have been dropped by an enemy officer in Massacre Bay. Was ordered to evaluate a detailed map of Massacre Bay and Holtz Bay which was in the possession of Capt. Robt. J. Edwards, Adj. of Col Smith. Got tired and went to sleep. First Lieutenant Ujiie is in charge of translation.

MAY 20, 1943

Dr Nakamura speaking."

Holding the instrument to his ear, he seated himself on a nearby canvas stool and solemnly contemplated the dried mud on his boots. The last operation had not been successful—a shattered spine who, by every measure, shouldn't have lived at all. Two hours on the table and not giving a single sign that he knew or cared. A Samurai's death, classic in its simplicity. Sighing his disappointment, Tomi had removed mask and gloves and begun thinking of tea. Then this radio call—

"This is Lieutenant Ujiie. Good morning, Acting Officer Nakamura."

"Good morning, honored sir." He kept his voice carefully polite.

"There is a matter which greatly disturbs our revered Colonel Shima. Last night our communications people picked up a radio signal in English from Chichagof Harbor. It was thought to emanate from your hospital. The message was, 'Big Boy One, this is Eagle Four,' repeated several times about zero-four-hundred hours. Can you possibly explain it?"

Tomi blinked his surprise. Eagle Four? Michael? It could only be Michael. But the radio. How? "No, honored sir. As you know, I spent the night at the church."

"Of course. Our esteemed colonel requires, however, that you investigate the matter and report the facts to me personally, at once."

"At once, honored sir." Further comment became academic; the honored Lieutenant Ujiie had disconnected.

For a moment Tomi sat in silence, stunned. Michael, Michael, you will kill us both.

He felt both blessed and cursed by Americans. Jones, too, was a problem to be dealt with—in more ways than one. An hour ago, easing through the rows of litters, pausing to check each chart and offer a word of cheer and hope to each patient, he had found only cold disfavor. Most confusing. Why?

Hayasaka, almost in tears, had supplied the answer: "The black American! You have prescribed generous quantities of sake for him, and no one else. Others, good sons of Nippon, would also enjoy sake."

Tomi was for a moment speechless. "They think I am partial? But the fact is that we have no brandy or whisky, so I ordered sake—the only alcohol available. It dilates his veins. It increases the flow of blood through his feet—"

"But, honored sir, he is merely an American. You are giving him our sake."

"He is a patient and I am his physician. There is no other distinction. He needs the sake, others do not. Is that not apparent?"

"No, honored doctor." The boy had trouble speaking. "Not to everyone."

"To you?"

Hayasaka nodded reluctantly. "Now that I know."

"Then we remain friends."

Now he must deal with Jones on a double level—the patient's needs and the effect of such treatment on all others. Where to draw the line?

At the end of Jones's litter he said "Good morning" and bent to examine the man's feet. As he had hoped, the left foot had paled considerably, the hard brilliant red giving way to a near-normal brown. It would continue restoring itself. But the right foot was already acquiring that certain opaque, shiny-black appearance every surgeon feared. The first sour-sweet odor of putrefaction was there, faint but unmistakable. "How do you feel?"

"I ain't too hot, Doc." Jones moved his shoulders to ease the press of the litter against his back. Watching, Tomi became aware of how quiet the ward had grown, patients and wardmen alike watching without appearing to. He could feel their animosity: the American-trained doctor showing favoritism to one of them.

"The fact is, Doc," Jones was saying, "I'm-rabid-about-a-habit. I'm a hep cat, in-the-groove-an'-on-the-move. An' baby, y'all doan cut it."

"I beg your pardon. Would you translate that to English?"

"Like I'm sayin', it's this lousy rice. Ain't you got some food? Like pork chops. Or maybe a juicy steak an' taters? Somethin', Doc—anythin'. Who told you rice was food?"

"Rice is all we have, Private First-Class Jones. We used to have bean curd, but alas! no more. Have you tried rice wrapped in seaweed? It's called sushi, and it's really quite tasty."

"Doc, y'doan unnerstand. I'm hungry!"

"I'm sorry. It's rice or nothing."

"Okay. Then how about lots more? I mean, with my size I gotta have more'n you give these—other little guys. Maybe you doan know what real hungry is."

"Perhaps I do! We've lived on half-rations now for quite some time. We get much less than that now, a condition that will continue and probably grow worse. It's called slow starvation. You're lucky, you may share it with us."

"You kiddin' me, Doc? Ain't you heard of the Geneva Convention?"

"Private First-Class Jones, we'll share what we have, but—"

"Okay. Y'wanna see somethin' funny? Watch this." Eyes shining with expectancy, Jones turned to Private Umeda. "Hey! Tojo is a two-faced, two-legged frog."

"Greta Garbo is a fat pig," Umeda said abruptly, his quiet voice filled with rancor. "Charlie Chaplin is a sorry fool; he isn't amusing. And Clark Gable is an unkind moron."

"See?" grinned Jones. "Jus' push a button an' watch the puppet. He lives, he breathes, he says funny things."

"You mustn't tempt him, bait him. Your humor he fails to—"

"Look, Doc, can't you find me a fork? These lousy chopsticks is okay for a midget like"—a dark thumb arced in Umeda's direction—"but I got only one arm to hold the bowl."

"We have no forks."

"A knife then. Down home we allus use a knife for eatin' goober peas an' beans an' all kindsa stuff."

Tomi shook his head, hoping the wardmen and all the patients would notice. "Prisoners are not allowed knives."

"It's chopsticks or nuthin'?"

"I think that sums it up. You'll manage."

Now Jones shook his head. "Doc, I thought for a while you was civilized. You was nice an' all. Now I'm gittin' the idea you doan like me."

Tomi hoped the idea was universal. "How's your head—still hurt?"

"It's jus' my feet, Doc. Fum the ankle down. They hurt sometimes worser than cottonmouth poison. Fix that, huh? An' then lemme outta here."

"President Roosevelt is an evil man," Umeda said, obviously angry at Jones. "That's why he's crippled."

"Shut up, bandy-legs! Doan y'all put down Pres'dent Ros-afelt. He the only good thin' that happen to my people since the damyankees went home. He a high rootin-tooter. He got us meat on the table twice a week, and shoes, baby! Sunday go t'meetin' shoes, fine for struttin' on Satiday nights, too. So doan you down-talk Pres'dent Ros-afelt."

"He's white! Two-faced! He's not your friend."

"Now looky here! Doan you start—"

"Jones, I have to amputate your foot."

"—none o' *that*, 'cause I know for a fact your own Emp'rah ain't so perf—" Jones stopped still and stared at Tomi. "Doc, what you say?"

"Your right foot. It has to come off."

Jones held up one hand, vertically, a gesture that said "Stop." "Nope, it don't got to. It gonna stay right there on the end of my leg. It's warm an' happy there, most times. It's gonna get well an' carry me anywheres I wanna go. It gonna take me dancin' an' sparkin' on Satiday nights, an' somewheres—fast!—when they gets pregnant. Nope, I got plans for that foot. I'm fond of it."

"It comes off tonight, right after your interrogation by Intelligence. It comes off or you can't live."

Tomi walked away, the sound of Umeda's voice unavoidable: "American Marines eat their grandmothers. Everyone here is aware of that. What foul beasts you Americans are!"

Japanese discipline, so ironlike, so dependable in the past, was beginning to break down, he knew. The results were subtle, yet everywhere about him.

Near the tent opening he found Private Hayasaka waiting to speak. "Honored sir, I bring news. In your absence during the night our soldiers searching the hills for the missing American airman found several pieces of muddy American clothing. Could you guess where? In our storeroom for discarded uniforms. Now everyone wonders how and when—"

Inwardly Tomi groaned. The hunt narrowed. The noose tightened another inch.

"Where," he managed to ask, "are our soldiers searching now?"

"In the caves along the ravine leading up to Umanose. If he is not in one of them, then it is believed he has taken refuge somewhere here in Chichagof Harbor."

"Then let us hope they find him." He felt thankful now he had not taken Michael Andrews to one of those caves. Though he hadn't thought of caves at the time.

"By the way, Hayasaka, who was the radio guard on duty last night between twenty-four hundred and zero-four hundred?"

"It was I, honored sir." His tone seemed usual, yet somehow guarded. "Is anything wrong?"

"Did you sleep at all while on duty?"

"Oh, honored sir!"

"Hayasaka, it's important! Did you sleep? For even a few minutes?"

The boy hesitated only a second, then hung his head. "Only for a short moment. I tried hard not to. But—"

"I understand. But you must not sleep on radio guard duty again. May I depend on you?"

Hayasaka nodded and wandered away, head down, leaving Tomi fully aware of which radio Michael had used and the risk taken. *Michael, have you no brains?*

During an idle moment, Hirose said, "I spoke to a friend of mine at headquarters. The opinion there is that American casualties are very large. Everyone seems to agree. They must soon bleed themselves into surrender or defeat."

"I have no facts," Tomi said, watching Sergeant Okasaki measure out the patients' rations of rice. "Yet, I would assume a large attrition rate. On the other hand, there are many thousands of Americans remaining on the island."

"That many more to kill."

"Did your friend at headquarters mention anything about a strange radio transmission last night from nearby?" He omitted saying "in English," though later he could insist he had.

Hirose raised his brows. "Was there one?"

"That's what I'm told. No unauthorized person used our radio?"

"How should I know? Between supervising most of the day and operating half the night and then trying to snatch a few hours of sleep—" Hirose cut himself short, his eyes bloodshot and face drawn from a sleepless night. "I'm going to the barracks now. Have Sergeant Okasaki replenish our operating supplies, would you? Several items are in low supply."

"At once," Tomi said, turning his attention to the matters which worried him most. Since returning from the church he'd had no chance to speak with Michael, for Okasaki had been there, directing and observing a half-dozen sleepy, bumbling wardmen. Always Okasaki, watching, aware.

The result was that Michael had gone all day and night without food. And water. Without a bedpan. No assurance that all was well, whether it was or not. No explanation of why he'd been neglected. Now the man's mind would be filled with doubt.

"The burn case troubles you?" asked Okasaki, suddenly at his elbow. "Before dawn this morning I discovered him returning from the latrine."

"In his condition? But he mustn't rise yet!"

"I spoke, asking if he needed assistance. He did not answer. Yet he must have heard."

"His ears are damaged," Tomi said quickly, the first thought that rose to mind. "I am not yet sure how badly."

"Is that why he rejects my assistance?"

"You've given him directions?"

"Only to see to his needs. He refused to be turned in his litter. He is very rude."

Tomi kept his voice calm, even. "You must not concern yourself with the burn case, Sergeant Okasaki. He is my responsibility alone."

Okasaki's eyes narrowed a fraction. "And he has a strange odor, very musky. Why is that?"

Okasaki's persistence was close to becoming impudence, even outright disobedience. But a heavy word of discipline now would only rouse Okasaki's curiosity. Tact, that was the tactic.

Tomi knew precisely the source of the odor. Beef or pork or lamb eaten in sufficient quantities three times a day will provide a body odor that is unmistakable. Conversely, a steady diet of fish will produce a distinctly different smell. Hence the old arguments about the acrid Asian odor and the musky Caucasian smell each had merit. Was Okasaki, an intelligent man, aware of this?

"The burn case has a disease that is not yet diagnosed, not to my satisfaction. His odor must stem from that."

But even to him the comment seemed shallow, perhaps inane. "Have you noticed any unauthorized person using our radio telephone of late?"

Okasaki gazed at him, obviously curious. "No, honored sir. Is there a problem?"

"I am not certain." He turned away, found a rice ball and wolfed it down, but so little food could not ease his hunger. He pushed himself through the rows of litters, stopping first beside Michael Andrews to peer down at the dark, gargoylelike goggles. In quick Japanese he asked: "Are you in pain? Resting well?" His fingers, however, pressed Michael's bandaged wrist in what he hoped was a reassuring gesture. Leaning low, he whispered in English, "Tonight! Bear with me."

The attack yesterday had failed miserably, but Murphy and the kids and all of Dog Company had been held in reserve. This morning the shelling of the bowl had been a magnificent thing to watch. A spotter plane overhead and a rolling barrage, that was the only way. Fourteen-inch Navy shells. Hell, bury the Japs deep with all those big shells and geysers of earth leaping high like fountains of spring water. One after another, *wham! wham! wham!*, a hundred or more until your ears hurt and eyes boggled, thankful that Japs and not yourself were on the receiving end.

With the barrage finished, there had been ample time and cover for the entire company to enter the bowl, scale the knolls and check for Jap survivors, finding only a few groggy, confused, helpless-looking little men, each of whom had reached for grenade or rifle and had died instantly with 30-caliber lead through his head. Stupid way to die, Murphy had thought. Situation hopeless and all they had to do was hold up their hands and wait. They could have lived. Yet they preferred to die. Murphy didn't understand.

At any rate the bowl was now American territory. From his foxhole on the southern rim of the bowl Murphy could peer the length of a long ravine that led down to Chichagof. A blue haze there hung over much of the area. Looked for all the world like coal smoke.

Chichagof Harbor he found fascinating. There was movement there, life. Japs—their friggen headquarters area. Two miles away, he guessed. It was hard to see specifics; he needed better binoculars. Yet there was a thin column of men he could barely see bearing—litters? They were moving like ants along the beach heading northward. Litters? Why there? There wasn't a red cross to be seen anywhere.

A hum of planes. He eyed the sky—there! Navy planes coming in from the south, all blue and silver and lumbering pregnantlike through the air, flying just under cloud level. They turned rather than wheeled, fell rather than dived. The shriek of wings and whine of motors grew as they angled down toward Chichagof Harbor.

In a slow dive of 75 degrees, the first plane appeared to hang in the air, took forever to take on a larger dimension. Diving brakes set and motor adjusted just so, round nacelle gleaming, the stubby plane filled the sky with noise and Murphy's mind with keen interest. A small dark object soon broke free and fell like a stone. Fascinated, he noted the course of its fall, down past mountaintops and snowline toward plain and harbor. It'll miss, he thought. The friggen thing'll fall in the bay. Damn Navy can't bomb worth shit.

Each split second the object grew larger, darker, more cylindrical, whistling a faint hollow wail as it neared the earth. Then it struck. In the depths of the village church a dark flower instantly blossomed, separating itself into tiny pieces of wood and stone and dark torn earth, all tossed like unwinnowed wheat and topped by roiling smoke, together with a muffled distant *boom!* that sailed hard upon the cold wind.

"Jumping Jesus H. Christ!" said Swensen. "Y'see that, Sarge? Just like the fucken movies."

Even before the debris had fallen to earth, another fountain rose high, then another and another: Car-*ruumph!* Car-*ruumph!* Car-*ruumph!*—all too quickly for the mind to grasp. From the comfort of his foxhole Murphy saw the village destroyed in less than a minute—the church, the school, all ten little houses and everything that moved.

Finished at last, the planes began lumbering southward, back to the carrier. The wind moaned. Below, the smoke thinned in the brisk wind.

1990/

Swensen found himself staring hard at the scuffed and muddy toes of his boots. God, God! Of their own accord his hands had abruptly clasped hard together and kept pressing one against the other. That's the only way he could control it—this strange trembling of late that plagued him. Where did it come from? What caused it? He didn't understand, couldn't explain. Certainly he didn't feel cold, not inside.

"Sarge," he said, desperately eying the water warming over canned heat, "did I ever tell you how I got this rash in my armpits? There was this girl I knew in high school, y'see. Lotsa wild ideas. She was an acrobat and had athlete's foot. So one night we . . ."

The village—a total loss. But the esteemed Garrison Commander Colonel Shima was safe and unhurt. That was all Tomi knew. For hours he had been tending the survivors in surgery, and only a moment ago emerged, hoping to find a moment of peace in the ward tent. But Lieutenant Ujiie was there, waiting. "I didn't expect to see you, honored sir," Tomi said, motioning to a canvas stool by the radio phone, the only seat available in the ward tent. But Ujiie remained standing.

Tomi slowly removed his blood-stained operating gown. At last the ward was quiet, he thought. No more confusion. Coma, sleep, stoicism, all served as a welcome change of pace from the shelling.

"I am here in place of the respected Lieutenants Oda and Hirona," Ujiie said. "Both died gloriously for the Emperor in the village church just a few hours ago. My mission is to interrogate the American prisoner. He is conscious? Alert? The esteemed Garrison Commander Colonel Shima suggests you attend. Your English is more fluent than mine, and your ear is more closely attuned to the American idiom."

"Of course. Whatever the esteemed colonel suggests."

One more task, he thought, always one more. The many operations finished, he and Hirose had agreed they now had nothing to do but sleep if fate allowed and then see to the needs of ninety-two patients, a third of whom were newly injured. "The black American is conscious."

Behind the mellowness derived from much sake, Private First-Class Jones seemed to accept Tomi but not Ujiie. "You got my name, rank an' serial number, Mister Jap. That's all you git."

"We also know your division, battalion and company," Ujiie said in a gloating tone. "The general in charge is named Landrum."

"Tain't so. I know, an' you know, it's ol' Gen'ral Brown."

"General Brown was relieved of command several days ago for reasons we haven't determined, specifically. We think he failed to advance fast enough. His many trucks and tractors sank to their wheel hubs in mud and his troops proved soft and unprepared. They were soon quite exhausted."

"Sonuvagun! Mired, tired an' fired, all in one day. Ol'-Brown's-down, he-ain't-aroun'."

"American, do not be facetious. It's insulting."

"Be what? Hey, Jap, you callin' me names?"

"Of course not!" snapped Ujiie. "I merely demand that you be serious. I do not care for American humor."

"Oh, I'm serious. Ain't I, Doc? No-flip-o'-the-lip, not me. No, jus'-part-o'-my-heart. Or don'tcha wanna dance?"

"I beg your pardon?"

"Doan beg, Mister Tojo. I hates to see a grown man on his knees." Jones grinned victoriously at Tomi.

"See here, Private Jones—"

"Private Fust-Class, to you. Doan forgit agin—boy!"

"Lieutenant," Tomi interrupted, noting that Michael Andrews had propped himself on one elbow, watching, his eerie figure perhaps too intent. "May I suggest you get on with the interrogation? You mentioned the American general being relieved of command. Is that relevant to Private First-Class Jones?"

"That is what I wish to explore." Ujiie frowned, turning again to glare down on Jones. "We also question General Brown's use of poison gas. Was it not a factor in his dismissal? It's barely possible. Did he not use enough? What are current American attitudes concerning his criminal use of poison gas?"

"Poison gas? What poison gas?" Jones's eyes were suddenly wide and alert, suspicious. Tomi decided the man was more in command of himself than his consumption of sake would suggest.

"I refer to the poison gas used against Japanese troops several days ago. It was white, very white, foul-smelling, and fortunately blown away by the wind."

Jones grinned, his big white teeth lighting his entire face. "Oh, thaaaat! The lootenant, sonuvagun, he call for smoke shells so we could see where we was shootin'. That's all. An' the Navy it fired an' the smoke it went *blooey!* Like that. *Blooey!*—all to hell an' gone an' real purty. Then all your little Jap people suddenly started jumpin' up like they got bees in their unnerwear, slapped gas masks on an' skedaddled like scared poh-licemens for a better hole. Back a-ways they went."

"Smoke shells? I don't believe you."

Jones waved a hand, disregarding Ujiie. "We couldn't believe what happened neither. First we jus' laid there in the snow, goggle-eyed an' lookin' around an' scratchin' our skulls an' wonderin' what-in-de-worl' is goin' on? Y'know? Lootenant, he doan know nothin'. Then sergeant he git the idea. We move in where you poor boys had jus' left—y'know, alla time firin' more smoke shells an' laughin', laughin' all the way. So hi-de-ho-an'-away-we-go! A great way to fight a war. You Japs really thought it was gas?"

"Indeed. We still do."

Umeda was listening from the next litter, his eyes shining. He nodded at Tomi, smiling.

"I ain't lyin'," Jones said. "Tha's-a'-fact; it-ain't-no-act."

"I think you lie! All you Americans lie at the slightest whim. A nation of liars."

Jones paused to take a deep breath. "Looky, Mister Twinkle-toes. We's the big boys. We doan gotta use gas or nuthin' like that to whup you-all. All we gotta do is cut off your food an' oil an' every-thin' else an' let you follow li'l ol' Hi-ro-hito right to hell."

"Insolent dog!" cried Ujiie, and slapped Jones's face. Too late Tomi leaped to intervene.

But Jones merely stared, his eyes wide and sure. "Doan do that agin, y'hear? I got no legs to work with an' only one arm. But tetch me agin an' you'll wish you didn't."

"American pig! How dare you insult—"

"Oh, I dares anythin'," Jones said, a lazy, dangerous smile growing on his face. "Some thin's I dares more'n once. Feel lucky? Try slappin' my face agin."

"It was gas! Our men cannot be wrong. Be truthful! Tell me it was gas."

"Nope. Y'wanna know why? It's like this: the men what made the gas would know it was gas—right? Same for the dock loaders; can't fool 'em a-tall. Same for the Navy boys who stowed the shells jus' so in a nice cool place, and who fired the shots. An' if we knowed there'd be gas floatin' around, doan you think we'd wear masks our own selfs? Yas-suuuh! But we throwed them down, first day, on the beach. Got rid of everythin' we didn't need."

"All lies! Just a cheap rationale—"

"Doan interrupt! I jus' told you there's thousands o' men involved. Can't keep no secrets, not with flap-happy, snoop reporters from newspapers all around, jus' lookin' for somethin' like that. Y'think it could be kept secret? Not a chance in all-de-world."

"President Roosevelt arranges anything he likes."

"Not nuthin' like usin' gas! Nohow! He be kicked right outta office—*blooey!* Jus' like that, WPA an' new shoes or no. Can you do that with Hi-ro-hito?"

His face livid, Ujiie leaned close. "And who is Eagle Four? Who is Big Boy One? Whom were you calling and for what purpose? Are you an agent from American Military Intelligence? Where did you hide your radio? How many more are with you?"

Tomi could only stare at Ujiie. Jones said, "Slow down! Who is what? Hey, how come they let you outta the cell?"

"The radio, where is it?"

Jones frowned in confusion. "Only radio I know about is the one the Lootenant used. He call in smoke shells an' *blooey!* Jus' *blooey!* An' the li'l Jap fellers all got up like jack-in-the-boxes an' ran off-tippy-tippy-toe."

Ujiie, speechless and quivering in suppressed rage, turned suddenly and stomped from the tent. Jones laughed once, a snort of derision, and turned toward Tomi, no longer smiling. Tomi read the message: anything Japanese was Enemy, now very much hated. For a moment they gazed at each other, the wind moaning outside.

"I have been told," murmured Umeda, "that President Roosevelt is now sleeping with nigger girls."

Jones gave Umeda a long appraising stare. "I doubt if he do," he murmured at last. "But if so, he shore knows what's good."

He lay back and closed his eyes, a hint of a smile touching his lips.

Less than an hour later Hayasaka reported that a certain patient, a junior officer, claimed the theft of his pistol, a nine-shot, ivory-handled weapon purchased before Pearl Harbor at great expense. Tomi listened without comment, but thought it very curious: the officer's litter lay near the entrance of the ward tent, almost elbow to elbow with that of Michael Andrews.

May 20. The hard fighting of our 303rd Battalion in Massacre Bay is fierce and it is to our advantage. Have captured enemy weapons and used that to fight. Mowed down ten enemy coming in under the fog. Five of our men and one medical NCO died. Heard enemy pilots faces can be seen around Umanose. The enemy naval gun firing near our hospital is fierce. Drops about twenty meters away.

MAY 21, 1943

I t was the damnedest thing I ever saw," Swensen was saying in a taut voice, trembling. "She had these wooden legs, y'see. Both of 'em, all the way up. Oak or ash, I dunno. Well! So when I learned that, I started the old pitch. I says, 'How about a good sand job? Been varnished lately? How's to let me polish you up a bit? Or should I rub you right—we'll make sawdust.' She looks at me funny and I says, 'What the hell you afraid of—I'll give you termites?' "

"Jesus," said Jeeters, chewing K-rats, "you didn't."

"Shit," muttered Hall. Absently he picked pimples. "She knock you on your can?"

"Not old Swensen. So I works on her for months and months and suddenly one night I'm right there, between the logs. Like making love in a sawmill, really. And y'know what I picked up from that fucken babe?"

"Clap?" asked Bennett, forcing himself to use forbidden language.

"Syph." Baker nodded, positive he was right. Wasn't he always right?

"Slivers! All up and down my goddamn legs. Nothing but a bunch of lousy slivers."

Murphy turned away, unable to watch Swensen. He knew exactly why. It was that host of freckles, that snub nose, that brash expression—Johnny's bold face he saw each time Swensen grinned. Bigger, older—but Johnny. Murphy hadn't meant to get overly attached to Swensen. Had fought it now for over a year, tried hard not to play favorites. But the fact was there, undeniably: Swensen and Johnny often merged in his mind, became one.

It wasn't fair, he thought. Johnny was dead. Why should Murphy be constantly reminded of gutters that flowed red and black with blood and oil, and gray with water that swirled everything down the sewer?

"Your wounds are all clean and healing," Tomi whispered to Michael Andrews. "It is a sign of God's protection. A few more days' rest and you will be out of danger."

At this time of night the ward tent was almost totally dark. Only a single candle by the radio telephone flickered in the frigid air, and in its glow Wardman Ouye sprawled in his canvas chair, sound asleep while on duty. An unforgivable sin, but it left Tomi this golden opportunity to remove Michael's bandages, to feed him and speak. "I regret there is not more rice."

"Me, too! But do I have to wear this damned catheter? I'm getting sore down there."

"A few more days. Circumstances determine everything. We shall see how events develop."

"Let's create our own events. That Negro—Jones? I heard you talking to him."

"Ignore him. He is not important to you. Make no attempt to contact—"

"Doc, do you realize that if Jones and I both had guns and five minutes at that radio, we could bring the whole American Army into Chichagof Harbor? Talk about opportunity—it's undefended from the sea."

"No! No guns, no radio. I will not hear of it. You must rest. I will do all I can to save your life, but you must not use that radio again. It's too dangerous."

"Think of the lives we'd save, like yours and mine and Jones."

"That is speculation and very disloyal for me. I cannot be a part of it. Besides, Jones has only one foot. And now there is an ivory-handled pistol missing. Stolen. Did you take it?"

A moment of silence. Tomi peered blindly through the black. Michael would not be a good liar. Christians were not trained to lie. "Please do not use the gun."

"Look, it's this way, Nakamura—"

"Tomi."

"Okay, Tomi. I stay here, like this, and it's only a question of time before somebody adds it up. Then my butt's in a sling, and yours, too. I got to get out of here."

"It's too early. You're still too weak. With great exertion that artery wall could hemorrhage. You must wait. Soldiers are look-ing for you."

"Well, I'm weak, I admit. Coming up that slope from the latrine last night—"

"That was foolish."

"But necessary, believe me."

"You were seen. Sergeant Okasaki—"

"The big guy, with a belly? He sees everything. He keeps poking around, watching, even sniffing. He suspects something."

"Even so, we must wait until you are stronger, then for the right moment. I will know when it comes. You must trust me. And pray."

Above all, he thought, pray.

Prayer was okay, Michael thought. Prayer was just fine as far as it went. He didn't want to negate God, but he'd noticed many times before that when a man asked God to do something it helped to have a good, workable backup system ready. Then give it all you got and nine times out of ten God came through. The best of both worlds was an undeniable advantage.

Prayer! Tomi was *maybe* a nice guy, maybe a brave and unselfish man, maybe had his neck stuck out a mile. But nobody worked for nothing. What was Tomi's angle?

In any case, Michael couldn't sit back and wait for unpredictable, unforeseen events to dictate his future. Or lack of same. Not after overhearing the interrogation of Jones last night by that scrawny little Jap everyone seemed in fear of. Who is Eagle Four? the man had wanted to know. What is Big Boy One? Okay, so Jap Intelligence knew about his use of the radio, knew he'd gotten no answer in those few seconds before the little Jap sleeping nearby had stirred. By now the Japs would have troops searching high and low with orders to shoot on sight. That was good to know. It only stressed the need to do something now. Like move his freight out of here. Nothing rash or crude. Something well thought out, that had a chance.

One immediate snag was Jones. He was back now, borne by litter-bearers struggling under his great weight. Unconscious even yet, his face was slack, mouth slightly ajar, a mask that hardly looked alive. The stump of one leg bulged white with bandages, just below the knee. Forever a crippled giant.

So the idea of using Jones with stolen rifles and the radio to bring a rescue party into Chichagof Harbor was out. So was a quick escape together. Jones must remain here and hope he, Michael, could get away and return quickly with help. Futile thought! Weak as a damn cat and thinking of running. Whatever, he'd need special clothes and equipment. . . .

He was fumbling and he knew it. His mind wouldn't work right. He needed a plan, solid and workable, not this wishful thinking. That plan required a focus, a key. Jesus, he thought. What the hell am I looking for?

Okusan—honored wife, Tomi wrote in his usual awkward style. He stared at the otherwise blank paper, then set down his pen.

What could he possibly write?

● That he had saved a certain man's life, and if that fact were known his name, honor and life would all become forfeit?

• That he felt drawn in friendship with this man who had eyes like those of Jesus, who was also a fellow humanist and man of good will—who was also an enemy?

• That day after day good Japanese boys and men were dying needlessly for a half-frozen scrap of terrain they didn't need, couldn't use and wouldn't want?

• That the specter of slow starvation lay hard in his mind?

• That the cold today was the bitterest of the whole campaign, with fresh snow falling now on the peaks, with wounded men exposed to frostbite as they lay helpless on litters?

• That coal and gasoline supplies were dangerously low? That there weren't enough woolen blankets now for the wounded? That Americans were brave and overpowering and would not be defeated?

No, he told himself, he could write nothing of the sort. Even without the censor, he wouldn't want to worry her, his Sumiko. As always, he might write that he was well and strong, vigorous and confident, but a glance in the mirror made a lie of all that. Gaunt cheeks, haunted eyes, a ragged mustache and now an itching, unkempt beard—that was the grim truth, and he wouldn't lie. Especially to Sumiko.

Oku-san, he thought. Woman of my heart. Oh, to share a moment in your company. To gaze again upon your lovely face, to tease the glow to your cheek and that delightful impish twinkle to your eye. To stroll again amid the irises of May, all purple and white; to enjoy the fragrance of green leaves and the quiet warmth of sunshine.

The azaleas of Haruna, do you recall them? We walked among them without words, for such beauty is felt in the heart and needs no translation. I remember the cherry blossoms in our garden. Are they in full bloom, fragile and smelling sweet? The tender lotus blooms, chrysanthemums, gladioli, the lilies? Oh, I remember.

I remember, too, your flower teacakes made of bean jam. I remember my father's house and the moment I first met you. How mischievous you were! I remember those days of delight, our courtship and marriage, and how I feared in my heart you'd refuse me.

With infinite joy I remember the birth of our first child, gazing upon her beauty as delicate as yours and knowing the wonder of this miracle God had given us.

I remember many things—my daily hot bath and clean fresh clothes, the smell of incense, a sated belly. I remember hope and promise and deep restful sleep.

At night I remember music.

In the wind I remember warmth.

At all times I remember laughter, the glowing, singing of heart and soul in tune with yours. I remember life and love and happiness.

Oh, Sumiko—*oku-san*—above all I remember you. . . .

From the barracks up the ramp to the ward tent Tomi fought a strong snowy wind that sliced through small holes and gaps in his clothing and chilled him through. He hurried, his left knee stabbing with each step. Inside the ward tent he ignored Michael, the safest thing to do, and found Hirose near the stove supervising the removal of a fresh corpse.

"I can't explain it," Hirose growled on seeing Tomi. "By every measure I know the man should have lived. His progress to this point was excellent. Then suddenly—"

"It sometimes happens; it's not your fault. Hirose, I have heard that Americans have taken the pass that leads from Massacre Bay to upper Sarana Valley, plus a small hill nearby. They now assault the mountains on either side of the pass. What is your opinion; will they succeed? If so, what then?"

"My opinion does not matter," Hirose said, his tone flat and somehow patronizing. "What does the enemy's great number matter? Size is not everything. They will take the terrain or they will not. In either case, it is not our problem. Our task is to repair the wounded, if possible, and send them back. Personally, I have no time for other matters."

"What happens to us if the enemy keeps advancing?"

"They will not. I assure you of that. We shall be reinforced. The Emperor himself has promised."

"But suppose something happens? Something unforeseen. Suppose for some reason we aren't reinforced?"

"Then eventually the Americans will arrive at this point. Simple, isn't it? They will kill us, or we shall die by our own hands and spare them the trouble. Either way, it will all be over and nothing will matter. Did you sleep well?"

Half angry, Tomi reminded himself that, unlike Hirose, he had no intention of dying, certainly not without a good reason and, even then, not if he could help it. Somehow he must retain control of his immediate future, for Michael's sake. He had dire need of a good idea, a plan. . . .

Meanwhile he merely grunted, "Sleep? The American artillery makes sleep impossible."

"Nakamura," Hirose murmured, a half-smile playing around his eyes. "You are very jumpy these days. Do not worry so! How many times must I tell you? This outpost is vital to the Emperor, remember? Help will come."

"I wish I were as sure of that as you."

"Give the High Command time. Keep an open mind. Everything will turn out all right. Trust me."

Tomi recalled saying the same thing to Michael.

"Which reminds me," Hirose said. "A patient reported that someone was whispering in English in the ward tent this morning before dawn. You were on duty. What do you know of it?"

"Eng—English?" He was dumbfounded, couldn't think of what to say.

"Didn't you hear me? It was definitely English, but undistinguishable. Strange, wouldn't you say?"

"Oh, very! Perhaps the black American, Jones."

"He was under heavy sedation. Last night you amputated—"

"Of course. Then it must be—" He almost said Umeda but thought better of it.

"Must be what?"

"That someone heard me reciting quotations from the Bible.

The Psalms—yes! I once memorized them in English, you see, and every once in a while—"

"Dr. Nakamura, you must cease doing that at once. It creates much confusion and doubt." Abruptly he rose and hurried away without even a bow.

Tomi sighed his relief. He knew he hadn't carried it off well, but the surprise . . . He was sweating, feeling ashamed and unsettled. But Hayasaka was nearby and waiting to speak. The boy seemed fearful of being overheard.

"Honored sir," he whispered, "I am confused about the burn case. Each time I remove his container of urine I hear his stomach rumble fearfully. So I bring him his daily ration of rice and he refuses—"

"By my orders." Tomi tried to appear calm but forceful. "Have you not been instructed to remain at a distance from him? His disease is very—"

"But, honored sir, the urine must be removed! Besides, I have no fear of contagious disease. Once, but no longer. Jesus will protect me."

Still shaken, Tomi had no ready answer.

"Last night I knelt beside this patient and prayed to Jesus. I asked that his health be fully restored and that he prosper all his life. Do you think my prayers will be answered?"

Tomi almost choked. "We both wish so. How did the patient react?"

"He said nothing. He, too, seemed to be praying. Then a strange feeling came over me. I dreamed that with practice I might also perform miracles. Imagine!—to merely touch each of these patients, and each would rise, well and whole again."

Heresy? Tomi could listen no more. "We will speak of this another time. Is the black American conscious?"

"Honored sir, I do not know. He has stirred several times on the litter."

Approaching Jones, Tomi felt better, more in command of himself. Last night the operation had gone well, quickly, and with no complications. Little chance of other infections existed, but one could never be sure.

Jones's temperature, pulse and respiration were within acceptable limits. Blood pressure was high but not bad. He'd consumed sixty cubic centimeters of water since midnight and voided nothing. Obviously dehydrated. Few nursing notes, of course, due to lack of quality and quantity of trained personnel, lack of time, lack of everything. So, with luck, Private First-Class Jones would be all right.

"You took it off," Jones muttered in a blurred listless voice. "You put somethin' in my likker. I started sleepin'. An' you cut it off."

"I saved your life. Your life! Does anything else matter?"

"That foot was good, not like you say."

"No, it wasn't. When you were admitted here, your right foot had ice crystals through and through, including the bone. I could tell by the color—waxy-looking and yellow. The skin was frozen solid to your ankle; it wouldn't move. Then the edema—"

"What's that?"

"A swelling. Water expands as it freezes."

"A good foot." Listless, yes. But now his eyes held a glint.

Tomi shook his head. "It wasn't even a marginal case, as your other foot was. But I tried to save it. I amputated only because the first stage of gangrene was well in evidence. Anything less than amputation would endanger your life."

"It was my leg! It was good. I could feel it."

"You felt morphine, that's what you felt. Without morphine you'd have experienced intense pain. You'd have begged me to operate."

"You . . . butcher. I gonna kill you. No matter where."

Tomi managed a smile. "You've been watching too many American movies. Now about your recovery. I want you to drink more water—"

"Go 'way, Jap! It was a good foot."

He sighed his disappointment. "I'm sorry you feel that way." He turned to Hayasaka. "Give this man all the water he wants. See to it now. If he suffers pain, give him two aspirin."

What more could he do than tell Jones the truth? A man as shortsighted, ungrateful and vindictive as Jones was depressing.

Tomi struggled to understand. What other logic, what other arguments, could he have used? What other tactics? Last night he'd had no time or energy to play games, to ask or coax or plead. Without fuss or confusion he'd simply done the obvious—prescribed chloral hydrate, waited for Jones to fall asleep, and got it over with. Granted, in America such tactics were illegal; he'd need a signed permission form or court order. But Attu wasn't America, not yet. Meanwhile, he had saved a man's life. And he hadn't castrated anyone. When would Jones think of that?

Okasaki, he saw, had stationed himself near the burn case, was now staring down on the bandaged head, face, arms and hands; his face wore a puzzled expression. To call him away now would only invite suspicion. So no matter what happened—until it happened—Tomi could only continue in his duty.

Rumor said the Japs are crumbling; everything is going our way.

It was true that Holtz Bay had fallen, that Jarmin Pass had been taken, that the great bulk of Gilbert Ridge was now under American control. But the enemy still held the peak of Point Able, overlooking Sarana Valley and the route to Chichagof Harbor, and therefore the terrain below was, for Americans, untenable.

Rumor said the Japs can't last much longer. A day or two, maybe three. We got 'em just where we want 'em.

But the small brown men, seen at a distance but rarely, clung tenaciously to high ridge and ravine; they hid in fog and foxhole and had to be found and dug out and killed one at a time; no Jap would surrender. It was hard, dangerous work, and Murphy was weary of tasteless K-rats and coffee that never got hot, of sleepless nights and pressure that never eased. Meanwhile there was weather that wouldn't quit, the wind drove in and pained like a knife cut. What the hell, he thought; what the goddamn hell . . .

"Hayasaka, what are you dreaming about?" Tomi asked. The boy had been feeding a patient, a quadriplegic, and had finished but made no attempt to remove the empty bowl. He sat without motion, staring blankly into space.

"Oh!" The boy jumped. Embarrassment flooded his face. "My thoughts? Merely that this is the month of May. It is spring everywhere but on Attu. I cannot help but remember an old haiku: 'The spring departs—birds cry and tears fill fish's eyes.' "

"Very appropriate," Tomi said in a sharp tone. "But men in pain go hungry while you remember poetry. Come now, we mustn't be selfish, must we? Hayasaka, we must remember duty."

He disliked his own tone of reprimand; it wasn't his usual method. But he felt tired and in this case scolding was necessary.

Umeda was waving from across the tent. It took Tomi only a moment to arrive at Umeda's side.

"The American is less than a man," Umeda hissed gleefully. "His missing foot pains him, for he groans. Do you hear him? So does mine, but I bear it like a man. It gives me joy to know he suffers."

Tomi fixed his eyes upon Jones. "I'm told you are in pain."

"Natchurly." The voice was soft and mellow, the eyes hard. "But I ain't askin' for no favors. None of that lousy likker, not from you. Otherwise I might wake up an' have no head."

"That's ridiculous. We have a quantity of aspirin. Perhaps that would help."

"I doan want nothin' from you, Jap. You ruint my whole life."

"See how the American pig lies," said Umeda in Japanese. "No doubt his mother sells herself like an animal in the streets."

"Mind your own business, Private Umeda. Private First-Class Jones, understand me. I haven't ruined your life. An artificial leg will serve you almost as well. You can go to school and learn a trade. You can still do most things."

"Doc, don't be foolish! You know what a hot, sweet-lovin' little mama say, all cuddly in bed an' seein' me take off a wooden leg? She say, Go 'way, nigger boy. I wants me a man, a whole man."

Tomi sighed, escaped from Jones and sought out Hirose. "What shall we do about the black American? In a few days he can be moved. I want him out of here as quickly as possible." For more reasons than one, he thought, with Michael in mind.

Hirose grunted and Tomi smelled sake, stale and foul, on his breath. "In ordinary circumstances he'd go to a prison hospital. But we have no means of sending him to one. I'll pass the question to our illustrious and devoted Captain Yamamoto, the champion of all us downtrodden practitioners of the medical art." He tilted his head loosely, his eyes overbright. "Will that satisfy you?"

"I'm not sure." He'd known since his arrival last March that Hirose used sake, a little here and there, not often overindulging. But this was new—drinking in the ward, on duty. To make it worse, the amount Hirose had consumed this day must be large, for his speech, both slurred and verbose, was unlike his usual style. "The worthy Captain Yamamoto will probably do nothing."

"How can you say that? Trust him. Yamamoto, a man of action! He will pass the problem to a higher, more noble authority, just as I am, and await their earth-shattering decision."

Tomi hoped that Okasaki and the wardmen were unaware of Hirose's condition. Carefully he steered the man toward the tent entrance where few of the patients could hear.

"Honored sir, if you wish to rest in the barracks a few hours, I will accept the responsibility for the ward and for surgery. I would consider it an honor if—"

He was interrupted by the bell at the entrance to the operating tent, a harsh jangling of immediate priority. Its first clamor still hung in the air as Tomi entered the operating tent. He began washing his hands, aware that Hirose had arrived and was also scrubbing. Apparently he intended to operate, under the influence of sake or not.

"I can manage the operating, honored sir, for there are only nine wounded. If you wish to supervise the ward tent . . ." He tried to sound as smooth as possible, normal, casual. "The way the wardmen are conducting themselves, they need more supervision than an enlisted man can provide."

"Okasaki can handle the ward tent."

"But Okasaki is here to assist me in surgery. Behind you, also washing his hands."

Owlishly Hirose peered around at Okasaki. "So he is. Well, no matter." He offered a leering grin. "I see through your strategy,

Nakamura. Very clever and commendable. But your psychology is terrible."

"I mean well. I keep thinking of the patients. Are you offended?"

"No, merely touched to the bottom of my black heart. I am not drunk! I repeat, I—am—not—drunk. But even if I were, I could still operate quite well. Always have. Perhaps even better than when sober. Thus I have spoken. I ask you to remember that."

Without another word Tomi accepted his own lack of military authority, donned his gown, gloves, mask and cap, and with a heavy heart walked to his table.

Okasaki and the others were there, waiting. Beneath the yellow lantern light, amid the smell of gasoline, antiseptics and blood, lay the center of attention and the purpose of all these gleaming tools: the first patient, unconscious, prepped and draped, a gunshot wound in the left thigh.

Tomi could tell by the condition of the wound that the bullet had traveled a considerable distance. He remembered reading somewhere that the average service rifle bullet had an initial muzzle velocity of about three thousand feet per second, plus a spin of nearly three thousand revolutions. After traveling a hundred meters or so, the spin and velocity diminished, the bullet often tipping in flight and sometimes striking its target sideways with devastating effect. That was the case here, a wide section of femur comminuted into powder, the soft tissues dreadfully pulped. Pieces of bone had themselves become secondary missiles, slicing into nerves, tendons, blood vessels and muscle. As a result, Tomi didn't have much to work with.

Working quickly but without enthusiasm, he began the amputation. He could not, however, concentrate on his work. Hirose, debriding a torn abdomen, kept keening a tuneless, off-key dirge. It distracted everyone. An eerie, nerve-racking sound, it became in Tomi's mind a prime example of unprofessional conduct. One should focus on essentials during any operation, let nothing from the outside intrude.

But that, he reminded himself, was an ideal—and narrow—

judgment. Exceptions were all too frequent. But it proved he was only human, very tense about Andrews, quite fatigued and in need of adequate food, proper food. Like everyone these days, he felt nervous and irritable, perhaps even frightened. And the strain was showing.

Like Jesus, he should help others bear the burden, not criticize.

"You sing well," he said deliberately, accepting a clamp from Okasaki. "A bit of music always helps relieve the tension."

"Don't be sarcastic," Hirose growled, slicing a section of perforated intestine free. The fine edge derived from alcohol was wearing off; the letdown seemed in full swing. "And don't use that stupid psychology on me again. I'm tired of it."

"I beg your pardon." Tomi felt sorry now he'd spoken. "I meant no offense. Yet it's true. There is an old American saying, something about music soothing the savage beast. Or breast. Saw, please."

"Don't be pious, Nakamura. I detest pious people! Give me an honest hypocrite any day. So I drink! If you hate me or what I do, why not just say so?"

Tomi stared past Okasaki to Hirose, bending over a misplaced mass of gray squirming intestine. "Why, I don't hate you! Where did you get such an idea?"

"Never mind. Just leave me alone."

Tomi fell silent, troubled as always at his total inability to understand Hirose, an enigma. Perhaps he'd fare better by confining his conversation to medicine, a safe area of discussion. On that subject they could usually agree.

He sutured the flap, bandaged the stump and called for the next patient, a victim of artillery fire. The lower right arm had all but been torn from the elbow; shredded, mangled flesh was the only connection. He reached for the scalpel.

He was slicing deep along the bicep, the knife tip grazing bone, absorbed—

"Air raid! Air raid!" The alarm clamored. "Everybody into the trenches." Hayasaka and Okasaki both shuffled their feet. "Of all times," groaned Hirose. Someone coughed but no one fled. "Sponge," Tomi said, knowing they should all run and hide. He wanted to flee quickly, before the planes knifed down and killed him. He could hear them coming, already diving, the soft scream of engines rising in volume. Distant machine guns began coughing. "Clamp, please." Hayasaka sniffed, his hands shaking.

"Control yourself," said Okasaki quietly to Hayasaka.

A quick ear-shattering roar broke above them—a plane skimming the ground, throttle wide open—a roar instantly upon them and instantly gone, frightening, startling. Everyone jumped. Hayasaka cried out and ducked. "Damn!" cried Hirose, a fountain of scarlet blood pouring from his patient. "The aorta—I cut it in two."

"Release the clamp," Tomi said to Okasaki, and Hirose and his crew fled. He sutured the small vessels, irrigated, applied sulfa, sutured the flap, bandaged—

Another roar, another plane. Machine guns, a chilling sound, like the rattle of bones in a coffin. Hayasaka now was sobbing. An abrupt ripping sound, a hundred holes appearing in the tent top, two neat rows. He applied the last strip of tape. There! Nothing more to be done here; the other patients must wait. No sense in risking his entire operating crew longer than necessary.

"Into the trenches," he said calmly, and hurried past Andrews with the others, his left knee screaming its protest and bullets churning the mud around him. Each moment he expected to be torn to bits.

In the wet trench, holding Hayasaka's sobbing frame, he peered up into the blinking red eyes of machine guns, his mind ablaze with raw fear barely under control. "Don't be afraid," he soothed. "Don't be afraid," knowing that in all this din Hayasaka couldn't possibly hear him.

His life wasn't worth two cents right now and Michael knew it. Canvas was no armor, a blanket no shield against 50-calibers. The din was God-awful. He forced himself to lie as still as a stone, gazing at other patients, all the while wanting to shout to his friends above, "Quit it, you guys! There are people down here."

He wanted to rise like a shot and run to find a hole to dive into. Somewhere nearby there should be a nice big hole just his size. One corner of his mind, however, remained coldly analytical, recording the raw data displayed before him. Among the Japanese a radical change of behavior had occurred. It seemed terribly important to know why.

During previous attacks and shellings he'd observed the stoic Japanese at his very best. Not a man in the tent had so much as blinked an eye, or made a sound. The patients had lain as still as statues, the attendants moved like robots, each man acting as if death in large numbers, and the threat of death, was not occurring just outside the tent. It had seemed eerie, almost inhuman, this calm, unperturbed exterior. Within a day or so after arriving he'd realized that to a Japanese duty was paramount to all else, perhaps a sacred obligation to the Emperor. To show fear or even concern in any way was considered unmanly. Fate was a big deal in Japan, blindly accepted and never resisted. He'd heard of—hadn't believed the propaganda—the implacable Japanese visage. Now he'd seen it firsthand.

Strangest of all, he'd begun to admire it. At least in part.

One of the keys to such behavior, he must admit, was Hardnose himself. Hardnose was a superb supervisor; he did everything by the book. To him regulations were sacred, routine an inviolate law. High officers with infinite wisdom had decreed the most efficient system possible, perfected it to the smallest detail and ordered its use. So it must be. One did not question such wisdom, such perfection. One obeyed. It was the Emperor's wish and command.

And that, Michael had decided, was the weakness he'd been looking for. The Japanese system was totally inflexible.

Logic then posed a question: How to exploit this weakness? There were two general avenues of approach. He could plan to create confusion, find a monkey wrench to throw into the works; a diversion of sorts, while he and maybe Jones slipped away. Or he might use the system itself, make its rigidity the very force that would permit escape.

So he'd thought. Now, however, only minutes ago, he'd seen another side to that so-called implacable Japanese visage. Immediately after that first low, ear-shattering pass—that would have been Eddie—the attendants had suddenly dropped catheters, blankets, bedpans, all other implements and medicines and they'd run. Almost in panic. Why? What had changed them? Where was Hardnose's iron discipline? Where was Hardnose himself?

Ten dollars against a doughnut hole said the big bastard was outside crouching like a mole in a hole. So much for the fantasy of the fearless Japanese.

On the other hand, no man in his right mind would choose to do otherwise, given the chance. Michael wished he were there with Hardnose, sharing the deepest hole in the island.

A few patients, too, had fled from the tent. That was the important thing, maybe the key to all he'd been seeking. If patients could leave, he could, too.

So it figured: an air raid at the right time of day. Say just before dark. It might be the very diversion he'd been looking for.

May 21. Was strafed while amputating a patient's arm. It is my first time since moving over to Chichagof Harbor that I went in an air raid shelter. Enemy plane is a Martin. Nervousness of our commanding officer is severe and he has said his last words to his NCO's and officers that he will die tomorrow. Gave all his articles away. Hasty chap, this fellow. The officers of the front are doing a fine job. Everyone who heard this became desperate and things became disorderly.

MAY 22, 1943

After graduation, with Phyllis meeting and falling in love with his parents, Michael had found that summer of '41 hot and dry and—because Phyllis was home with her folks—far too lonely. After being admitted to graduate school, he remained on campus helping with certain experiments and counting the days until her return. That day he had never forgotten. "I'm back," she had cried, stepping down from the bus. "All set for the fall semester, and I missed you, Mike. Really I did."

"Humph!" he said, letting his eyes devour every detail. New clothes and a fresh suntan, but all else was the same. Rebellious hair. Smoky eyes. Big grin and a warm kiss. "You've gained weight."

"No, I haven't. Oh, Mike, you look wonderful!" She kissed him again and he liked that. "I won't ask if you missed me. Of course you did."

"You're right, I did." With one hand he picked up her grip; with the other he clasped her own. "I missed you like everything."

"You did? You really, honestly did?"

"I've been hungry a lot."

"Oh-ho-ho! I won't bite." She bubbled. If he could just bottle all that effervescence, he thought, he could make a fortune. They began walking toward the campus.

"How's Jim?"

She glanced up, now on the defensive. "Like I wrote, just fine. He was there two weeks but he's gone now, back to New York for interning."

"You tell him about me?"

"Yes." She walked a while in silence. "Mike, are you jealous of Jim?"

"No. Why should I be jealous?"

"Good question. I just thought you sounded jealous. . . ."

"No, I'm not jealous. I'm not that type." He watched his shoes moving against the sidewalk. "He kiss you?"

"I kissed him good-bye. Just a little peck, Mike. He's an old family friend."

"Sure. What did you tell him?"

"Everything. That I didn't love him, really, and could never marry him. That I'd met a guy here at school who seemed pretty nice—"

"Seemed? You said that?"

"I said that! And that in any case I wouldn't marry anyone until after I graduate. That's in '43."

"You really said that?"

She gave him a glare. "He took it pretty hard. Said he'd worked like a fool to get out of school, get his license and start practicing so we could marry. Now this. I feel sorry for him."

"You do?"

"Didn't I just say so? Honestly, Mike! He asked me not to do anything rash. Like eloping. I agreed. When he gets through interning he expects to open a practice in Berkeley. So I should keep an open mind about him and give him a chance to fight back, that's all he wants."

He frowned at the sidewalk. "And you said?"

"Mike, I swear you're jealous."

"Like I said, I'm not jealous."

"You are! I can tell by the way you act. You're very jealous."

"Dammit, I'm not jealous! Only idiots get jealous. Morons. Children and other monsters. How many times do I have to say I'm not jealous?"

She stopped to face him, hands on hips. "Then why aren't you jealous, Michael Andrews? Am I your girl or not?"

"You're my girl—"

"Then why aren't you jealous? Unless you're some way not normal—"

"I'm normal, I'm normal!"

"Then?"

He expelled a lungful of air. "All right, dammit! You're my girl and I'm jealous. I'm jealous as hell! Every time I think of that low-class goon, that perverted anatomy hound, touching you or kissing you or just being with you, it . . . it fries my hide."

"Oh," she said, suddenly smiling. "Well, that's better!" Again they were walking.

"Phyllis," he said desperately. "Please listen! There's something you have to know. Now. I love you."

She looked at him, kept walking.

"You know I love you. You've known from the very first."

"This is the first time you've said so, Mike. In so many words."

"Okay, but you know it's true. I never knew if you'd believe me."

"Oh, I've believed you from the very first, too. Your style is unorthodox, to an extreme, but sincere."

"Well?"

"Well what? I want to hear you say it several more times. Until the novelty wears off."

"Phyllis, I *love* you. I love *you*. I love you! I LOVE YOU—"

"Mike, you're shouting! People are staring."

"Let 'em stare. Well?"

"You haven't called me 'honey' yet."

"Honey, I love you." He waited. "Well?"

"Well what?"

"You know damned well what! Do you love me or not?"

She grinned wickedly. "You told me six months ago I loved you. Remember? Why do you doubt yourself now?"

"Now who's playing games?"

"Oh, I'm not playing games, Mike. Not about us! You want to hear something really serious?"

"Phyllis, if it's about Jim—"

"I've dated several times this summer and tried to have fun and made a real effort to get you out of my mind. But—wouldn't you know? You wouldn't go."

"I'm the stubborn type. You keep reminding me."

"So I've thought a lot about you and me. An awful lot. What do you think of that?"

"You should see a doctor. There's pills for problems like that."

"Mike, did you hear me? Look at me! It's been a long summer. I've been counting the days until—"

"You have? My God, maybe you really should see a doctor."

She frowned. "I didn't mean anything like that at all! Mike, damn you, do you know what I'm saying?"

"Of course not. Do you?"

"Yes. I love you! I love you so very much. Can't you see that?"

He paused to calm his leaping heart and study her gray eyes; they gleamed deep and true. "You feel all right? No fever? Headache? Maybe you have athlete's foot."

"Mike, please—"

"Since when?"

"Why do you think I was in the library?"

For a full half-block he thought about that. The idea of her actually pursuing him had never entered his mind. It changed everything. "I suspect," he said softly, "that you're a master at tactics."

"Feminine finesse, I think, is a much nicer phrase. And I'm not a master of anyth—"

"Mistress?"

"You're quick, aren't you? I have to watch myself with you, all the time."

"Phyllis." He gazed down on that adorable profile. "Will you marry me?"

"Yes! Michael Andrews, I've been here with you for ten minutes. How come it took you so long to ask?"

"When? How soon?"

"Down, boy! The day I graduate, plus or minus a week or two."

"Two years? Why so long?"

"Mike, I'm not ready yet. I mean, to settle down and have babies. You're not ready either. We both have to finish school."

She was right and he knew it. Why was she always right? "Okay," he murmured as smoothly as possible. "But we don't have to wait for everything—do we?"

She stopped in the middle of the sidewalk, her eyes shocked. "What—exactly what—does that mean?"

"It means—" Grinning, he set down her suitcase, then fumbled in his pocket, brought an object forth. "It means that once upon a time a handsome young prince held the hand—like this—of a beautiful gray-eyed princess. And he said: Kiddo, this glittering trinket is the real McCoy; it's worth a lot of green stuff. But that's okay—you're my Gorgeous Wench. And *that* means that from here on into the sunset I have no truck with other female type people. No extra carousing or sexual browsing."

"How utterly romantic."

He eased the ring along her finger. "And the princess answered thusly: Dear sir, magnificent cur, you have torn my heart in twain. But with this ring my heart shall sing; will the band on my hand turn green?"

"Oh." She blew a wayward tress from her brow. "That doesn't rhyme."

"I know. I got desperate."

"Such original drivel." Suddenly she was crying. "Y—you wonderful idiot. Mike, it's beautiful!" He kissed her long and deep but not hard, savoring her lips and the softness of her body pressed against him. Never had he wanted anything as he wanted her that moment. Finally, too soon, he pulled away. "I love you, Phyllis."

"And I love you, Michael Andrews. But you mustn't kiss me like that again. Not—"

"Not again?"

"Not until we're married."

"Oh."

The grip again in hand, he eased hand in hand with her along the sidewalk. "Happy?"

"Ecstatic. Hungry?"

"Starved."

In a way she was right, he thought. Walking about before half the town with an erection like his was an embarrassing and damned awkward thing to do.

According to Sergeant Okasaki, quoting a friend at headquarters, the officer in charge of the search for the American airman had been certain that the body would be located in some remote gully or crevice now that the spring runoff was gaining momentum. That was a week ago. Now the lack of such success was disappointing but not yet a defeat. Until the body was found and properly identified, the American could not be presumed dead. Though the soldiers engaged in the search were badly needed elsewhere, the frustrating task would continue.

It was also said that a large American warship offshore was transmitting an uncoded message twenty-four hours a day, every thirty seconds: Eagle Four, this is Big Boy One, over. To the best of anyone's knowledge there had been no response.

Tomi told Michael nothing of the transmissions from the American ship. That the search continued he reported in full.

"All the more reason to leave," Michael said. "I'll need warm clothing, some food if you can spare it, and a compass. First chance I get, when it's darkest, I'll head west alongside Lake Cories toward Massacre Bay."

"Our outposts are stationed at regular intervals all across the valley," Tomi hissed. "You will be intercepted and shot."

"Then north along the beach below Fish Hook Ridge, around the point and back to East Arm of Holtz Bay. There's Americans there, and I can make it."

"No, you cannot! Six miles of trudging in soft sand, in this cold rain? In this wind? You are not that strong. Our men of the Sea Defense Command will see you."

Michael said nothing. His eyes, however, were guarded. Suspicious even yet.

Tomi could admit now he would never understand Americans. Why could they not accept life as it is and not have to change everything? Too much change led to instability, then fragmentation, which in turn created anarchy and chaos. And Michael Andrews at times seemed a very chaotic young man, ready to rush about in several different directions at once. Where, in all this turbulence, was the sober, dedicated, well-ordered giant destined to feed the poor of this world, including the poor of Japan?

Yet he knew his first decision had been right. Michael was that giant. Tomi could see it in his clear eyes that were far older than his years—confident, sure eyes that said anything was possible; all one need do is dare.

"By the way," Michael said with studied casualness, "remember that silver cross I wore? I lost it somewhere in the boondocks. I feel . . . naked without it. Think you could look around a bit?"

Tomi was speechless. The cross! If found nearby it would point like an arrow to the very spot the American was hiding.

He didn't know for a fact exactly where he had lost the silver cross. It was gone; he missed it. Its sentimental value was large, a present from Mom. Cost her fifteen bucks, a lot of money with a lot of better uses. But she'd insisted and who could say no to Mom? Okay, Mom! Worn it every day, like brushing his teeth and donning clean underwear.

The cross. Goddamn! He'd worn it when he went down to the john. No Tomi to guard him and no Hardnose to watch for. Alone. A simple no-alternative trip. Returning, there in the path was this dark singing creature, weaving as he went, soaring within himself and totally oblivious to the world about him.

In his left hand he carried a flashlight.

Flashlight? Like a bomb the idea burst in Michael's mind. He bowed low as the Japanese all seemed to do. The drunk in his path responded. "You sonuvabitch," Michael murmured. A hard jab to the belly and a quick right to the jaw settled the issue; the man fell. Michael grabbed the flashlight and fled. Not until later did he miss the cross. How, in God's name, and exactly where, had it come loose?

Tomi had to find it. Because if anyone else saw it, recognized it—well, that would be the ball game right there; close the gates. Then Phyllis could forget all about ol' Mike. They'd shoot Tomi, too.

His body pressing the frozen snow, Murphy peered across a long thirty yards to where Swensen and Hall waited behind a huge boulder. They were closest to the Jap, who was all alone there in the snow. A live Jap, deserted by his buddies. Bandaged head, arm in sling. But wounded again, this time in the legs or lower back. Couldn't walk or crawl, had dropped his rifle but was armed with grenades. Dangerous as hell.

If Murphy had his way he'd shoot the sonuvabitch now and keep going. But the brass wanted a prisoner.

Was this a trap, the Japs using their own wounded for bait? They had done it before. Murphy's scalp drew tight at the thought.

It was logical to send Swensen and Hall to do the job, with Murphy and the squad offering covering fire if needed. Logical. But Murphy held back, ashamed that he didn't want to risk Swensen, especially. It bordered too much on killing his own son. . . .

All the kids were waiting for orders, Baker eying him a bit too closely. Baker was right! Never play favorites. Clenching his teeth, deliberately he waved Swensen and Hall forward.

They rose promptly, Swensen hunched low and for once without a swagger, Hall dropping his cigarette and scuttling half sideways like a crab. Each held his rifle at port arms. Wrapped as they were in dirty, baggy, never-quite-dry OD's, they looked distorted, like mere caricatures of men. Hall had one bootlace dragging across the frozen snow. Swensen was still chewing the last hurried bite of a fruit bar from a K-rat box, had unbuckled the chin strap. His helmet sat cocked at a jaunty angle.

One circled left, the other right. In silence they closed to within ten yards of the Jap. Then Swensen paused, watching the wounded Jap and also the darkest part of the slope; that's where ambushing Japs usually hid. As he stared, a high crack of a light rifle carried on the wind and Hall went down hard.

Oh, shit! Murphy could see no enemy and he cursed the Jap's smokeless powder. Another shot, two, and Swensen, surprised, slow to react, was suddenly rolling in the snow.

Murphy half rose. Swensen! Oh, God . . .

A stir on the hillside and there a Jap was standing, hands fumbling at the bolt of his rifle. His jaw and lower face was one huge bandage, his left hand another. He fired wildly and by that time Murphy was erect, his rifle alive in his hands—a full half-clip into the sniping Jap. Even before the body hit the slope and began sliding redly in the snow, Murphy was charging. "Swensen!"

All the kids were up now, staring—Bennett, Jeeters, Young following Murphy across the snow, each shouting. It was Murphy, cold inside with growing dread, who was closest to Swensen when the wounded Jap suddenly moved an arm. Then Swensen rolled, his rifle arced a quick half-circle—two, three shots. The Jap's body bounced and slid a bit with each hit, and the grenade he held fell limply between his legs. Murphy dived low as the grenade exploded. The Jap's body lifted lazily, turned end over end and fell bloodily with a dull thud ten feet away.

Murphy found himself crawling toward Swensen, his mind blurred by dread. He saw that Hall had taken a round low in the gut, dead center, was conscious but dazed, his pimples aflame in an ashen face, slack mouth oozing blood. The medics were just arriving with morphine, plasma, the works. Swensen was sitting up, saying, "I'm okay, it don't hurt." His side was bloody as hell. Murphy rose, trembling, throat still tight with fear for Hall, concern for Swensen, and saw the kids gathered close to watch. "Go back and take cover!" A snarl in his voice he couldn't help. He watched the medics take Hall away, conscious but well drugged. "Easy now." He helped Swensen rise and ease back to cover, submitting then to first aid for a gunshot crease just under the armpit and above the ribs. Wounded in action. P᾽ ple Heart. He saved my life, Murphy thought, his heart swelling with pride. Johnny saved my—

"No, I'm not going back," Swensen insisted, lighting a cigarette. "Just bandage it up and I'll stay here."

"You're going back," said Murphy, near tears. "That slice needs more attention."

"Shit! I'll stay here. With the squad. With you."

"Swensen, you need medical atten—"

"Sarge, they'd just gimme steak, ice cream and beer. Who needs it?"

Murphy was too shaken to argue. One of the medics said that Hall would be okay; another that Hall wouldn't make it—a chilling thought. Jesus! Another one of the kids . . .

By this time Swensen had puffed hard at a cigarette. Stripped to the waist, a medic binding the wound, he began shivering like mad in the cold, face twisted oddly and talking far too rapidly: " . . , this girl I met on Main Street. One night by accident she pushed the cigarette lighter in my Dad's car with her foot, and at the first smell I thought jeez!—she's really hot. But then of course I realized . . .

At 0600 hours they came again—Lightnings this time, about a dozen dull-khaki twin-tail planes all skimming the water as the pilots apparently liked to do. Michael's squadron again, without doubt. At full throttle they angled in from the north and were upon the camp and firing before anyone knew. The first casualty was a drum of gasoline; it was holed and caught fire. Then another, a half-dozen, and even more. Surprised men began running, shouting, diving into trenches. Someone screamed, a hollow sound that seemed to come from everywhere at once. Tomi, returning from the latrine, hugged the sides of the barracks' trench hole and peered up at the planes arcing freely in a rare patch of clear sky.

Less than fifty feet high, a plane zipped past dragging a flurry of loose snow in its wake. Tomi raised his head to watch the next in line. Full throttle, wings level, a half-mile out—fire! Its nose immediately blossomed with blinking flame. He heard the distant hollow coughing, like a man gasping for air, the snapping and whistling of bullets above his head.

A man was still screaming, and Tomi saw him now. Hayasaka! Still in his operating smock, snowy-white against black churned mud, caught in the open between latrine and barracks. He lay a full thirty meters away, unable to move, yelling and helpless, staring up at the next plane knifing inland from the sea. From here his wound was not apparent.

In such noise and against the wind, with Hayasaka's mind closed by fear, shouting was useless. Hayasaka, an obvious target, was as good as dead. Surely the next plane would get him.

Without conscious thought, Tomi found himself lurching from the trench hole toward Hayasaka. How much time? Ten seconds, twenty? He could make it, he knew. He could make it, he could make it. . . . A fiery pain stabbed his knee with each stride. Go! Run!

But halfway there it became clear: time had already run out. Certainly the plane would fire before—

From the corner of his eye he saw a new figure racing toward Hayasaka. A big man, white-clad, familiar shoulders—Okasaki! Like an American fullback driving toward the goal line, Okasaki sprinted the distance, reached down in full stride, gave an arm a mighty tug as the plane fired. Bullets popped the mud, whipping two long trails of upflung earth. Both men fell. The plane streaked past, its pilot glancing coldly down, and another began its run. Panting from exertion and sudden knowledge that he, too, wore surgical white, Tomi halted and knelt beside the pair. A miracle, both still lived, one's face filled by fear and the other's by pain.

"Okasaki—"

"I'm all right. See to the boy."

"Hayasaka, can you hear me? Can you crawl to the snow?"

"They'll kill me! The planes, the planes—" The boy's eyes were wide, irrational; he appeared beyond self-control. Sharply Tomi slapped his face. "Crawl to the snow!"

There wasn't much time; the next plane was nearing. Hayasaka, still sobbing but understanding now, suddenly half rose, scuttled crablike to the snow and threw himself down, digging himself a mantle of snow.

"Damn you!" shouted Okasaki, shaking one fist at Hayasaka. "May Buddha curse you forever." Blood covered one thigh. His left wrist jutted at an odd angle. "Honored sir, save yourself."

Tomi was already tugging the man upright, gritting his teeth with the effort. The plane, the plane! Hayasaka was right.

Okasaki weighed at least 180 and Tomi now about 125. He had no fear of hurting the big man; pain was unavoidable. It was important to move quickly. Okasaki suddenly uncoiled and came quickly erect, one good arm about Tomi's shoulder, and together they struggled toward the snow.

Watching the plane, he saw the first blink of red flame. He glimpsed the trails of whipping mud coming straight and true. He had time for one desperate lunge, pushing himself and Okasaki sideways into the mire, thinking how hopeless it was even to try keeping wounds clean. Okasaki grunted as his injured arm struck the ground, but the bullets buried themselves only in sodden earth and lay hissing in their graves. Little jets of steam rose in four straight lines. The plane zipped past, the next one arrowing in.

"Let us try again," Tomi panted, amazed that his voice sounded so small and thin. They stumbled forward together into the bank of snow, not far from Hayasaka.

Fighting for breath, he cut Okasaki's trouser leg and examined the wound. No large amount of blood, merely an entry and exit. "It is not serious," he announced. "The bullet touched no bone or major vessel, only good Japanese meat. We shall clean it and bind it tight. After a few days of soreness, it will serve you well. Let me see your arm."

"My arm is nothing," Okasaki muttered, then ducked low and waited as the next plane *whoooshed!* past. "The ulna and radius were both fractured when Hayasaka fell upon them. But not too badly. A simple cast will protect the arm. I can still supervise the wardmen."

Okasaki turned suddenly upon Hayasaka, who peered up with eyes brimming and lips quivering. "Except you! You were not wounded at all. Fool! Idiot! Moron! Coward! You allowed yourself to panic like a silly girl who finds a mouse in her kitchen. Have you no shame?"

"Have mercy! I couldn't help—"

"Can you not look about you and see what must be done to preserve yourself? Are you a woman, frightened of the world? You are miserable, a disgrace to the Emperor."

"Please! Please understand!"

"Do not call yourself Japanese, Hayasaka. We disown you! Henceforth, stay out of my sight, for I am now a greater enemy of yours than all the American Army."

Hayasaka cowered down and away, hiding his face. He seemed incapable of comment. Tomi leaned close, aware that such a person should never have been sent into combat. "I shall talk to you soon, Hayasaka. In the meantime, don't worry. Remember Jesus and have no fear."

Okasaki snorted but said nothing more. Together they lay deep in the snow and watched the planes complete their second runs. Soon, ammunition exhausted, they rose like gulls breasting the high wind and flew away. Back to warm barracks, clean beds, hot baths and food—and fresh apple pie, Tomi mused. The thought brought intense pangs of hunger.

Okasaki refused assistance. He walked slowly and with scarcely a limp up the ramp and into the operating tent and sat with the others, scowling at everyone awaiting attention.

Meanwhile Tomi scrubbed, a time-consuming procedure, changed his gown and was prepared to help Hirose in the operating tent when the radio phone guard signaled. "Headquarters, honored sir. They wish to speak to you."

Tomi took the phone. "Dr. Nakamura."

"This is Lieutenant Ujiie. Why haven't you reported to me about that radio transmission in English?"

"Honored sir, my investigation is not yet complete. I need more time."

"Have you turned up anything at all?"

"Nothing. None of the staff or patients has reported any unauthorized use of—" A click. Tomi held a dead instrument.

In the operating area he found Hirose already in surgery and Sergeant Okasaki waiting, jaw clamped and eyes hard, his face drawn and pale and beaded with sweat, but on his feet in his usual place across the table. He wore a fresh gown, mask, cap, and glove on one hand. His left wrist wore a splint. As Tomi entered he pulled himself erect and waited in silence for Tomi to take position. In the yellow glare and soft hiss of the lantern they stared a long moment at each other across the table.

"I thank you for my life, honored Dr. Nakamura." Okasaki spoke quietly.

"You are welcome indeed, honored Sergeant Okasaki." At that moment they became friends, bonded together by more than a common cause, a common risk, a common task. Different in age, education, religion and life experience, they nonetheless respected each other. On the surface it seemed no more than that.

On a deeper level, however, Tomi saw much significance. By saving Okasaki's life he had committed the man to a lifelong expression of gratitude—an *On,* a continuing duty or debt, a moral obligation, an unwavering loyalty. Much as all Japanese were indebted to the Emperor, so was Okasaki now indebted to Tomi, but more personally, more intently. Okasaki would seek every possible opportunity to pay his obligation but never succeed, for such an *On* was a lifetime burden.

"He insisted on being first," Hirose interrupted as if he'd been conversing casually with Tomi for hours. "Wanted to be ready when you entered. No medication for pain, refused it. He wanted nothing that might affect his efficiency. So I cleaned the hole in his leg, sewed it up and set his arm. All he did was sweat. A very ox-headed man."

"Ox heads are very important," Tomi said, knowing how embarrassed Okasaki must feel. "Especially to the ox."

He bent to examine a patient, a not uncommon case. The man's scrotum had been shot through in its lowest part, and the testicles were now supported only by an artificial bridge of tape attached to either thigh. Tomi sighed, for the operation would be difficult and challenging.

"Let us begin," he said to everyone. With a scalpel he carefully sliced open the scrotum to form a crude gutter.

"The Americans have advanced very close now," Hirose muttered, plucking a splintered rib from its bed in a lung. His patient was Wardman Tanaka, a night-duty man. "That explosion last night, so close to the barracks. I assume it woke you up."

"Of course." Everything seemed clear now. The man's right testicle must be removed, for the spermatic vessels were badly injured. Too bad, but it could not be helped. The problem then was to save the left testicle in such a way that it would not atrophy later, with a complete loss of function. Both the left epididymis and carpus Highmore were intact, so the prognosis appeared favorable. Many a good man had lost a testicle and later fathered children.

"Why do you say the Americans are so close?" he asked. "Because their ships can reach our barracks with artillery?"

Hirose grunted, eying a pneumothorax. "That was not naval gunfire. That was a trench mortar if I ever heard one."

Regretfully Tomi sliced away the man's right testicle and sutured the vessels, then began cutting away the herniated parts of the left testicle and excising the damaged margins of the wound. "Trench mortars don't make that much noise," he murmured, concentrating. "Nor that big a hole."

"Nakamura, you are naïve! Some American trench mortars are very large. They make lots of noise and dig big holes. I learned that last year on Bataan."

"Oh? I hadn't known you were there."

"For a while. Very boring. Hot and humid. The beer was sour and so were the women."

Tomi irrigated the wound. The next step was to suture the tunica albuginea and tunica vaginalis. "Needle, please."

Okasaki had it in hand, the proper gut already in place. He was breathing heavily, sweating. No sense at all, thought Tomi. The man should be resting his leg.

"Perhaps you haven't heard," Hirose said as if to himself, debriding as he spoke. "That big hill dividing Massacre Bay from Sarana Valley? The Americans seized it last night. They have artillery on it already, shelling our troops. The revered Garrison Commander Colonel Shima, I hear, is very disappointed in the loss, and very angry. He will counterattack, of course, but—"

"You sound pessimistic now." He thought briefly of Michael Andrews, the optimist. To his credit, Michael evinced a feeling of guilt because he'd been captured. He was bedsore and constantly hungry but delighted to be alive, determined to escape and felt he could beat the world.

Tomi worked slowly, taking small stitches and drawing each one tight before going on. He gave it all his attention, his tongue caught between teeth and lips. Several minutes passed before he spoke. "It really isn't like you to be pessimistic, Dr. Hirose."

"I am not negative. Help is coming tomorrow." Hirose fell silent a long moment, then sighed, stepped back and nodded to the waiting litter-men to take the corpse away. "An adequate wardman, I suppose, but as a patient he was hopeless. Two fifty-caliber holes in one chest—"

"Why do you say tomorrow?" Tomi began gathering the scrotum together, needle in hand. "Are you clairvoyant?"

"Not at all." Another patient was hoisted to the table and Hirose gazed down on a simple scalp wound, a grazing of the skull and a possible hairline fracture. Very minor. This one would be back in a trench hole tomorrow, armed with a brutal headache and a rifle that would jar him mad with every shot. "You see, it's very basic. Our High Command, using inspired wisdom and magnificent judgment, always attacks on Sundays. A fetish, I think. Or does it merely seem—"

He broke off this incredible and dangerous satire before going too far. Yet his inference was clear. But what was worse, Tomi realized with a start, was that today was Saturday, Tomi's Sabbath and day of rest. The second Sabbath in combat. And he'd forgotten, always so tired, so busy. He suddenly felt ashamed.

Done at last with suturing the scrotal wall, complete with drainage tube, he ordered the patient removed, positive that libido, erection and ejaculation would eventually occur, given the proper motivation. So, tired or not, he felt good. This was what made a career in medicine worthwhile, this satisfaction of restoring a diseased or broken body to health and production, to a normal life.

All surgery was complete by early afternoon. Tomi hurried to the ward tent and paused near the entrance to wipe his spectacles dry. Michael Andrews lay as usual, his bulk covered by blankets and bandages, his dark goggles like ludicrous twin black moons. There had been no sign of the missing silver cross, and that worried Tomi. Soldiers could come at any time, probing into every crevice, asking questions, their eyes unyielding. The firing squad would show no mercy.

It was Sergeant Okasaki, not Wardman Hayasaka, who greeted him with a bow and a bowl of hot rice. A full bowl, not the meager half-portion of the past two weeks. Tomi at once suspected Okasaki of sacrificing his ration in favor of his *On* man, Tomi. He saw no way, however, of refusing the extra portion or sharing it with Okasaki, not without causing the man embarrassment—"loss of face," an American would say—by having his gift rejected. "Thank you," he murmured with a bow of his own. "I am very hungry."

"The worthy Captain Yamamoto awaits you," Okasaki said, as if nothing unusual had happened. "There beside the stove, with the honored Lieutenant Hirose."

Yamamoto had changed considerably since Tomi had last seen him. His unshaven cheeks were thinner, eyes sunken, lips a straight merciless line. The effect was sharklike, or perhaps wolfish. Mud caked his boots and dabbed his uniform. Looking at Yamamoto was in many ways like looking into a mirror, he thought as he advanced. Thanks to the war, the battle, fate itself, everyone had sunk to a physical state of low order.

"Good afternoon, worthy Captain Yamamoto," he said, bowing first to Yamamoto and then to Hirose. "Lieutenant Hirose and I are honored at your presence."

Yamamoto did not return the bow. "Do you always greet a

superior officer with a bowl of rice in your hands? One that holds twice your allotment of food?"

"I beg your—" Tomi glanced down at the bowl of cooling rice, at a loss to explain. Okasaki stood unobtrusively within hearing distance; he must not be shamed. On the other hand, Yamamoto was waiting; he would not be denied. "I've been in surgery," he explained. "Only now have I returned."

"To wolf the food your patients should eat?" Yamamoto turned abruptly toward the tent entrance. "Ah! How punctual."

Tomi saw the entrance choked by a full squad of armed soldiers, one of them close beside Michael's litter. Just as he had feared. "But they can't—"

Yamamoto grunted. "The American airman was here. The communications officer is positive the signal came from this hospital. Corporal, begin your search."

Tomi could do nothing to stop them. The corporal and two men detached themselves from the group and began picking their way between litters in the aisle, eying shattered bodies and brown Nipponese faces. One man stopped to stare at Michael; the goggles stared back. Tomi waited, praying without words. The soldier neither spoke nor moved.

The corporal motioned toward Jones. "This black American is for carrion. On the night of transmission, he was here?"

"Right there," Tomi replied. "Under sedation, with frozen feet." It bothered him that the one soldier kept staring at Michael.

"Why do we bother with him now?" said Yamamoto. "He has been interrogated. Yet he occupies precious space, he eats precious food. Far too much, I'm sure."

The corporal grunted, shrugged, and with his companion eased toward the entrance. He paused beside the soldier staring at Michael. "What is this?"

"An officer," Tomi blurted. "He is burned. He cannot speak or hear."

The staring soldier now turned to the corporal, cupping one hand beside his mouth. "A sleeping snowman! My esteemed father and I once made a sleeping snowman." Laughing as only the thoughtless laugh, they walked from the tent. Tomi, sweating, was limp with relief. He did not dare look at Michael.

"I think the need is clear," said Yamamoto, tenacious with his subject. "We must kill him today."

"The black American?" asked Hirose, brows uplifted. "Why not? I have no respect for him, no more than I had for the thousands we captured at Bataan and Corregidor. They surrendered! Such cowards are beneath contempt. I don't mind ordering this one beaten or starved; he deserves it. Such treatment is automatic for prisoners. Personally I refused to treat him. But he is Nakamura's pet."

"The American is not my pet," said Tomi, staring directly into Yamamoto's hooded eyes. "He is my patient. And I do not give orders to kill."

Yamamoto's eyes began gloating. "You are not only insolent, Nakamura, but incompetent as well. Your medical and moral judgment does not meet Japanese standards. I am considering sending you to the front, as a mere soldier with a rifle. There you will defend yourself or die. Perhaps both."

Tomi bowed, accepting his fate. To the front he might be sent, but he would never kill or use a weapon of any kind. No one could force him.

On the other hand, if he were sent to the front, Michael would have no one to protect him.

Without warning or precedent Sergeant Okasaki stepped to Tomi's side and stood silently, thus intruding his presence into officers' affairs. He glared at Yamamoto. Both were dangerous things to do. Yamamoto was armed with a pistol and, as an officer, had every right to kill, given the slightest provocation. Also, he could bring charges and ruin Okasaki's career. Or he could simply slap or beat Okasaki, who could only follow tradition and accept, submit— But Yamamoto stood quite still, his keen eyes searching Okasaki.

"What . . . what is it?" His tongue flicked across dry lips. His voice sounded husky. But he had just given Okasaki the right to speak.

"The honored Dr. Nakamura saved my life, worthless though it is, only this morning," Okasaki said simply. Then he fell silent and stepped back, having said enough. But he'd said everything—the *On*, the obligation he now owed, the gratitude he felt, the responsibility he accepted for Tomi's well-being. It was both a statement of fact and of eternal dedication.

It served the purpose. Yamamoto seemed to wilt inside, to change from his usual commanding and arrogant self to something far less, as if he could no longer assert himself, Tomi thought; as if the sergeant had somehow gained power over the captain.

Without warning Yamamoto bowed, turned away and hurried from the tent—escaping, Tomi felt sure. He felt numb, his brain sluggish. One vital question thrummed in his mind: What old experience, what history, did Yamamoto and Okasaki have in common?

"This burn case of yours," said Hirose. "Is there a good reason why he shouldn't be returned to the front?"

"The burn case?" Frantically Tomi tried to think. "Why, he's far too weak. The ruptured artery, the loss of blood—"

"No more so than others, I suppose. He can walk and throw grenades?"

"Oh, I doubt it. Not for long. And his eyes! They—they were also affected, you see. Singed a bit."

"They were?" Hirose peered at him closely. "How very unusual. Why didn't you mention this before?"

"There was little need. We were both quite busy."

"Another thing; a nagging thought. Why does a small burn require such a large bandage?"

Why indeed? His mind raced. "Because—I'm experimenting. Just an idea. I heard in America—"

"Ah, America! This case intrigues me more all the time."

"The patient is my responsibility, Dr. Hirose, not yours. And in my judgment he should not yet be returned to the front."

"I see. Well, I'll want to examine him. I shall wait until tomorrow. Then—"

Jones's high cackling laugh suddenly rang through the ward tent, followed an instant later by his angry shout: "Nigger—I ain't no nigger, you damn Jap!"

Tomi turned in time to see Jones's good fist arc across the short distance between litters and strike Umeda's cheek. And just as quickly a urinal in Umeda's hands, just filled, emptied its contents upon the American.

"'Merican dog!" cried Umeda. "You will pay! I shall kill you myself."

By the time Tomi and Hirose had fought their way through the throng of litters to halt between Jones and Umeda, four wardmen were already struggling to hold Jones down, an impossible task if Jones weren't already weak from loss of blood. The black man fought, veins in neck and temple distended, but his one huge fist crashed without force against his captors and he grew steadily weaker. "Stop it!" Tomi commanded. "I will permit no fighting here." He waited until Jones gasped for air and fell back, chest heaving, glaring at Umeda.

Hirose shrugged and yawned. "I shall retire to my quarters and leave the American to you, Nakamura."

Tomi nodded, relieved that Michael, for the moment, was safe. He turned to Wardman Ouye. "Give him a damp cloth to wash his face. Nehira, replace his blanket." Then in English: "Private First-Class Jones, remain silent while I speak to this man." He turned to Umeda. "Why did you empty the urinal on him?"

"I am justified! He called me a slanty-eyed butcher, a murderer, a rapist! Dirty, sneaky little Jap, he said! Bandy-legs, he said! Runt, he said—and what is that? These lies I will not allow, especially from an American gangster who kills children on the streets of Chicago and then eats their flesh. No, I shall be avenged."

"Kill the American," someone said, and the onlookers stirred.

"Feed his eyes to the birds and his manhood to the fish," said another, glaring across at Jones. "Then let his carcass rot."

"Let me kill him," added a third, raising a bandaged head. "I have fired at many but struck no one. I wish revenge for my wound."

"No! I shall kill him," Umeda cried. "He belongs to me, for my hate of him is greater than any other's. Tonight, when he sleeps."

"No one will kill him," Tomi said firmly. "Umeda, you feel virtuous, I know, in resenting his insults. To be virtuous is the mark of a man. You wish revenge, another of our better Japanese virtues. I don't blame you. But you will not kill him because there is no manhood or honor in killing a helpless, unarmed man. No measure of courage is required. So all virtue will be lost."

"Why do you protect the American?" Umeda wanted to know. "Are you sympathetic to Americans?"

"He is a human much like yourself. He is also my patient. There are no other reasons. To you and to the American I urge self-restraint. Only in self-restraint is there virtue."

These were telling arguments to the men of Nippon, he knew. No man of honor, no matter how disoriented by hunger, hardship and hate for Americans, would truly shame himself. But Umeda may be a different sort. "Why do you detest Americans so blindly?" Tomi asked. "Have you visited America?"

Umeda did not hesitate. "Once. With my parents I journeyed to San Francisco. We were not well received. We were not trusted."

"There must be a reason. Of what profession was your father?"

"A merchant. He used his life's savings to make children's toys—fine products, the best in all Japan. He wished to sell them to Americans. Yet, they called him cheap, his products worthless. Junk, they said, and refused to buy. Thus the Americans shamed him in his own eyes. They deprived him of self-respect. We returned bankrupt to Japan. My father then committed hara-kiri."

"And for this you blame the Americans?"

"Why not? They killed him with their sneers."

"And is that why you hate?"

"Now I live only to kill Americans. Twice on Attu I have been successful. He will be the third." He pointed at Jones, who lay still, glaring, fists clenched.

"You will ignore him, Umeda. That is an order."

He turned to Sergeant Okasaki and gave instructions to have Umeda's litter removed to the opposite side of the tent, as far from Jones as possible. But—regrettably—near Michael Andrews. To Jones he said, "Your humor is not understood or well received; it angers them. So you must do nothing to antagonize the other patients. If you do, I cannot guarantee your safety. Speak to no one but me. Most of all you must pray."

"I pray for damn sure. Jus' let me git my hands on his scrawny throat an' I pray for strength. No man calls me nigger. No man sprays me with piss. I tell you true, he gonna git his."

"Get that idea out of your head at once. They'll kill you."

"They have a helluva time tryin'."

No use, no use at all. He passed the order to Sergeant Okasaki: a guard at Jones's head all night long—a guard who would also deter Michael Andrews from using the radio again.

May 22. 0600 air raid again. Strafing killed one medical man. Medical man Okasaki wounded in right thigh, and fractured arm. During the night a mortar shell came awfully close.

MAY 23, 1943

T hat guy staring at me like I'm a fish in a monkey tank," Michael whispered in the dark. "And that inquisition squad! Five bucks says they'll be back."

"Perhaps. One never knows."

"It's a good bet. So what do I do then, give with the mummy act? I gotta get out of here."

"There is a time to stay and a time to go. Be prudent. Please accept the idea that remaining here is the wise—"

"Staying here is dangerous."

"So is leaving. Which is the greater of two dangers?"

"That guy sent chills right up my back. His eyes were like two black rocks, as if he had no feelings at all."

"That of course is not the case. Michael—"

"This is a trap. I feel smothered. I'd rather die in the open, in the wind and rain where at least I got a chance to save myself."

Michael's attitude was more than disturbing: it frightened Tomi. He had given much thought to the reasons for Michael's distrust. As yet he failed to understand.

His own life was also in great peril. Surely Michael was aware of that.

"Oh, I'm very fond of dandelions," he told her. "The pollen, you see. One good whiff and I go mad for sexy young geraniums. The pink ones especially—"

Her lips shut off his voice and he fought to keep his hands about her waist where they belonged. When she eased away, short of breath and eyes glowing, he crossed his legs to help hide the problem growing in his crotch.

"I'd better warn you," she murmured in his ear. "I'm a very affectionate girl."

"Be warned yourself. I'm a very passionate man. And only human."

"We have two years to go."

"Twenty months and two weeks. I've been counting."

She eased from his arm and placed both feet firmly on the floor. "We're going to have a problem with my parents. They're prepared to dislike you."

"But we've never met; they don't know me." He studied the perfection inherent in the lobe of her ear. "After all, to know me is to love me."

"Mike, they've had this dream for years about me and Jim. He's going to be rich, maybe even famous. Pop didn't say much, but Mother thinks I'm a fool to throw away all that security just to marry a . . ."

"Country bumpkin?"

" 'Hick' was the word she used. She's very modern, sophisticated, urbane. What she has against farmers I don't know. May I apologize for her?"

"No need." He, too, placed both feet on the floor and gazed at his shoes without seeing them. "Phyllis, I suppose I could get into something that would make a lot of money. The next few years will see a lot of changes in agriculture. There's no question: opportunity galore is right next door. But I don't really want—"

"Don't change any of your plans, Mike. They sound good to me. Very necessary work, fulfilling and satisfying to the man who does it. Without people like you, the changes you talk of aren't going to happen."

"But I'll never make much money. We'll have enough, be comfortable and secure but never rich. I want you to realize that."

"We'll be together! There's that. Besides, Mike, I could never be happy with an ordinary man, even a doctor. Not after knowing a guy who loves sexy geraniums." She eyed him with an analytical air. "So I've got myself a big problem. My mother regards you as a 'country hick.' Anyway, you're the raw material I have to work with. So, for the next two years, what do I do with it?"

"Why not just feed it, pet it and keep it warm?"

"And hope blindly for the best? You fool you."

"You prefer direct action?"

"I won't answer that. Do you know what a big problem you really are? Look at you! Your shirt isn't clean and you need a haircut. There's a big hole in your shoe stuffed with cardboard. You're way too thin—"

"If there's lipstick on my collar, it's yours."

"And you look tired. Obviously you're not competent to deal with the mundane facts of life by yourself."

"That's what I keep telling you. Third helpings are necessary."

"Smart guy! So nothing short of a martyr can even begin to make you presentable."

"You want the job? Pay's lousy, but the fringe benefits are topnotch."

"Well . . . " She paused to touch the hair curling back of his ears. "I guess somebody has to . . ."

The Jap binoculars were really fine, the lenses far better than those of Lieutenant Scott's. The enlargement was greater, detail sharper, and Murphy could damn near read the Japs' minds.

Earlier in the day he had focused on the bombed-out ruins of Aleut Village. Beyond those was a big Jap landing barge catty-wampus halfway up the sand. To the south was a low broad hill and tucked beyond that was a wreckage of sorts—a plane? For a second those sticks had looked almost like the twin-tail booms of a P-38.

On a short hill to the left of the ravine he'd found two coal-soot-colored cones snugged in the hollow of a knoll. Now, in the ravine itself, he could see a surprising number of white smock-clad figures huddling in foxholes. That fact, plus the litters seen earlier, made him wonder if there wasn't a Jap hospital down there.

There were two ships at the harbor's mouth. A destroyer and maybe a gunboat? The gunboat kept pounding the shore with 20- and 40-millimeter AA's, plus a three-inch cannon. Farther out, a lean gray destroyer was firing its twin-mount five-inch rifles slowly, almost casually, yet with precision. Both ships were practically dead in the water, brazenly so, without opposition or return fire of any kind. At point-blank range they fired at anything that moved or looked suspicious. Overhead a small Navy float plane circled lazily, without doubt sending fire-control messages to the ships. Smoke was rising black and full from a warehouse and from the ravine.

This battle, Murphy thought, is all but over. The Japs were now confined to only one narrow corridor on Attu. Yet they fought on, fury undiminished. In a way he had to admire them.

It must be hell to be a friggen Jap on Attu.

By midafternoon Tomi felt numb with fatigue. He sprawled limply against the damp, oozing side of the trench hole, his feet anchored in three inches of icy water, gazing at Hirose without really seeing him. He heard the explosions all about and without interest watched the black eruptions of earth. He had prayed, hoped, waited in vain; the shells kept coming. Before dawn and all morning long he'd told himself, bear up, old fellow, this will soon be over. This afternoon, however, he felt far too tired for such self-deception. His legs no longer ached from his cramped position; both had lost all feeling long ago. His head throbbed and his bladder cried its need for release and the rain fell, a cold steady drizzle, as it had now for hours. And the wind, the cursed wind! He and Hirose were both soaking wet.

Beside him Hirose wept openly, and Tomi felt much the same. When would the shelling end? He peered upravine, beyond the administration barracks, where smoke from burning gasoline drums rose thick and full and black at the base, then thinning in the wind. The fire had spread to a nearby pile of stores covered by a camouflaged tarpaulin. More troubles, more problems, more shortages, he thought. Had he the strength, he might have groaned. In the operating tent the alcohol was nearly gone. No more plaster for casts. Oxygen was exhausted. The ten-centimeter bandage compresses had all been used. Tomorrow would see the end of all hydrogen peroxide. At the present rate of usage, the tincture of iodine would last two, perhaps three days at most. But sake seemed in plentiful supply, a point Hirose could confirm. To the trench hole he'd brought a full two-liter bottle of sake, now empty and thrown aside. Hirose, mouth slack and eyes bleary, sobbing quietly against the trench-hole wall, looked more like a derelict than a fine physician and surgeon.

The shells from the gunboat were creeping close again, pounding the tundra and rock of the lower slopes above the ravine. Would they never run out of ammunition? The 20-millimeter bursts were short, four, five, six rounds each to avoid overheating the guns. The latrine was virtually destroyed. The tent tops had been holed several times, despite the excellent camouflage. But the lower sections—and Michael Andrews—were protected somewhat by a long fold of earth. Tomi believed all the patients were safe. Barring, of course, a direct hit or shrapnel bursting in the immediate vicinity.

Suddenly he wanted to laugh. Everyone on Attu was safe— barring getting shot to death or blown to bits or burned to a crisp. Everyone was safe, so why worry? Why not find a place to sleep, forget it all? Why not, indeed?

He swiveled his head to eye the terrain between here and the underground barracks. Thirty, forty meters. He could manage that, perhaps by crawling through the snow water in the stream bed to that tall rock, inching through the covering clump of knee-high thistle and dashing the remaining distance to the barracks door. Yes, he could do it, bad knee or not. Yes, he'd be even safer once he got there, snug and warm in his blankets. Then he would sleep. It was worth a try; anything was better than this.

First a deep breath. Brace himself against the trench-hole wall. Plant his feet firmly. Now!

He pushed from the wall and began rising, but nothing happened. His feet felt numb, like two inert stilts at the end of his legs. They refused to move; he couldn't stand. His knees remained bent. A fine thing, he thought. Thirty-three years of age and already an old man.

He began pushing his feet against the trench-hole wall. He wiggled his toes and fingers, moved his arms and shoulders in rhythm. Anything to improve circulation. Get the heart pumping, the blood pressure up, the adrenaline flowing.

"Hirose, stir yourself! Do something—anything!—to assert yourself. Do not surrender so easily. Move your arms and legs."

Hirose stared dully, not comprehending, a stranger lying in the mud.

"Come, get up. Save yourself!"

A crack sounded higher and sharper than any explosion. Tomi whirled about, peering up the hill to see the top of the ward tent billow like a fat man puffing his cheeks, and settle slowly into itself. *Whoooosh!* Michael! Michael! Only one thing could cause such a collapse: a bullet or shell hitting the tentpole. Inside were more than fifty patients, most of them helpless. Was Michael all right? The tent was heavy, but its weight was distributed over a wide area and should not greatly burden anyone. Michael should be all right. In the meantime, no one here could help anyone inside. Any movement now across the tundra would draw a steady torrent of fire and result in the rescuer's quick death, to say nothing of endangering the patients. Bravery was one thing, foolhardiness something else. The patients would have to wait.

As if the fall of the tent were a signal, the enemy ships in the harbor suddenly were moving, white water churning astern and shimmering waves of heat rising from their stacks. Slowly they moved about, heading seaward. The stern guns kept firing, an aimless and even insulting gesture, Tomi thought, for the fire kept everyone's head down an extra quarter-hour, in the rain, trembling, feet encased in icy water, the wind slicing like a raw burn through sopping clothing. For an instant Tomi hated Americans, those cruel and unforgiving men who thought of themselves as Christians.

"All out! All out!" cried Sergeant Okasaki. His voice rose hoarse and strained against the wind. He stood alone in the rain, a giant ignoring the elements. "All wardmen to the ward tent at once! Do not delay. Corporal, rise from your trench hole or I'll pull you out. You, Superior Private, find new lumber and lashings. The rest of you, line up here. Snap to it!"

With difficulty Tomi crawled from the hole and tried to stand erect. His knees shook from strain. His shoulders trembled from cold. His hands seemed out of control. A chattering came from his own teeth and he couldn't feel a thing. Never had he felt so sleepy. He peered down at Hirose, lying without comprehension in the bottom of the trench hole.

"Come," he whispered, the best he could manage, "I'll help you." Where the strength would come from he couldn't imagine. Why he bothered he didn't know. Hirose wouldn't move. Tomi hobbled slowly to Sergeant Okasaki. "The honored Lieutenant Hirose needs assistance," he croaked, hoping he'd be understood. Without waiting to find out, he hobbled toward the barracks.

Inside the warmth of his room the temperature gauge read 33 degrees Fahrenheit. He stripped down, examined his bare feet and rubbed them until the pains began. He strode back and forth and kept waving his arms wide, faster, harder. Soon he began panting for breath, felt himself begin to sweat and immediately quit exercising. First, fresh underwear and clothing. Then dry woolen stockings, two pairs, drawing them smooth and well up his calf. A pair of dry boots. Puttees. The pains in his feet grew intense; very good, the blood was now flowing full and rich. Dressed at last, he hobbled through the rain up the ramp to the ward tent, found it already repaired and usable, thanks to

Sergeant Okasaki. A makeshift two-by-four replaced the splintered original pole. Two patients were dead, one impaled by the ragged upper end of the tentpole through his chest; the other, a quadriplegic, a victim of suffocation. Both were quickly taken outside to lie in the snow and await the body disposal team.

Fourteen hours of steady, intensive bombardment. The time now was 1630 hours. At last the day's work could begin.

The first patient was Dr. Hirose, a mild case of chilblains. "Strip him down," Tomi told Wardman Ouye. "Cover him well with blankets. Give him fifty milligrams of Benadryl. Then rub his feet briskly until he screams. Ignore his orders. Hot tea is fine, but no other liquids without my permission."

To Sergeant Okasaki he gave orders that all hospital personnel should change to dry clothing and boots as soon as possible.

In the midst of reorganizing the ward, he was called to the radiophone. "Dr. Nakamura," he said. Tinny in his ear, in the background, was the distant rumble of American artillery.

"This is Lieutenant Ujiie, aide to the revered Garrison Commander Colonel Shima." The voice sounded thin and blurred by static. "The revered colonel requires your presence in order to deal properly with radio transmissions allegedly emanating from in or near your hospital. You will be prepared to answer all questions."

"Yes, honored sir." On top of all other burdens, why this?

"Tomorrow the revered garrison commander will be visiting the distinguished Battalion Commander Nagumo at battalion headquarters. You will present yourself at zero-eight-hundred hours."

"Honored sir, I am not familiar with the new location of batt—"

"It is adjacent to Captain Yamamoto's hospital cave near Umanose. Just go up the ravine."

"I understand. I will be there." He hung up the phone.

Observing the ward, he found all moving in good order. The patients were being fed what little food was available, while Michael watched. Okasaki, limping noticeably, had just ordered a body removed. Hayasaka was delivering a bedpan to a double amputee. Umeda kept staring at Jones, who was eating rice with his fingers. Hirose lay awake and squirming, not deep in a sake dream as one might expect.

"Leave my feet alone," he kept saying to Wardman Matsumoto as Tomi approached. "I do not wish such attention. Do you hear? I gave you an order."

Wardman Matsumoto kept rubbing. "My instructions from the honored Dr. Nakamura are to ignore your commands and rub your feet until you scream. You have not yet screamed."

"Nakamura!" cried Hirose. "Remove this misbegotten son of a cow from my sight. My feet are killing me."

Tomi bent down to examine the feet. They were somewhat red and swollen. "Do they itch?"

"Yes, dammit!"

"Hurt? Tingle?"

"Yes! You know very well they do."

"So do mine. But I'm on my feet and working, pain or not."

"Tell this maniac to stop! This is sadistic treatment."

"Which I hope will soon have you up and about." He turned to Matsumoto. "You may stop now. Bring the honored lieutenant a bowl of hot tea. One also for me."

"Sake," Hirose said. "I prefer sake."

"No sake," Tomi told him. "You and I must talk."

"Talking is easier with sake. And I outrank you."

"I am your physician now and I say no sake. Come now, I wish to talk of Captain Yamamoto and his past experiences with Sergeant Okasaki. What do you know of them?"

"Very little," said Hirose, frowning. "Only that they served together in China. A forward medical detachment, I believe. In '38 or '39."

"That's all? You know nothing more?"

"Nothing." But the man gazed at the shredded tent top, not at Tomi at all.

"Were you there with them at that time?"

"I served in the rear. I know nothing of what happened near the front line."

"Yamamoto somehow disgraced himself? Perhaps a court-martial?"

"Perhaps. I don't know. It was not my concern. As I say, I was far to the rear."

"Of course." Tomi sighed his disappointment. "Are you ready now to rise again and become a physician?"

"With these feet? I doubt if I can stand."

"It's difficult, I confess. Yet, if one tries—"

"Damn you, Nakamura! I've warned you, don't use that stupid psychology on me again. It won't work."

"You are correct," murmured Tomi as Hirose sat up. "My humble apologies." He bowed and left Hirose to himself.

The American, Jones, was also sitting upright, gazing down at the stump of his leg. "Hear the music, Doc?" He jerked a huge thumb in the direction of American artillery, which seemed louder now than it had this morning. "Tha's my squad. They're comin' to get me soon. Then we see who's the big man." He nodded as if to himself. "That's when I fry your hide."

"How's your leg—still hurt?"

"Some, now and then. Doan tell me you care, Doc. I knows differnt. Any man what takes a puffectly good leg—"

Tomi swept the comment aside. "Are you sleeping well?"

"Nope. Never dare close an eye with all you Japs—"

"*Japanese*, if you please."

"—all you Japs around. Somebody knife me in my sleep an' who does I complain to?"

"Nonsense! No one's going to stab you. There's a guard posted every night to prevent that very—"

"Yea, but who pertects me fum him?"

Tomi gazed along the wall to where Hirose stood, now almost fully dressed in dry clothes. The man already held a small bottle of sake from which he sipped occasionally.

Hayasaka brought tea and seemed far too quiet. "What troubles you?" Tomi asked, far more depressed than he sounded. "Are you ill?"

"I am going to die," Hayasaka said in a low voice. "Tomorrow. I have no choice. It is my fate."

For a moment Tomi merely stared. Then: "You mean *seppuku?* Why?"

"When the enemy ships came early this morning, I became afraid and did not wish to shame myself . . . again."

"You did not seek shelter in a trench hole?"

"No, honored sir. Instead, I gave myself a measure of opium."

"You what?" Tomi peered closely at the boy. "Where did you get it? If you broke the lock, you are in serious trouble."

Hayasaka hung his head. "There are . . . ways, honored sir. Not all of the drugs go to the patients."

"I see." Another matter for investigation. "Continue."

"Then I lay upon your operating table and slept all through the bombardment. As I slept an angel came to me and said, 'Tomorrow you will die.' "

"An angel? Which angel? What did it look like?"

"Oh, honored sir." Hayasaka raised his head high, his face aglow. "This angel had no name or appearance. It was there! An angel is something one feels."

"Interesting," mused Tomi, deciding to humor rather than challenge the boy. "I've never before known a man who spoke to an angel. It is an event of a lifetime. I am honored to know you, Private Hayasaka."

"Thank you." Hayasaka's eyes shone with pride, or perhaps exultation. Very eerie. "I shall not mind the pain. I am told the first thrust of the knife is all one feels. Once that is over . . . " He finished with a shrug.

"I shall miss you very much, Hayasaka. Of late my fondness and concern for you has grown by the day. Without you, who among us will recite haikus?"

"Aaaah," breathed Hayasaka, clasping his hands as if in prayer. " 'Think not of yourself as nothing. Festival of Souls.' A fitting epitaph."

"Very. Tell me, Hayasaka, have you made peace with God?"

"Yes, honored sir. I have made peace. I am calm. I have no fear. I welcome rebirth."

"You must remember, Hayasaka, that *seppuku* and all other forms of suicide are a great sin among Christians. Thus I ask of you a favor: pray to God for guidance. Talk to Him and say what is in your heart. Then come speak to me again. Will you do that for me?"

"Hara-kiri is a sin? How can it be? In Japan—"

"In Japan they do not fully understand the principles of Jesus. In time He will come to them, but not yet. Meanwhile, you must pray."

"Yes. Yes, I must. . . . " He wandered away, the glow on his face replaced by confusion. Tomi felt a bit confused himself, wondering if destroying the work of an angel was balanced by saving a man's life. If not, would he be forgiven?

"Dr. Nakamura!" Hirose, standing beside Umeda's litter, was frowning. Tomi picked his way through the crowded ward to find Umeda's stump unbandaged and exposed to the air. The odor and one glance told him all: gangrene. The entire area was red, swollen and warm to the touch.

"Fever? Chills? Headache?" They had no means of testing for leukocytosis.

"All of those," Hirose said, breathing heavy fumes of sake. "I want to know why this man wasn't discovered sooner. Our only recourse now is another amputation."

"You're very unfair," Tomi said. "Do you recall that both of us were operating until past midnight? Then we both spent fourteen hours in a trench hole? So why do you charge me alone with this neglect? You have had as much opportunity as I to discover Umeda's gangrene."

Hirose gazed coldly at Tomi. "May I remind you, Dr. Nakamura, that you are my subordinate? I do not appreciate quibbling. I insist that you strive to increase your level of competency."

Tomi felt his face go hot. Angry retorts leaped to mind. He wanted to lash out blindly, hurt Hirose to the depth of his being. "May I suggest, Dr. Hirose, that you strive to concentrate more on medicine and less on sake?"

In the long silence no tinge of friendship softened Hirose's eyes. "That will be quite enough, Dr. Nakamura. We shall discuss this matter another time, in private."

"I welcome the opportunity." Turning away, he knew he had erred. By withholding mercy and charity from Dr. Hirose, he'd been very unchristian. Tonight he must pray for forgiveness. These days he seemed to need a lot of forgiving.

He searched his mind for explanations. Of late Hirose had changed his attitude toward Tomi. As to what had triggered this change, he had few clues. One possibility: Hirose had evaded the whole truth about Yamamoto and Okasaki. Why should he avoid truth? Another possibility was that Tomi had denied the man sake, a demeaning thing to do to a grown man, a superior officer. But necessary! A third possibility: in the trench hole Hirose, in his drunken state, had allowed himself to appear as a weakling, a man who sobbed without restraint and who succumbed to fear. Such lack of self-control was alien to Samurai tradition. So Hirose's change of attitude could be rooted in any of these, or all of them.

Or perhaps the answer was physical—the lack of food, sleep, strained nerves or digestive upset. Tomi shook his head. As always, Hirose remained a mystery.

On the positive side was the fact that so far today Hirose had not attempted to examine Michael Andrews. Had he forgotten? Or was sake to blame? Or fear, or perhaps self-concern?

Curtly Tomi ordered Umeda's litter taken to the operating tent. Along with Okasaki and Hayasaka, he scrubbed while Umeda cursed him. The raucous voice droned on and on, sharp, acid, fearful, angry. It ceased only when the ether cone covered his lower face.

Peering down on his patient, Tomi felt sure he could save the knee. The inflammation was concentrated at the stump, low on the leg where the lean shafts of fibula and tibia began enlarging to meet the ankle joint. The redness was not well defined, quite typical of gangrene, but faded gradually upward into hues of healthy tissue. In his mind there existed no doubt: the knee could be saved.

Concentrating, he made the first incision and found the scalpel moving smoothly, as though independent of his hand. Flesh, muscle, tendon, nerve. He clamped an artery. . . .

Only when he returned to the ward tent did Tomi see the empty litter. In the crowded ward it stood out starkly, struck him like a blow. Michael Andrews had disappeared.

Michael hadn't counted on the force of the wind, or its coldness. It came howling and gusting down from the northeast, like a lancing knife across the vast frozen plains of Siberia and along a thousand-mile stretch of icy Arctic sea to strike him, without mercy, here on the bleak shore of Attu. The air itself was probably not quite freezing, but high humidity combined with this driving wind made the chill factor far below zero. His clothing was light—no heavy underwear, no cap or gloves or overcoat. No woolen stockings. So he gasped and shivered, cursed to himself, huddled down in the lee of a small gully and peered out on the heaving, frigid sea.

His escape had been simplicity itself. In all the confusion following the shelling, with Tomi, the Oily One and Hardnose in surgery, he'd merely blended in with the other walking-wounded heading toward the latrine. The flashlight and pistol he had hidden in his clothing. He'd made sure he was last in line, remained inside until all others had returned to the tents on the bluff. Only then did he emerge. All quiet except for feverish activity about the tents. He was alone and no one was watching. Five long steps carried him into the hip-deep fronds of the lower ravine, through which he crawled toward the beach to lie there and wait for dark.

Now the wind punished him and the cold crept in like a knife on his flesh. He studied the dark sea. Where was the goddamn Navy when you needed it? Nothing out there but waves. Big Boy One, you sonuvabitch, where are you? Eagle Four is loose and waiting in Chichagof Harbor. Jesus, the cold!

His crossed arms sheltered his hands in his armpits. There! A shadow. A small length of black only a shade darker than the sea around it. A destroyer? A mile or two offshore, no more than that. At last, thank God. . . .

The cold had stiffened his hands into awkward, fumbling claws. Even so, the flashlight did not drop. He aimed its length seaward and pressed the switch, released it. *Dot. Dot. Dot.* Cringe down from the wind. *Dash. Dash. Dash.* Hey, you guys, wake up! *Dot. Dot. Dot.*

No response. Again the SOS. Again nothing doing. Bastards asleep at the switch out there. *SOS. Eagle Four.* C'mon, earn your pay! *Dot. Dot. Dot.*

He blinked and rubbed his eyes. A light? A tiny glint of flickering light had appeared from the black shadow of the sea. Not a big signal lamp meant to carry to the far horizon but a single little nothing he could hardly make out. Some goddamn looie jg with mush for a brain, only a flashlight in hand, not wanting to show a decent light.

He strained his eyes into the dark. *I*. Okay. *D*. C'mon. C'mon! *E*. Oh, God, the wind, the cold! *N*. Please hurry. *T*. Ident? Identify! *Y*—

Eagle Four! Eagle Four! Eagle Four! Assistance need—

Without warning the snowbank beside his head exploded, tossing bits of ice against his cheek. He peered back to see where the shot had come from. There against the blue-white of the snow, a half-dozen or so dark figures sweeping down from the slope of the mountain, firing as they came and heading like avenging angels directly toward him.

Run! cried his mind. His legs felt like wooden stilts. He rose in the biting wind and staggered like a drunk along the gully, thinking how much nicer it would be to be shot to death quickly than to lie in the open and freeze.

May 23. Seventeen friendly medium naval bombers destroyed a cruiser off shore. By naval gun firing a hit was scored on the pillar post of tents for patients and the tent caved in. Two died instantly. From 0200 to 1600 stayed in trench-hole. Days rations: 1 go, five shakers 1.5 lbs. Nothing else. Officers and man alike in front. Everybody looked around for food and stole everything they could find.

MAY 24, 1943

Y our burn case has returned to his unit?" asked Hirose, his eyes still swollen from sleep. "Nakamura, why was I not informed?"

"Honored sir, I—"

"I wished to examine him today; his treatment intrigued me. Now the opportunity is lost." Hirose eyed Tomi with dark suspicion. "The burn case's sudden strength is surprising."

"No less surprising to me, honored sir. He requested immediate return to the fighting. I honored his request." The lie came easily; that, too, was surprising.

"You could have informed me."

"As we emerged from surgery, honored sir, you wished only to sleep."

"Now I wish answers. Common courtesy demanded—"

"Honored sir, I will not be cross-examined."

Hirose sighed. "Go get some sleep, Nakamura. Then we must talk."

He struggled from the depths and understood only vaguely what the voice kept saying. Hayasaka? The boy's mouth moved, words tumbled forth. Sleep fought to reclaim him but Hayasaka insisted. Tomi focused and let the message enter: the missing American airman had been located, perhaps. A few hours ago a lone figure was seen fleeing across the low slope below Hokuchin Yama toward the East Arm of Holtz Bay. Ordered to stop, the man fled. Pursued, he retreated through crevice and gully, his footprints in snow and mud leading toward the main trail in the headquarters ravine at Chichagof. Somewhere, somehow, the spoor had been lost, but a silver cross that only an American would wear had been found near the latrine. All personnel were therefore warned: the American airman was believed to be skulking in the immediate area; he must be found, forced to reveal where he had hidden for days, then shot.

The worst had happened. All he had tried to prevent was now fact. Soon he, too, would be dead and his name forever dishonored.

Minutes later he entered the ward tent to find Sergeant Okasaki blocking the aisle, his eyes glowing with a strange inner fire. He bent low to whisper. "I must speak to you at once in private. A matter of urgent necessity. Can you meet me at once in the operating area?" His gaze gave no hint of what lay in his mind.

"I must check on a few patients," Tomi said, his curiosity aroused. "Shall we say fifteen minutes?"

"What were you two whispering about?" asked Hirose a moment later. He seemed overly suspicious.

"A private matter of no consequence," said Tomi. "Have today's rations arrived?"

"At last! The off-duty wardmen were carrying cartons from headquarters most of the night. Today at least we can eat. Tomorrow, I don't know."

Again the pessimist speaks, thought Tomi. He noted Hirose's red-streaked eyes and haggard features. "You didn't sleep well? How do you feel?"

Hirose turned to stare, his eyes cold. "Does it matter how I feel? Don't patronize me, Nakamura. Understand this: I have come to realize that your aggressive behavior has promoted you to a false position of dominance in this hospital. You think I haven't noticed? At first I didn't see, being quite busy with . . . very important matters. So, may I remind you, honored doctor, that you are but an acting officer and I am a full lieutenant? That means I am in charge here, a matter that in other circumstances I should not find necessary to bring to your attention."

"It escapes me how I have offended you, but I thank you for your honesty. I, too, am concerned. With every sip of sake you stand more and more as a living example of what a responsible physician should not do. The patients see, and they wonder. May I suggest—"

"You may suggest nothing. Not you, Nakamura. Someone has stolen my flashlight. Was it you? I demand you return it at once."

"Honored sir!" Had he heard correctly? "I know nothing of your flashlight."

"You took it yourself. You, a colleague. A man whom I trusted. Is this then the depth of your degradation?"

"I have not seen the flashlight in question. I do not have it and will no longer submit to this abuse." He bowed again, aware that Hirose was too irrational to connect the absent burn case to this sighting of the missing American airman. "With your permission, honored sir, I shall see to one of my patients."

He found Umeda conscious, barely, though weak and nauseous, a typical aftereffect of ether. According to the chart, Umeda's blood pressure was normal, so no large hemorrhage had occurred. Umeda, a strong and healthy young man, was progressing quite well.

"I understand now," Umeda breathed hoarsely, "how the American feels."

"You understand nothing," Tomi said with a frown. "And do not blame anyone for your gangrene. It happens all too often, despite every precaution."

"That is simple for you to say, honored doctor. You are not the victim."

"In the future, Private Umeda, you must guard yourself against making unjustified accusations. At all times be sure of the facts before you speak. Hayasaka? A bowl of hot tea for this man, and half a gram of sodium benzoate at once. Umeda, at the moment that is the best I can do for you."

"Bah!" moaned Umeda. "The American drinks sake and I get sour medicine."

Tomi ignored him. He walked from the tent only to find Hayasaka following. "Honored sir! Please, a moment of your time? Perhaps here beside the tent, out of the wind."

"It's important, Hayasaka? More news of the American? Or another angel?"

"Neither, honored sir. Before I die today I wish to thank you for all your help. You have been like a father to me. I honor you. I am grateful. You must know, also, that I am not afraid."

"I am glad, Hayasaka." Tomi tried to read the boy's mind, seeking an explanation for this strange fixation. "You needn't die, you know. You are needed badly here. The patients need you. I need you. Who would serve me as scrub nurse?"

Hayasaka smiled sadly. "I have no choice, honored sir. I understand what I must do, though not why. Am I to die for the Emperor or Jesus?"

"Why not live and work for both?"

"No, today I must die. That is my fate. All that remains is to choose the time."

"Well, don't be hasty! Wait at least until I return later from headquarters. Then we shall talk again. Will you wait?"

"If it pleases you." With his eyes avoiding Tomi's, the boy bowed deeply and returned to the tent.

Tomi continued on his way. In the tiny unlit gloom of the operating area he found the sergeant waiting, seated upon the surgery table with two small packages beside him. "I regret that I am late," he said. "I tried to hurry, but Dr. Hirose delayed me unnecessarily."

"Dr. Hirose!" muttered Okasaki in a scornful tone, handing one of the packages to Tomi. "Here, last night I foraged two American K-rations. Let us relax together as we talk and enjoy an American meal."

"K-rations?" Tomi hesitated. Ordinarily he would share such a rare boon with Hirose, the wardmen and the patients. Anything edible received from home was always shared, this unspoken rule always observed. But now— ?

The box was so small, its contents not even a small bite for each of the patients. The wardmen would gobble it down and have their hunger unrelieved. And as for Hirose . . .

His hunger suddenly seemed acute, all-powerful; he could think of little else. His fingers trembled as he accepted the box, hastily tore the heavy paper lid open. Awkwardly he plied the can opener around the can and eyed the contents. Beans, a mixture of bean mush. Delicious! Crackers, cheese, canned fruit and a fruit bar which he slipped into a pocket. In silence they ate together, neither caring if he appeared wolfish or greedy. Food was nutrition, nutrition was life and strength and perhaps survival, and it all tasted so fine and disappeared too quickly. Tomi sighed. The food glowed in his stomach. "Where did you find this delicacy? Do you mind my asking?"

Okasaki's teeth gleamed in the dim light. "Those idiots at headquarters have never learned how to hide things. That is all I can say."

"You are a resourceful man, Sergeant Okasaki. I am glad you are not my enemy."

"I, too, am very glad of that. At heart I wish to be no man's enemy. Except Hirose's."

Tomi sensed a second, more sinister purpose in this meeting. Not about the pursued American, but about Hirose. "Why do you say that?"

Okasaki smiled thinly. "He is a contemptible man! I have watched him strut and pose. He is like a Kabuki dancer who is ill-trained, an insufferable fool. I detest his manner, commanding us all with such a lordly air. It will give me joy to see him humbled." He paused to eye Tomi, gauging him. "I see by your alert attention that you wish to hear more."

"I do." Tomi sucked on a sugar cube. "I am very curious."

"My information comes from what I saw and heard long ago. It is not widely known, this disgrace. For years I have kept the secret. Now it is time to speak."

"About the honored Lieutenant Hirose or the worthy Captain Yamamoto?" He guessed wildly.

"Both. One night in China, years ago, they sat together and drank much sake. They talked and sang and drank, as men will. They became unconscious, or nearly so. I have heard one story, then another."

"What happened?"

"As they drank, a certain small band of Chinese soldiers came patrolling behind our lines, seeking information from prisoners. Sad to say, they came upon the worthy—"

"Both of them? They were taken by the enemy?"

"One hears different things. One version said they were taken. Another said they surrendered rather than die by burning. Personally I don't know which. Does it really matter?"

"I think not." In either case it meant a lifelong disgrace for both men. "Is that why the worthy Captain Yamamoto has no higher rank?"

"I don't know. No official report was made later of their recovery, but I suspect so. Informed people in high places hear. And they remember."

"But neither man committed hara-kiri. Very strange."

"Indeed, as any man of honor would choose to do. Now their names are soiled, their honor swept away as if by flood. Even yet they choose to live." In the gloom Okasaki's eyes kept regarding him. "What is generally not known is that both men gave the Chinese all the information they sought. Of course they were tortured."

"Of course." Tomi studied Okasaki a long moment. "How do you know this?"

"First, the Chinese attacked at dawn and slaughtered a full battalion of our troops who were not yet in position for defense. Our counterattack repelled them and also recovered the worthy captain and the honored lieutenant. Both had lost their swords of the Samurai. Also both had been drugged, but the captain was conscious. I personally attended him in his own hospital. I saw his blood, his wounds. Second, the captain wept like a child. In a weak moment he told me all. Now he fears me. He knows that I know."

"And Hirose does not?"

"I do not know. Nor do I care."

Tomi nodded. The great mystery was solved, though a large question remained. Okasaki had just broken a pattern of silence; it was not like him. "Thank you for telling me of this matter," he said gently. "May I ask your reason for doing so?"

Again Okasaki's teeth gleamed as he eased from the table. "I knew you would ask. Let me say this: it gives a man no pride to speak of another's shame. So be it. Now, however, you have the means of protecting yourself. Do not hesitate to use it."

Having made another payment on his debt of gratitude, he bowed deeply, briefly, and strode away.

Heavenly Father, Tomi silently prayed. Of Thee I ask nothing for myself. I pray on behalf of a good and honorable man, Michael Andrews, a lost and lonely soul now wandering through bitter cold and wind and rain and mud. He is in great danger. And helpless. Please guide him to safety. Protect him from all harm. Preserve his life from those who would destroy him, for he is Thy servant on earth. Give him strength and courage and the will to do Thy work. Restore him to health, I beseech Thee, for he is my cherished friend. I ask this boon in the name of my Saviour, Jesus Christ. Amen.

The cave was neither large nor deep but at one point a man could stand erect. That was where Michael placed himself, flashlight in one hand and pistol in the other. He kept waving his arms and moving his feet, a poor attempt to run in place. Jump! Hop! Kick! Swing those arms! He could feel his strength dwindling. In all his life he had never felt so weak, tired, lost. His situation, though desperate, was not hopeless. Although he had no food or water, was chilled through and through by exposure and felt thoroughly exhausted, the fact remained he was alive and functioning, armed to some small degree and in a cave out of the bitter wind.

Tomi haunted his mind. Tomi, who by now would know he was gone. What had Tomi thought, felt, done at the sight of the empty litter? It was apparent now that Tomi had been right in so many ways. Tomi knew Attu, understood the intense cold, the strength of the wind, the blinding fog. The whereabouts of the Jap troops? Just ask Tomi. Tomi had laid the whole package on the line for Michael to see. And what did the world's greatest idiot do? Ignored the whole damn thing!

Tomi—friend, companion, rescuer and mentor. Brother and father, too. He knew it now. But now was too late.

For the future . . . Many long hours from now, night would come. Until then he must remain here in the dark of the cave, constantly moving to keep his blood pumping. Then in the dark he would venture forth, flashlight in hand, and try again. With luck the Navy would send a boat. . . .

He couldn't explain to himself why he hadn't been caught. Granted, in the dark one gully looked a lot like any other and he'd changed gullies several times. Instead of fleeing down to the shore as they apparently expected him to do, he'd edged higher, ever higher, a tactic not born of brilliant intellect but more a product of animal cunning, blind instinct. He'd almost missed the mouth of the cave.

The encouraging thing was that at least he'd made contact. Eagle Four in Morse code; how many times had he flashed it? Four, five, enough anyway to do the job. The Navy wasn't stupid. They'd seen, known, understood, answered. By now Big Boy One would have the word: Eagle Four alive, loose, needing assistance in Chichagof Harbor. They'd come snooping, for sure. Whole goddamn Navy—battleships, planes, small boats. Coming for one of their own. Depend on the Navy that way. Fuck-up half the time but they'd try.

By now Coach would know, would be thinking of how he could

help. Eddie, ol' Joe and Jake. All cruising over the area, watching like hawks for some tiny signal. Like maybe if he tramped an SOS in the snow . . .

Soon Mom and Dad would be told. "Sir, last night on Island X a signal from the beach area was received. The content of the . . . " Dad, face unmoving but all torn up inside. "Y'see, Mother," he'd say, "he's all right. I said he would be. Mike may fall down but he gets up right away. Now no more worrying." Patting her shoulder awkwardly, helplessly, with a broad, gnarled hand. Mom, quietly going into the sewing room and closing the door . . .

Later, she'd call Phyllis. "He's alive! He signaled somehow last night. Still trying, still fighting, that's our Mike. Dear, don't cry so. With a little luck . . ."

Luck and be damned, he thought. He wasn't through by a long shot. Get killed on Attu? Freeze to death? Not him! Not Mike Andrews. He had fifty years to live yet, fifty at least. There was work to be done, people to feed, a whole new world to build and let shine, something new and wonderful growing every day. Most of all there was Phyllis. Phyllis, Phyllis, I love you, Phyllis. All warm soft breasts and clinging thighs. Smoky, happy eyes, big grin, a giving loving woman. He'd never been able to match her capacity for giving. Fifty-fifty? No, more like eighty-twenty, him the giant receiver and yet doing his damnedest to give and give—

Except for that certain day he'd arrived for supper. She met him at the door, eyes wide, tearful, frightened. "Mike, have you heard the radio?"

"Heard what?"

"The Japanese. My God, they've bombed Pearl Harbor."

He stared at her. "Y'sure? I don't under—Why would they do that?"

"It's no joke, Mike. The announcer said—"

"Hey, maybe it's another Orson Welles radio show. Y'know, they make it sound so real."

"It's on all the stations. It's true! You can listen for yourself. Mike, will you have to go?"

He listened to sketchy reports for all of two minutes. "Damn!"

he muttered into her wide gray eyes. Dreams and plans—gone! His timetable flushed down the drain. "Couldn't they wait till after finals?"

Tomi waited inside a barracks tent adjacent to Battalion Headquarters. He'd been here for more than an hour, pacing the uneven floor and hoping the revered Garrison Commander Colonel Shima would not interrogate him too thoroughly about the strange use of English on the hospital radio. He knew nothing— that could be his only argument. What he had deduced was another matter.

The tent flap suddenly brushed to one side, a gust of icy wind rushing into the tent. Captain Yamamoto eased inside, closed the flap and turned to Tomi, his black rubber raincoat and hat dripping. "I was told I would find you here."

Tomi bowed. "Worthy sir, good morning."

The man's clothing hung loosely on a frame wasted by hunger. His face was far too lean, even taut, the bones evident in a most startling manner. His eyes were deeper in their sockets than Tomi remembered, and they burned now with crisp intensity. He wasted no time.

"The revered colonel is too busy with much more important and immediate matters to speak with you. So I am here to question in his place. Nakamura, someone flashed a message early this morning to an American warship just offshore. What do you know of it?"

"Honored sir?" Dumbfounded, he gazed at Yamamoto.

"Do not play innocent with me. Answer the question."

"I know nothing of any such message." Flashed? A flashlight! It could only be Michael, an utter fool who seemed determined to trap them both.

"Your face denies your words, Nakamura." Yamamoto almost purred with delight. "Tell me all you know. Hold nothing in reserve."

"Honored sir. I know only this: since yesterday a flashlight is missing. The how and why—and who, of course—I do not know."

"Who else but the American airman?"

"That cannot be, honored sir. He would be seen and reported at once. Consider: Is it not possible that someone else—"

"That a Japanese would so disgrace himself? Unthinkable. Now, as to this matter of someone misusing the hospital radio— you have investigated thoroughly?"

"Worthy Captain." Tomi bowed. "Each man in my hospital is loyal and dedicated to the Emperor, as I am myself. Not one of us has flashed a message or misused the hospital radio." A true statement. All were innocent.

"Yet the radio was used."

"And you suspect me! All that night I was with Lieutenant Ujiie."

"I am aware of that. I am also aware that the communications people who were stationed in the village school reported a very strong signal emanating from a point in direct line with your hospital. Nakamura, such circumstantial evidence is over-whelming."

"I agree."

"You do?" Yamamoto gazed steadily at him, unbelieving. "Then . . . then who in your hospital, besides yourself, speaks English?"

"A superior private named Umeda, whose foot was amputated, and the black American, Jones, whose feet were frozen. It was neither of them."

"Then who, if not you?"

"Worthy Captain, the result of my investigation reveals no unauthorized use of our hospital radio. That is my full report."

"Perhaps you haven't really tried. Nakamura, I always trust my instincts, and they tell me now that you speak falsely, like an American. Perhaps you know more than you report."

"If you doubt me," Tomi said with sudden surging glee, an inadvertent smile quickly erased, "you may confirm my statements with Sergeant Okasaki."

Yamamoto seemed to shrink. "Nakamura . . ."

"I don't suppose the past really matters. Not anymore. This is Attu."

Yamamoto blinked, having expected one response and received another. "I don't understand you. Perhaps it is the American influence. Once a man is tainted he can never again become pure."

"I am tainted, worthy.Captain, in the same degree as you. Only the manner differs. God help us both."

Somehow Yamamoto gathered strength and dignity. "Enough of this. You may report to your unit. The revered colonel, however, will contact you by radiophone."

Outside, Tomi found a driving rain and howling wind. So thick was the rain that the hospital cave and the slopes on each side of the ravine were totally obscured. The gusts of wind staggered his body.

He paused, questioning now what he should do. One alternative was to retrace his steps to Misumi Barracks and wait out the storm with Captain Yamamoto, which he preferred not to do. Another was to seek refuge in the hospital cave itself and wait there, another distasteful solution. The third was to brave the weather, advance through it and seek a haven where he belonged, among his own patients, with his own work. So the cold, wind, rain, what did they matter? If he walked quickly, he was sure to keep warm.

Ignoring the vague, perhaps intuitive warning that surfaced in his mind, he found the path. The wind now came from behind, pushing him down the ravine. It felt good to be moving, to be doing something positive. His knee ached, but he'd learned to live with pain.

After the first hundred yards the downward slant of the ravine eased and walking was easier. Soon the rain became sleet, vicious pellets of ice half the size of golf balls that hammered his back and head. After his first gasp of surprise, and after searching in vain for some kind of shelter, he felt grateful for the thickness of a woolen cap he wore under the furry hood of his coat. Otherwise he might be pounded to unconsciousness. As it was, his only alternative was to endure and to move along as rapidly as possible. And to pray.

A quarter-mile, a half-mile. The sleet kept coming down. He

kept watching the downhill path, for if that was lost, so was he. It would be easy to lose himself here and flounder about blindly in search of the path or some familiar object to guide himself by. He would gradually lose body heat, grow weak and fall and not be able to rise. One could freeze to death quite easily here on Attu. A comforting thing, this muddy, oozing path stretching clearly before him, a black rut in dormant tundra. He could see its length a good thirty yards. Follow it, that's all, and in less than an hour he would be safe and relatively warm in the barracks or ward tent, drinking hot tea—if any was left—and dealing tactfully with Hirose, Hayasaka, Okasaki and three-score patients. He looked forward to that with pleasure.

Walking was good. But, aside from the constant crescendo of wind and thud and crackle of sleet on his raincoat, he could hear nothing. Sight was limited both in distance and quality. He could smell dank earth and nothing more. Neither could he feel much of anything and he thought about that. At first his boots had struck hard against the path, the accustomed jar traveling the length of his body. Now, though he saw the boots still pounding forward, strong, sure, in perfect control, he felt as if he were floating on air, a not unpleasant sensation.

He laughed, despite himself. It seemed as though he and his body were not working together. His body, a strangely autonomous creature, continued on its way—*left, right, hup! two three four!*—while he, the mind that saw and sensed everything, merely relaxed and went along for the ride. He felt like a child suddenly let out of school. He was free! No responsibility, he had escaped. . . .

No, it was a refuge, a haven, that's what it was. He'd found a place a man could retreat to, wait deep inside himself, and watch all that happened out there. He could rest and gain strength, prepare himself, and when the need arose, emerge and again take command. It was here, in this snug, warm chamber of his mind that his earlobes no longer ached, his fingers ceased to tingle, the sharp ache in his chilled and burdened lungs ceased to exist and the clear, sweet, haunting strains of *Clair de Lune* filled the air. How strong the bass notes, how delicate the treble! It was he who was playing, he could see that now. Sumiko sat beside him, her eyes soft and sweet as the music. Debussy, Strauss, Chopin, Tchaikovsky, Rachmaninoff, Gershwin, Foster—he loved them all. Without effort his fingers roamed the keys, the strong beat keeping time with the hard, sure, stroking of his boots against the dark earth . . .

. . . dark earth, rich black soil and endless waving golden fields of grain, waving in rhythm, left right left . . .

For what reason he didn't know he found himself struggling to clear his mind. Function! Think! Assert yourself! Where were the barracks, the ward tent, the path itself? Nothing but yellow-white tundra grass, covered by little silver pellets of ice, lay about him.

Though the chill in his lungs stabbed fire with every breath, he shouted downwind. No response. Should he retrace his steps? Had he gone too far? Perhaps he should wait a moment or two; the sleet came now in smaller pellets without its former force. If he could only see something familiar!

He shouted again, a small and forlorn cry in the wind. Would anyone hear? Surely the barracks and ward tent were somewhere nearby. Perhaps in that direction? Or over there?

The cold drove into him. But what did mere cold matter? Cold could be overcome by moving within it and through it, hunger by holding a figurative toothpick between one's teeth and smiling, exhaustion by an exercise of iron will—that was the Japanese way, derived from the ancient code of the Samurai, the warriors, the elite. Thus no man should acknowledge pain or fear danger. The Japanese were above such things.

Yet he felt weaker now, his legs weighing tons. He staggered as he walked. It would be nice to sink down into soft tundra and sleep—beautiful sleep!—but of course that would be fatal. Sumiko. He must keep going for Sumiko. For little Yoko, the baby Keiko. For Michael and Jesus, for the work yet to be done, for his patients. Everyone needed him. "*Hoooooo!*" he cried again. Only silence answered, terrible in its presence. Alone, alone . . . Trembling with cold, he stood still, with the last of his strength, howling: "*Hoooooo!*"

No one answered. He waited in the driving sleet, helpless, the world a gray wet blur. Which way should he go?

A dim movement caught his eye. A bear? A white bear? But no bear lived on Attu. Nothing but small blue fox. Yet it was white and huge and moving swiftly, a great rushing form that emerged from the snow, ice, sleet and wind; it closed in without a sound and with one arm lifted him high as one would a child. He felt himself borne quickly away, a prize for the victor. Deep in his mind Tomi found himself laughing, for this was the only lumbering bear in the world that wore a white lab coat, splints on one wrist, and bore the grizzled motherly features of the much-honored Sergeant Okasaki.

Michael could delay no longer, that was self-evident. It was now and quickly or not at all. Now! Before he collapsed from sheer exhaustion. Tired to the bone from running in place, tired from forever waving his arms. But outside the cave there was nothing to see. Just fog—dense white, blinding goddamn fog. The gleam of a flashlight wouldn't penetrate five feet, much less two-three miles.

Tomi had been right—he was far too weak. Now he felt utterly spent. Already his throat hurt. Lungs burning with cold. So stay here to starve and freeze? He laughed without sound or strength. His options had narrowed to one. Tomi! Tomi giving Jones the best he could. The same for himself. Now, without Tomi he would die. Had to apologize to Tomi. Keep faith in Tomi. Get back to Tomi. Somehow make contact . . .

If only he lived long enough to get there.

The light seemed to come and go. Tomi waited for it, watched it, found it held no patterns, had no purpose, sought no reason. It was simply there, now white, then gray, sometimes yellow. Or it was absent. He could do nothing about it.

He was warm. Exactly when he realized *warmth* he really couldn't tell. But undeniably a small mountain of blankets covered him. Time had no meaning. After a while he recognized the barracks, his own tiny room and bed, Sergeant Okasaki in too-busy attendance, the taste of hot tea that burned his throat and the sound of explosions that seemed far too loud, far too near. Rocks and bits of loosened sod kept falling from the roof. He wanted someone to make it all stop. Michael—

"An air raid?" he whispered.

"A naval bombardment, courtesy of the American Navy." The voice was deep and soft and soothing. "Now you must sleep."

May 24. It sleeted and was extremely cold. A great amount of shells were dropping from naval gun firing. Mud and rocks flew around the room and fell from the roof. In a trench-hole five meters away, Hayasaka, a medical man, died instantly by a penetration of shrapnel through the heart.

MAY 25, 1943

T omi!"

The voice was low and hoarse and came from the shadows, seemed everywhere at once and compelling in its urgency. At this time and place, used with such carefree informality, it could only belong to one person. Yet Tomi failed to recognize the voice. It rattled rather than rang, seemed filled by infinite pain. Could it be Michael? The voice lacked the firm measured tones Michael normally used and in any case failed to carry with either strength or conviction.

At the moment, just after dawn, all enlisted hospital personnel were on duty, feeding, bathing, tending the patients. Here in the barracks Tomi held his breath as the shadows stirred. From a pile of twisted blankets far in one corner came a figure, moving with agonizing slowness. It grunted and groaned and wheezed and coughed repeatedly, breathing far too heavily, and at last reached Tomi's side. "You were right. I couldn't make it."

Such a foolish comment! Even as he sagged with sweet relief he noted that Michael looked fully as ill as he sounded, gaunt as a skeleton, pale yet feverish, his blond-bewhiskered face lined by agony and his eyes stricken by the depth of this new experience.

Yet those eyes remained fierce, undaunted, determined as ever. Christlike . . .

Little mattered, however, except Michael was safe, alive. "Come with me." Tomi led him back to his own tiny sleeping area. In the yellow light of a single candle Michael's face looked as if he had aged ten years. He was also incredibly dirty.

"Tell me all," Tomi said quietly. "From the moment you disappeared."

"There's not much to tell." An understatement. His voice rasped; with a trained ear Tomi listened to the guttural grating of a very sore throat. "I went to the latrine. From there into the fronds in the ravine. I crawled toward the beach and waited there till dark, cold and wet as—"

"And no boots? In bare feet? It is a wonder they did not freeze."

"I had boots. I hid in a cave. This morning, halfway back in the fog, I took off my boots to change the tracks. Y'see? I did everything to get back here okay. I made it. No strain."

Another understatement. "And the flashlight? Tell me of the flashlight."

"Oh!" A pitiful attempt at a smile. "You know about that."

"Possibly the entire Japanese contingent on Attu knows. They seek to capture you, force you to reveal all. You risked both our lives! So foolish, Michael. So very foolish."

"I'm sorry. Really! But think . . . of all the fun I had."

Americans! "You might have been killed."

"They're lousy shots, really."

"One of them might have been lucky. You thought of that? I warned you, Michael Andrews. Now you have chills and fever. There is a definite possibility of bronchitis, even pneumonia. Why don't you trust me? Why don't you listen and obey?"

"I'm sorry! You were right. So now I trust you. We still friends?"

Tomi's heart leaped. "You are hungry?" From his pocket he drew the fruit bar from yesterday's K-ration. "Remove your wet clothing. Wash up; there is the basin. Water is in that container. I shall return in a moment."

It was a risk, one he could not avoid. Okasaki, however, was busy in the ward tent. From the operating tent Tomi brought bandages, a pair of woolen trousers, boots, stockings, a bowl of cold rice and a strong solution of salt-water gargle. Michael's wounds, unaccountably, proved to be clean. Even so Tomi washed and redressed them and wrapped Michael again as a mummy, leaving eyeholes to be covered by goggles, plus a small gap for a water straw. As they strode together up the ramp in the cold half-light, Michael said, "You call the shots, Tomi. I'll do as you say." *Cough! Cough!* "But let's not wait too long—okay?"

Americans!

He stationed Michael in a litter directly across the aisle from Jones and adjacent to Umeda, for better or for worse. All that was needed to return him to his own people was a bit of time and a great deal of luck. Somehow Michael Andrews seemed to thrive on luck.

Meanwhile, burdened by a multitude of responsibilities, Tomi knew he must bear up, endure. Hayasaka was dead, the victim of shrapnel through his heart during the shelling last night. Dead— the boy had been right! But he could not allow himself to think overly much of Hayasaka. It served no purpose and hurt too much to enter the tent and not find the boy's eager face; to turn about, expecting him at the elbow and find the space vacant. Now the boy belonged to yesterday, a time that no longer mattered. Today must be dealt with, the focus of all thought. But how, alone and confronted with insurmountable problems, could one deal with today?

He continued in his duty; it was as simple as that. On his early morning rounds, however, he saw nothing but problems piling up on problems. A total of nine patients had died during the night, three from internal hemorrhage, one from nonfunction of a shot-riddled liver, four from causes as yet unspecified and one from shock on the operating table—a victim of Dr. Hirose's uncertain hand. It helped not one bit to know that at 0800 hours Hirose remained in bed—as the Americans said, sleeping it off. That was good in the sense that Hirose could not, at the moment, impose his newfound anger upon the ward. Yet that was bad because Hirose was needed, and Tomi wished he were here.

As for himself: before dawn he'd recovered well enough to analyze his own condition—hypothermia, an abnormal reduction of general body temperature. His was not a serious case. After rescue he'd merely felt uncomfortable, though not entirely conscious. He should have remained in bed at least a day, resting. But with Hirose in that condition, Tomi had risen to tend the patients.

The immediate result was that he felt dizzy all too often, especially when rising to his feet or turning his head too quickly. A minor affliction, of course, one that would disappear as the day wore on and he recovered gradually from last night's exposure.

He sat on the edge of a litter, an unprecedented act, pretending to read a chart but really resting. He couldn't remember ever feeling so weak. He needed rice, lots of rice. He wanted fresh milk, cold lettuce, hot noodles, a large fillet of red snapper, even the American fruit bar he had given to Michael.

"You feel well, honored doctor?" Sergeant Okasaki, face impassive and impersonal, again hovering about him like a mother hen with a disabled chick.

"I am fine, thank you. Merely resting a moment."

"You would care for water? If you are hungry, I can always find an extra portion of rice—"

"No more than my share."

"Of course." Okasaki's eyes flicked toward the west wall. "I see the burn case has returned. Is that not unusual?"

"Yes, he was too weak to return to the front. Halfway there—"

"I understand. He has acquired a dry cough. Please call if I may assist you in any way."

He watched Okasaki stride away, his splinted arm swinging free. Tomi felt grateful to Okasaki. Last night when the sleet began, Okasaki had stationed himself at the entrance to the tent, watching the path and worrying, though he'd refused to admit it. "I felt the need for fresh air," he'd said to everyone who asked.

Even so, he'd saved Tomi's life and now the *On* was balanced; they were even. Though Okasaki would probably never admit it.

Earlier this morning he had confronted Okasaki. "Honored Sergeant, I have this to say: Thank you for my life."

For a moment Okasaki had stood in silence, regarding Tomi. "You owe me no thanks, honored sir. I did not save your life. You saved your own life."

Tomi raised his brows. "How is that possible?"

"If you had not saved my life a matter of days ago, I would not have been there to pull you in from the sleet. A simple matter of logic."

"Yet you did rescue me. I am in your debt."

Okasaki almost smiled. "I will compromise. At worst our debts cancel each other. At best we must each recognize our debt for a lifetime. Which do you prefer?"

A lifetime of friendship with Okasaki? "I prefer the latter, of course."

"Of course." Okasaki did smile, just a bit.

Turning again to the chart, Tomi found no morning notations as to vital signs. He groaned inwardly, confronting his new problem. The esteemed Garrison Commander Colonel Shima's order had arrived—transfer four wardmen at once for duty at the front. Four wardmen! With the death of Hayasaka and a wardman killed two or three days ago, plus this departure of four inadequately trained but badly needed wardmen, only ten enlisted men remained to staff the hospital. As of 0300 hours, the patient count stood at sixty-three, twenty-one of them critical.

What can we do, he thought. Good men will die for lack of care.

Michael Andrews coughed, once, twice.

Tomi found himself gazing down on Private First-Class George Washington Jones. "Good morning," he said in a listless tone. "You are well today?"

"Feelin'-fine-an'-getting-mine!"

"You seem very cheerful."

"Them guns is closer now. Closer every day. You sayin' your prayers regular? If you ain't, you sho' better start, cause we're-shootin'-right-with-all-our-might. That's the American way."

"You should try writing lyrics for songs. I see your leg is healing nicely. No complications at all."

"That's cause I bin eatin' pork chops all my life. Two-chops-a-day-keeps-the-cops-away! Just ask my sweet mama. Nuthin' like pork chops to make a good man heal right."

Tomi was annoyed with nonsense. "Jones, we need your litter. Today I want you to try crutches. Move around and loosen up. Tonight, I don't know. We'll find some place for you to sleep."

"Atta boy, Doc! In-my-ear-your-word-is-clear. First thing, I'm gonna find me some food."

"Don't wander into forbidden places. You're weak and mustn't overdo it. Also, you might get shot."

"Not me! Tell you what I do. You gimme more rice, an' when my friends come I'll put in a good word for you."

"Are you serious?" A bribe—he was actually being bribed!

"You-gimme-the-rice-I'll-treat-you-nice. How about it?"

"I thought you wanted to kill me."

"I sure did—day before yesterday. Today I wanna eat."

"Don't we all?" A cramp churned his stomach. "I'm sorry, but a ration is a ration. When I pray tonight, however, I'll put in a good word for you, too."

Jones frowned. "Y' better pray for yourself, Doc. 'Cause I don't like people sayin' no. What's more, I want my night guard back. I ain't safe in here without one. An' that little medic with the moon face, I want him, too. This new one smells bad an' ain't worth nothin'."

The cramp was making him sweat. "No guard, not anymore. You'll have to take your chances. That little medic? Yesterday the American planes killed him."

Without waiting for a reaction, he moved along the aisle, thinking of poor innocent Hayasaka, dead so young, and what could one say? At least he died quickly and with honor, a hero now to all Japan. A sacrifice for the Emperor, of course. Yet Hayasaka had been one with God, decent, faithful, repentant.

Michael Andrews coughed again, repeatedly, a bandaged hand

before a bandaged face, and a sudden thought froze in Tomi's mind. After all Michael's struggles and Tomi's care, would Michael now die in the breathless agony of chronic broncho-pneumonia?

Michael would have slept and could have slept, he knew, if only the coughing would cease. The chills persisted, with sharp pains in his upper chest and throat and with a bitter saliva he swore looked pink. Cold as ice, shivering, he kept sweating as profusely as a hard-running athlete. The ache in his head, dull and throbbing at first, seemed to increase with each gasping breath. When would Tomi's medicine begin to work?

There were blankets heaped upon him; he felt the weight. Tomi came with frequent salt-water gargles and Michael was immensely grateful. For everything! He wanted to say thanks in some meaningful way, to swear friendship forever, to ask how he might repay such kindness. But someone was always near, watching or listening, and often his mind drifted away to visions of heavily laden vines and fields of golden wheat, all mixed with Dad, Mom, Coach and Eddie and a host of fond old dreams blurring together. He felt tired of fighting blankets and chills. It seemed such a simple thing to let go, close his eyes, feel the warmth invade and see her rise again to meet him at the door, wearing blue satin pajamas and a darker blue satin bathrobe, both new. Her hair was combed in soft lovely waves. A touch of lipstick, and those warm gray eyes . . .

"I brought wine," he said, holding her close and letting her hair tickle his nose. Her body trembled and there in the curve of his shoulder she sniffed loudly.

"Why a whole half-gallon? Oh, I know you. You'll try to get me drunk and then seduce me. Wretch that you are."

"Never trust an Air Force man." Tonight everything should be kept lighthearted, he thought; make it as easy for her as he could. "Seduce 'em keen and leave the scene, that's our motto."

"Crush a poor girl's bleeding heart and then dash off for another easy conquest. You taken the oath yet?"

"This morning. So I'm in, it's official. The train pulls out at seven in the morning."

"Okay, so I'll go to the station with you."

"In the rain? It'll be cold, wet, miserable, awfully crowded. Why not sleep in?"

"I want to be there."

"You have an eight o'clock class. You'll miss breakfast."

"Mike, I'll be there. I want to."

"But, Phyllis—"

"Dammit, Mike!"

"Okay. Y'know you're beautiful when you shout? That a new robe? What's the occasion?"

"This rag? Oh, I'm entertaining a gentleman tonight. One should come along any time now."

"Anyone I know?"

"Heavens, no! He won't be handsome at all. I like real dunderheads with a superman complex who go dashing off to war so poor little girls like me won't be raped by hordes of Japan—" Suddenly she burst into tears, "Damn! I swore I wouldn't cry."

"You look real cute when you cry. Like a little doll."

"You're not helping any." She sniffed and he gave her his handkerchief. "Why the tie? You never wear a tie. You look like a waiter."

"Special date tonight. Banker's daughter. If I string her along maybe I can marry the whole bank. Isn't that interesting?"

"Lousy puns"— she blew her nose both lustily and daintily, a combination only she could achieve—"are a product of a degenerate mind. Let's have some wine."

He poured red wine and joined her on the divan. "I sure hope they'll let me fly. I'd give almost anything to be a fighter pilot."

"It sounds dangerous, Mike."

"What isn't? Mother says I should fly low and slow. Dad says this war is no worse than the last one. Eighteen months and we'll all be home."

"I wish! But Mike, a year and a half is a long time. A lot can happen. I have nightmares about you lying dead—"

"C'mon, none of that! Here's to our wedding day, the day you graduate."

"Oh, Mike, to think—"

"Don't start that again. That's my only handkerchief. It's already wet."

Sniff! "Mike, I'll write every day, I promise. I'll send pictures and packages. I'll knit and help every way I can. Whatever you want or need I'll send."

"Don't strip your gears, honey. Just study hard. We'll need lots of chemists. Have some more wine?"

"Mike, you won't do anything dangerous, will you? You're just the type to— I mean, some crazy stupid thing . . ."

"I consider myself absolutely indispensable to the war effort. And to you afterward. How else would all our kids get born? Anyway, at heart I'm a coward."

She looked doubtful. "And I hear so many stories about girls in other countries, what they do and say, so . . . available. I mean men are only human, so—"

"So I love you. You! No one else. Okay?"

"Okay." Her eyes kept brimming. "Oh, I'm going to miss you, Michael Andrews!"

He nodded, set down the wineglass. "Hey, c'mon. Where's my bright-eyed little Phyllis? Where's the flip lip with a hip quip?"

She blew her nose. "Oh, poor me! To think I have to listen to drivel like that for the next fifty years."

"A fate worse than death. Hey, I brought you something." From a side coat pocket he drew a flat, square box. "Open it."

Eyes wide, she did. "A necklace? Pearls? Are they real?"

"They're real."

He gathered the necklace, as she leaned forward, her face only inches from his. The necklace seemed to clasp itself and lie smoothly upon her throat, a perfect match for her eyes.

Ah, her eyes! Within the glistening warm gray were flecks of distant stars he'd never noticed before; stars that twinkled and beckoned. Her skin smelled faintly sweet, of woman musk. He thought of kissing her and suddenly forgot to breathe. Somehow she was waiting, poised, watching him, and he knew then he could have her, knew how very much he wanted her. All of her—thighs, breasts. Her hips held in his hands, churning; lip pressed upon lip. Joined and surging . . .

"It's all right," she whispered, her eyes steady, very sure.

A touch, a gesture, a word, a kiss; anything he did would be good and right, so very necessary. His loins thundered a hard message: now! now!

"Mike, it's all right. I love you. . . . " She eased his hand to her breast. Somehow the robe came apart. The buttons of her pajama top became undone. Her flesh was smooth, warm and sweet, the rise of her breast soft and incredibly mellow, its hard little tip a discovery of pure joy.

"Mmmmike." She kept kissing him, arms clinging about his neck. "Mike."

"Yes."

"Oh. Mike. Now?"

"Yes."

"Please?"

"Yes." She seemed a feather in his arms as he bore her along the hallway.

"The last door. In there," she breathed into the hollow of his neck. "Oh, Mike. Honey . . ."

Murphy lay sprawled in the snow, cold and miserable and trying to catch his breath; no breathless man can shoot straight. Three feet behind him Jeeters was quietly cursing, a series of rich and round Anglo-Saxon oaths. Ten feet ahead lay the western end of the Jap trench.

Arriving at this point was no accident. He'd followed orders up to a point, crawling behind a low fold of land, unseen, unheard. From here, the line of fire would lie straight down the length of the trench, and two men could command the entire area. No Jap could escape. Simple, he thought. Nothing to it.

"This is close enough," he said softly to Jeeters, who nodded and flicked the safety off the BAR.

Jeeters was now the squad BAR man, replacing Jones. Jeeters was a good choice. He could play that BAR like a piano. Took an artist to do that. A BAR was heavy—twenty-two pounds, empty. It had a slow rate of fire and a man who knew his weapon and had a light touch could squeeze the rounds one at a time. That was Jeeters. And no man in the company could reload as fast.

There were perhaps twenty Japs in the forty-yard trench but Murphy had seen Japs ducking into and out of a hole dug horizontally into the mountain—-an underground compartment? The hole was at the far end of the trench and upslope a few feet. Above, a small smokestack jutted vertically from the mountain and a soft haze of blue smoke could hardly be seen through the snow.

One of the Japs was an officer, a colonel or general. He wore a sparkling fresh dress uniform with gold trimming and lots of bright medals. A dress uniform—*here?* He's for me, Murphy thought. His ass is mine.

His breath steaming in the air, Murphy laid a half-dozen grenades in the snow close at hand. Jeeters did the same. Together they placed spare ammo clips and magazines alongside.

"You ready?" Murphy saw Jeeters's short nod, jaw clenched. "On the count of three." He took a deep breath, picked up a grenade. "One." Downslope he could glimpse Dog Company—a row of round, half-egg helmets jutting up from the ravine.

"Two."

In the trench the Japs were keeping their heads low, only occasionally peeking down into the ravine below. Some were laughing, others standing quietly and waiting. All friggen armies were the same, thought Murphy.

"Three!" He pulled the pin and threw—a short lob just barely into the trench. Quickly another grenade, this one tossed a bit farther. Then a third. Jeeters had done the same; six grenades now in the trench or on the way before the first exploded. Then *bam! bam! bam!*—like firecrackers. Chaos in the trench, men screaming, falling, turning, not knowing where to fire. One grenade after another as fast as he could pull pins and throw. Then prone with the rifle, Jeeters beside him, smoke clearing from the trench. There—a few stunned, bewildered men staggering to their feet. Jeeters began firing slowly, calmly, one shot per man. Four rounds in all. Each man went down, lay still, and with no targets all fell quiet. Murphy stared into a trench where nothing but snowflakes now moved. They were white and cold and incredibly soft on his cheek.

From the underground compartment Japs came boiling into the trench. Jeeters began firing in short bursts, Murphy as fast as his rifle would fire. Japs fell, dropping their rifles, but others kept coming, stumbling and fumbling, peering this way and that for the source of gunfire. Someone shouted, pointing. Jeeters got him. Murphy quickly reloaded and kept firing, the rifle bucking in his hands and his mind filled only with the sure knowledge that bodies were piling up but still the Japs came, no sooner out of the lower compartment and in the trench, erect and seeking the enemy, than suddenly dead or wounded. Murphy saw no blood and heard no screams, merely small black holes in bulky clothing. In a way it was like watching a movie—a dramatic bang and a distant figure falls. It didn't seem real, no cries, no pain. Cold forgotten, snow ignored, Murphy felt nothing, concentrating only on hitting his targets.

Abruptly no more figures emerged like moles from the recess cut into the mountain. Except one. The last to emerge was the officer, glittering with gold epaulets and bright medals, armed only with a sheathed sword. He stood straddle-legged with hands on hips among his crumpled dead, staring directly at Murphy. Both Murphy and Jeeters, surprised, suddenly quit firing.

The wind howled and snow swirled. For a long moment the officer neither spoke nor moved. Then, commanding their full attention, his gaze never once leaving Murphy's, he placed one polished boot upon the humped buttocks of one of his fallen men and used him as a stepping-stone up and out of the trench. He seemed oblivious of cold, snow and all danger. He began striding toward them.

"Don't trust 'im, Sarge. He got a grenade?"

"Do you surrender?" called Murphy. "Then raise your hands."

No reply. The officer was calm, deliberate in his approach, his expression a total mask.

"Shit!" said Jeeters, his BAR now centered on the officer's chest.

"Raise your hands!"

For a split second Murphy thought the man understood, was obeying. But the hands moved not upward but to the sword at his side. At the same time a high battle cry burst from his lips, a fanatic glare from his eye. The sword was half unsheathed when Jeeters fired, all three rounds finding the left chest. Like a dropped stone the body fell, the sword skidding to a stop in the snow, its hazy blue steel stained a bright arterial red.

It took only a moment to summon Lieutenant Scott and the platoon. Two wounded Japs, unconscious, were taken prisoner. Those who were conscious had to be killed—armed, they would have it no other way.

Murphy could only stare at the Jap officer. By every measure he had ever known the stupid sonuvabitch had committed suicide.

Sergeant Okasaki was pulling a blanket over the still face of a corpse—a thorax case, Tomi recalled; multiple penetrating wounds of the right thorax, right leg and both feet. The patient had been doing well, though yesterday Tomi had been unable to check. If anything had gone wrong, Hirose would be responsible. "Sergeant, what was the cause of death?"

"Honored sir," Okasaki murmured with a warning glance, "may I speak to you of this in private?"

Tomi gestured toward the tent entrance, an area too cold and windy for patient comfort. Okasaki ordered the corpse removed before joining him. Meanwhile Tomi noted the weather—the wind blowing hard, as usual, but now carrying large flakes of snow. From the look of a sky filled by low dark clouds, snow would fall most of the day with only an occasional pause. But at least the clouds and snow kept the planes away.

"Honored Sergeant Okasaki." He bowed. "The cause of death?"

"Honored Dr. Nakamura." Okasaki bowed a bit lower than Tomi had. "I regret to inform you that the patient in question committed *seppuku* by slashing his wrist with a bayonet."

Tomi allowed no reaction to touch his face. Inwardly he felt aghast. A suicide! A man who surely would have recovered, now a soul eternally damned to hell. "Do any of the other patients know?"

"I can't be positive. But if only one or two know, then all will know. These matters cannot be kept secret."

"Of course. There was no warning?"

"None. The patient lay quietly at breakfast time. He refused rice and asked only for tea. But—we had no more tea."

Tomi understood. It was he, last night, who had consumed the last of the tea, without knowing. Okasaki had seen to that. Yet he now felt a twinge of shame. "Then apparently the patient had planned—"

"Apparently. But one as busy as I can never anticipate such matters."

"No one blames you," he said quickly. "I least of all. I suggest, however, that we search the ward for weapons. Confiscate them without exception." He did not dare look at Michael.

"At once, honored sir. But you are aware that this is the third instance? Last night two others led the way. They are included in the morning report under Unspecified Deaths."

"I see." All this was his own fault, he told himself. If he had given the matter a second thought he would have known, would have seen—he *should* have seen. But who had time to think? That was part of the trouble, so short of manpower that no one had time for more than essentials. "I will discuss this matter with Dr. Hirose."

"What matter?" said Hirose's voice, and Tomi turned to find

the man approaching, his cheeks puffy and eyes red, brushing snow from the shoulders of his heavy coat. He must have ears like a cat, Tomi thought. He omitted his usual "Good morning" and bow.

"Three suicides among the patients," he said as curtly as possible. "Sergeant Okasaki can verify them all."

"So it's started, has it? Odd it should take so long. Is there any hot tea?"

"You anticipated?" asked Tomi, finding this concept incredible. "Then why didn't you have the weapons removed?"

"Very simple. The battle will soon be finished. At the end, all of us are doomed to die. So what difference does it make if a few patients remove themselves a few days early? What we should do is distribute bayonets to everyone, not take them away. Then you and I and the wardmen wouldn't have to work so hard. Or so long."

"But we are physicians, surgeons!" Tomi cried. "As long as life exists, our sworn duty is to—"

"Our duty is to ourselves." He gave Tomi a glance of pure contempt. "Besides, I'm tired of all these idealistic banalities. Sergeant, don't you agree?"

His face expressionless, Okasaki gazed at Hirose, his voice stiff: "I cannot accept death merely for the sake of death, as you seem to do. In battle one fights and lives, or fights and accepts the consequences. But *seppuku* is a last resort for a brave man, not a first resort for a coward."

"Well said," murmured Hirose. "For a fool you use words well. Now bring me some hot tea."

"There is no tea." The omission of "honored sir" was more than evident; it weighed heavily on Tomi's ear. Hirose seemed not to notice.

"Hot rice, then."

"There is no rice. There is no coal."

Hirose eyed Okasaki a long moment. "Sergeant, you will correct your tone of voice and your attitude or we will also have no sergeant." With a chilly glance at Tomi he swept into the tent, ignored patients and wardmen alike, and headed toward the locked cabinet that held the sake.

Okasaki sighed. "Honored sir, I anticipate a long and difficult day."

"Honored Sergeant, as always, you are correct. This day will stretch far into the night."

Discouraged, Tomi continued making the rounds. At the foot of Umeda's litter he tried to avoid looking at Michael Andrews, coughing again in the adjacent space. Otherwise Michael might make some gesture, or he himself might inadvertently flash some secret message with his eye, and Umeda would see and possibly begin to wonder. Right now no one should begin wondering about the burn case. The secret was too fragile.

He found Umeda watching him, eyes dark and unfathomable. "Good morning, how is your leg?"

"It is there, I suppose, what's left of it." He spoke simply, as if conversation wasn't worth the effort.

"Is there pain at all?"

"No, not if I lie quietly, though sometimes it feels as though my foot hurts. Tell me, do you plan now to chop me up bit by bit? Or are you satisfied with this much practice?"

"Oh, come now, Umeda! Your leg was diseased and I saved your knee. Isn't that encouraging? Think of how much easier walking will be."

"If I ever walk again it will only be to the front, on crutches. None of us here has cause for great joy."

"How about small joys then? Your blood pressure is fine. The stump appears clean and healthy. You seem in fine condition, except your eyes are bloodshot and you are tired." He paused. Across the tent Lieutenant Hirose was standing openly before the assembly and sucking his bottle of sake.

Tomi dropped the chart and headed toward Hirose, a move duplicated across the room by Sergeant Okasaki, both converging on their superior officer. Hirose observed them, his face twisted in a sardonic grin. Only the sound of the wind broke the stillness; various patients sat up to watch and listen.

"Honored Lieutenant Hirose," Tomi said as Okasaki joined him, "will you accompany me to the operating tent? We must speak together in private."

"No, I'm staying here. Say whatever you want to say, if you think you must."

"I do not wish to embarrass you in front of—"

"Then say nothing and go away." His face was dark, ugly, resentful.

Tomi shrugged and glanced at Okasaki, who nodded. "Honored sir, I speak of a personal habit. Your consumption of sake while on duty must stop at once. It cannot be tolerated further. I am prepared to appeal to the highest authority."

"Go ahead," muttered Hirose. "What can they do, send me home in disgrace?"

"Your consumption of sake while on duty is unprofessional, ungentlemanly, something one doesn't expect of a Japanese officer."

Hirose laughed. "Did you know that Yamamoto's hospital below Umanose is full, running over, can't take another patient? So from now on we'll get them all."

"We can handle them much better if you will cease drinking sake on duty. Otherwise, men who have a chance to live will die."

"The front line is being moved, too, you know that? Retreating! That's because the Americans built an artillery position on a hill so close—"

"The issue here is your drinking on duty. At the moment nothing else matters. I don't want to report—"

"Report, damn you! Report and have it done and don't bother me any more with your childish moralizing. And you, too, Sergeant. Wipe that damned sneer off your face."

"Honored sir," Okasaki said in a calm, deliberate manner, "do you wish these patients and headquarters to hear of your shame in China? I will not hesitate to report the facts, if that's what is necessary."

"Ch—China?" whispered Hirose. "How did you learn of that?"

"You have three choices: duty, exposure or *seppuku*. I don't care which you choose."

"Ah, Sergeant! Dr. Nakamura!" His sudden half-smile was more like a sick grimace. "I wish to explain my position. May we discuss this matter elsewhere, in complete privacy? The barracks, perhaps?"

Okasaki led the way down the ramp and into the ravine. The snow had quit and the clouds thinned. From the east a broad patch of pale blue sky was approaching, a harbinger of air raid and blood and a long night of operating. What they needed was more snow and sleet and rain and fog, Tomi thought. And a few miracles.

Inside the barracks door, Hirose tried to smile, his face flushed with embarrassment. "Ah, this matter of China. Exactly what did you hear? Something amusing?"

"I was there," said Okasaki. "I saw you unconscious and attended you. I know everything that happened to you and Captain Yamamoto. So does the honored Dr. Nakamura. This information we will use if—"

"Listen!" Hirose's face now twisted with rage. "Damn you, do you know what torture is like? The Chinese are ingenious—nothing crude, you understand. Just a few needles, little pinpoints of fire, a razor, all exquisitely used in the most tender parts of the human anatomy. Given with a smile and sweet request. I tried to be strong, brave, to bear pain as a true Samurai should, to sink into myself and not let the pain find me. But it was not to be. One is helpless. They slice off a tiny bit here and insert a needle just so there, and the flame—oh, the flame!"

"I understand," Okasaki murmured. "I saw the wounds."

"Then you do understand! At least you share what I felt, the agony, the suffering—"

"I understand but do not sympathize. You allowed yourself to be taken, like a dog seized for the cooking pot."

"And I've been impotent ever since! Can you understand that? You have been so tortured? Then who are you to stand in judgment of me?"

"We do not judge you," Tomi insisted. "We merely demand that you drink no sake while on duty. Is this asking too much?"

"You are judging. I see it in your eyes."

"No sake, honored sir," Okasaki said. "It's that simple."

"All right, no sake. Damn you! Now are you satisfied?"

Tomi hesitated. The victory, so long resisted, had been far too easy. Instinctively he knew Hirose could not be trusted. Yet, no other course came to mind. He found himself staring at Hirose's hands, the long, smooth, gentle hands of a surgeon or fine artist.

"One more question, honored sir," said Okasaki, his eyes studying Hirose. "Why did you never commit *seppuku?*"

"Why should I? Does anyone really want to die? I don't want to die. I shouldn't be forced to die—it's wrong! In fact, I'm afraid to die. Is that honest enough for you?"

Okasaki turned suddenly and walked from the barracks. In silence Tomi gazed at Hirose, wondering what evasion the man had in mind. Another mystery. Then he, too, left, feeling soiled and not a bit proud of what he'd done to Hirose in the name of the patients.

May 25. Naval gun firing, aerial bombardment, trench warfare, the worst is yet to come. The enemy is constructing their positions. Battalion commander died. At Umanose they cannot fully accomodate all the patients. It has been said that at Massacre Bay District, the road coming to Sector Unit Headquarters is isolated. Am suffering from diarrhea and feel dizzy.

MAY 26, 1943

S o you were right, Tomi," Michael Andrews said. "I have to get better equipped." His voice grated through a sore throat in the dark, here out of the wind in the lee of the barracks. The time was shortly past midnight. In the half-light he spoke quietly. His face appeared drawn, haggard. His spirit had not flagged, but his present lack of physical strength was apparent, Tomi thought. Such natural vitality demanded more than a mere cup of rice per day. Michael should have cottage cheese and lots of fresh fish, raw vegetables and all the sweet fruits—such futile thoughts.

It helped not at all to know that Michael Andrews also suffered from diarrhea, a not uncommon occurrence when proper sanitation practices were not strictly observed. Ordinarily there would be no problem, as Tomi knew well, for the Japanese are by tradition and practice meticulously clean. But too many patients, too many tasks, too few wardmen and too few hours in a day— that's when human errors multiplied.

For Michael Andrews diarrhea was particularly dangerous, not only for the general dehydration of his body and consequent weakness, but because he must make frequent trips to the latrine. Exposed white flanks, if seen by any Japanese, would at once raise the alarm and trigger Michael's death. And his own, as well, Tomi thought wryly. Hence the liberal dosage of phenobarbital, the most potent weapon of its kind in Tomi's limited arsenal.

"I'll need wool stockings, wool underwear, good watertight boots, warm clothing, heavy overcoats and maybe raincoats."

How dangerous to gather all that! If anyone should see, become suspicious—

"Also a compass and a map. And food, Tomi. I'll need lots of food."

There was no retreat. He must go forward. No escape from death or dishonor. He wished he could understand thoroughly what forces had brought him to this state. Perhaps it had worked like steps on a ladder. The first step had been preserving the life of Michael Andrews, the second the decision to hide him and protect him from the firing squad. Another step involved getting acquainted, becoming friends. Somewhere in the process, perhaps only last night, it became quite apparent that maintaining a status quo, with Michael ever on the razor's edge of discovery, was not enough. To ensure his life and safety, Michael must escape. To escape, he needed certain basic equipment. For that he turned now to Tomi. Thus Dr. Tomi Nakamura, a devoted and patriotic Japanese gentleman, was now plotting to help in the escape of an enemy of his country. Yet, he thought, what else can a man of God do? One duty demanded a given course of action; another duty required the opposite.

"I promise that you will be properly equipped. It will take two days at least. Then if you are sufficiently strong, it becomes a matter of timing."

"You give the word. We'll also need rifles."

"No rifles. That in all conscience I cannot do."

"But we have to have rifles. Don't you see that?"

"You must do without. I insist! I will not arm you for killing my own people. You wouldn't kill, would you?"

"Tomi, listen—"

"Is it truly necessary to take Private First-Class Jones? In his condition, on crutches, he can only delay you. Speed will be a vital factor."

"We'll go together. I won't leave him behind. That big sergeant of yours will kill him."

"Okasaki?" On that point perhaps Michael was right.

"Or that little snippy guy next to me. I don't trust him."

"Umeda? Perhaps."

"So we go together, okay? Now wrap me up; it's time I got back."

Quietly reentering the near pitch-dark of the tent, Michael paused at one side of the aisle. In the faint light of a single candle near the far wall the duty radioman sat asleep, his head resting on the hard surface of the radio table. No Hardnose present, no one else stirring and that was good. The snores and muted whistles and assorted small pops and bubblings of sleeping men were the only sounds. Was anyone at all awake, perhaps lying awake and alert in the dark? Impossible to say.

A lot would depend on Jones. The guy was no dummy. He'd picked up the signals and read them right. From across the tent Michael had nodded or shaken his head a bit each time Jones spoke to Tomi or Umeda, an even bet that eventually Jones would detect the subtle movements of the white mask and dark glasses. When the idea had entered Jones's mind was hard to say. But in time Jones began gazing at him, frowning, curious and suspicious. Then came Jones's quiet little V-sign with two fingers, the Churchill V, followed by Michael's nod and a slow stretch of arms into another V. Jones's sudden smirk said it all; he knew a friend was near at hand.

Now, given this golden opportunity, Michael eased along the aisle to the foot of Jones's litter. Was he asleep? Making contact this time of night was dangerous, for Jones by his own admission feared an attack in the dark. A mere touch on any part of his body could result in an explosion of shouting and violence that Michael didn't even want to think about. A wrong sound might do the same thing. So how—

"Hmmm?"

It was a soft croon almost lost amid the chorus of snores.

"Hst!"

"Hmmm."

"Hst!"

A long leg moved a fraction. The shadows shifted. A sighing whisper: "Aw *riii*ght."

He edged forward to kneel near Jones's head, his voice low and guarded. "Jones? My name's Mike."

"How I know that? You the guy all bandage up? Where you from?"

"California. I have a plan. If we stay here, they'll kill us. Soon! We have to escape, okay?"

"You're half smart. How long it take you to think of that?"

"I have a gun. I'm assembling supplies—no questions! I know a little cave where we'll be safe, at least for a while. You'll need crutches. Practice all you can. When I go, you go with me." No more time. A pat on Jones's shoulder and Michael eased away to his own litter. Everything had gone just fine; a step in the right direction.

"Honored Dr. Nakamura," Okasaki said, holding forth an ivory-handled pistol, "in my search for firearms and bayonets hidden among the patients, I found this handgun within the blankets of the burn case. This weapon was stolen a few days ago from an officer-patient, adjacent to the burn case, who since has died."

"Is this the same weapon? You are positive?"

"It fits the description exactly."

"Then are you implying that the burn case is a common thief?"

"Honored sir, at face value the evidence suggests he is."

"Thank you, Sergeant Okasaki, for bringing the matter to my attention." Reluctantly he accepted the weapon, wondering who else knew of the matter. "I shall investigate at once."

It sure was odd, Swensen thought. Everybody in the squad had borrowed Sarge's binoculars and seen the litters down there and the guys in white smocks. Collectively the squad figured those two little tents for a Jap aid station. There could hardly be any doubt. So Sarge had passed the word upstairs—Swensen had heard him do it. Surely Scott had told battalion and battalion told division and division told the Navy and Air Force. But it somehow made no difference; the shells and bombs kept falling in the lower ravine anyway.

Swensen found it frustrating to report something really important like that and have it all ignored. Somebody should do something. Made you wonder about things and people, really wonder.

These days nothing seemed to go right. A half-hour ago in the rain he had relieved Baker at the foxhole. Climbing out from under the half-shelter, all soaking wet, Baker had said to keep a good eye on "those two tents down there—a guy, looks like a big-ass, one-legged Negro. Maybe it's Jones! He's hobbling around on a crutch. Let's try to confirm it before we pass the word."

Baker was a corporal and he should know best. Swensen had accepted the binoculars and crawled into the hole, learning immediately why Baker had gotten wet. The half-shelter was useless: the rain came pelting directly into his face. The next two hours would be cold, wet and endless. Jones! he thought.

Quickly he'd set out grenades and spare ammo clips on a little earthen shelf, eyed the snow and black earth of the terrain before him for skulking Japs, then focused the binoculars on the ravine below.

At least he'd tried to. The rain, however, kept blurring the glass. He'd had to remove both gloves, unbutton his heavy jacket and all else beneath, fumble for a handkerchief, already soiled, button again and wipe the glass, don the gloves over his now-chilled hands and again peer down on the tents. Immediately the glass was wet, blurred and useless.

Worst of all, the handkerchief got wet, too, so it seemed no use. All he could do was wait for the rain to quit or change direction before trying again.

Jones? One leg? Godamighty! To be a cripple . . .

A not-too-distant but muted coughing broke out to the rear. He recognized the sound. Mortars. American, thank God, lobbing shells down into Chichagof Harbor. He would like to watch the results, but the rain . . .

Dammit, he thought. Like always, nothing ever went right.

Car-*ruumph!* Car-*ruumph!* Car-*ruumph!*

The American mortar shells were hitting closer now, on the slopes of Hokuchin Yama and on the ridge directly above the hospital. Tomi tried to ignore them but failed. American infantrymen couldn't be seen as yet, not even with binoculars, but according to all he'd heard it could only be a question of time.

Eying the ward, he saw all was now as normal as possible. Eighty-three patients lay shoulder to shoulder in an area designed for no more than forty. By 1040 hours all except Michael had been fed, bathed—or given wet cloths to bathe themselves— rebandaged if necessary, given appropriate medications and generally made comfortable. The latest suicides and other dead had been removed and at the moment no operations were pending. Best of all, Hirose was sober, a big help. Across the tent he was laughing and talking amiably with a patient. Tomi frowned, for this was new and strange behavior he hadn't had time to assess. Okasaki had been instructing a wardman. Now he rose and began approaching Tomi. Waiting, Tomi watched the black American, Jones, struggling near the tent entrance with a too-small pair of crutches. Jones's expression flickered from annoyance to determination and back again. After twenty minutes he was tiring, proof that he lacked the strength and physical stamina to flee with Michael. Tomi would give him five minutes more.

Car-RUUMPH! Car-RUUMPH! Car-RUUMPH!

Okasaki bowed and thrust his uninjured hand into a pocket of his white smock. "Honored sir, I have this for you." He pulled forth a battered New Testament, the one Tomi had loaned to Hayasaka.

"If this book had been in his breast pocket, where he carried it, it would have been badly damaged but might have saved his life. I found it in his hands. He had been reading, and, I'm told, praying." His tone carried a strong flavor of disapproval. He laid the book in Tomi's hand, bowed again and moved with straight shoulders along the crowded aisle, leaving Tomi aghast and torn over these new details of Hayasaka's death.

He stood listening to the occasional car-*ruumph!* of American shells—shells fired by American ships that should have been attacked by Japanese planes.

Hirose had worked his way through the litters and now stood only a few feet away. "A delightful day," he said with a smile. He lounged against the square black bulk of the radiophone, mounted on its table. The shelling on the slope above had no visible effect on him. "Too bad there's no more tea. I would really enjoy a bowl of tea."

His pupils, Tomi saw with a shock, had narrowed to mere pinpoints of hard light. "We would all enjoy tea," he murmured. Indeed, he missed the morning tea very much, for nothing of late had given him as much simple pleasure as a hot, aromatic bowl of tea. Another big void, he told himself. The pattern of life was now becoming one void after another. "Honored sir, how long have you been using morphine?"

Hirose gave an idle wave of the hand. "Have you been outside the tent this morning? First there was rain and then fog. I think the fog is lifting. At least some of the signs are there. Another thing. Do you suppose we could send someone fishing? I'd truly enjoy some fresh fish."

Car-*ruumph!* Car-*ruumph!*

Tomi dismissed the proposition as too impractical to consider. "Honored sir, may I draw your attention to our lack of fuel? The scraps of wood we gather in the old village are inadequate for—"

"We could send a patient or two down the beach, rig a pole for each, a line and a few safety pins for hooks . . ."

"Honored sir? Our problems of sterilizing our operating equipment are growing beyond—"

Car-*ruumph!* Car-*ruumph!* Car-*ruumph!*

"Of course. See to it, won't you, Dr. Nakamura?" Hirose began strolling along the crowded aisle, pausing here and there to smile and bow to patients. Tomi watched him go, feeling an added burden of responsibility he had never felt before.

One immediate duty was to release all walking wounded for service at the front, always a difficult task for Tomi. He had no wish to say who should go and fight—and die—and who should stay and rest. He wanted all to stay, heal properly and grow strong, but the policy of the High Command, implemented by the esteemed Garrison Commander Colonel Shima, directed by the worthy Dr. Yamamoto and dictated by military necessity, all said no, someone must select.

The process of selection, however, was unexplained. Could he remove a boy's arm, numb his pain and send him back while his stump was still oozing blood? How barbarous! A delay of three or four days seemed the minimum.

Then there remained the question of strength. Every patient in the ward had been weakened by loss of blood. It was to Tomi a ridiculous and callous waste of human life to send a weakened man up the slippery, rocky, steep mountainside and forward to the front line trench holes, there to gasp in the cold air for breath, perhaps fall asleep from sheer exhaustion, or peer out upon an advancing enemy and realize he had no strength left—no power to fire rifle or machine gun, no power to rise and hurl grenades, no power to thrust himself from trench hole to trench hole. Too weak to fight, too weak to run. There remained only the final choice of surrender or *seppuku*, and nothing of benefit to anyone had been gained by his death.

The term "walking wounded" itself needed clarification. For even a blind man could walk.

Car-*ruumph!* Car-*ruumph!*

Reinforcements! Where in the name of God were the promised reinforcements? Where was the vaunted Japanese air arm? Why couldn't they parachute desperately needed supplies?

On second thought he knew only too well. Of course all use of parachutes had been discouraged by the Japanese High Command. No Japanese airman who considered himself manly, truly brave, would allow a parachute in his plane. After all, war and flying was a life-or-death risk. Nothing in between. Only cowards thought of parachutes. So the parachute industry in Japan had never really developed.

Car-*ruumph!* Car-*ruumph!*

Brooding, Tomi watched as each of twenty-three patients listened to Sergeant Okasaki. Each rose, his face stoic, dressed and came to stand before Tomi. Each bowed low, murmuring "Thank you, Dr. Nakamura," and walked from the tent. As the last of them left, he found the radio guard watching him.

"Don't stare at me!" he shouted. "Mind your own business! Why don't you do your work?"

Instantly he regretted his outburst. "*Gomen nasai,*" he said, bowing. "I am sorry."

Calming himself, he saw that Jones, returning to his litter, had paused near Michael's feet and was grinning now to everyone in the ward tent. "Poker, anybody? Blackjack? I'm a gamblin' man. I'm-glad-you-came; I'll-play-your-game. I'm ready. Let's go!"

It was apparent to Tomi—and he hoped to no one else—that Jones, while addressing the crowd, spoke only to Michael. Michael gave no response other than a quick and almost imperceptible nod. And he coughed; Tomi frowned. The two men had made initial contact and nothing good could come out of that.

"Private First-Class Jones, please be silent and return to your litter. Men are sleeping." Jones ignored him.

"I'll play any game you want, any time. I'm ready."

"Jones! Be silent!"

Now Jones stared down on Umeda. Neither spoke. They merely gazed long and soberly at each other. Then Jones turned, fighting the crutches, and hobbled across the tent between the litters. And every eye in the room, unreadable, watched his progress, marking his every move.

"An amusing fellow," Hirose said, nearing Tomi's elbow. "Is he a professional clown? What did he say?"

Tomi explained: the black American was bored, wanted to play card games, had talked sheer nonsense, as Americans were prone to do. Nothing of any importance.

"How very strange."

Then Michael coughed, a dry tortured hacking that racked his shoulders. Definitely bronchitis, thought Tomi. And what was the man's temperature now? He needed large dosages of vitamins A and D, a steam inhalant—

"When did your burn case return?" asked Hirose. "He now has complications. He is progressing well otherwise?"

"Quite well. He remains weak, however, from loss of blood. Then exposure to the elements, and diarrhea—"

"Let us examine him." In an instant Hirose was edging through the litters toward Michael.

"I hardly think that is necessary! Dr. Hirose?" Hirose seemed deaf, in fact was already there, beaming down like a little brown Santa Claus on the white mask.

"Aaah, and how are we today? Better? I am Dr. Hirose, and I wish to remove your bandages."

"There is an amputation case in the operating tent that should interest you," Tomi said quickly. "A splintered femur—"

Hirose reached and Michael abruptly thrust Hirose's hand away—not a gesture that might be considered accidental. It was deliberate, forceful, an act of cold rejection. No Japanese would ever be so direct. Hirose gasped. "Did you see that? Nakamura, he—he pushed! No one has ever . . . What manner of man is this?"

The dark goggles turned from one man to the other.

"Honored sir, this officer is not responsible, a result of too many bombs and too many shells exploding nearby. My instructions—"

"Shellshock, you say? Battle fatigue? Nonsense! No Japanese—"

Abruptly the air raid siren began clattering, a horrible, nerve-racking sound he would never get used to. Thank God! thought Tomi. Instantly he regretted the thought, for this fortunate respite granted to Michael would cost many Japanese lives. Tonight he must pray for forgiveness.

She wrote that she wasn't pregnant—he was almost sorry she wasn't. She was still seeing Jim, now an M.D. at Oakland Naval

Hospital. He resented that, resented her mother pushing Phyllis and Jim together. Especially without him there to protect his future, his rights, his Phyllis. She had given him her love and body. Forever. Hadn't she? Hadn't she?

She wouldn't forget him, ignore him, drift away. Or would she? Oh, God . . .

The planes were coming in low, just under the overcast that barely cleared the tops of the mountains: and slow, arrogantly so, the pilots apparently positive they would draw no return fire. The bomb-bay doors were open. The planes droned in steady, careful fashion, with all the grace of bulldozers, Murphy thought. Mitchell bombers, an even dozen from Amchitka. Even from this distance the sheen of wet propellors reflected soft, dainty, rainbow circles of light.

"I betcha the smokes out of my next K-rats they score a hit on those two Jap tents," Swensen said, happy to be with Sarge. "They can't miss."

"You're on. The Air Force can miss if anybody can. It's a special skill." He hunkered down better to escape the bite of the wind.

Already the first long string of bombs was dropping from the lead plane. They fell silently, lazily. Down and down they came, closer . . . Then a sudden trail of bursts, one after another, that ran zipperlike across the flat, a straight line of a score of machine-gun-quick explosions, all in just one short half-mile.

Interesting, thought Murphy. Like something you saw in a newsreel back home—the Army testing some new wonder weapon—that sort of thing. But not really dramatic, not these painless, harmless-looking spurts of earth. It was just too remote to be dramatic. The sounds, carried away by the sweep of the wind, could hardly be heard. He found himself yawning.

"Shit," murmured Swensen. He watched the second, third and fourth string of bombs. "The Air Force bombs like the fucken Navy."

Murphy waited. More planes, more bombs. A warehouse crumpled. A tent high in the ravine began burning; the two below remained unscathed. "Maybe if they'd try to miss they'd get a hit. Think so?"

"Wanna double the bet? I got plenty of cigarettes."

"Double's okay. Bennett won't mind giving me his."

It was fascinating how close these bursts of earth came to the tents, all around the area, without touching. Meanwhile it was cold, just squatting. Boring, too. By the time the ninth, tenth and eleventh planes had unloaded and wheeled away, cocked on the wind like huge hawks, Swensen said: "It's no use. I guess I just lost a half a day's supply of butts."

"Have one of mine," Murphy said. But Swensen had turned away, not bothering to watch the twelfth plane. Its bombs were already falling.

CAR-*RUUMPH!* CAR-*RUUMPH!*

A finger in each ear closed out much of the mind-splitting roar, yet the earth shuddered with each explosion, the rank smell of gunpowder joined with the wind and Tomi found his fists clenched, jaw held tight and body trembling. He couldn't help it, couldn't stop the groan and half-sob locked behind his teeth. He caught one glimpse of Okasaki sitting erect on the floor of the trench, his legs folded together in the Zen position, lost to all, with eyes fixed blankly on the wall before him; another of Hirose cringing against the black oozing wall of the trench, his puny cries lost in the thunder of bombs. Again the storm struck—*wham! Wham! Wham!* He felt the earth leaping beneath him and smashing him asprawl in the mud.

This was no way for a man to die, he knew. Not crouching in a wet hole, cringing like a trapped animal. Not tossed in the air and shredded to bits, his various parts and blood mingled with mud and rocks and frozen grass, all of him scattered and buried deep without honor and his bones never found. No, only a man full of years and wisdom should know death, a man lying warm and comforted in his own bed, surrounded by family and honored above all, filled and sustained by faith in Jesus and a love of God in his heart.

He found his breath strangely whipped from his lungs, and he gasped for air. The sky was dark and raining great clods of earth, pebbles, snow, wisps of tundra and slivers of wood. The trench wall slowly collapsed with a long sigh and half buried his legs. The sounds of bombs were distant now, he knew, though he could hear nothing. The earth still leaped and danced and kept smashing his chin. His face ached, not from clenching his jaw but from the force of a blow. He felt his cheek and looked dully at fresh blood smeared the length of his hand.

He'd been hit. The knowledge crept slowly into his mind. How badly? Exactly where? Tentatively he touched himself but found no wound, felt no stabbing pain, could move every muscle if he tried, could seize quick lungfuls of sweet precious air, hear and see—

He gazed about him, left, right, around and down. There! On the floor of the trench he found the missile. A human hand. A hand with long artistic fingers, no calluses. A complete hand and wrist. He saw the ulna and radius jutting forth like flagpoles. Strands of tendons, nerves and small vessels. Very little blood. He gazed at it, uncomprehending, knowing only this: the hand was not his own.

He tried to rise but could only claw without result at soft mud. The collapsed trench weighed on his legs. He half rolled, freed himself and sat up, sucking air. He felt empty, drained, wanting to hear nothing more, smell nothing more, feel nothing more. Okasaki lay beside him, barely conscious but also in the need of air, beginning to come around. Weakly he slapped the man's face. "You all right?" He turned for help and found, a meter away, slumped against the trench wall, Hirose, his face contorted in a soundless cry and his eyes locked on the limp shreds of flesh where hand and wrist had once been attached. From the midst of splintered bone, scarlet blood spurted in regular beats.

Tourniquet, thought Tomi vaguely. Hirose should apply a tourniquet. Hirose should quit screaming. Hirose should start thinking. Hirose should do something. Hirose should—

He forced his legs beneath him, began crawling that long

distance of one full meter. Arms not coordinated with legs. Stop! Try again. With an effort, this leg. Then the other. Fine! He thrust his arms forward. Good! Again. He peered up and found he was there. He saw his hand reaching, with strength that surprised him, and clamping the brachial artery at the elbow. His thumb trembled with the effort, but the blood flow no longer pulsed; it merely oozed. Staring into Hirose's fear-crazed eyes, he wondered how long before his thumb grew tired.

Tourniquet. He tried to say the word but nothing emerged. The task of making wrapping motions with his free hand—no, he hadn't the strength or will. To communicate, that was the problem. It overwhelmed him. He turned his head to peer at Okasaki, pleading with his eyes. Come. Help.

Mud stained the man's face. Okasaki looked old, very old. Yet he nodded yes, pushed his wet, muddy length along the trench and with an effort began unwrapping his puttee from one leg. Ideal, thought Tomi. Why didn't I think of that?

"Put it back!" screamed Hirose suddenly, his gaze finding the hand a full meter away. "It's mine! Sew it back!"

The words meant little to Tomi. Okasaki handed him the puttee, a long, narrow strip of brown wool; his thumb replaced Tomi's on the brachial artery. Slowly Tomi fashioned a tourniquet, slipped it high over the jagged stump and tightened it down with a bayonet sheath. Just so, the lower arm was becoming pale and yellowish, the pulse below the elbow soon gone. There—the immediate danger had passed. He would operate later. Without great concern he watched Okasaki search for the medical bag, find it and begin a saline IV. No morphine, no, despite Hirose's frantic pleas. Already he'd had enough.

Without thought or energy he sat beside Hirose, staring across the trench at Okasaki. Neither spoke. Gradually he came to realize that the bombers had gone but Lightnings were strafing. He could hear their engines, a strange muted sound that seemed a million meters away, though their tracers came close. Did it matter? An excited superior private Tomi had never seen before cried that far up the valley a tent was burning, that Misumi

Barracks had blown up. Tomi didn't care. His head throbbed with every beat of his heart. His legs ached, shoulders were sore. Tired, so tired. No energy or interest remained, and his eyelids kept drooping. Without resisting he let them close, let the sweet cool dark close in and find him.

He found himself suddenly blinking at the slime of the trench wall. Okasaki was gone, Hirose gone. They would need him. He rose at once and climbed from the trench and hurried up the ramp to the operating tent.

In the yellow lantern light Okasaki was debriding and cleansing mud from the remnant of Hirose's arm. Hirose lay unresponding, withdrawn, his gaze blank and fixed on the lantern overhead.

"Honored sir," Okasaki breathed, "I welcome your presence. The honored lieutenant needs attention and I haven't the skill—"

"You have done well." He bent to peer at the arm. Nothing unusual here. "We shall tie off the vessels and fashion this section for a flap—"

He caught himself thinking, at least Hirose is no longer a threat to Michael. But that idea was bad, almost a sin—to rejoice because a man had lost a hand. Tonight he would have much to be forgiven for.

The operation went well and quickly. He lost himself in his work. Other patients arrived and Hirose was set aside in the recovery area, his eyes wide and blank. Only the regular rise and fall of his chest proved that he lived.

In late afternoon Tomi finished the last operation, a simple jaw fracture caused by a man being tossed into the air. Emerging from the operating tent, he paused with Okasaki and listened to strange voices on the wind. At headquarters a group of men were singing!

"Why?" he asked. "What song is that?"

"One I do not wish to hear," Okasaki said in a low tone. "It tells me that our esteemed Garrison Commander Colonel Shima has read the Imperial Edict to his officers and staff. Through him the Emperor speaks. The final attack—*banzai!* Now we shall each die in battle, firing our guns until no more bullets remain, wielding bayonets until they are torn from our grasp, grappling with clawing hands until we are dismembered, kicking, too, until our feet are chopped away. Then with strong teeth we shall bite the enemy's throat until he kills us."

"A dismal prospect."

Okasaki shrugged. "Life, too, is dismal. However, now more than ever we are committed to die gloriously in battle for the Emperor. That is well. It is better to die fighting than commit *seppuku*."

"But the song—"

"One of dedication to the Emperor. It is part of the formal ceremony."

"We are committed to die," breathed Tomi, gazing down on the floor of the ravine toward headquarters. The Imperial Edict, an official death notice, had come from that direction.

So would the Americans.

May 26. By naval gun firing it felt like Misumi barracks blew up and things shook up tremendously. Consciousness became vague. One tent burned down by a hit from incendiary bombs. Strafing planes hit the next room. Two hits from a 50 caliber shell; one stopped in the ceiling and one penetrated. My room looks like an awful mess from the sand and pebbles that come down from the roof. Hirose, first lieutenant of the medical corps, is also wounded. There was the ceremony of granting of Imperial Edict. The last line of Umanose was broken through. No hope of reinforcements.

MAY 27, 1943

By 0600 the attack had covered at least a quarter-mile with only occasional firing, mostly on the lower slopes. Then the mountain abruptly burst with Jap fire—mortars, MG's, rifles and grenades, everything the Japs could bring to bear. That first savage volume of fire dropped several men—six, eight. Murphy, diving for cover, couldn't be sure. He knew that Young gave a startled "Oh!," dropped his rifle, crumpled and slid ten yards down the slope. He left a broad crimson trail in the snow.

Prone in mud and ice, his heart like lead in his chest, Murphy peered up at a perpendicular outcropping of black rock rising from the steep slope. Under it and all across the upper incline were Jap MG's and a series of foxholes—lots of them, each topped by a half-dome of Jap helmet. The round of blobs kept popping into view, firing and disappearing, impossible to aim at and hit.

From where he lay Murphy could see no way to scale that vertical wall and drop grenades from above. Artillery might help, but artillery couldn't bear on this position. Friendly troops were too close—that ruled out an air strike. One of the new flamethrowers could do the job but the division wasn't yet supplied. Meanwhile the attack had bogged down and Young was dead. Young—oh, God! No doubt of that. Too much bright red blood . . .

He thought about Young—a normal, everyday kind of kid, fine and decent. Young had owned a quick mind, a shy and sensitive nature and a smile to melt some little girl's heart. It hurt—all that humanity and promise suddenly and brutally gone.

The body lay spread-eagled on the snow, open eyes gazing in mild surprise at the overcast, arms outflung as if in greeting some heavenly host. Now and then an arm or leg twitched, or the torso bounced, as Jap bullets still struck. Who would die next—Swensen? Not Swensen! Murphy turned again to peer at the heights, a sense of cold detachment settling over his mind. He knew what he must do, saw it all with a certainty as cold and clear and pure as the ice glinting beneath his hand.

Without further thought he rose to his feet in full view of Jap and American alike. A momentary hush fell across the slope. Necks craned and eyes stared as Murphy began trudging methodically upward. Behind him the air began cracking with the sounds of the squad's covering fire, trying, he knew, to help keep the Japs' heads down.

Bullets from both sides were whistling about like superangry bees. He ignored them, his mind starkly objective and set on his goal; his heart like a lump of ice. Only one thing mattered—to continue climbing from rock to rock, snowbank to snowbank, higher and ever higher. Only this one tactic would work.

That uneven raspy, sobbing sound he heard could only be his own ragged breath. Such triviality he thrust aside. He felt strong, confident, never more sure that all this was right. His hand and eye were steady—that's all that mattered.

Reaching the level of the foxholes he found the first round hole and stalked toward it. On its lip he paused to gaze down on a small brown body huddled ostrichlike in the hole; it jumped as the bullet struck. Twenty feet away, another hole and another hiding Jap—then still another, a long sequence of foxholes. He didn't count them, merely kept going and ignoring all else about him— one round per cowering Jap, no more, well placed in the back of the helmet.

At the base of a vertical rock, reloading as he went, he turned left and deliberately began working westward. Two Japs crouched over a machine gun—both died. Two more popped up from a foxhole and he calmly felled them both. From a cave to his right a Jap appeared, grenade in hand, and Murphy fired, the grenade exploding in the man's hand as he fell.

Below him the entire company now came storming up the slope. Swensen, Baker, Bennett, Jeeters—all that were left of his squad. But all okay. Murphy reversed course, reloaded and kept firing into foxholes. He felt no cold, no icy blasts of violent wind, only a blind and unreasoning certainty of heart and mind. Young was dead. Murphy would find and kill the Jap who fired the shot. If a hundred died, two hundred—that was fine. The more the better. Kill them all and get the killing over with.

Downslope a Jap officer suddenly stood, pointing a pistol, and caught three rounds in the gut. A machine gun swiveled but remained silent, its gunner instantly dead. A figure tossed a grenade that fell woefully short; the thrower died before it hit the ground. This was all good work, Murphy knew. But he took no satisfaction. Lewis, Cooper—both dead. Hall badly wounded, Jones missing. Now Young . . .

The company overtook him and swept past, each man dedicated to finishing what Murphy had begun. He felt suddenly spent, a tired old man with nothing to do, vaguely aware of a sense of disappointment he couldn't define.

Behind a shelter of rock he paused to light a cigarette, the wind proving too strong. "Shit!" he muttered, peering downslope at Young's broken body.

That's where the kids found him, huddled over the body with stains of tears on his cheeks. No one spoke to him. Gazing at the heaving of his shoulders, wanting to help, no one knew quite what to say.

Three hours of sleep was not enough, Tomi thought, entering the ward tent. Three hours, rather, of restless tossing, his mind too alert, always aware, flitting from one fantasy to another. First too warm, then too cold, his bladder demanding relief. Men had snored. The building had creaked. The wind had sighed over the roof. Only time had passed without his knowing, so technically he was forced to call it sleep. Yet he could take an oath on the Bible that he'd lain awake all night long.

"Honored sir?" Sergeant Okasaki had been waiting for him, his face far thinner than it had been two weeks ago, still gray and deeply lined from yesterday's ordeal. It was framed into its usual implacable mask, but his manner now was tense, concerned. "There is a matter I feel compelled to bring to your attention at once."

More bad news, Tomi understood immediately. Favorable news had become a stranger since the Americans landed. Any news now was bad news, requiring one adjustment after another. "It's Lieutenant Hirose? More suicides? A new American landing?"

"None of these, honored sir." Okasaki pointed. "The American."

He almost blurted, Which American? But one glance told the story. Private First-Class George Washington Jones, U.S. Army, lay on his side without benefit of blankets, one eye half open and glazed with death. From his back protruded the hilt of a bayonet, the tip of its blade, he assumed, buried deep in Jones's heart. Under his touch the body was already cold. Last night, he thought. In the dark.

He gazed about the ward tent. Michael's dark goggles stared back, impersonal, cold, like the eyes of some monstrous machine. Beside Michael, Umeda seemed asleep and all others averted their eyes. He knew it would be useless to ask about the culprit. "What information do you have?"

"Only what you see, honored sir. He lies as I found him. No one saw or heard in the dark."

Okasaki's attitude seemed matter-of-fact, uninvolved and perhaps not truly interested, as one might expect. Okasaki would be thinking: Does one dead American really matter? Isn't killing them part of our mission?

And of course Okasaki was right. Jones's death in itself wasn't important. But his manner of dying seemed all-important. Jones, a Christian of sorts, had been killed while under Japanese, and Tomi's, protection. A personal affront. One thrust of the knife had negated all the skill and care Tomi had given the American, all the time and knowledge he'd applied, all the hope and promise of seeing the man recover. In a way it was like being robbed. And being robbed of his labor he viewed as a most demeaning insult.

An insult! Of course no Japanese gentleman worthy of the term could, or would, accept such an insult without some sort of retaliation. It was expected. One's manhood, one's sense of stature and self-esteem, demanded revenge. In Japan revenge was in fact a virtue; it proved that one was both courageous and not to be taken lightly, as one would a child. In American history, as Tomi recalled, a certain flag expressed the same sentiment by depicting a coiled viper and the slogan: "Don't tread on me!"

In this mood he approached Umeda and his small group of followers, for now he realized they had defied him almost from the beginning. Complainers! Slyly disobedient! Perhaps baiting Jones. Blindly following Umeda's lead in all he did. But all that was finished now. This stump, that fractured clavicle, the splinted metacarpus, the temporal skull wound, the torn knee cartilage, the shrapnel-slashed thigh—all were healing beautifully, no complications. So on each chart he wrote, with much satisfaction: *Release: return immediately to unit.*

"But, honored sir, I cannot walk. How do you expect—"

"Use crutches! Or your friends may carry you on a litter. Your means of transportation is not my concern."

Only Umeda himself Tomi excepted, to his regret. Umeda's stump needed more time and perhaps another operation, this time above the knee, though Tomi couldn't be certain. The color seemed a bit strange in this light. No sour odor yet, but perhaps this afternoon— In any case, professional ethics required that Umeda remain for further treatment.

"Thank you, honored sir," each of them said. He felt sure they knew the reason they were leaving at this particular time, yet no sign touched their faces. Sobered, each of them bowed, murmured the ritual phrase and departed, the one-legged man hobbling painfully on Jones's crutch.

Within a half hour, however, Tomi regretted what he'd done. He'd acted too hastily, with anger and not with reason. There was nothing of Christian mercy and forgiveness in deliberately and perhaps unnecessarily sending men to their deaths. He had sinned, terribly, and his deed could never be undone. It would lie like a stone on his conscience all the days of his life.

On the other hand, was he not human, imperfect and subject to error? He assumed Jesus knew that. The fact was that now he always felt tired, always hungry to the point of weakness, trembling often without apparent cause, working on raw nerve. He was irritable and frightened, dreading the ordeal that surely was soon to come, even worse and far more dangerous than anything he'd already experienced. With Hirose wounded, the entire burden of medical supervision fell on him alone.

Yet this was not the time to excuse himself for human failure. Nor the time to ease up. He must continue to work intelligently and objectively to aid his fellow man. He must do his very best. If he erred here or there, Jesus would understand.

Gazing about at his patients, he wondered how many were also exhausted in mind, body and spirit, hungry as never before, discouraged beyond any shred of hope, frightened of this vast unknown called death and uncertain of how it would find them— or not find them. Perhaps they might be only wounded, crippled, lie unconscious in the mud or snow, be captured and forever disgraced and unable to return home, would thereafter slink about the edges of life in some alien land and know within themselves they were unworthy of all respect.

He wished he could talk to Hirose, but Hirose lay quietly upon a litter, like all other wounded, his eyes open but seeing nothing, now a man without a mind, having escaped first through sake, then morphine and now this. In his present state nothing could touch him, hurt him, degrade him or force him into any decision or action. At last he was free, no devil to plague him, no hunger or pain, no harsh army or demanding Emperor, no daily succession of crushed and broken bodies to agonize over, no memory of a bitter past and no concern for the future. Utopia, Tomi thought, as he began making his rounds.

The first patient along the row had quietly died in early morning, a victim finally of a large splinter of wood through his groin. The second pleaded to be sent without delay to the front, skull fracture and partial paralysis of the face or not—Tomi agreed. The third simply shrugged when told of a gangrenous leg; he, too, desired immediate duty on the line. The fourth asked only for morphine. A great deal of morphine.

"You wish to die?" asked Tomi.

"Honored doctor, the battle is lost. Is there purpose in living a few more painful hours?"

Last night on the operating table the man had merely wanted the bleeding stopped, a long shrapnel tear in his calf sewn up and an immediate release to what was left of his unit—they needed him. A commendable attitude, Tomi had thought. But the posterior tibial artery had been nicked and any activity at all could lead to sudden hemorrhage and death. The man must rest his leg for at least a week. "The battle is not lost! Not yet."

"But we have failed to defeat the enemy. Is that not evident?"

A political, social heretic, Tomi thought. Even so, medical needs must prevail. "I do not wish my patients to be disheartened by your opinions," he said.

"It is not opinion but fact," the man said, and by now others were listening. "Besides, the patients know that most of the combat troops are now dead. Perhaps only a thousand Japanese remain alive on Attu—that's all. These are mostly clerks and repairmen, not accustomed to firing rifles, and untrained in fighting techniques. So how well can they fight these persistent Americans? How long can they hold this tiny corner of Attu? I tell you, the end is near."

"That is not so," said a second man nearby. "All events to this point were ordered by the High Command. We are part of their grand plan. The battle proceeds in good order, as they predicted. We are not defeated, we merely follow the plan."

"They intend to lose Attu?" asked an amputee, his eyes wide and unbelieving. "They plan that we should die?"

"Indeed, we are privileged to die in the name of the Emperor. Think! The American Navy here is all but destroyed, the Army shredded. In attacking us on Attu the enemy has used tremendous numbers of shells, rations, men, planes, ships, and a huge store of supplies badly needed in the Solomon Islands. Thus, in the far south the enemy grows weak and Japan grows strong."

"A children's story," muttered a superior private. "Despite our strongest effort we were defeated soundly at Guadalcanal and are being driven methodically from all of the Solomons. Where did you hear such lies?"

"The nightly broadcast from Tokyo. It is truth! We on Attu are now heroes to all Japan. We are already immortal. Our names will ring in haiku and legend for a thousand years. Streets and cities will be named after us. Statues will be erected in our honor. Already maidens wail songs of lament."

"That is not what I hear," growled a man across the aisle. "These facts come from headquarters itself. A secret weapon has been perfected. It will be used soon against the enemy. Here on Attu."

"A secret weapon?" asked the amputee.

"If it is secret, how do you know of it?" Tomi wanted to know. "What kind of weapon is this?"

"From all accounts it has a devastating effect on all Caucasians. A matter of pigmentation, to be sure. One drop can kill thousands. There is no defense against it."

"This is a liquid? A gas? Dropped from a plane or fired from—"

"I do not know. As I say, it is a secret."

Tomi had heard enough. He escaped quickly along the aisle, positive the future held little doubt. The reading of the Imperial Edict settled all that: every Japanese on Attu had been ordered to die for the Emperor. In combat, of course. Except for *seppuku*.

But death was not for him, he knew. Not now. Not on Attu. As God's agent, he would live. And Michael would live. Michael had the will, determination, the courage to live, the indomitable American spirit that might accept a small surrender but not total defeat. Lose a battle, but win the war.

Now, however, was the time for a personal gamble. He found Wardman Ouye near the entryway. "Please remove all the clothing and boots of the head wound who died last night in the operating tent. The clothing is to be placed in my quarters."

The man nodded, his manner one of blind obedience, which was well. The head wound case had been a man of about Michael's size and weight. The clothing was relatively clean, considering.

Right now it was the best Tomi could do.

He confessed to a new sense of urgency about Michael, a reversal of opinion. With Jones's death, delay in removing Michael from the hospital could no longer be tolerated. Expedite—that was the key.

But where could Michael go? And when? The dilemma caused a frown, a sinking sensation. Earlier he had felt so good. Now . . .

"Honored sir, may I speak?" Okasaki remained at his side, interrupting. "About the burn case?"

"Yes, please continue."

"I am disturbed! In what remote corner of Japan was this man born? Is he an idiot? He appears to know nothing. Upon leaving the tent for the first time each dawn, en route to the latrine, he fails to bow to the Emperor. An officer, he does not precede the others in line. Nor does he acknowledge when I stand aside on the pathways for one of officer's rank. And yesterday, rudely thrusting aside the arm of Lieutenant Hirose—"

"The man is a special case, as I have explained before. I can tell you nothing, for the esteemed colonel himself has sworn me to silence." It was a good lie, as lies go. He felt almost proud of it. Yet a lie was a grievous sin.

Okasaki gazed at him. "Honored sir. Is Dr. Hirose informed of this man? It appears not. Only yesterday on the radiophone he discussed the merits of the case with Captain Yamamoto and seemed unaware—"

"And the result of the discussion?" Tomi felt shaken. Would

Yamamoto now start asking more questions, challenging his lies?

"I did not hear, honored sir. I was busy with—"

"Thank you for your concern. But all is in good order. Now may I have my ration of rice?"

How long, he wondered, could he hold the sergeant at bay?

Tomi was staring at a patient's chart but didn't see it. He kept thinking of his *On* of responsibility to Okasaki, a stern and rigid soldier, yet fair to all, at heart a good man. Also his responsibility to Sumiko and the children, for they depended on him for all things. Also to the Emperor, the moral and spiritual leader of all Japan, whom Tomi had honored and admired for a lifetime. Also to the United States and all the Christians he'd known there, for in America he'd gained knowledge, insights, understanding, a direction he wanted his life to go. Certainly to Michael Andrews, a young man whom God favored, a new kind of savior for all mankind. All this responsibility—such a heavy load! Yet he felt grateful, wanted somehow to return these gifts in kind. Particularly to the patients: the hand stretching forth, frightened eyes pleading, all demanding his strength, courage, leadership, assurance . . .

But he was only one man, weak and alone and very tired, yet lending moral support to everyone he touched. Sometimes the overall burden seemed too much to bear.

Especially now with stomach cramps returning; he felt half sick. The rice, he thought. Is it the rice? He'd had no time of late to oversee the preparation of food. Had it been properly boiled? Handled in every respect in sanitary manner? He must look into the matter. Meanwhile the cramps were sharp, strong, very painful and would not be denied. He hurried toward the latrine.

So Jones was dead. To a large degree Michael blamed himself. If only he had played it close, as Tomi said; if he hadn't tried to play hero and chitchat on a party line with Jones, the poor bastard might still be alive. There was of course the outside argument that Jones, his own worst enemy, had brought destruction down on his own head, but only maybe. Michael would never know for sure which truth prevailed.

Meantime, they were closing in on him now and he knew it. Whoever "they" were. He'd talked to Jones and now Jones was dead; ergo, someone had heard and understood. Granted, it had been dark and perhaps no one, at this moment, could point an accurate finger. But someone knew.

So now he had two nemeses: that unknowing someone and old Hardnose, the Asian bloodhound. What if they got together and compared notes? Hardnose would say, "Everybody seems okay except this guy with all the bandages. Y'had a good look at him? He's a real oddball. He don't act right, don't look right. When does he eat and who gives it to him? Little doc, who speaks English, that's who." And the someone would answer: "Y'mean Bandage Head who looks like a cabbage? Why, he was talking just the other night in the dark with Jones—"

And *boom!* He and Tomi would both be dead. Just like that.

So something drastic had to be done. Now! Tonight! Or the same bayonet that got Jones would also get him. Then Tomi—a firing squad. Tomi deserved better than that. Tomi deserved . . . everything good.

Michael thought hard about Tomi. It was abundantly clear now—and mentally he kicked himself for not thinking of this earlier—that everything he did or didn't do could have dire and immediate consequences for Tomi. So if he, Michael, should tear again into the wild blue yonder in some sort of half-ass escape plan, it could well cost Tomi his life. That stood to reason. And one thing Tomi didn't deserve was a stab in the back from a guy he was trying hard to help.

So what was best to do for Tomi? Going, staying—both presented risks. Going without adequate preparation meant capture or death from exposure, and both would negate everything Tomi was trying to do. Staying . . . well, the odds of survival seemed slim. But the possibility remained that maybe, with a bit of luck, time would work things out. Time. That's all Tomi wanted, and it was high time he began respecting Tomi's judgment. It wouldn't hurt, either, to start cooperating with Tomi and quit acting like a wild-eyed Custer attacking the Sioux. Learn a little humility, he told himself, and get Phyllis really confused.

Cooperation, however, meant doing nothing. Not one lousy thing. Doing nothing was difficult, if not impossible. Never in his life had he successfully done nothing. Besides, in this case it took guts, no other word for it. Did he have the guts to lie in the dark alone, listening to all the snores and snorts and farts and bubblings of four score or so men, just waiting for some brown-skinned runt smelling of fish and rice to slide between litters and stick a knife in his ribs? Jesus!

He sighed to himself and settled back on the litter, waiting behind dark glasses and watching Hardnose's every move. Waiting as always for Tomi . . .

Returning, Tomi found Lieutenant Ujiie waiting impatiently with Okasaki, beside the radiophone set near the stove.

"Nakamura!" called Ujiie in an imperious tone Tomi resented. Tomi approached, bowed and waited, expecting a question concerning Jones's death. But Ujiie merely waved a paper. "This document was dropped near headquarters this morning by an American aircraft. The esteemed Garrison Commander Colonel Shima requires that you translate it. Do so at once."

Another insult, Tomi thought, accepting the paper. The man had given no thought to "How is your health, your work, your friend Hirose"; nothing of personal concern. Even the word "please," fundamental to Japanese nature, was ignored. Any direct order without "please" or some other softening word or phrase became demeaning, an insult. Ujiie knew that. Why was the man deliberately rude?

He glanced at the paper—one page, single-spaced, neatly typed. The message itself set his pulse racing. In his hand was the instrument of escape. It meant life, freedom, a future for everyone.

Slowly he began translating, writing carefully:

May 27, 1943

TO COMMANDING OFFICER—
JAPANESE GARRISON
ATTU ISLAND

Your attention is called to the fact that your forces are now in a hopeless situation, and that because the United States forces control the air and sea lanes, there is no chance for reinforcements for your troops. Therefore in accordance with the rules of land warfare, I ask for the unconditional surrender of the Japanese Garrison of ATTU ISLAND.

Your defense and soldierly conduct of your troops has been worthy of the highest military traditions.

It is requested that the Commanding Officer, accompanied by not to exceed four Staff Officers, proceed openly in broad daylight under white flags in a southerly direction in CHICHAGOF VALLEY to the vicinity of the south end of LAKE CORIES. This party will not be fired upon, and will be met by guides who will conduct it to the place where the surrender will be received.

After the surrender, your forces will be entitled to and receive all privileges due prisoners of war according to the rules of land warfare.

COMMANDING OFFICER
AMERICAN FORCES OF ATTU

The completed translation he gave to Ujiie, but now he felt no elation. Surrender at this time made a lot of sense, and the means lay at hand. But of course the esteemed Garrison Commander Colonel Shima would never agree. Not Shima or any other Japanese commander. The American general must be well aware of that. So this was merely a humanitarian gesture, well meant but empty of real meaning. A thousand more Japanese would be forced to die without reason, and nothing could be done to stop it. The Imperial Edict would see to that.

Ujiie was peering suspiciously about the tent. "Why do you have so many patients? Are all of them badly wounded? Why haven't half of them been returned to the front? This man so greatly bandaged, can he not walk, see, fire a—"

"Honored sir," said Tomi quickly, fearing Okasaki might overhear and have his suspicions aroused, "the overcast is lifting and soon the American planes will arrive in force. If you don't wish to be caught here, where shelter is inadequate, may I suggest—"

With every courtesy he escorted Lieutenant Ujiie to the tent entrance and got rid of him. If Tomi hadn't been in such pain he might have laughed. Instead he stifled a groan, clutched his stomach and hurried again toward the latrine. From overhead he heard the droning of the first planes of the day.

It was later that Sergeant Okasaki reported. In the ward tent were wild but firmly believed rumors that a second American was present or close by; in the night he'd been clearly heard making escape plans with the black American, Jones.

May 27. Diarrhea continues, pain is severe. Took everything from pills, opium, and morphine, then slept pretty well. Strafing by planes, roof broke through. There is less than 1000 left from more than 2000 troops. Wounded from Coast Defense unit, Field Hospital Headquarters, field post office—the rest are on the front line.

MAY 28, 1943

I know the radio frequencies my squadron uses," Michael was saying.

They sat together in the wreckage of Tomi's room, among the debris of the roof shattered in yesterday's air raid. Hunched over the uncertain, flickering light of a single candle, Michael looked thin, tired, too pale, the results of wounds and hunger and lack of sunlight. Occasionally he coughed. Through the hole in the roof the wet wind whistled down and ruffled his blond hair, the effect reminding Tomi of cream-gold grain waving in the sunshine. Imagine—from one horizon to another, countless acres of grain and rice. Imagine millions upon millions of well-fed bellies . . .

"If I got my hand on a radio I could contact them next time over. I'd tell them, this is a hospital! They'd veer off, pass the word."

"No, Michael. Our Intelligence people claim the reverse. You Americans always attack—"

"A hospital? Nonsense! We see a red cross and lay off. Without a red cross—"

"None of our medical people wear the red cross. Neither are our hospitals marked. Why? To protect them. A bright red cross is such a good target."

"Take it from me, you guys got it backward. Tomi, no American—"

"It is too dangerous for us both. You see? We must avoid any and all use of a radio. Now, as to more urgent matters. Here is a map I have drawn, also a compass we no longer need. By nightfall I shall have acquired three pounds of rice. Soon, very soon, you must go. I have, as you say, a hunch."

"Okay, I got the same feeling. That kid next to me—the scrawny kid that Jones had that trouble with? He got up the night Jones got killed. Crawled away in the aisle. I couldn't see well in the dark, or hear much with all that snoring. Somebody groaned or grunted, I don't know. But next morning Jones was dead. Kaput!" For a moment Michael was silent, lips compressed, staring down at his hands. "That kid's been watching me. Then he rattles off to that big sergeant."

"Okasaki?"

"I don't know his name. The kid talks and stares at me—round big eyes. And quiet, like he's waiting. So something smells. Tomi, it's time to go."

"Yes! If I only knew just when the best—"

"Now, Tomi. Tonight."

"No—"

"Yes! Let's suppose I go tonight. Your guys find me and *boom!* I'm dead. If I stay, they get you, too. That's too high a price to pay. Face it, Tomi. I can't risk your getting killed—not just for me, not anymore."

"The time is not right."

"But the risk should be mine."

"Neither of us has a choice, Michael. Not now. So listen to me. With Okasaki so alert, you will no longer masquerade as the burn case. A new disguise—"

"And location? Why don't I stay here in your roommate's place?"

The solution at once popped into his mind, crystal clear. The most seriously wounded cases, all comatose, could be transferred to the gloom of the barracks area. There was plenty of room here.

Michael could be one of those undisturbed in the gloom, especially if his blond hair was hidden by a bandage, if he shaved and if his face and hands were bathed in tincture of iodine to darken the flesh tones, if he kept his eyes closed and pretended to be comatose.

Possible. It was clearly possible.

Now Tomi could nod, even smile to himself. Clever fellow! Like magic the peculiar burn case would disappear and—presto!—the hospital would acquire another anonymous and hopeless head wound, comatose and in fact not worth bothering with.

Murphy kept thinking of Jones. Early this morning he had peered through binoculars and seen Jones's big black body, naked and frozen, one-legged, sprawled amid a pile of dead Japs. No mistaking the body—that long, narrow head, so familiar, and huge white teeth, no longer grinning but drawn back in a ghastly grimace; those long lean limbs seen hundreds of times in a shower. So Jones was dead—a sickening thought. Murphy had hoped against hope. But now that was four. Four fine young men he'd hoped to bring home safely.

His first reaction had been to grab the whole friggen platoon, march down the long snowy, muddy slope with guns blazing and clean out those two goddamn tents. That was a hospital? More like a butcher shop. Look at those mangled Jap bodies. Look at Jones—just a bandaged arm, the stump of a leg. No other wounds. So they'd killed a wounded prisoner. Goddamn! Enough to make a man's blood boil.

But no such rash action could save Jones now; a man couldn't go off half-cocked. Why kill the rest of the kids just for the sake of revenge?

"A roster of patients is almost impossible to maintain," Sergeant Okasaki said, his face haggard from lack of sleep. "At eighteen hundred hours last night we listed ninety-two patients. Of the thirty-seven sent to us from the worthy Captain Yamamoto's hospital, only twelve survived, the others being caught en route by machine-gun fire from strafing planes. The fighting last night sent us nineteen more. This morning we released sixteen to the front. During the night eleven died, four others committed *seppuku* and an undetermined number simply rose from their litters—the burn case among them; he is gone—and returned to the front. Amid such confusion, how is one to record numbers, let alone names?"

"It is difficult, I know," said Tomi, almost trembling with relief. "But Lieutenant Ujiie insists on name, rank and unit, as regulations require. Somehow we must please him."

"We can do that easily, with twenty more wardmen."

They stood at the edge of the bluff peering out at a rain cloud threatening from the east. In the ravine below, Michael was now safely disguised and hidden among more than a dozen comatose patients, including Hirose. Tomi tried to imagine Michael's experience: lying motionless all day and most of the night, alone, hungry, waiting for a miracle.

Okasaki was saying: "I do not think the roster is now of primary importance, honored sir, despite all that the honored Lieutenant Ujiie says. The Imperial Edict has been given, and it is a fact widely known that our garrison commissary holds rations for only two more days."

"That's all? What are you suggesting?"

"That in two days Lieutenant Ujiie and the esteemed colonel and you and I will all be dead and no one will remain to worry about a medical roster. The patients, too, will be dead."

"You have a point." He peered down at the black mud at his feet. He could not accept the premise that his grave might be dug here, on Attu. "I shall find the means to placate the honored lieutenant," he said. "Meanwhile, you foraged last night for additional medical supplies?"

"I did, honored sir. I found Captain Yamamoto's hospital near Umanose besieged by American mortar fire. The patients who could not walk or be easily moved were given overdoses of morphine, a total of four hundred injections, I'm told. The tent which held the reserve stores was struck a few days ago by an

American firebomb and all stores were lost. There is none other available to us."

"I see," said Tomi, still gazing grimly at the ground. In just one brief hour last night he'd exhausted his last stocks of tetanus and alcohol. As of this morning the gauze flats were gone, adhesive tape gone, gasoline for the lanterns gone. In woefully short supply, but possibly adequate for two days, were ether and chloroform, tannic acid, magnesium sulfate and diuretics, pentobarbital sodium. . . .

"Tell me, honored Sergeant," he said, needing to know details only Okasaki would know, "about this rumor of an English-speaking intruder talking to Jones. What conclusion do you come to?"

"I have no conclusion, honored sir. I have nothing but facts. Superior Private Umeda heard Jones and another American plotting their escape. The other American is called Mcik and is believed to be the American aviator shot down a week ago."

"But how can that be?" said Tomi, desperately gambling now on the usual rigidity of the Japanese mind. Neither Okasaki, Yamamoto nor Ujiie would think creatively and now look where they hadn't looked before, under their very noses. They saw only the obvious and therefore limited their vision. "Surely by this time the American pilot is dead."

"Not necessarily. His continued presence at Chichagof Harbor is possible only if he has shelter and a source of food. But where?"

"Where indeed." Now he smiled. "Perhaps he dines nightly with the revered Garrison Commander Colonel Shima. Or is possibly a member of the searching party."

Okasaki frowned away this frivolity. "Our soldiers have vigorously searched each cave in the ravine. Every building in the area has been examined. Personally I question if the search has been that thorough. The dedication of young enlisted men today is not high."

Okasaki turned to see if the wardmen were working properly. "Honored sir, may I speak to you of a personal matter?"

"Of course, friend Okasaki. I am honored."

"As I spoke before, it is not too late to turn to Zen. In Zen there is much strength from within, and comfort. Certainly a man facing death . . ." His voice trailed off in embarrassment and he did not look at Tomi.

"Thank you, Okasaki, for your concern. It pleases me to know that Zen does for you what Jesus does for me, a source of strength and comfort. That is good. At such a time as this, what more can a man ask for?"

Okasaki bowed his head, not knowing how to proceed. He remained silent.

"As you know, Okasaki, all my life I have been a Christian. I must remain so." He turned to gaze at the other and let a smile touch his eyes. "To reverse matters, it is not too late for you to turn to Jesus."

"No, I cannot—" Then Okasaki also smiled, and Tomi felt as though the sun itself had given him warmth. "To each his own. Is that not a famous American phrase?"

"Very American and very old. Sometimes even Americans express things well."

Tomi watched the first raindrops splatter against the mud near his feet. The wind had changed and now swept from east to west. The same wind touched Japanese and American alike, he thought, an evidence of God's impartiality and love of all mankind. Yet, one passage from the Bible crept into mind: "In flaming fire taking vengeance on them that know not God, and that obey not the gospel of our Lord Jesus . . ."

It hurt to know that Okasaki and all other Japanese on Attu would suffer the flaming fire. That was their fate, ordained by the Emperor. But he, Tomi Nakamura, Christian and lifelong devout believer, was fated to survive, to live and work a lifetime to help improve the lot of mankind. He and Michael. Tonight or tomorrow night Michael would go. Time, circumstances and Michael's magical luck would provide the opportunity.

From above came the muffled sound of mortar shells—American mortars from atop the ridge above the hospital. It wasn't safe anymore to walk about in the ravine upstream from the hospital. American snipers had hidden themselves atop the rocky cliffs and in clear weather kept firing into the valley, a matter of only three or four hundred yards. En route to or from headquarters, one man had already been killed and two others wounded. Soon, perhaps even today, the Americans might add rifle grenades or even mortars, at which time the hospital area would be untenable. Was it possible, he mused, to evacuate all these patients while under fire?

He wondered what might happen if he should suddenly step forth in his white surgeon's smock, turn toward the cliffs and shout in English, "Hey, this is a hospital!"

Foolish fantasy! They would shoot first and listen later, as any sensible man would. Yet the idea held a certain merit. At the proper moment, when the Americans came close . . .

Inside the ward tent, he eased along the line of litters. "Good afternoon," he said to the first patient, glancing at the chart. "Your shoulder is feeling better?"

"Maggots!" the man gasped, lying on his uninjured side. "They're all over me, eating me up."

"Maggots?" Tomi eyed the neat row of stitches down the man's side. Very clean, healing well, a wound only four days old. "There are no maggots on Attu. Maggots come from flies. It is too cold here for flies."

Release, he wrote on the chart, and moved to the second man. Brain damage, comatose, hopeless: *transfer to barracks ward.* The third litter, a leg amputation, clean and healing: *release.* Then a shrapnel-slashed buttock: *release.* A fractured radius: *release.* Down the line: *release, release, transfer, release.* The next man—"Good morning, Private Umeda."

Umeda remained silent. Stone-faced, he merely stared at Tomi, his eyes pinpointed by preoperation sedatives. Or was there a special glint hidden within? Animosity, perhaps? Or a suspicion or knowledge of the burn case, his former neighbor? A stomach wound case now occupied the adjacent litter.

"You're scheduled for surgery late this afternoon, as soon as the instruments are once again sterile." That, too, was another nagging problem, the lack of adequate fuel combined with the smallness of the autoclave; it wasted much time. "I regret you must lose your knee."

Tomi knew what the man must be thinking. Butcher! Incompetent quack! The fact remained, however, that even among the best of sterile conditions gangrene arose without warning from sources no one could quickly or easily determine. Here, under these wretched field conditions, it did not proliferate, a victory in itself. Yet it could not be eliminated.

"I understand we are faced with final defeat at last," Umeda said in a monotone, his tongue thick and in the way of clear speech.

"That appears to be the case. I suppose it was inevitable."

"No one is trying hard enough. That is very clear to me, if not to you and others. All of you are fools! I wish to return to the front immediately."

"Sorry, I cannot approve."

"Nakamura, listen to me!" No "honored sir," no respectful terms at all. "I prefer that you do not interfere with my destiny. I wish to die a glorious death for the Emperor. I demand immediate release."

"Demand all you please. I will not send a man under sedation, burdened by a gangrenous leg, to the front. It's next to murder."

"Others are going who are no better than I."

"But not you, Umeda. You are special. Do you know why?"

Umeda stared, at first frowning then raising his brows. "The American . . ."

"Yes, the American—Jones. He wanted life and you gave him death. Now you want death. I will give you life."

"Life? I don't understand."

"When the Americans come, and they will, you will be unconscious. You will be my gift to the Americans, in place of Jones. The trade, however, is a bad one, with the Americans the loser."

"You would do that—surrender a Japanese to the enemy?"

"Indeed, especially you. May God help me, I will enjoy it! What's more, it is very legal and moral and within my religion."

Umeda closed his eyes and turned his face away, his jaw muscles taut.

The heat and close smells within the tent were suddenly too much. Tomi escaped into the icy gusting wind at the top of the bluff. The cold sharpened his mind.

Sergeant Okasaki soon came to join him, bowing. "Honored sir, there is a matter of great personal concern. May I speak?"

"Of course, Okasaki." The man was acting quite strange, eyes averted.

"It is said throughout the ward tent that once we are dead the Americans will wrench the teeth from our mouths to extract the gold. Can this be true?"

Tomi blinked his surprise. "The great number of Americans, no. But there may be one or two among thousands. As it is in any army, there are always a few bad ones."

"I do not wish to be mutilated. That is my only concern."

"I would not worry. It's a possibility, but remote. I do not think it probable."

"It is also said the Americans regard testicles as a delicacy. Is this a fact?"

"It is true, but only the organs of animals—sheep, goats, pigs and cattle. Mostly in the western area and only among people with strong stomachs. Personally I have never seen them eaten."

"And brains—they do not split a man's skull, remove his brains and fry them?"

"No! Again only the brains of animals. I've heard Americans say that the brains of beef are very good. But Americans are not cannibals."

Okasaki nodded, his eyes clouded with doubt and worry.

Tomi gazed along the beachfront. The waves kept washing the sand, back and forth, thrusting themselves against the land as they had a thousand years ago and would a thousand years hence. "Okasaki, forgive my intrusion into your privacy. Do you perhaps have a family?"

Okasaki turned to gaze at him, his eyes both curious and holding something akin to affection. "I have a son dead at Midway, another at Guadalcanal."

Then he fell silent, his eyes brooding down upon the ravine, leaving Tomi to imagine the rest—a score or more of nameless sons the man had never seen, nor wished to perhaps, all born of delightful and willing women of various nationalities who had once served him well. Truly a man of the world, he thought.

"And your wife?"

"Dead in the great Tokyo earthquake of twenty years ago." He paused to study Tomi. "Why do you ask?"

"Merely curious. You have done much to smooth the path before me, to assist also with my problems. I wondered if I might assist you with yours."

"Hah!" Okasaki cried, and he laughed, his teeth gleaming with gold and white. "Thank you, honored sir. But I have no problems that cannot be solved by victory. *Banzai* to the Emperor!" With a bow he excused himself and strode away to berate a young wardman who had curled himself into a dry corner to sleep.

Tomi wanted to sleep also but dared not. To sleep, perchance to dream, he thought. Very tempting. Once asleep he'd never want to wake up, might even prefer to lie comatose in the barracks, as Hirose was, awake but not awake, present yet somewhere else. Hirose—locked forever in some remote prison of his mind, safe and secure from unsolvable problems, hard decisions and enemies of all kinds.

"Bennett's got a real problem," Swensen announced suddenly in an oddly grating tone, his hands clasped hard together. "Constipation! You can tell by looking at him. He's full of shit."

Bennett sat quietly, enduring. Say nothing. All this will go away.

"For instance, look at his eyes. Browner'n hell! All brown-eyed people are full of shit. Otherwise—"

Murphy wasn't listening, one corner of his mind far away, long ago, and warm with the memory of soft, scented flesh and a taut nipple that clung to the clutching nest of his fingers. Oh, Helen! Nested together, the two of them, naked, satiated, cooling in the breeze of a June night. Her long and contented sigh warm upon his cheek, neither feeling the need for words. It was always enough to lie close together, so aware of each other and filled with the wonder of the moment. To know such happiness; to appreciate, too, that for a while all was right with the world.

Life with her was all too perfect. He should have known it could not last.

After the funeral he was still a man, had felt the same physical ache she had eased so often—that dull but often acute pressure in his loins. Insistent, persistent, demanding. For months he had thought of little but Helen, wanting her, needing her. Sleepless nights. Endless days. The thought of bedding another woman hadn't entered his mind.

Here, however, on Attu, that dark thought had come to life. A woman! Silky soft. Warm. Loving. Sweet. Flesh sliding on willing flesh. Lip to lip and loins locked together. He could see it, feel it, there in his mind. He admitted he wanted a woman. God help him, almost any woman would do. If only for a while.

The thought shamed him, brought a quick hand to cover his eyes and shield his shame from the world. Jesus! What would Helen think? Not two years dead and already her own husband was disloyal, unfaithful, committing adultery deep in his heart. . . .

"Sarge, you okay?" Swensen got no answer but that didn't stop him from watching out for ol' Sarge. When Sarge felt bad, like right now, Swensen felt bad, too. But what the hell could a guy do to help? Kidding or laughing—shit! If he had a beer right now, he'd give it to Sarge.

He hunkered down, their shoulders almost touching. "Here, have a smoke."

"How is the fighting going?" Tomi asked a sergeant whose scalp had been miraculously sliced by a bullet that had not touched the bone.

"It goes on," the man said in a weary tone. "I don't mind the fighting or the danger, but sometimes it is hard to sleep in all that noise."

"You are fighting at present on Umanose?"

"In the vicinity. The Americans have advanced north of the pass, but there are pockets of us emerging behind them, first here and then there. To kill us they must first find us, and that is often a difficult thing to do."

Tomi gazed at the long wound; it had been bleeding freely and now must be closed. "I have no novocaine. This will hurt."

Actually he did have certain painkillers, but the sergeant had already been given a full quantity of morphine, and other drugs available would keep the man out of action too long. Tomi bunched a section of the scalp, ran the needle through, and the sergeant gave no sign of pain, except he blinked.

"You have seen the distinguished Battalion Commander, Colonel Nagumo?" Tomi asked. "He is still alive?"

The sergeant gave no answer; however a waiting superior private with a shattered, fingerless hand said, "It is said he is dead. In dress uniform, with sword in hand, he charged the enemy, shouting the Emperor's name."

"He was a fine soldier, a good man," Tomi said, tying the first of a long series of knots.

"A tactician without equal, one of the Emperor's best," said the superior private. "It was he who taught us to lie in the snow as if dead, let the Americans hurry past and then rise and shoot into their backs. A most satisfactory tactic. It worked well, for a while."

"For a while," agreed another man; he wore a makeshift arm sling. "Then the Americans began shooting into the bodies of both pretenders and dead alike. Very barbarous, these Americans."

Tying a second knot, Tomi nodded, not because he thought the Americans barbarous. Americans, so individualistic, were quick to learn, very adaptable, and positive in their actions, desirable and worthwhile qualities in any man, he thought. Thus he, too, would listen and learn and be flexible, and his idea for surviving this battle, the idea now growing in his mind, would take final form as circumstances might permit. Perhaps Michael would advise him.

Okay, so she saw Jim occasionally, claimed there was nothing wrong with that. An old family friend. Dinners. Went dancing once. No movies, no kisses. Yes, Mother kept insisting. But nothing will come of it. Love you. You alone. Want you back. Please be careful. But really, Mike, I'm very upset because you don't trust me. . . .

May 28. The remaining rations are for only two days. Our artillery has been completely destroyed. There is a sound of trench mortars, also AA guns. The company on the bottom of Attu Fiji has been completely destroyed except for one. Rations for about two days. I wonder if Commander [Nagumo] and some of the men are still living. Other companies have been annihilated except for one or two. 303rd Battalion has been defeated. [Nagumo] Battalion is still holding Umanose. Continuous cases of suicide. Half of the Sector Unit Headquarters was blown away. Heard that they gave 400 shots of morphine to severely wounded and killed them. Ate half-fried thistle. It is the first time I have eaten something fresh in six months. It is a delicacy. Order from Sector Commander to move field hospital to the inland. It was called off.

MAY 29, 1943

M ichael?" whispered Tomi into the shadows of the barracks. At best he could see the gray blurs of various bandages worn by patients. In the still cold air the aisle lay straight and true toward the rear of the building and his own tiny room, but he had to feel his way in the dark.

He stumbled across some object in his path and remembered now that the aisle was strewn with clods of earth, pebbles and bits of tundra fallen from the roof, a result of air raids, plus various items of mislaid clothing and equipment. Such clutter annoyed him, but these were unusual times. No one had time for proper housecleaning.

"Michael? I have brought your rice. Wait a moment; I will find a candle."

He eased along the aisle. In his room the light was better, for the grayness of dawn filtered down through the damaged roof. The wind for a moment delayed the lighting of a candle. In its dull glow Michael loomed in the doorway, a grotesque-looking creature, bandage askew and blond hair exposed, his iodine-painted face appearing a sickly green in the pale light.

"Rice?" said Michael, his voice sounding much more normal

today. Continual gargling with salt water was producing the desired effect. He coughed far less frequently now. "I'll eat anything—termites, snakes, old shoes. I'm near starved to death."

"This is your ration for today." Tomi presented a tea bowl heaped high with cold rice, the combined rations of four patients who had not survived the night. A lot of rice, in these circumstances, for just one man. It was four times the sample Tomi would eat, but Michael soon would need all his strength. "And in this package are emergency rations for your journey. Guard it well. The time now is growing close."

"You won't believe this, Tomi. But in a way I hate to leave. It's been nice knowing you. You've taught me a lot. And I won't see you for quite a while."

Warmth flooded through him; he did not trust himself to answer. "Michael, listen to me. The radio guard on duty overheard various orders concerning the shifting of troops—Japanese troops. They descend even at this moment from the mountain heights into the low country. At this time there is no area that is not dangerous for you to venture into. Stay hidden! I shall be alert for the proper moment, the proper route. I will notify you the instant I know."

Michael coughed, twice, three times. Then he gazed at Tomi. "How can I ever thank you?"

"You owe me no thanks."

"But I do! By the ton. It took me a while to catch on, but now I know. You risked—"

"Just live, Michael! Go home. Work and study. Grow food for all the world."

"But, Tomi—"

"That is all I ask."

"I'll find a way." Michael bridged his embarrassment by gazing at Sumiko's picture pinned to the wall. "A gorgeous dish! Nice eyes, pretty smile. I have a girl too. Blond with gray eyes and a sassy grin, cooks like a million bucks. Strictly class, but the home type, too."

Tomi smiled his happiness. "I wish you contentment and many children."

"With luck. Thanks to you! But there's a long way to go."

"Soon! Now I must return to my patients." He rose and reached for the candle, inhaling and ready to blow it out. Then from the barracks came a sudden flurry of boots clumping upon the wooden floor. Tomi had time to turn and glimpse the far door bursting ajar, the flash of a small white-coated figure running from the building. It was over in an instant, and Tomi stood aghast in the full knowledge that someone, obviously a malingering enlisted wardman, had seen him with a large patient with blond hair, conspiring together in English.

In both the operating tent and ward tent Tomi found all wardmen present. Nothing seemed changed. Each man went about his duties in a normal fashion, unhurried, as thorough as limited knowledge and time permitted, without undue compassion for the patients. Tomi sought occasion to speak to each wardman in turn, finding no revealing flick of eye or strangely reserved behavior, no new awareness, sadness, contempt or alarm. He wondered why. On one hand they each had many sterling qualities, yet the fact remained that as a group they were dull and plodding fellows. That Tomi knew well, and it often angered him. Had they been men of wit and spirit they never would have been assigned to medical work.

But one of them had seen and heard. One of them knew too much. But who? When would he report it to Okasaki? Until he did, Tomi could only continue his work as if the discovery had never been made.

The runner from Sector Unit Headquarters appeared without warning in the ward tent just prior to 1300 hours, a rare and significant event. Wardmen and patients alike suddenly fell silent, watching as the runner fought his way through a multitude of litters in the aisle, found Tomi and bowed at last, sucking in his breath in respect. "Dr. Nakamura? A message of greatest importance from the esteemed Garrison Commander Colonel Shima. Sign here, please, honored sir."

The first paper was the standard "message received" form, used only for secret, vital or emergency communications. In a quiet that pervaded the entire ward, Tomi signed on the appropriate line.

The message itself, on a mimeographed sheet hastily prepared, he read quickly:

CHICHAGOF HARBOR
Attack order of the Second Sector Unit

1. By the combined attack of the enemy land, sea and air units, the Battalions of the front line have been defeated. However, our morale is excellent and we are holding in some important points. We will attack and annihilate the United States forces.

2. The Maruyama Battalion will hold in their position and cover the assembling forces, then will be prepared to attack on the left in the direction of the Sarana-Massacre Pass.

3. The Nagumo Battalion will form on the right of Lake Cories and will advance on the right in the direction of Sarana Pass.

4. The Aota Battalion (AA) will cease the defense of the sea frontier and will advance in the center in the direction of Sarana Pass.

5. Lieutenant Tsuroka (Navy) will command the detached naval personnel and will advance as Third Reserve in the rear of Headquarters.

6. The Cryptographic and Wireless Section will destroy all documents and will act under the command of the adjutant.

7. The Field Hospital, after direct assistance to the patients, will advance as part of the reserve under command of the adjutant.

8. The time of the attack will be announced later. All units will send liaison officers to headquarters prior to 2200.

9. I, in the advance for the attack, will be in the center rear of the front line.

> Shigero Shima
> Colonel, Infantry
> Commanding

The finale, Tomi thought. The great denouement. Everyone knew it had to come. Everyone knew it meant death for all Japanese on the island. But no one could do anything about it.

It also meant that the Japanese forces would be forming generally in Chichagof Valley, near Lake Cories. So the long descending spine of Hokuchin Yama, leading down to the sea, would soon be free of all Sea Defense units. Over the low hills of the peninsula and along the beach of West Arm of Holtz Bay toward the American forces there—that would be Michael's route. When? That was what he must next determine.

Until the final attack, however, life must continue and so must work. He gave the message to Sergeant Okasaki, assuming the patients would hear its contents, dismissed it from immediate concern and glanced about the ward tent. On the surface everything appeared normal. Last night's *seppukus* and other dead had been removed and the litters freshly filled by wounded men, the charts and reports either brought up to date or forwarded as required, and the patients bathed and given their noon meal. In surgery the instruments lay shiny and sharp on cloth-draped trays, sterile and ready for instant use. The safety valve on the autoclave kept bubbling and emitting tiny bursts of steam. Outside, the clouds hung low and dark and ominous. The wind blew as usual, and even the deep car-*ruumph!* of mortars and tenor *dah!-ah!-ah!ah!* of machine guns caused no alarm. Such sounds were, after all, expected, an everyday occurrence.

But below the façade of business as usual Tomi found a certain disturbing mood settle upon the ward. The patients had become much too quiet, in utter resignation, lying with blank gazes fixed either on the ceiling of the tent or on the bleak snow-and-mud world outside the tent entrance. A few had not eaten their noon dabble of rice, and all seemed withdrawn to one degree or another, no longer allowing themselves to feel, not wanting to think or remember but merely accepting the inevitable. All must die, and soon. Only hours remained.

The radiophone suddenly buzzed and all eyes turned to watch the radio guard on duty lift the instrument, listen and motion to Tomi. "This is Dr. Nakamura sp—"

"And this is Lieutenant Ujiie, chief assistant to the esteemed Garrison Commander Colonel Shima. Listen carefully—"

Everywhere he looked Tomi saw eyes watching him, knowing, yet not wanting to know. No one moved. No one spoke. The only sound was the low, hollow dirge of the wind skimming the tent top.

"Here are your orders, in two parts. Part one. By eighteen hundred hours this afternoon you will have released every patient who can walk and carry a weapon. These men will report to headquarters for further instructions. All other patients will be permitted *seppuku* or be sacrificed by appropriate means. I stress this point: no patient will remain alive to be captured by the enemy. Is all this thoroughly understood?"

"It is, honored sir. Perfectly." The prospect, however, sickened him. "And the next order?"

"Part two. In company with all medical and attached personnel, you will report for orientation and instruction at headquarters promptly at twenty hundred hours. You will join us in our final attack. *Banzai!*"

"Final attack. At twenty hundred—yes, honored sir. *Banz*—"

Without warning the radiophone went dead in his hand.

His mind flicked with certainty: as of 2000 hours Michael's route would be clear. The daylight, however, would be much too strong. For ultimate safety, wait for nightfall.

Surrendering the instrument to the radio guard on duty, he turned to stare at the patients. But they already knew—death, eternal death for them all. That seemed obvious from the sea of set, expressionless faces. Each had already gathered his courage and prepared himself to die.

Tomi sought out Okasaki. "How many patients have we left?"

"Eighty-seven, honored sir."

Nineteen of those were now in the barracks ward, Hirose included, the men Michael hid among. These were the critical cases: head wounds, pneumothorax and abdominal penetrations, one paraplegic and one quadriplegic, another sightless, a few mindless, all of them comatose and set aside to die quietly. They would have to be given an excess of morphine, but not by Tomi. He would have nothing to do with killing, especially his own kind. His soul felt already burdened as never before by sin and guilt. Providing the weapons and opportunity for *seppuku* was morally wrong, deeply so, though he had no alternative. But he needn't commit deliberate murder. Tonight, he decided, he would fall upon his knees and make peace with God.

"You know what to do, Sergeant Okasaki," he said quietly. "You alone are in charge. To the extent possible, however, each patient must have his choice."

"Of course, honored sir, I understand. At once."

The remaining patients were divided evenly between the ward tent and the operating tent. Without comment or involvement he watched Okasaki work.

"Morphine or grenade?" the sergeant quietly asked each patient, bowing low in a gesture of last respect.

"Grenade." A low tone, a grasping hand.

"Grenade." Indifferent, seemingly.

"Grenade." As though asking for tea. Polite.

"Morphine." A quaver in that voice. Young. Afraid to die. Afraid of pain.

"Grenade." Quick, sharp. Wants to get it done.

"Morphine." Sliced and chewed by shrapnel. Lots of pain there—but no more. Best just to go to sleep.

"Grenade." A braggart's tone. Big man pose, showing off.

"Grenade." Calm and accepting. No hope, had given up long ago.

"Grenade." A half-smile, bitter and godless.

Okasaki wasted no time. Four injections of a half-grain morphine each, and soon they slept. Others held grenades in their hands and appraised them thoughtfully, a bit curious but much resigned. One man sighed long and loud and closed his eyes, his chin quivering briefly. Another blinked back his tears and thrust one undamaged arm over his face.

Slowly Okasaki worked his way along the line, and Tomi watched Umeda squirm. Doomed to be surrendered. . . . The man's eyes darted toward Tomi, then back to Okasaki and the carton of grenades. His purpose was quite evident—steal a grenade. Or perhaps share a grenade with a comrade. Of course Tomi could stop him, simply sedate him and have his body removed to the barracks. But why bother? Did Umeda really matter? Tomi felt too tired now, too discouraged, too weak from hunger and too concerned about other matters to bother much with revenge. Jones had died a million years ago.

"Morphine or grenade?" asked Okasaki.

"Grenade!" cried Umeda, reaching with both hands as if the grenade were a gift or long-coveted prize.

How nice for him, that he may now die with the others, thought Tomi coldly.

With Okasaki occupied, Tomi hurried down the ramp against a strong, bitterly cold, icy wind toward the barracks and Michael.

En route he felt glad that Sumiko knew nothing of his various struggles and hardships and the way he'd been forced to live here on Attu. His thinness would horrify her. Also the lines that now scored his face, his scraggly beard, his red-streaked, weary-looking eyes and the new tremor that all too often overwhelmed his hands.

Someday he would tell her the story of Attu. Not immediately, not when he first saw her again. But someday, years from now, sitting close together before a warm fire and with the wind crying outside, drinking good fresh tea, he would remember this clammy fog, this freezing cold and snow and mud, this moaning eternal wind, these flapping brown tents hugging the frozen earth, those hills and mountains of incredible beauty that stood aloof from the small doings of man, these hidden valleys where one's sense of loneliness becomes overwhelming—all these were locked in his mind like a dream that would not fade. Someday he would tell of this trial and horror. He would speak slowly at first and then more rapidly. The adventure. The friendships: Okasaki, Hirose, Hayasaka, Jones and Michael, Colonel Shima and Nagumo. How deeply he missed her and how often he thought of her.

But he would not tell her of war, of the hundreds of broken, splintered bodies, each tossed like a carcass of beef upon his table; the arms, legs, eyes and other organs he had removed; the agony, starvation, loss of hope and faith; the planes angling in like lean and eager sharks, spitting fire from their eyes; the naval shells sighing downward, erupting and spewing black earthy vomit and warm red blood upon the lovely snow; the fear, exhaustion, tension; and men becoming automatons, struggling night and day without rest or freedom from pain and each changing in often subtle ways.

Had each man been tempered by war, like steel in a forge? Become unsure, or more certain? Fatalistic? Religious? Competent or careless? Mentally or morally or emotionally deranged? Some men became braver than ever before, others more cowardly. Many blindly sought a measure of release, became frivolous or irresponsible. If Tomi had learned anything at all on Attu, it concerned the extent to which a troubled man will go in order to escape a certainty too horrible to bear. Each in his own way thus adjusted to the stark, unrelenting horror of war. Each bore hidden scars and, if he survived, would never again be the same.

He shook such morbid thoughts from his mind. In the barracks he paused to let his eyes become accustomed to the gloom. All within was silent.

Here the hopeless, critical patients lay on platforms on each side of the aisle. Nineteen, including Hirose. They lay as if already dead, the only signs of life the slow, almost imperceptible rise and fall of their chests. It saddened him. In a modern, well-equipped hospital he could help them so much more.

He glanced about toward Hirose, hoping the man's condition had improved, but found himself staring at an empty litter and a gray pile of tumbled blankets.

"Where—" This morning Hirose had lain there, breathing and staring but not seeing and not hearing, a living corpse. Now Hirose was gone.

"He's in there, your room," whispered Michael's voice from the dark. It sounded hollow, eerie, raspy. The words were followed by the scrape of his boots on wood.

The back room smelled faintly of moldy earth, old sweat and unwashed feet; it was also a mess—medical books tumbled to the floor and now sodden with rain and mud, Hirose's and Tomi's clothing ripped from nails in the wall, personal effects scattered about, and, at his desk, Hirose, slumped over, bandaged forearm outflung, a bottle of sake near an elbow, a service pistol in his remaining hand and a small blue, powder-ringed hole in his temple.

Tomi stood in his tracks. For a moment he simply stared. Then, knowing how futile it was, he checked Hirose's pulse. None. Reflex action? None. The body was still warm but cooling rapidly. Tomi stood back, looking down. Oddly, he felt no sorrow or remorse for Hirose. He felt nothing at all. Nor did he think twice of Hirose's *seppuku*. It was that which concerned him. Had he grown that numb to death—that callous, that indifferent? Or was he merely tired beyond caring? He didn't know, couldn't answer. He knew only that Hirose had committed the final unreasonable act of an utter fool.

"It happened only a little while ago," Michael said softly from the doorway. "Two of your guys came in talking, like they were excited. They got some stuff and left. Then this guy suddenly comes to like a zombie rising from the dead—really scary, Tomi. And he stumbles in here and *pow!* Just like that! No warning, not a sound, just *pow!* Why? What's the deal?"

Tomi couldn't explain. Nor would Michael ever understand. In any case, Hirose wasn't important now. "Michael, your place now is in this room. Get into Hirose's blankets. Stay there! Do not under any circumstances leave this room until I return. Wardmen will be coming to these barracks." He didn't want to add, to kill the comatose patients. Michael would be safe here, if all luck held.

He didn't want to talk; his numbed heart now seemed too full. Rather, he thanked God that his own New Testament was undamaged by rain or mud. He slipped the book into an inner coat pocket, paused to look longingly at the picture of Sumiko, turned abruptly and walked quickly from the barracks.

Outside again, he found the weather hadn't changed. The wind whipped, as before, down from the ice and snowcapped peaks to the west. The overcast remained thick but was darkening. It would rain soon, and that was good. The weather retarded the enemy advance, the only positive thing about it. All the garrison lacked was an earthquake or two mixed with volcanic eruptions. That's all. Then toss in a hurricane, a typhoon and a hundred-foot tidal wave and perhaps the garrison might be saved from the enemy.

Such wishful thinking! He knew, even if other Japanese didn't, that these days modern miracles were mass-produced only in America.

"Word just came down from battalion," Lieutenant Scott said to Murphy. Scott, muddy and unshaved, looked as worn as anyone else; hard to tell him from a lowly GI. "Intelligence says the Japs are up to mischief, nobody knows just what. There's a sudden increase in field radio traffic, most of it in code. There's troop movement but none yet that fits a pattern. Everybody at battalion's having a shit-hemorrhage."

"Don't they always?"

"The word is this: all combat units are to draw extra ammo and be especially alert. Stress that to your men. In addition, battalion wants a patrol to reconn Buffalo Ridge. We're in reserve, a logical choice. We move out at twenty-three hundred, if possible exploring the whole of Buffalo Ridge. Any questions?"

"That's all? Just all of Buffalo Ridge?"

Scott nodded. "I know it's a large area, but you are getting five replacements. Also, we're to take prisoners if we can. Intelligence says a prisoner is our first priority."

Murphy pursed his lips. Scott knew better—that no Jap, conscious and in his right mind, would willingly surrender. Not one on Attu ever had.

Trust her? Of course he did. Absolutely. It was Jim and his foul motives he didn't trust. And her mother. All that pressure, plus school. Write and say, I love you. Please wait.

He was helpless. And jealous—granted. Did he have reason for such jealousy? Or within himself was he so damned insecure that . . .

Tomi peered about the tent. All was finished here, Ouye, the Senior Wardman, waiting for orders. Tomi turned to Okasaki. "The wardmen are prepared to leave?"

"In five minutes. We shall all march to headquarters together."

"The patients are instructed as to when *seppuku* is appropriate?"

"They are. The exact time will be decided among themselves."

The mechanics of it . . . Would someone organize a death ritual? Perhaps a sergeant or superior private. "On the count of three we all pull pins. Ready? One! Two! Thr—"

He felt anxious now that someone bent on looting or some idle wanderer could stumble into the room and find Michael. Certainly one of the wardmen knew, could report at any time to headquarters or to Okasaki that the once-honored Dr. Nakamura had been speaking English to a supposedly comatose patient.

But such thoughts were self-defeating and he thrust them from his mind. Because of his rank he led the others—Okasaki a step behind him—down the ramp and along the narrow path that led through half-frozen, half-muddy tundra toward headquarters. No one spoke, for the wind whipped the breath from their mouths and they leaned into the blasts. Tomi pushed his boots hard into the path and wondered how the wind could find every little gap in his clothing, force it wide and fill it with cold.

Wonderful weather for the attack, he thought. In this wind, in the dark, the Americans in the rear would be huddled in sleeping bags and gathered in tents, the sentries curled deep in their trench holes, unexpecting, not alert. Once the front line was breached, nothing would stop the Japanese.

Two hundred meters upravine from the hospital tents Tomi found garrison headquarters, a log-walled, sod-roofed building identical to his own barracks. Here, partly protected from the whining force of the wind, were several hundred ragged, heavily clad men bunched in front of the building. Not all were properly or adequately armed. The majority carried rifles, though many held nothing but pistols or grenades. Others were armed only with sticks, or rods, with bayonets attached. A few had no weapons at all.

"There are no rifles available?" Okasaki asked a waiting private.

"None. Most of the weapons remain in trench holes now held by Americans. A pity! You must arm yourself."

"*Arigato*. I shall do so."

"What is the news?" Tomi asked a second man.

"News? You haven't heard? The American radio in San Francisco lies! They claim we are beaten, defeated, without force or purpose. Yet tonight we attack! Tomorrow they will know the truth."

"Of course," said Tomi in his most courteous tone. "As will everyone."

Everywhere about him, sprinkled among the crowd, were the uniforms of the Sea Defense Command. Good! Perfect! That meant Michael's route was now open.

"Aaah, Nakamura! I see you have come to the party," said a voice at his elbow. Captain Yamamoto, thin, glassy-eyed, as supercilious as ever. "I am overjoyed to see you. If we cannot be brothers in life, perhaps we may do so in death. Where is the honored Lieutenant Hirose?"

"He is dead, worthy Captain. By his own hand, only hours ago."

Yamamoto blinked. "Hirose dead? So soon. Then he will not march with us—"

"He will not," growled Okasaki, intruding into the conversation and omitting all courtesy. "Why don't you leave us alone? Is it not strange that now you wish the company of others? Are you a coward, afraid to die alone?"

Yamamoto's eyes suddenly shone with great hatred. He gave no answer, but pivoted stiffly and faded into the crowd. Tomi felt relieved. With luck, he would never see Yamamoto again.

Watching Yamamoto disappear from sight, as if fleeing from battle, Okasaki snorted once and turned to Tomi. "Honored sir, we must find weapons for ourselves."

He paused, for the garrison headquarters' door had opened and the esteemed Garrison Commander Colonel Shima emerged from the building, followed by Lieutenant Ujiie. To a man the assembly snapped to attention. The two officers strode a few feet up the side of the ravine, turned and planted their feet in the mud, facing the troops. Shima wore no heavy coat. In a clean, freshly pressed, bemedaled full-dress uniform, he stood at parade rest and gazed down on the remnant of his command. A tall man, thick of body, strong of muscle, he raised one arm.

"Soldiers of Japan." His voice boomed across the ravine. "I salute you! Before the sun rises again we shall reverse the course of this battle. Soon we shall attack the enemy. This attack will become a maximum effort, a total effort. Our objective is the enemy artillery position in the pass from Sarana Valley to Massacre Bay. We shall capture those guns and use them at once against the Americans. En route to the battle, you must cut all enemy telephone lines, destroy the American field radios and slay the enemy. Destroy them! But do not hesitate as you run; stop for nothing! Continue with full force toward the objective and victory will be assured. *Banzai!*"

"*BANZAI!*"

"I will lead you!"

"*BANZAI!*"

"Follow me to victory!"

"*BANZAI!*"

"*Banzai* to the Emperor!"

"*BANZAI! BANZAI! BANZAI!*" The cry swelled like a rising sea from hundreds of throats. "*BANZAI! BANZAI!*"

Satisfied, Shima stepped aside and gestured toward Lieutenant Ujiie.

"Soldiers of Japan," Ujiie cried in a high voice, "rifle ammunition and grenades will be issued at the armory. Three pounds of rice per man is available at our headquarters kitchen. Remember, each man must kill twenty of the enemy! *Banzai* to the Emperor!"

"Idiot!" muttered Okasaki. He turned to face Tomi. "Honored sir, we must arm ourselves without delay. I know where. There are many unclaimed weapons hidden at our hospital."

"I will go with you," Tomi said, wanting now to speak to Michael. "Also, we may await the attack in the warmth of the tent."

"Come." Okasaki led the way from the group. They began climbing the side of the ravine.

"Where are you going?" cried a sneering voice. "Are you running away?"

"We go to seek weapons," snarled Okasaki. "We shall return in time to join the attack. Then we will run our bayonets through your insolent bowels."

The wind pushed them along the narrow path to the barracks and tents where Okasaki disappeared up the slope and Tomi paused, eying the tents, torn between concern for his patients and worry about Michael.

The tents, he saw, remained as before. Though torn by enemy gunfire, faded and soiled by long exposure to the elements, the tents showed no recent damage. But the patients—were they all dead? Curious, he hurried up the ramp and inside the operating tent and found a large number of patients waiting with set faces and grenades in their hands. Others, perhaps a third of the total, were already dead from an excess of morphine. Their faces sagged. Half-open eyes stared emptily. Thick yellow mucus drained from noses and mouths. It could not be said they appeared to be sleeping.

"I fail to understand," Tomi said to an abdominal case. "You have the grenades. The time is growing late. Why haven't you used them?"

"I don't know. Someone said 'wait.' We see no need to hurry."

"Something might happen," said one of yesterday's amputees. "I don't know what, but something. Maybe the Navy will come, or the air arm. The Americans might suddenly quit. They are soft, aren't they? Cowardly? Who knows?"

"Who knows, indeed," said Tomi in a sad, gentle tone. He checked them all, adjusted an arm sling for greater comfort, changed a bloody bandage, furnished a bedpan, an extra blanket, a bowl of water, a quarter-grain of morphine for pain. Futile, he knew, but habit was strong. The dead, pallid faces he covered with blankets, then strode from the tent, aware now that as long as one of his patients lived he must be near to tend their needs. That was his task in life, what he had trained for from the very beginning.

After all, he told himself, I am more than a Japanese. I am a physician. I am also a Christian.

In the barracks he walked past the dead near the entrance and to his room at the rear. "Michael?" he whispered and found Michael staring back, half-raised with Hirose's gun in hand, aimed hard at Tomi's heart.

No one spoke. Michael grunted, flicked the safety lever down. The gun disappeared into a pocket. Tomi ignored the matter. "Michael, remain here as you are. I shall be nearby, standing guard in the barracks."

Ignoring Hirose's body, he removed his New Testament from an inner breast pocket, then settled himself among the corpses in the barracks area to read and wait for Okasaki.

May 29. Today at 2000 we assembled in front of headquarters. The field hospital took part too. The last assault is to be carried out. All patients in the hospital were made to commit suicide.

I am grateful I have kept the peace in my soul, which Christ bestowed upon me. At 1800 took care of all the patients with grenades. Goodby [Sumiko], my beloved wife who has loved me to the last. Until we meet again, grant you Godspeed. [Yoko], who just became four years old, will grow up unharmed. I feel sorry [Keiko] born Feb. of this year and gone without seeing your father. The number participating in the attack is a little over 1000, to take enemy artillery position. It seems the enemy is expecting an all-out attack tomorrow.

Life facts:
1. March 6, 1929; graduated from Koryo Middle School, Prefecture of Hiroshima.
2. Sept. 1929; graduated from Frazier English Academy. Sept. 15, 1929 to May 22, 1932; Pacific Union College, Medical Dept, Agwin, California.
3. Sept. 1, 1933 to June 1937; College of Medical Evangelist. Received college Med. License Sept. 8, 1938.
4. Jan. 10, 1941; inducted into First Replacement in 1st Imperial Guard Infantry Regiment.
5. Jan. 13; transferred to 1st Imperial Infantry Regiment.
6. May 1; ordered as Officer Candidate.
7. July 1; promoted to superior private, Medical Dept.
8. Sept. 1; promoted to corporal.
9. Oct. 24; graduated from Army Medical School.
10. Oct. 31; promoted to sergeant-major. Ordered by Probationary Officer.
11. Acting Officer since December.

MAY 30, 1943

The fog was either a curse or a blessing, Murphy couldn't decide. Ten yards of visibility. It hid them from the Japs and vice versa. Today, for no valid reason he could think of, the fog set his teeth on edge. He preferred to see where he was going.

The only good thing about the friggen fog was that it seemed to be thinning.

A half hour ago his reinforced squad and the entire platoon had passed quietly through the forward A Company line of foxholes. The advance had not been rapid; it was best to feel one's way in the dark. Detachments of two or three men each had explored each ravine, knoll and fold of ground. There were many signs of Japs—empty foxholes, a half-dug trench, a few helmets and bits of assorted equipment, two bodies with bandages neatly applied and a fresh round hole in each forehead, and even a heavy machine gun complete with belts of ammo. That was puzzling. Why would the Japs abandon a perfectly good machine gun?

The extended line of foxholes on Buffalo Ridge revealed only one other item of information—one small tin cooking pot poised over a glowing tin of canned heat. It held a few ounces of burned rice. "The guy who cooked this mess," Murphy said to Scott, "was here not too long ago. Less than a half hour. And he left in a big hurry."

"That's important—the timing. Intelligence will want to know."

A figure loomed from the dark. "Sarge?" Jeeters's voice, hoarse with intensity. "Me and Swensen found something. Come look."

Murphy and Scott followed Jeeters and Swensen down the gradual back slope of Buffalo Ridge. "Watch it right here," Swensen said, motioning. "This kind of level place, it's a roof of one of them underground buildings. The door was wide open, everything quiet, so Jeeters and me went inside. There's maps on the wall, a desk and papers and lots of field radios. It also stinks of fish, mostly."

"HQ of some kind," mused Scott. Fog dripped from his helmet.

"Abandoned, like everything else."

"It doesn't make much sense."

"Sarge, there's something else. In that big cave—see that big bluff?" Jeeters was pointing northward across the beginning of a ravine to a huge slanting slab of black rock towering into the thinning fog. Murphy recognized it, had seen it from the crest of Fish Hook Ridge. And this ravine, that path, led directly down to Chichagof Harbor and those two tents on a low hill where Jones's body lay.

"Just under the bluff," Jeeters said, teeth shining from the shadow under his helmet. "That's where the cave is—that wide, black gap—looks like a mouth. We heard Japs in there, singing. I guess it was singing."

"You're sure?" Scott asked. "You saw them?"

"Heard 'em. Chattering like fucken monkeys."

Scott ordered a two-prong advance, one squad left and one right, each up the hill to flank the cave and provide cross fire. There were armed Japs up there. "But remember, our orders say to take a prisoner."

"Right. We'll try."

Climbing, avoiding the crevices to prevent being outlined against the snow, Murphy led Scott and the squad through deep mud which kept sucking against his boots and sliding away under-foot. The wind was rising now, a desolate moan filled with cold and loneliness. But the higher he climbed the more he became aware of an odor, bitter and sharp.

Another twenty yards brought him even with the lip of the cave at its west side. Jeeters and two of the new men he sent to the center under the lip of the cave. For certain there were Japs in there. Far in the black depths the glow of a lantern shone on a low ceiling, and there were voices, high-pitched and staccato and filled with bravado and broken laughter. Drunk, Murphy thought. Drunker than a proper Irishman on Saturday night.

As to their number, Murphy couldn't see and didn't know. From the sound of the voices he could guess perhaps five or six, not an awesome number, but potentially dangerous. Now and then a figure passed in front of the lantern.

"That's a hospital in there," Scott breathed into his ear. "Smell the medicines? It's like a chem lab."

"Sarge?" Swensen's voice hissed through the dark. "I'll crawl in and take a look-see, okay?"

"No!" He didn't mean to sound so harsh. "Not yet."

In the cold they waited, the wind gusting and wailing. No rain, no sleet, no snow and now no fog—thank God. The movement inside increased.

The lantern inside suddenly went dark. A flashlight flickered, wavered, moved. Floating, it neared the cave entrance, then went out. Someone stumbled, muttered what could only be a curse. Abruptly on the lip of the cave, mere feet from Adams, Jeeters and Nelson, a dark lumpy figure paused. Then another—more, a half-dozen all bunched together. All were silent. Then metal suddenly glinted and someone below them fired. Instantly Jeeters tripped the trigger of the BAR and the huddled mass disintegrated into limp black forms suddenly sprawled on the cold earth.

"Goddammit!" shouted Scott. "Jeeters, you sonuvabitch!" He was shaking from cold or anger, Murphy couldn't be sure which. His glare now focused on the sprawled forms.

One of the Japs was moving. Slowly, painfully. Like a shadow emerging from the sea he rose to his knees, hard to see in this dim light. A hooded parka hid all features. One arm hung limply to his side, and his voice carried clearly downwind. "'Merican! No shoot! Me Joe! Me Joe!"

Scott moved two paces forward, hoping to see better. Murphy's instinct said fire. He kept the rifle aimed dead center on the Jap's chest.

Scott leaned forward. "You surrender, Joe? Get up. Raise both hands." Another pace forward. A fourth, pistol held waist high.

"Me Joe! Me Joe!" The man wavered, seemed unable to rise. Suddenly the wounded arm moved, struck a metallic object against a rock, and an object flew toward Murphy, who fired—too late, he knew. Scott gasped his surprise and men dove for cover. All but Swensen. In a flash he darted forward like a shortstop fielding a pop fly. Then the grenade exploded, a white-hot instant glare. The blast lifted the lieutenant and tossed him over the lip and crashing down the slope. In shocking silence, smoke whisking, powder smell thick, Swensen lay unmoving. Slowly then, in the dark stillness he began a soft whimper. "S—Sarge? I . . . oh, God! Where . . ."

"Jeeters, Bennett, Baker, check inside for Japs!" That was first, most important. Then: "Medic! Medic!"

"Saaaarge . . ."

Murphy threw all caution aside, hurrying to kneel beside Swensen. Oh, Christ! His face was all bloody, looked like chopped meat. Black—like blood and oil oozing in a gutter. "I'm here! Lay still. Help's coming, so keep calm."

"It hurts . . . like, oh, Jesus . . ."

Two medics arrived and began working on Swensen. Without emotion a new man reported the lieutenant dead. Jeeters returned from the cave. "Sarge, you gotta come look at this. F'Chrissake, I can't believe . . ."

Dully Murphy moved into the cave. The Jap flashlight revealed six rows of Japs on litters, all bandaged in various ways and all quite dead, eyes closed gently as if in sleep. Dried mucus stained

noses, lips and chins. A disarray of medical equipment lay everywhere—used vials of morphine, bandages, empty bottles of sake,
pots and trays and operating tools. Behind the odor of medicine
was another, a combination of urine, feces and vomit. Murphy,
holding his nose, almost gagged. This was not a macabre tomb but
a charnel house.

But why? he wondered. Why would anyone want to kill their
own wounded?

On the lip of the cave he knelt beside Swensen, futilely patting
the boy's hand. A bandage was wrapped about the boy's head and
he was already drowsy from morphine "Sarge? I . . . can't see.
Everything's all black. What does . . . do you think . . ."

"We'll get you back to a doc, right away. Just don't worry! Think
of all the girls. . . ." Even to him the words sounded false. His
voice too tight, throat aching, he broke away. Swensen, he
thought. Like Johnny. Oh, dear God . . .

It took only a moment to radio in the report: no live Japs
anywhere on Buffalo Ridge. Then he led the platoon toward
American lines, Swensen on one litter and the bloody remains of
Lieutenant Scott on another. A rare treat, the sky was totally
clear, a few stars dimly blinking. They looked strange and
wonderful, out of place in this cold, alien, merciless land.

Numbly he wished Swensen could see them.

Tomi sat reading the New Testament. The candlelight flickered
and weird shadows danced among the dead. Nothing else moved.
The wind moaned and gusted over the roof. From time to time
Michael coughed faintly, the sound muffled in the tiny room at
the opposite end of the barracks. Tomi sat in silence, absorbed,
staring down on a certain passage: ". . . and with many other
words did testify and exhort, saying, Save yourself from this
untoward generation."

Okasaki arrived just before midnight bearing a four-foot
broomstick, a blue-shiny bayonet strapped to one end. A small
pistol protruded from his belt.

"Honored sir, my quest for weapons took longer than I first

expected. The cache of weapons I gathered from the patients had been raided. Everything was gone. This is all I could find, by robbing the bodies of the dead. Do you prefer pistol or bayonet?"

From the odor on his breath, the strange glassy appearance of his eyes and his new glib manner of speech, Okasaki's use of sake was both obvious and regrettable. The quantity consumed Tomi could only guess.

"I see you have fortified yourself for the task ahead." He spoke in a flat tone, no censure in his voice. His disappointment must remain his own.

"And why not?" Okasaki frowned. "A man has every right to choose his own style of death. I shall die deep in sake. As in the past it will give strength to my arm and power to my mind. I shall be among the first into battle, with only the esteemed Garrison Commander Colonel Shima ahead. I shall die at his side, shouting *Banzai!* and singing the glory of the Emperor."

"Truly a warrior's death," sighed Tomi, too tired and too discouraged to discuss the matter. From the opposite end of the barracks came the sound of muffled coughing, and Okasaki gazed along the length of the dark aisle. Tomi spoke quickly: "I suppose it really doesn't matter how you die, or why or when if that's what you're determined to do."

Okasaki gazed again at Tomi; he blinked and seemed confused. "Honored sir, shall we not die together as brothers and comrades? Here are our weapons—inadequate, of course, but they must do. Which do you choose?"

"Neither," Tomi said quietly. "I shall remain with the patients."

"Honored sir!" Eyes wide, astonished, Okasaki stared.

"True, all expect to die soon. But perhaps not. While they live my duty is here."

"But you have orders! The Imperial Edict—"

"I have divided responsibilities."

Okasaki stared at Tomi, unbelieving. "Honored sir, I do not understand."

"I am not going, Sergeant Okasaki. I do not wish to die in

battle, not without cause. Neither will I commit *seppuku*. I intend to live for many years."

"You cannot!" Okasaki shook his head. "The Americans will come. They will . . . they . . . they are not to be trusted."

"I have no fear of Americans. Okasaki, strong companion, old friend—understand. I cannot discard the principles upon which I have built my life. Jesus himself would turn his face from me. Thus I refuse to die for the Emperor. I choose to live for Jesus."

"You choose—?" A soft sound of coughing filled Tomi's mind like artillery explosions. Okasaki swiveled his head. "What is that?"

"The wind," Tomi managed to say. "It whips a wet loose blanket against the wall, a minor annoyance. I regret it interrupted you. Please continue."

Okasaki tried to shake the fumes from his mind. Focusing again on Tomi, his eyes slowly hardened. "So you choose to defy the Emperor! Hah! So at last I know the worthy Captain Yamamoto was right. You are not a true Japanese! Your heart is soft, your blood thin and pale. You are but a pseudo-American."

"No! I am as much Japanese as you. I revere the Emperor. But I am also a Christian, a doctor of medicine, a husband and father. Why should I discard all these—and my life—for nothing?"

"Nothing? Your country is nothing? Your people are nothing? The Emperor is nothing?" The concept addled his brain. He waited, angry and confused, pondering the matter. At last he straightened, coming to a formal stance of attention. "Honored sir! I am a loyal Japanese. I go now to die gloriously for the Emperor. I ask—I beg of you—join me!"

Sadly Tomi shook his head. "You have a gun and a knife but I have a better weapon. It is this." He raised the New Testament from his lap. "This is all the weapon I need. As long as I live I shall heal the sick and cast out devils. Freely have I received; freely must I give. Now do you see?"

For a moment Okasaki stood silently, gazing without hope at Tomi. At last he said quietly, "So! It is as I feared. I have lost my third son."

He did not bow. He turned his head from Tomi and headed toward the door.

Okasaki's departure was lost in the sudden blur that affected Tomi's eyes. He could not watch the man go. Rather, he stood for a moment alone, eyes tightly closed, in the ageless quiet of the barracks, a living creature among the mute dead. At last, candle in hand, the New Testament tucked in a breast pocket beside his diary, he walked to the room where Michael waited, wrapped in blankets, his face haggard but rock-hard with determination.

"Come. Everyone has gone."

"For good? You sure?"

"I think so, at least for now. But one never knows what might happen tomorrow. Now is the time you must go."

"Thank God!" Quickly now, Michael rose.

"Go over the low hills below Hokuchin Yama and double back along the beach to my old hospital at East Arm of Holtz Bay. The way is clear and the Americans are there. The journey is several miles. You should arrive there at zero-seven or eight hundred hours. You will be quite weary, but a hot breakfast awaits you."

"Come with me, Tomi! You saved me, now I can save you. The whole world needs guys like you. We're a team. C'mon."

To save Michael's life was one thing, a fine thing to do. But he could not desert to the enemy. "My duty is here. My patients—"

"You can't help them now. It's all over. You guys can't win."

"You must go now while no one else is here. May God bless you."

"Tomi, after all you've done for me, I can't abandon you."

"I will be quite well here. I insist! Will you go now?"

Michael sighed, shaking his head. "I can never repay you enough, Tomi. Maybe someday, when we meet again, I can—"

"You warm my heart. It is enough to know that you live. Michael, sayonara and Godspeed."

Tomi bowed his respect, then eased erect to find Michael's extended hand. He gripped it with all his strength. In Michael's eyes he thought was a bit too much moisture and he himself began blinking rapidly. Neither spoke. What good were words?

At the barracks door he watched the half-light of midnight absorb Michael's figure. The footfalls faded and all that Tomi knew of Michael Andrews was lost in the night. Except for the memory, of course. He felt both sad and immensely relieved now that Michael was gone. All problems, anxieties and even fear had faded away. He was again free. Free. But he had lost a dear friend. . . .

That, too, was fate. He wanted no reward. In time, the world and its people would have the reward.

It was enough to know that Michael would survive and mature and accomplish great things. Tomi felt quite sure of that, for Michael had become an extension of Tomi himself, and that was a warm, comforting thought.

Yet he felt undecided about which was the greater, his shame of such disloyalty to the Emperor or his pride in saving Michael's life.

He would wonder, he knew, to the very last day of his life.

Michael now had no fear of discovery. Thanks to Tomi, his only enemies were the cold and the wind, and his lack of strength and endurance that continued to haunt him. Yet he felt confident. Well clothed and warm, he was on his way at last to East Arm, to life and home and Phyllis.

Here in the darkest hour of night, like dusk at home, he needed no compass. He could easily see the brooding, looming black height of Fish Hook Ridge on his left. All he need do was keep it there as he climbed the low spine of ridge, descended the other side to the shore of Holtz Bay, turned left and followed the shoreline toward the old Japanese airfield. Somewhere along that shore some distrustful, eagle-eyed GI with a twitchy trigger finger would challenge him. But he'd thought of that; he'd be ready.

Climbing the slope, staggering at times from the blasts of wind, he paced himself with measured steps. His instinct was to hurry, for time might be short. Too short for Tomi. Yet logic demanded a steady, almost leisurely pace that allowed him to husband his strength, proceed without stopping and arrive at his destination as soon as possible. Then pass the word about Tomi. It was the least he could do for him, the very least.

The terrain seemed vaguely familiar, this series of erosion gullies he'd used during his first escape attempt. In one of these was the small cave opening he'd found, crept into and waited in the cold, left the flashlight in. He felt glad now he hadn't tried to find the cave with Jones. All these gullies looked alike. He couldn't have found the opening, so probably he and Jones would have been caught and killed.

It took a long time to reach the crest of the ridge and start down the other side. The gray glistening mass of Holtz Bay lay straight ahead, dotted here and there by the black bulks of anchored transports, freighters, destroyers, whatever. The snow here on the north slope was deeper, crisper, harder, much like ice. He slipped several times, the wind combining with gravity to push him downslope on his back. Compared to climbing, the descent seemed to take hardly any time at all. The incessant washing of the waves against the shore rode faintly on the wind, became louder and constant. Wet sand soon pushed against his feet. He wondered if he were hallucinating, or sleeping on his feet. Where had all the time gone? To his right the sky had grown bright. Dawn already? To his left the dark mass of East Arm waited only three or four miles away, perhaps not even that. He saw his feet moving.

Walking on the wet sand seemed easy enough. Yet he sensed he was tiring, and he wanted to stop, rest, breathe deeply, perhaps even sleep. No! That wouldn't be fair to Tomi. Must go on. He had a friend in need, a debt to pay. It was Michael's turn now. Tomi deserved his very best effort.

He focused hard on the curve of the shoreline far ahead. That's where they were—the GI's, hot food, clean sheets, rest and sleep and a dream again of Phyllis. Oh, her soft clinging hungry lips! Her smooth warm waist and pert little nipples that rose so tautly at the touch of his tongue. Lying with him in the dark, sated, fulfilled in the curve of his arm, whispering into his ear.

Oh, yes, he had to get back to little Phyllis, very soon. Some-where nearby was a lumbering hospital plane waiting to fly him home. Convalescent leave. Two weeks from now appearing at her graduation, Class A uniform, all ribbons and wings and a Purple Heart; loving her with his eyes, she walking forth to receive her diploma; surprise and wild joy lighting her eyes as she found him waiting at the bottom of the stairs . . .

Three days from that day they would get married. Nothing—no Army Air Force, no red tape, no doctor, no transportation prob-lems, no mother or father or that guy Jim would stand in his way. Then for the rest of his natural life he would protect her with all his strength from every man except himself. With him she'd simply have to take her chances. Come what may.

It sounded both marvelous and perfectly natural. Mrs. Phyllis Andrews . . .

Such dreamy warmth became a flickering knowledge of terri-ble coldness. The wind. It was the wind. The damned killer wind that sapped what little strength he had and drove his knees to the sand. No! He clenched his teeth. Up, dammit, up and into the force of the wind. Fight it, drive into it. Full light now, and there only a half-mile away . . . Familiar flag, movement, people. "Hey, I'm here! Gimme a hand."

Dressed in Japanese clothing, he knew how vulnerable he truly was. From an inner coat pocket he removed his pass to safety and freedom, a pure white lab coat taken in a moment of quiet from the belongings of the Oily One, Tomi's roommate, whose body still lay slumped over the desk in Tomi's shell-battered quarters. Now held high, gripped in both hands, the lab coat whipped and snapped like a tortured thing in the wind. They'd see it, oh, soon they'd see it. Now he weaved as he walked, always plunging ahead, falling but rising and going on. "Hey, you guys! I'm Eagle Four!"

Where it came from he never knew. One moment he reeled alone on a wet bleak beach, the next instant a sharp command: "Halt!"

Stop he did, as if striking a stone wall, clutching the precious white lab coat and watching blurred figures approach warily, surround him and catch his sagging body. Into a mass of bearded, weary, wide-eyed GI faces he gasped, "Andrews! Air Force. Take me to . . . Intelligence!"

Borne on a stretcher, he knew that. Warmth. Hot coffee he gagged on and gulped eagerly and burned his lip. Hot gooey eggs and Spam—and never had anything tasted so good. Spilling out his report to a questioning, sympathetic major—the need, the imperative urgency, to send a force at once into undefended Chichagof Harbor, seize a friendly Christian doctor named Naka-mura, save him—

"We'll do all we can," the major said. "At the moment, howev-er, we're involved in a full-scale battle, apparently a *banzai* attack, near Sarana Valley. If you listen when the wind is right you can hear the guns."

"This must be done at once," Michael insisted. "If his own people don't kill him, ours probably will. He saved my life at the risk of his own. He's one of us at heart, really. Give me a boat, a squad. I'll go."

"Someone else perhaps; not you. Our doctor says you're not physically capable of walking across the airstrip, let alone—"

"Bullshit! I got here! I can damn well—"

"Lieutenant, please understand. I'd like to help all I can, and I will, but at the present time any incursion into Chichagof is considered a maximum risk."

"It isn't, believe me. Please—"

"But you don't know that for an absolute fact. Neither do we."

"I'm telling you, goddammit! I just came from there. There's no—"

"That risk—for one lousy Jap?"

"*Japanese*, dammit! Now send that message to the area com-mander. Or I will."

"Okay! Just as soon as—"

"Don't sit there, f'Chrissake! Send it! Now!"

"Lieutenant, control yourself! Don't get hysterical. It takes only a few minutes to go through proper channels."

"Look, don't argue, okay? Send it now! Please!"

"Okay, I'll do all I possibly can. But I trust you understand. With our ground forces presently engaged in heavy combat, this will be a low priority message."

For a while Tomi slept lightly, his body resting on a litter among the dead but his mind tuned to the sounds of the night. He heard the blasts of wind above the barracks, the frenzied rustle of fronds in the ravine, the ever-teasing murmur of water in the stream. Later, aware of the distant cry, *Banzai! Banzai! Banzai!*, he stirred in his sleep and knew they were on their way. At last.

To die for the Emperor. *Banzai.*

Without knowing, he noted the passing of time. Morning twilight began about 0240 hours; he knew it had come. Enough light for visual artillery sighting arrived close to 0500; he heard a dull, persistent rumble. Dawn came quietly at 0644, and he rose, stepped outside and eyed the brightening eastern sky. May 30—in America a day devoted to the memory of sons, brothers, husbands and fathers killed in battle. On Attu, a day used to increase that number.

En route to the tents atop the low bluff, he thought it strange to see no messengers, no litter-bearers, no wardmen bustling about. All was too quiet, deserted, yet remained the same—the sky threatening rain. The cold. The ever-present, hated wind.

Michael by this time would be nearing the Americans at Holtz Bay, would soon be safe, warm and well-fed. Tomi sighed, remembering days of safety and warmth, the delight of good food.

Nothing had altered the tents. The only sounds and movement were the whine of the wind, a flapping of torn canvas and a few whipping tent ropes. He climbed the ramp and heard a sudden garbled cry:

"It is Dr. Nakamura! Restrain yourselves!"

From what? Tomi wondered. Pausing just inside the entrance, he found a battery of alert dark eyes intent on his arrival, each man clutching a grenade, fingers white near the pins. "Is all in order here?" he asked. "Is anyone in need?"

"What is the news of the battle?" cried a man with a fractured pelvis. "We heard the guns."

"Tell us of our glorious victory."

"Why do you return? Why did you not die with the others?"

"Are the Americans coming? How soon?"

Two wounds were draining and needed new dressings. He gave water to the thirsty, a quarter-grain of morphine to those in pain, extra blankets to all who felt the cold. He wished he could feed them, but no rice remained.

"Why did you not go with the others?" asked a man with a fractured femur.

Tomi eyed a gangrenous leg; it really should be removed. "Because it is not my fate to die today."

Here he had done all he could do, alone. In the ward tent he found the patients also nervous, unwilling to use the grenades until all hope of survival was gone. Except Umeda.

"I have changed my mind," said Umeda. "I prefer to die of morphine."

Tomi shook his head. "I will give you sufficient to ease your pain. But no more than that."

"Morphine!" Umeda's eyes were bright with fever and challenge.

"No morphine."

"Rice!"

"There is no rice."

"Water!"

Tomi gave him water and turned to the others. Most of them had turned inward and needed nothing. They ignored him and left him feeling empty. For a fleeting moment he thought the unthinkable: perhaps he should have gone with Michael. . . . An unworthy thought; he forced it from mind.

He found a spare blanket, spread it wide on the tundra grass at the top of the bluff and settled down to wait. It felt eerie, this being so alone. He gazed down on a crater-marked plain now empty of men.

But not for long, he knew. They would come. All he must do is wait and see them appear on that low, windswept hill across the harbor. Who? A few Japanese, perhaps, returning from a temporary victory in battle? Or a horde of grim-faced, vengeful Americans advancing upon the harbor? Whoever, they would come.

For an hour he read the New Testament, the wind rustling the thin pages. Then he dozed until midmorning. Later he watched the gray, heaving, restless sea, the gray overcast tumbling about the mountain peaks, the white curling waves abrading the shore. He listened to the wind, blasting and roaring, then mournful, hollow—

Michael would be there by now, perhaps talking to some incredulous Intelligence officer of the wondrous Japanese doctor at Chichagof Harbor who had preserved his life, fed him and hidden him and helped him escape, all at the risk of his own life and honor. But possibly Michael would not be believed. No matter. Michael would never forget the friendship they had shared. . . .

The sound of frantic gunfire carried clearly over the field radio. That, combined with the howl of the wind, made it difficult to hear the captain. With one hand Murphy covered his exposed ear, saying: "Repeat, please repeat."

"I said Intelligence wants a certain Jap doctor for interrogation."

"A what?"

"Jap doctor, that's right. His name is Nakamura. N-A-K-A-M-U-R-A. He's said to be in Chichagof Harbor, at a hospital there. Your job is to find him and bring him out."

"Go get him, yessir." Nothing made any sense anymore.

"Bring him in alive and not wounded. Treat him with every courtesy."

"Sir, has Intelligence ever tried to take a Jap prisoner?"

A short laugh. "Not that I know of. I suggest you take a route you determine is best. The safety of you and your men is an important factor. So is speed. Intelligence is very anxious."

"I'll try my best, sir. Anything else?"

"Not at present. Good luck. Report to me by radio when you have him. Over and out."

Murphy stared blankly at the dead handset, his heart a dull sad thumping in his chest. Another Jap prisoner?

In the ruins of Aleut Village, moving slowly and blending with the landscape, was a lone figure. Tomi blinked, wiped his eyes and stared. The figure limped and sometimes staggered. Yet it kept coming, hurrying as best it could. Okasaki? Tomi's heart leaped with gladness. He'd come back!

Then he looked closer, aware that the figure lacked Okasaki's height and bulk. Too, its head and back seemed bowed, and a welcoming shout died in Tomi's throat.

He watched the figure slowly cross the plain, dip into the ravine and struggle to cross the stream. Emerging, the man raised his head, exposing a weary, bloodied face. "Captain Yamamoto!" Tomi's surprise matched his disappointment. Discarding both, he hastened down the ramp to help.

They met among the knee-deep fronds of the lower ravine and Yamamoto sagged into Tomi's arms, his lower left leg drenched by blood. "Nakamura? Help . . ." His uniform was torn, perforated by a dozen or more small black-edged holes. It was also dirty with vomit, spotted and streaked by blood and mud.

"Nakamura! Has anyone . . . been here? From up the ravine? They said . . . help me! I have such news! Get ready for . . ."

"Ready for what? We have won the battle? Or are reinforce—"

"They'll be here . . . very soon. They said—"

Together they stumbled toward the ramp. "Who are you talking about?" asked Tomi. "Our Navy is coming?"

"Radiomen! From headquarters. There's a submarine . . . out there. One of ours. If we can . . . make contact. . . . My leg!"

"Take your time. Easy up the ramp now." Tomi could offer a shoulder and arm but no reserve of strength. Yamamoto leaned against him, was heavy. Tomi half carried the man up the ramp, a tedious process, one agonizing, breathless step at a time. At last they reached the top. Tomi pointed toward the operating tent. "Only a few steps now."

"No. Take me . . . where you were . . . the blanket . . . on the bluff. I'll wait there. I'll see them."

"But you're hurt. Your leg—"

"A grenade, I think. Or a small shell. The concussion . . ."

Tomi hurried into the operating tent, seized dressings and bandages, Vaseline, tincture of iodine, a vial of morphine. He scooped them up and hurried to Yamamoto's side. The man was watching the ravine. He had removed coat and trousers, was trembling under the icy blast of the wind. His frame was woefully thin.

"You would be more comfortable in the operating tent," Tomi said.

"No. I must watch for them, be ready."

Tomi shrugged. "All I have as antiseptic is iodine. The pain will be great for a moment, so I brought morphine."

"No! I wish no morphine. I must remain alert. I must function well."

"I can help you watch."

"Thank you. But I can stand the iodine. I must! Just that, sew me up and apply a few bandages. Please."

Please, thought Tomi. The man had said "please."

"Hurry, Nakamura. Then, with a little luck, if the radiomen arrive in time, perhaps I can take you with me."

"Tell me of this radio and submarine." He applied iodine slowly, knowing how much it hurt. Hospital and radio personnel, he remembered, had been lumped together this morning as troops in reserve.

Yamamoto's fists clenched against pain. His gaze held to the upper ravine. "During the battle a radioman confided that he did not destroy his radio as ordered. Why? Because he'd been in contact with a Japanese submarine that waits nearby, for what purpose he did not know. Perhaps its captain is watching us this very moment."

Despite himself, Tomi glanced toward the sea, saw nothing but gray, white-crested waves and spray whipped by the wind.

"The tide of battle had already turned against us. We could see that. So we argued: Should we—a half-dozen or so highly trained, valuable men—commit *seppuku* with the common herd, or should we try to serve the Emperor in the future in other campaigns?"

"You decided on the latter course, obviously."

"It seemed a wise thing to contact the submarine by radio and attempt to evacuate. Why not gamble? We have little more to lose." Craftily now he eyed Tomi. "Of course you will be included, if there's room."

"Thank you." Tomi hid the leap of his heart. In Tokyo at this hour the sun would be shining in the garden. Sumiko would be working among the vegetables, her mind alert, as always, to the sudden wail of a sleeping child. Imagine! To appear suddenly at the gateway and find her kneeling on the damp soil, a cheek smudged, old clothing soiled, her hair perhaps in mild disarray. How surprised she would be! How wonderfully furious to be caught in such disorder. But only for a moment.

"Where is this radio? And how soon are these radio people to arrive?"

"It is hidden up the ravine, in a cave not far from here. They are already late, I'm sure. We planned to go together to the point of this spur between Chichagof Harbor and Holtz Bay, contact the submarine and wait for rescue."

"And if the Americans arrive here first?" The path on the far hill was still barren of people, he saw. So was the ravine.

"I cannot run. It is useless to hide, and starve. So *seppuku* . . . I have a pistol. Or you could supply morphine."

"So we wait."

Tomi applied iodine, Vaseline, dressing bandage. Yamamoto sat gazing at the empty ravine. "I looked for you in the column, with Okasaki. He refused to speak of you."

Tomi remained quiet, wanting to avoid discussion and argument.

"You didn't go, did you?"

"There is a small piece of shrapnel here in your hip. Removing it will be very painful."

"Nakamura, how could one not go? It matters, you know. The Emperor demands that you give your life—"

Their eyes met and Yamamoto glanced away.

"Tell me of the battle," Tomi said, his hands busy with gauze. "We have definitely lost? What happened?"

Yamamoto kept watching the ravine. "In the upper valley, near the joining of Sarana Valley, our advance elements found an enemy field hospital—tents, patients, everything. Such equipment! Such a store of supplies! Oh, I envied them."

"But what happened?"

"Our soldiers attacked only with bayonets. Or tried to. At first all went well. Patients, wardmen, officers, even an American colonel, all were surprised in the night and bayoneted in their sleeping bags."

Tomi winced to think of bayonets flashing down in the dark, driving into the vitals of sleeping, helpless, already wounded men.

"Despite orders, a few rash idiots used grenades and others rifles, so of course the alarm was given. Time became precious then. We hurried toward our objective, the American artillery on that low hill between Massacre Valley and Sarana Valley. With that artillery in our possession we could blast the enemy from the peaks and restore ourselves to the same positions we held two weeks ago. Sound strategy! Then if reinforcements arrived from Tokyo—"

Tomi nodded, carefully applying Vaseline to Yamamoto's hip.

"We were held in reserve, waiting for orders. That pleased everyone except Okasaki. I could see our forces were spread across the width of the valley. As full dawn approached I saw no order—no encirclement, no enfilade, no frontal assault. I saw nothing but chaos in which both sides seemed to be confused, groping. We had bypassed certain American units and surrounded them. They surprised me! They did not hide or quit, as we were told they would. No matter how desperate their circumstance, they merely seized whatever weapons lay about and began shooting."

"I could have told you that. They are very competitive. In playing baseball or football—"

"Never mind! 'Go get them,' I said to Okasaki. 'Attack the Americans. Kill them all with that little toothpick-tied-to-a-broomstick you have in your hands.' I laughed, but it was not a laughing matter. I soon saw how the situation had reversed. For the first time since the American landing, the enemy held the hills and we Japanese were caught beneath their guns, in the depth of a valley."

"Aaaah!" breathed Tomi as Yamamoto paused to bear the pain of iodine. "Always the American wants the upper hand. Give him time, and usually he gets it."

"What do hands have to do with it?" growled Yamamoto.

"Merely an expression. About Okasaki—"

"We received no orders by field telephone. The adjutant told us to wait; he would seek orders. He failed to return, so we waited and waited. Okasaki raged, demanding action, until I ordered him quiet. Then we talked, the radioman and I. And we watched. I tell you, the esteemed Garrison Commander Colonel Shima erred! The American artillery rallied, depressed their barrels and were firing into our troops. Point-blank range, no less! Japanese were dying by the score. All around the big guns were heavy trucks, tractors, earth-moving equipment. Everywhere the Americans were swarming like ants—thousands, I'm sure—firing madly, as if bullets were cheap and plentiful and could be easily replaced. It sobered my thinking."

"You gained a new perspective about Americans?"

Yamamoto glanced sourly at the ravine. "Why don't they come? They were all well and strong. It's a simple matter to climb the hills and retrieve the radio from the cave, stop by here—"

"Why didn't you go with them?"

"My leg. Climbing the hills seemed too difficult. You saw nothing of them?"

"Nothing. About the battle—"

"Nowhere on the battlefield did I see a bold Japanese advance. No single-minded, concerted drive into the heart of the enemy. All our action had become defensive. Our brave, honored soldiers were hiding in trench holes, in eroded gullies and swales, behind a small rise. I asked myself, why should this happen? A thousand Japanese moving fast and without pause, using all the advantage of surprise, should be unstoppable for a short distance. In the beginning the Americans would be confused, ignorant of opposing numbers, not knowing the exact area of advance or our direction of attack. Their communications would be disrupted, difficult, in some cases impossible. Orders would be superseded, each order given frantically and each demanding priority. They would rush to protect one area and leave another exposed, perhaps even fire into their own troops. Fear and hysteria would reign. And in the midst of it all, driving through a narrow gap like a scalpel slicing flesh, a thousand organized, determined, dedicated Japanese bent on one objective. How could we possibly fail?"

Tomi peered down on Yamamoto. The man was not talking to him. He was attempting to explain to himself this disaster for Japanese arms. Pain was forgotten, cold forgotten, Tomi forgotten.

"In time the answer came to me. Our troops had spread themselves in an arc from hill to hill across the valley. The driving wedge was in fact not a wedge at all, but a blunted, diffused weapon. By spreading, our troops had lost unity, purpose, force, direction. So at the very moment our esteemed Garrison Commander Colonel Shima needed the power of numbers, he found himself virtually alone."

"I understand." Tomi was well aware of how it felt to face a crisis alone. "The reserves were not committed to battle?"

"No, never! But we couldn't have helped. The one unspeakable error had been committed; we allowed the enemy time to adapt, organize, respond. Americans do that so well! That artillery and those engineers, they pinned us to the earth. We could not move."

"Very predictable. Perhaps even inevitable."

Yamamoto grunted. "Everything that happens is inevitable. Anyway, then the worst began. Without warning, three of our soldiers nearest the enemy suddenly rose as one, bowed toward Tokyo and the Emperor, pulled pins from grenades and committed *seppuku.*"

"Aaaaah!" cried Tomi bitterly. "*Seppuku!* Yet they still had guns, ammunition, grenades?"

"Yes, and that saddens me. However, we instantly guessed the cause of such action. Our esteemed Garrison Commander Colonel Shima was dead in battle, so why go on? Surely that was it. Why else—" Yamamoto's voice cracked in a half-sob, and for a moment he closed his eyes, ignoring the ravine.

Tomi began wrapping the last open wound. "How many survived?"

"*Seppuku* continued," Yamamoto intoned, in his mind reliving the battle. "A small group here, another there—the bow, the grenades. Always in groups. Five nearby. A dozen over there. *Pop! Pop! Pop!* went the grenades. A quarter-hour later, half a platoon. The *seppukus* soon totaled a hundred, then two."

No American would understand, Tomi felt sure. With the death of Colonel Shima it became futile, if not ridiculous, to continue a lopsided battle. All this fruitless endeavor must cease. Why prolong one's thirst and hunger, the entire agony of defeat and utter disaster?

Indeed, why attempt to exact a bloody toll from the enemy when your little bullets cannot find him on the hill, but his big shells easily seek you out and crush you?

Who among them had the will to go on? Who owned the physical strength?

To cease fighting, then—agreed. But surrender? Never! Better death of the vilest sort than eternal disgrace, dishonor and utter contempt given to one's memory. *Seppuku,* then, was the solution, the only means. *Seppuku,* the escape, the way out.

"How many of our men committed—"

"Who knows?" Yamamoto said. "Perhaps we lost two or three hundred in the fighting. Perhaps more. If so, then all the others are dead by their own hands."

"Am I to believe this? Seven hundred, eight hundred, all armed with rifles and ammunition—grenades—and all committed *seppuku?*"

"Does it matter now? They are dead; it is finished. After all we have done, we are totally defeated. Who would have thought this would come to pass?"

"And Okasaki?" asked Tomi softly.

"Gone. At the very last, in a wild rage he tore loose from our group, seized a rifle and alone charged the American artillery. A magnificent death! But stupid. His rifle jammed without firing a shot. He advanced no more than fifty yards."

"So you saw him die?"

"Yes." Yamamoto offered a sly smile. "Cut down by a burst of machine-gun fire. I enjoyed watching him fall."

Tomi closed his eyes. Good-bye, he called to the crying wind. Sayonara! He imagined the streamlets of the valley tinged pink by blood, mostly Japanese.

If only the Japanese had possessed more of everything, he thought. Especially food. Even Japanese cannot fight indefinitely on empty stomachs. He remembered all the rice and beans and flour abandoned earlier at West Arm of Holtz Bay, enough for 10,000 men in a dozen campaigns like Attu. But all gone—*poof!* Food is energy, power, courage, life itself.

It was the Americans who had everything, he argued. And they used it all—guns, ammunition, artillery shells of every kind. Such firepower! Their fire fell like rain, quaked the earth and scorched it, seared men's souls and shriveled them, destroyed everything it touched. Ever since the American landing the world had been one of unending labor and darkness and continual pain. Even the weather had plagued the Japanese—white frozen cold driven by a wind that at every turn blew in one's face.

"Okasaki, a stupid man!" hissed Yamamoto. "His charge brought our reserves to the attention of the American artillery. They fired toward us. There were more sudden explosions all about, one very nearby, and . . ."

"And here you are. All in one piece, a radio near at hand and a submarine waiting." All very convenient.

Who would arrive first, the radiomen or the enemy? Tomi eyed the sea. On the far horizon a gray shadow moved almost imperceptibly, a patrolling American destroyer. Between here and there lay an undersea haven offering warmth, food, unbroken sleep, to say nothing of a future.

"You are mourning for Sergeant Okasaki?" asked Yamamoto suddenly. "Do not! He was not your devoted friend. At the very last he came to regard you with great contempt. As I always did. And which you truly deserve."

He could hear the waves working against the shore, the never-ceasing wind gusting up the ravine. His heart felt like heavy ice in his chest.

Yamamoto said, "Aren't you curious? I will tell you. Walking past Lake Cories to the battle, your Senior Wardman Ouye asked Okasaki, Where is the honored Dr. Nakamura? I heard Ouye say he had grown confused—why had the honored doctor spoken English late at night to the burn case? Almost every night! And Okasaki halted in the midst of the path. Others kept bumping into him as he clutched poor Ouye and cried, 'The burn case?' He recalled how strange your patient had been, how only you had treated him, how the man had disappeared, then returned with a heavy cough and suddenly vanished again. Okasaki remembered also the strange cough in the barracks as he bade you farewell. Only then, on the long march to his death, did Okasaki realize this shocking truth. 'An American!' he cried. The burn case was American, the aviator! He wanted to return here to kill you but was denied permission to leave the column."

As Yamamoto spoke he seemed to gain in power and old arrogance. "Is that correct, Acting Officer Nakamura? Admit it! You harbored an Ameri—"

"I did! An airman shot down within our lines. He was—is—a man of great promise who will someday benefit all mankind, including Japan. He lives! I am glad I did it, even if I die for it. I thank God for the opportunity."

"And you are proud? Nakamura, you dishonored yourself! Disgraced—"

"I would do it again."

"You! I should kill you in the Emperor's name."

"You haven't the strength, or the will. Nor do you have assistance."

"Nakamura, if I live, you will die! I promise, your name will be forever—"

"We both want to live, Yamamoto. Admit it! I, because I wish to serve others. You, only for yourself."

"Coward! Traitor! Despicable—" Suddenly he paused, staring. Now pointing. "There! There they—"

Tomi saw them. But not in the ravine. In the east, on the trail upon the low hill that led from the battlefield and Lake Cories. Little brown specks of movement, like crawling ants. A half-dozen. No, a squad. Well spread out, rifles held aslant and ready. Grim, silent, determined. They were moving steadily, with that infantryman's unique combination of caution and confidence, down the hill and toward the harbor, toward the ruins of Aleut Village, toward the ravine.

Yamamoto swallowed hard, his mood entirely changed. "Well," he managed to mutter at last, "we have unwelcome guests. It seems I have been followed."

Tomi waited in silence. Only now, in the wake of Yamamoto's shouting and with the sudden appearance of the Americans, did his idea come into focus. He knew at last what he must do and how to do it. There was time. No need to rush or be foolish. Yamamoto was gauging the nearness of the enemy, turning to peer at the empty ravine. "It can still be managed," he insisted aloud to himself. "But they must come. Now!"

But no one signaled or came down the ravine. Rather, like a machine moving inexorably onward, the Americans moved into and through the ruins of the old village, poking cautiously at the rubble, eying the underbrush. For long minutes they milled about. Then, the area clear, they began approaching a large underground storehouse, now empty, on the flat plain. The ravine would be next. And the hospital tents.

With a futile glance up the ravine, Yamamoto said: "It is over.

The battle. My career. My life. Finished! What a fool I was to hope."

"Perhaps," Tomi agreed. "On the other hand—"

"Shut your traitorous mouth! Nakamura, I want six vials of morphine. Now! And of course the same for yourself. I insist!"

"You'll find them in the operating tent, in one of the chests. But none for me." He held up a restraining hand. "No lectures. Do as you will. I shall do as I must."

"I detest you! You—I would not have taken you aboard the submarine. Not a half-American, disloyal—"

"That's enough! I owe you nothing. Die if you wish. Just go!"

"I have one more order for you, Acting Officer Nakamura. Come into the tent with me. I will compose myself and bare my arm. Administer the morphine quickly."

"No! I will not murder you. You inject the morphine. I will pray for your soul."

"Damn you!" A frantic last glance at the ravine, another at the approaching Americans. With a curse Yamamoto stumbled erect and began hobbling toward the tent. Tomi paid no attention. He had been watching the infantry below. Now was the time. From this moment on, the patients were no longer his responsibility.

He rose, eased down the ramp and sought safety in the barracks. It would be easier here, behind long walls. He could wait and muster his courage.

For a full three minutes he stood among the dead, staring at a blank wall. He heard only his own breathing, felt the blood surging through his temples. Then he could wait no longer. Now! He cracked the barracks door a mere inch and peered along the lower ravine.

There they were, eight or so. Big men, the smallest of them several inches taller than Tomi. All of them ragged, dirty, bearded. They, too, were obviously weary, but not even that could hide the arrogant swagger of their shoulders.

They moved cautiously through the deep fronds up the ravine, eyes jerking tensely this way and that. One at a time up the ramp toward the tents. The tallest gestured, signaling the others into position. A big automatic rifleman stationed himself to one side of the entrance to the ward tent. The others kept out and away from a possible line of fire.

"Anybody in there?" shouted the tall one, a sergeant. His voice carried clearly downwind.

"'Merican die!" It was Umeda's voice, high and nasal and filled with his usual snarl.

"Come out with your hands up!"

At another time, another place, Tomi might have laughed. The tall sergeant seemed unaware that wounded, crippled men were inside. He also sounded a bit romantic, perhaps the effect of too many American movies.

The reply came almost immediately. Several grenades came flying from the entrance. The Americans dove quickly to the ground, the rifleman near the entrance rolling frantically to safety. *Pop! Pop! Pop!* Black mud still arced through the air as the Americans opened fire with rifles and automatic weapons. The din, Tomi thought, holding his ears, was far too great for a hospital area. He watched the tall sergeant begin throwing grenades of his own. The others joined him, some lobbing, others using the smooth, swift cast of a fast-ball pitcher throwing strikes. *POP! POP! POP! POP!* From inside came sudden cries, screams, shouts and wails, then from one side a wisp of black oily smoke, a tendril. A tiny flame appeared, both beautiful and horrible to watch. Snapping in the wind, it grew and spread and climbed. Higher, faster, brighter grew the flames, driven hard by the wind, and they quickly enveloped the top and sides. The heavy, double-walled canvas, well oiled to repel rain, burned with a dry sucking sound, a kind of long, drawn-out *Whooooooo!* that went on and on. Smoke billowed thick, black and foul from the entrance, from vents and holes; it whisked in the wind. The sound of more grenades exploding inside held the Americans in place, staring. Embers and burning bits of canvas began falling into the interior, upon dry wood and dry blankets. The flames flared high, crack-

ling now, and a high nasal scream, unintelligible, suddenly rose
and fell, rose and fell. Finally it quit, and the dry crackling of
orange-red flames became the only requiem.

Tomi had stood transfixed, gaping in dismay at the destruction
of his ward tent and his patients. Now he saw smoke and flames
consuming the operating tent, caused by embers on the wind, of
course. The result was like watching a movie the second time, the
same oily black smoke and horrible stench, the same long
whooooo! The same cries and crackles, the same sounds of exploding grenades and empty oh-God! feeling inside, and the same
helpless desire to somehow stop this madness, this carnage, this
useless death. Those were his patients, and the dry sob in his
throat was for them.

In minutes both tents and all within them were gone, destroyed. The tentpoles collapsed, each with a crash and a bounce
and a flurry of thin and dying smoke. The Americans peered at the
black carnage, shook their heads in utter bewilderment—one
vomited—and turned away and down the ramp and began heading toward the nearest building, the hospital barracks. Tomi
snapped himself alert. This was the time, the moment. He felt
certain now that in a few years, at war's end, he would be with
Sumiko again, in America, working, learning, worshiping and
enjoying fine music. From a back trouser pocket he pulled a
handkerchief. It wasn't as clean or white as normally it would be,
but it would do—it must. He seized a deep breath, slowly ex-
haled, counted to three and slowly pushed the door open.

"Jap! Jap! Take cover."

He wished they would say "Japanese." They were poised, he
knew. Rifles ready—a dozen deadly rifles would soon be aimed at
his heart. He hoped no one was overly nervous.

Body hidden behind the doorjamb, he eased forth one almost-
steady left hand and began waving the white handkerchief. The
wind caught it and billowed it full like a flag. No one could mistake
his signal, he felt positive. The Americans, as he remembered
from his own experience, were often ignorant of this matter or

that. Too, they were sometimes unthinking, as all people were, as Tomi was himself. But Americans, in general, were fair-minded. One could count on that.

Everything was working well.

He wished Michael were here to share this moment. For this was in fact not a surrender but a triumph of spirit and faith and God's will over all adversity. It was only a matter of time, a few short years, before he and Sumiko and the children would be well established in America. His children and Michael's children would play together, attend school together; their wives would exchange recipes and feminine confidences; he and Michael would again be comrades and grow old together. He would watch Michael's career and rejoice in the memory of how he had helped make it possible. . . .

He felt happy. Never in his life had he felt more joyful.

"Come out with your hands up!"

Tomi snapped alert. It was the same tall sergeant, of course, with his unconscious identification with the old Wild West—the noble sheriff and his posse, all filled with a sense of fair play.

Slowly Tomi edged forward, raising his hands high as he went. He smiled. They would see he was not armed. One step—on the threshold. Now he could see them well, dark gimlet eyes under helmets, above short ragged beards, hard behind rifle sights. And they him. Alert. Ready—

Two steps now, and well out from the doorway. Go slowly, he reminded himself. Make no mistakes.

"C'mon, c'mon, down here and away from that place. Move! Keep your hands up!" ·

"I am a Christian!" he shouted in English against the wind, walking forward as directed. "I am a Christian!"

"What? No tricks now. Keep your hands up!"

"I am a Christian! I call upon you to accept my surrender!"

"What? Bennett, can you make it out?"

"Not a word. Watch the sonuvabitch!"

"I say I'm a Christian! A man of God! Do you understand?"

"What y' say? Jeeters, flank him!"

"A Christian!" Did they think he said "question"? "See, I will show you."

He let the handkerchief fly from his hand and in one eager motion delved into his inner coat pocket for the New Testament, nestled there beside his diary. He felt it firmly in his grasp and was pulling it forth—

"Watch 'im!"

"Gun!"

"Grenade!"

Then the sergeant fired and Tomi felt a jolt in his chest. He felt no pain. His mind flickered with surprise, a dim realization and a fleeting sense of being thrown backward. There was nothing to grasp. He had no time to feel, no time to hear or begin to understand, no time for regret or complaint. Michael! he thought dimly, and the last thing he glimpsed was a red-splattered New Testament fluttering from his hand in the force of the wind.